DAMN NEAR DEAD 2

DAMN NEAR DEAD 2

LIVE NOIR OR DIE TRYING!

AN ANTHOLOGY OF GEEZER NOIR

EDITED BY BILL CRIDER
INTRODUCTION BY CHARLAINE HARRIS

BUSTED FLUSH
♥♣♥♥♥ PRESS
2010

DAMN NEAR DEAD 2: LIVE NOIR OR DIE TRYING!

BUSTED FLUSH
♥♣♥♥ ♥ PRESS

www.bustedflushpress.com
1213 N. Sherman Ave. #306
Madison WI 53704

TABLE OF CONTENTS

TABLE OF CONTENTS

INTRODUCTION

BY CHARLAINE HARRIS

SINCE I FIRST wrote this introduction, the bottom dropped out of the world, at least the mystery corner of it, with the death of my friend David Thompson. There is so much that can be said about David, by people who knew him much better than I did, but I can't bypass this opportunity to say how much I thought of David. His intelligence, enthusiasm, and encyclopedic knowledge of the mystery world made him a delightful companion and a challenging conversationalist. Along with countless others, I feel cheated of the chance to continue our friendship. Here is the original introduction I wrote at his behest:

DAVID THOMPSON HAS been one of my favorite book people for many years, so when he asked me to do an introduction for *Damn Near Dead 2* I was really pleased at the prospect. Now that I've seen the lineup of writers and read the stories for this anthology, I'm delighted that my name will appear on this volume.

Patricia Abbott's **Sleep, Creep, Leap** is a surprising story about Bob Mason, an aging man who's reluctantly trying to be a good neighbor. The results are … unsatisfactory. Neal Barrett Jr. contributes **Stiffs,** a story set in the future that changes the parameters of aging in a major way. C.J. Box (I'm a long-time fan of his) has a tale about **The End of Jim and Ezra,** in which the setting of 1835 Wyoming only proves that human nature hasn't changed. Declan Burke's **Out Stealing Buddha**, an Irish tale, is about a family with two aging members who are somewhat in the way of progress … the progress of the younger members of the family, that is. Two geriatric lovers have a star-crossed ending in **Love Story** by Scott A. Cupp. Christa Faust's **All About Eden** is about lovers, too—but Melanie and Eden are definitely not your average couple.

When you see Ed Gorman's name, it's a guarantee you're going to read something good. **Flying Solo** is a wonderful story about two friends still trying to make a difference in the world around them

INTRODUCTION

though they're both in chemo. Carolyn Haines's **Neighborhood Watch** is a specially wicked story about a retirement community where the main activity is spying on one's neighbors. Boredom can bring out the most interesting aspects of a retired lady's personality … **Memory Sketch** (by the multi-talented David Handler) is a reminder that it's never too late to pick up a new occupation. Gar Anthony Haywood drops into a nursing home to visit Vernon and Billie, a couple with a colorful past, as they take a Thursday evening jaunt in **Some Things You Never Forget.**

In Cameron Pierce Hughes's **The War Zone,** an old assassin on his last job meets with an unexpected hitch; someone's already killed his target. My friend Toni L.P. Kelner knocked my socks off with her story, **Kids Today,** about a retiree who will do a lot to keep his favorite waitress on the job. **The Old Man in the Motorized Chair** only wants to be left alone to enjoy Snake Week on cable TV, in Joe R. Lansdale's wonderful piece. Russel D. McLean's British nursing home inmate struggles for his life against an unexpected opponent in **Angel of Mercy.** Denise Mina's sly, wicked Miss Hartly (**Miss Hartly and the Cocksucker**) doesn't have everything her own way on a transatlantic flight. Marcia Muller's aging hero in **Sometimes You Can't Retire** has a novel way of liberating pets who have unworthy owners.

Since Gary Phillips and I served on the MWA board at the same time, I was anxious to read **The Investor.** Phillips delivers a story combining aging hippies, the mob, and the very modern green movement with comic gray affect. On the other hand, Scott Phillips retreats into the past in **Bill in Idaho,** in which a photographer tries to discover the whereabouts of a prostitute's baby. Then we take a trip into the world of moviemaking in Tom Piccirilli's **Zypho the Tentacled Brainsucker from Outer Space vs. the Mob.** Piccirilli's hapless moviemaker simply can't get out of his brainsucker suit. I've never read a story by Bill Pronzini that was anything but wonderful, and **Trade Secret** is no exception. Hit man Griff manages a last encounter with wonderful economy of effort.

The Summer Place is Cornelia Read's trip inside the head of a very old lady who is determined to kill her brother within a limited time frame. In James Reasoner's **Warning Shot**, a furniture store night watchman fires at a thief, changing the direction of his life. Another old lady, in this case Chinese, solves a kidnapping for her daughter, S.J. Rozan's famous detective Lydia Chin, in **Chin Yong-Yun Takes a Case.** Almost as much a reversal as notoriously difficult Chin Yong-Yun helping her daughter is Anthony Neil Smith's fabulous **Granny Pussy,** in which a pimp in his seventies tries to keep in the game. **Old Men and Old Boards,** Don Winslow's offering, is an elegiac look at the life of Bill Bakke, soldier, tile-layer, surfer, husband, and father, who gives his life an extra meaning on its final day.

This whole panoply of aging sleuths and villains has immense charm for me. I think my own approaching geezerdom has prepped me to appreciate that new genre, geezer noir. I've suddenly become invisible to a large percentage of the population. Only other people over fifty seem to be able to see me in grocery or department stores. It's like I put on that invisibility cloak of Harry Potter's. Harry will find out, when he passes fifty or sixty, that he won't need a cloak anymore.

With the graying of America (and lots of the rest of the world) I think the kids need to realize that we mature people—and some of us are *very* mature—are just as lethal as teenagers, and we're certainly capable of emotions that are every bit as dark and complicated. In fact, instead of brooding or boo-hooing about our problems, we're much more likely to take care of them … in very efficient, and possibly unpleasant, ways.

So hitch up your suspenders or put on your best granny pants, because you're preparing to enter … the gray zone. Proceed at your own risk.

EDITOR'S FOREWORD

BY BILL CRIDER

IT'S NOT OFTEN that an anthology like the original *Damn Near Dead* appears. Publisher David Thompson and editor Duane Swierczynski put together a lot of fine stories, one of which was nominated for an Edgar® Award by the MWA and another that was expanded into an Edgar®-winning novel. The rest of the stories in the book were equally good, as anyone who's read them will tell you.

But, as they say in those annoying TV commercials, there's more! *Damn Near Dead* broke new ground. It created a new sub-genre of crime fiction, *geezer noir*. So many people were taken with the idea of geezer noir that a sequel was probably inevitable. However, when David asked if I'd edit it, I was hesitant. It wasn't that he didn't offer me fame and fortune. He did, but I didn't see how he could possibly manage to bring together as many quality writers as he had for the first volume.

Then he told me who he wanted to invite. It was a can't-miss lineup, and it turned out that everybody David talked to wanted to be in the book. They were eager to contribute not for the fame and fortune (well, that, too) but because they wanted to write their own version of geezer noir. It seemed that everybody had a story to tell. I could hardly wait to read them, and I was sold on the idea of being the editor. I accepted the job. With a group of writers like that, how hard could it be?

When the first stories came in, I looked at the titles. The first one I saw was "Granny Pussy."

I called David. I said, "Uh, David, one of the stories is called 'Granny Pussy.'"

David said, "All riiiiiiiiight!"

So I knew we were on the right track.

Up above I referred to editing the book as a job. I shouldn't have. It wasn't a job. It was pure pleasure. How could it not be fun to be the first one to read stories by some of my favorite writers and to discover new favorites along the way? The same kind of pleasure's waiting for you in the pages of the book you hold in your hands. So have some fun. Go read them.

SLEEP, CREEP, LEAP

BY PATRICIA ABBOTT

LILLIAN GILLESPIE'S DOWNSTAIRS' lights had burned for at least seventy-two hours when her neighbor, Bob Mason, walked up to her front door. The cat's eyes glittered hostilely and it hissed when he put his eyes up to the mail slot. Bob stuck out his tongue, inadvertently allowing the metal door to slam on it. There was snow on the ground, and his shoes and pants' bottoms got soaked circling the house. He finally peered in through the one window he could see in from the back porch. Nothing. They'd been neighbors for more than ten years, but he didn't know Lillian's phone number. He'd agreed to keep a spare key after she locked herself out once, but couldn't warm up to the idea of using it now. Who knew what he'd find inside?

Reluctantly, he called the cops, returning to Lillian's door to wait for them. The two officers, neither seeming much more eager than Bob to enter the house, found Lillian sitting in front of the TV, a moldering salad on her lap tray. She was sixty-one according to the driver's license in her purse, over a decade younger than Bob. Standing outside in the dark, his wet pants' legs icing up, he answered questions as tersely as possible, wanting only to return home. "Did you know her at all?" the female officer finally asked, slapping her notebook shut and shining a flashlight straight into his eyes. "Ten years next door and you don't know where she worked? Where her children live?"

"HER PACEMAKER MALFUNCTIONED," Lillian's daughter in from Cleveland told him a day later. "You probably guessed it."

He nodded, although he'd no idea Lillian had heart trouble. She'd seemed active enough, zipping in and out of her garage in her little Cruiser.

"You'll probably see a realtor and some painters and plumbers around here in a few days." She smiled uneasily at his silence. "Just so you don't think the place is being robbed. Mother appreciated your neighborliness, Mr. Mason," she said at last. He was doubtful of this. Lillian and he had

1

barely had a conversation beyond exchanging pleasantries, wrongly delivered mail, and that key over the years. The daughter handed him a card with her phone number and email address before she left. He considered tossing it in the trash but placed it in his "Miscellaneous" file folder instead. His involvement with the Gillespie women was over as far as he was concerned.

THE HOUSE WAS on the market fourteen months. Would-be buyers trickled down to none in a short time. His street was patently undesirable, located two blocks from a major freeway. The houses were modest, sided in cheap vinyl and measuring less than a thousand square feet. The street needed paving and was unlikely to get it, and boarded-up windows were becoming commonplace. A squatter had recently been evicted a block away. This had been a respectable street ten years ago. Now it was on the circuit for cars with enhanced music systems. The possibility of late night drug deals had been raised at a neighborhood watch meeting a few months back.

TWENTY-THREE FEET lay between Bob's house and the one next door. He planted a row of hydrangea in the area between the houses the next summer, just inside his property line. He double dug the soil, peppering it with chemicals to make the flowers bloom blue. Even though it was the "sleep" year for the plants, they made a respectable showing. There was not a single plant in the yard next door except for some badly overgrown yews. He was tempted to divide a few of his lilies or hostas and plant them next door, but he let it be.

WENDY LARSEN MOVED in the next winter. A divorcée, he figured, as he peered at her through an upstairs window. She was standing on the sidewalk in front of her house, directing the moving men. The movers couldn't make it past her without making a slightly off-color remark or sneaking a look. Despite the cold, Bob raised his window just high enough to hear them. Laughing at what they said from time to time, the woman didn't seem to mind their flirtatious remarks. Twice she went inside to grab a cold beer for the men despite the frigid temperatures. The three of them sat, half-reclining on the ramp, tossing back their Miller Lights. When it began to grow dark, the men had to hustle to finish the job.

Wendy chose the room across from his bath as a bedroom and often forgot to close the curtains at nights. Bob wasn't sure why. He never saw more than a flash of bare skin, but watching for that moment passed the time. She got home from her shift at some downtown restaurant about ten most nights and was usually in bed by eleven. He began waiting for her light to go out before going to bed—it became a ritual.

WENDY WASN'T IN the house more than a week before she knocked at Bob's door. He peered out, and despite his aversion to getting involved, opened the door a crack. "I wonder if you could give me a jump. Car won't start." Her voice was throaty, warm. She waved an arm in the general direction of the street outside her house where an old green Saturn sat. She stamped her feet. "Lord, it's a cold one."

"Got jumper cables?" He'd bet a million bucks she didn't.

"My ex must have gotten them in the settlement." She laughed. "No, not really. Doubt we ever had 'em. He was the kinda guy never expected stuff like this to happen." She stamped her feet again, probably assuming he'd invite her inside. "Thought you might have some," she finally repeated when he didn't respond. "Mr. Mason, right? Saw your name on a piece of mail." She practically had her foot in his door. He nodded, pushed by her, and hurried back to his garage, coatless. She followed.

"Boy, you keep a neat garage," she said, looking around. Every tool in Bob's garage had its own peg—even implements like a barn fork and a flashlight. A series of tightly closed bins contained tools that wouldn't hang from a hook. He hated clutter, mess. Soil, fertilizer, and such were double-bagged and tightly tied. He had a dread of walking in and finding vermin.

"Most of the stuff's for gardening," he said, taking the cables from his car trunk. His words came out hoarsely and he wondered when the last time he'd spoken to someone had been. "When the ground warms up, I'll be outside getting the yard into shape." He didn't know why he was telling her this. From the length of her fingernails and the height of her heels, it was unlikely she did much manual labor. He couldn't picture her on her knees pulling weeds or handling a pair of hedge trimmers.

"Well, you keep the place real nice, Bob. Some men garden or cook, but I never met one who liked to clean before." He started to correct her, to say he didn't like cleaning per se—but let it go.

"I ought to warn you; I don't bother much with gardening," she continued. "Anyway, I might buy a dog and he'd probably tear up any flowers. You know puppies." He shrugged noncommittally, although the idea of a dog worried him.

The driveway was icy, but she negotiated it in heels without a slip as he slowly backed the Ford out. Her hair was twisted into some complicated design, a silver butterfly holding it in place. He didn't know what to call the style, but women had worn their hair like that when he was young.

She got into her car when he had the cables hooked up—inadvertently, he thought—giving him a quick flash of thigh. Thinner than he liked, but nice. "I don't feel right living here alone. A good guard dog might help." When he didn't respond, she rolled her window down further and said, "I guess you're not much of a dog lover, huh? Neither was my ex." She paused, thinking. "It was one of the few good things—after the divorce came through. I thought to myself that I could finally have a dog."

He got her car started, put the cables and truck away, and went back inside his house. It took some time for his pulse to stop racing though he held his wrists under the hot water tap, a trick his father taught him. "A woman will do that to you," the old man explained. "Warm water calms things down when that feeling you got ain't gonna do you no good."

THE PUPPY WAS outside the next week. She'd tied him to a post on her porch and he ran back and forth between the two houses on his long leash, barking in a tiny voice. The sound was slight, almost a squeak, but when the dog was full-grown, it'd probably sound deafening, and more than that—grating, nerve-wracking. A mixed-breed puppy, he didn't look like a dog who'd turn out to be small either. But she wouldn't pick something small for a guard dog.

Bob was not one for noise, hardly even listened to music. It was one of the issues that drove his once-upon-a-time wife, Edna, crazy. "What kind of person doesn't like some kind of music?" she asked him back then, whirling the radio dial this way and that while he shook his head. It was hard to explain it, but music was mostly noise to him, noise that played in his head for hours after hearing it. "I've heard of being tone deaf, but it's something else with you," she said, finally taking her vast collection of albums to another state.

"Cute, huh?" Wendy said now, coming out on the porch and down her steps. A large man followed her—the kind of man who looked like kicking a dog was not out of the question for him. His head was shaved, and he wore an old army jacket with the sleeves rolled up despite the cold. There was a tattoo on his neck and one on each arm. Cryptic symbols done in murky ink. Right off the bat, Bob hated him, knowing his type of man. "Dog's named Georgie. And this here's Buck," Wendy said, waving an arm at her companions and grinning.

Ignoring the introductions, Bob turned toward Wendy and said, "My hydrangeas will be blooming in a few months." He nodded toward the spot where the dog was taking a piss. The hydrangea plants didn't look like much yet, but come late June they'd bloom for six weeks or more. It was the creep year. Sleep, creep, leap, an old gardening adage.

Not getting it, Wendy nodded, saying, "That'll be nice. I bet I can see that patch from my kitchen window. What color are they? I always did like yellow flowers."

The man with her—Buck—laughed. "Don't you get it, Wen? He's telling you to keep your damned dog away from his flowers. Gardeners don't much like dogs trampling through their flowerbeds. Or taking a leak on them either." He turned to Bob. "I guess you know exactly where your property ends, right? Got some paper spells it out tucked in a drawer?"

The two men looked at each other for a few seconds. Then Bob looked over at Wendy and said, "Hydrangeas come in pink, blue, or white. Once in a while, you see one almost red."

The man laughed again. His laugh sounded even less happy. "Guess you'll have to live with pink, blue or white then, Wen. If you want to look at something yellow, you'll have to plant it yourself. I'm sure old Bob here can tell you which flowers to buy."

"Mine are blue," Bob said needlessly. They both looked at him blankly. "My hydrangeas have blue flowers." Then he turned and walked around to the back of his house where his cold frames needed a few more nails knocked into them. He split the first piece of wood from the force of the hammer and threw it aside disgustedly.

That man—Buck—had thirty pounds and thirty years on him. He remembered a time when no man would've spoken to him like that. A time when he could lift heavy equipment all day and think nothing of it. When he could handle hot, sharp, and dangerous machinery, barely needing gloves. He looked at his hands now. Gardener's hands and gardener's muscles. Negligible. He was an old man. No one would ever lose sleep over him again.

After dark, Bob watched Wendy Larsen and the man make love from his bathroom window. At least he imagined that's what was going on from the shadows thrown up. Every so often a sailboat seemed to glide across her wall. She must own one of those rotating lamps with cut-out shades that made shadows. A mood-maker, he'd heard them called. He opened the window and heard a groan or two, although it could have been the wind or the branches on the oak tree.

THINGS GOT BUSY as March turned into April and finally May. It was hectic in Michigan gardens come May. Everything had to be planted in a few short weeks. Wendy Larsen was often outside in the mornings before she left for work, Georgie sniffing around beside her. When Bob came upon her one day, she waved her cigarette in the air and said, "Buck doesn't like smoke in the house. Kind of a health nut." She frowned briefly and added, "In his own way, at least."

"It's your house, isn't it? Your rules?" Bob said before he could stop himself. He thought he saw a bruise on her neck, but maybe it was a love bite. Her eyes looked reddish, too.

"Yeah, but he's worth smoking outside for, Buck is. Probably keeps my smoking down. The price of it ..." Hearing some sound behind her, she turned calling, "Georgie!" The dog came swinging around the house, hardly a pup at all now. He barked with the volume Bob had expected, too. "I had one of those what-d'ya-call-it fences put in to keep Georgie from running into the street," Wendy explained. "Those invisible ones?" she added when he looked at her blankly. "You know."

He remembered seeing signs on neighborhood lawns. "But not *between* the houses," he said, looking down at the dog who was pissing on the flowerbed again. She looked at him blankly. "They didn't install a fence along here." He drew a line in the air.

Wendy flipped her cigarette, not even putting it out first. "You don't have to worry about Georgie, Bob," she said, misunderstanding. "One good shock and he's never gone near the street again. Georgie's no hero."

"Good, good," Bob said, giving up.

"I'm gonna get a collar for Buck soon, too," she added. "Wonder what voltage it'd take to keep him off the street."

EVERY DAY OR two that spring and summer, Bob made a circuit of the area, collecting more than a dozen butts each time. Using a shovel, he picked up dog feces that had scorched his lawn in several spots. Beer cans often sat on the fence posts in the backyard and litter of all sorts blew from her yard into his. Wendy's place seemed to be a magnet for refuse. She was simply oblivious to such things. Sometimes she even followed along, never connecting the dots. Georgie, wisely perhaps, settled into the deep shade that gathered between the two houses and watched.

Bob's windows were open nearly all the time by June, and he could both see and hear Buck, over there two or three nights a week. Sitting on her porch like he owned it, popping the tops on beers and yelling for her to bring him another one before he finished the last, hollering at the dog, listening to the Tigers' games on his boom box. Buck's nearly nonstop laugh was mean; Bob understood that laugh. He usually remained inside on those evenings, wrestling with the idea he was being intimidated. He concluded that he was and would have to live with it.

The first time he heard Wendy scream, he was on the other side of the house watching *The Killers*. Initially, he thought the scream was coming from the throat of Ava Gardner. But when the movie ended and he heard it again, he got up and went upstairs into his bathroom, trying to remember what a scream of passion sounded like as opposed to a scream of pain or fear. The house was dark, but Georgie was barking in some downstairs room. The barking was so cyclical, Bob wondered if the dog had been shut in. His stomach knotted. A door slammed, a thud or two followed, and then something fell and broke—probably a lamp. But there were no more screams. He watched for Wendy the next day and the one after, but didn't catch her. He wondered if she was avoiding him but decided that was a silly idea; she barely knew he existed.

The third day, Wendy and the dog were in the backyard again. He leaned over the fence and said hello. "Hi, Bob," she said, her voice subdued. She was sitting on a rotted picnic bench, her knees tucked up under her chin. Her cut-off jeans were streaked with paint and a short, ruffled pink blouse showed off her tanned middle. She waved a can of beer at him although it was only noon. "Come on over."

"Been okay?" he asked, surprising himself. He couldn't remember the last time he'd asked anyone such a thing. She looked so damned pathetic. Her yard was more untidy than ever. A row of brown plastic bags, some untied, lined the side of her garage. She must have missed several weeks of trash collection. His stomach turned at the thought of mice, and perhaps worse, running around the place at night. A messy yard was like a beacon for possums, raccoons, mice, stray cats.

"Sure, sure," she said. Then she paused. "Buck and me broke it off a few nights back." She looked down at the dog. "We've been keeping to ourselves. Not that Georgie was ever too fond of Buck. Or vice versa."

Georgie and Bob might have their differences on proper lawn etiquette, but on the subject of Buck, they apparently agreed. Bob took a deep breath. "Maybe it's a good thing. He always seemed kind of … mean. You know."

"Buck? Nah. Just has a temper. Seems most men do—or at least around me." She looked at Bob closely. "I bet you heard us fighting the other night." She waited for a response and when she got none, went on. "Well, so what. He's gone now anyway."

"What do you want a man like that for?" His voice was stiff, scolding. Bob couldn't believe he was saying these things. "A man who hits women," he added, chin out. He didn't know this for certain, but he knew he'd been that kind of man once himself. Edna had had the good sense to run away, packing her car up while he slept.

"Buck doesn't—" she started to say—when another voice broke in.

"Are you talking about me, you jackass?" They both turned, shocked. Buck stood in Wendy's driveway. "Are you giving Wendy advice about me?" His hands curled into fists as he spoke. "Do you hear me, old man? Are you saying I hit her? Smacked her around?" Buck took several steps forward. The dog began to growl. Buck gave Georgie a quick glance, and the dog fell silent. "What the hell do you know about it? Have you been peeping in the windows, getting your jollies from watching us?"

Bob sought out Wendy's eyes, but they were focused on a worn patch of grass. "Course not. None of my business," Bob said, kicking at an old piece of hose.

"You got that right, old man. And you better remember that if you want to be turning over that dirt in your yard next spring. Stick your nose where it don't belong again, and it'll be dirt turning over on you."

"You go on home now, Bob," Wendy said, finally looking up and motioning to him with her hands. She was actually chasing him away instead of Buck. "Buck and me, we gotta talk." She turned around.

HE'D BEEN DISMISSED. Deliberately closing the windows facing Wendy's house despite the heat, Bob put on the TV. The History Channel was showing a documentary about Albert Speer. He watched it with a small degree of absorption, followed by a bad Bette Davis movie, finally falling asleep in the chair, something he rarely did. But then, he seldom watched three consecutive hours of television. Walking stiffly up the stairs to his room sometime after one, he heard nothing outside except a gentle rain. Good, his flowers needed it. His sleep was fitful due to all the dozing he'd done. He got up at four AM and threw his bedroom window open. The rain had stopped, and he watched as Buck got into his truck and drove away.

"YOU SEEING HIM again then?" Bob was standing in the center of her backyard for the first time. She'd just dragged out another bag of trash to join the procession next to the garage. A butt hung from her lips. Wearing a pair of mules, she clopped back across the concrete. It was the clop-clop that had drawn him over. He'd thought of nothing except Wendy, his ears pricked for any sound of her outside or for a return of that truck.

She shook her head. "I told him not to come back. It's over." Her voice was shaking despite the firmness of her words.

"Think he'll listen?"

A shrug. "I know how to take care of myself. I got rid of my ex, didn't I?" She was unconvincing.

"Buck may be more persistent. Was your ex built like a sixteen-wheeler?"

She rolled her eyes, dropped the butt, and stomped on it with her foot. "Look, Bob, you gotta keep out of this. What you said to me last night— when he heard us talking out here—it just made him madder. You can't fool around with a guy like Buck. He takes special handling."

"And *you* know how to do that?" Her nod turned into another shrug. He made a derisive sound with his tongue, walked over to an open trash bag, and knotted it. "You're gonna get mice, you know. Maybe rats if you aren't careful." He pulled a cloth out of his pocket, wiped his hands, and looked up at her.

"I'm not the careful type—in case you don't know that yet. You'll just have to believe I can take care of myself with this. I doubt Buck'll be back anyway. It's over," she repeated. There was still some hesitation in her voice.

"Don't you get it? Only Buck gets to say when it's over."

"I gotta go," she said, walking back toward the house. "Put it out of your head. It'll just make things worse if he comes around and sees you here. I know what to do." But he knew she didn't.

HE TRIED TO take Wendy's advice, to go about his business and keep his eyes and ears where they belonged. But two nights later, Georgie began barking in the same hysterical way after the radio suddenly came on. Some sort of hip-hop station, blaring music. It sounded like music you might play to muffle other noises, music that would blend in with the traffic on his street.

Pacing the floor until he couldn't stand it, Bob picked up the phone. He'd looked up her phone number a few days before when the new telephone book arrived. Since then he'd glanced at the yellow Post-it so many times he had it memorized. He dialed it now and let it ring till the machine came on. Her voice sounded chirpy, inviting—he hadn't heard her sound like that in a long time. There'd be no point in leaving a message. What would he say? *Tell me you're safe, Wendy. Tell me Buck isn't around.* He tried three more times, getting the same useless message before slamming the receiver down.

He had to know what was going on in that house. Creeping outside, he circled it. Wendy's car was in the driveway, but there was no sign of Buck's truck. Buck could've parked down the street, of course, not wanting anyone, especially that old turd, Bob Mason, to see it. That's what Bob would've done. Bob/Buck would have burst in unexpectedly, taking Wendy by surprise, catching her off-guard. He could almost remember such an event. Remember what it felt like, how scared Edna had been. Or perhaps he'd dreamed it during one of the thousands of nights since she left.

There were very few lights on in the house: the kitchen's overhead fluorescent and a low-wattage bulb upstairs in Wendy's bedroom. He threw a stone or two at her window from the grass, hitting the siding with two loud clinks. Nothing. As he watched, the white curtains in her bedroom window turned themselves inside out, caught in some strong gusts of wind. Inside, Georgie was quiet, but the music played on, wailing tunes about women who'd done their men wrong. Why was that music playing? Wendy usually played soft rock.

Bob waited as long as he could. Then knowing a woman like Wendy wouldn't have bothered to change the lock on her door, he went home and got the key Lillian had given him years ago. Hurrying, he looked around the living room for some sort of protection to take with him, finally grabbing a shovel from the rack of fireplace tools. Minutes later he was stealthily opening her front door.

Georgie came trotting over at once, looking relieved to see him if such a thing was possible. The radio continued to blare its gloomy, percussive tunes. He peeked into the kitchen and saw a lightweight radio lying on its side on the floor. Had Buck knocked it there climbing in through the window? Or was it a casualty of the strong winds. Nothing else seemed amiss.

As he stumbled through the dark of the unfamiliar living room, the shovel clutched in his hand, the dog followed at his heels. After bumping his knee on a piece of low furniture and overturning a wastepaper basket, he ended up crawling up the stairs on his hands and knees, trying to avoid creaks, nearly impossible on an old wooden stairway he'd never climbed before.

Reaching the upstairs hallway, he looked into the spare bedroom. It was dark and appeared vacant except for some sealed boxes and a spare chair. The bathroom was empty, too. Only a nightlight lit it.

A thin ray of light shone from under the closed third door. Wendy's room. A sort of keening sound seemed to seep out for a few seconds. But then it stopped. Had he imagined it? What could she being doing in there? As he put his ear to the wood, leaning into it to hear better, the door was suddenly yanked open, and Wendy, standing in the doorway, fired a gun straight into Bob's chest. "I told you to keep away from me, Buck," she screamed. "You damned liar. I knew you made a key …" And then she saw it was Bob sliding to the floor.

She knelt on the floor beside him. "Now, just look what I've done." She moaned like a woman in labor, sobbing, her tears falling on him like a sudden shower. "I thought it was Buck. Calling me over and over, playing that crazy music, making Georgie bark like that. I was sure it was Buck creeping up the stairs. I told you I could take care of myself, Bob. Why d'ya have to come after me?"

Come after her? Is that what she thought? Bob looked at the gun on the floor beside him, looked at the woman leaning over him, now hysterical. He wanted to tell Wendy he hadn't come after her, explain how he couldn't let it go—knowing what he did about men. But decided instead to concentrate on staying alive.

If he could.

THE LONG LAST RIDE OF EL CANEJO (OR SUNSET)

BY ACE ATKINS

YOU GOT SIX months, probably less, and your wife asks you a simple question: What do you want to do with your time?

"Die?" you ask, grinning at her.

"We can go anywhere you like, you can get hospice anyplace."

"They shouldn't call it hospice," you say. "They should call it Die Son of a Bitch Die."

"It's your time. Do what you want."

And it's not a week later, that you're in the passenger seat of the Buick, always loving to drive, but the doctor saying it's not a good idea with all the painkillers and medications or horse pills and such. Your legs don't work so good either, now having to tool around in a wheelchair while the cancer goes to work on you. Throat cancer lighting up your hospital charts like a goddamn Christmas tree.

You decide to head south, back to the beach where you all started out after the war when you got out of the Navy. You moved down to Tampa where you worked as a newspaperman and then a sheriff's detective, busting up moonshine stills and illegal gambling. Down here they called you *El Canejo*, the rabbit. You were known. You were famous. You made the Mafia greaseballs shit themselves on occasions.

"Why don't you call up the old gang?" you ask.

"I think most of the old gang is dead," your wife says.

"What about Buddy?"

"We got a Christmas card."

"Still in Daytona Beach?" you ask.

She nods.

"Call him."

The wife has rented the condo for the month, a two-bedroom unit on the fourth floor. Sea Breeze 2. You gripe that it has a shit view, looking across the banyan trees and palmettos rooted in a little abandoned lot by the main road. You preferred something looking out at the Gulf.

"I can push you down to the dock," she says.

"And then I'm relying on you. I'd rather just be up here. I need a place to smoke."

"You've got to be kidding me."

"Yeah," you say. "It might kill me."

YOUR BOYS AND daughter come to visit. And there isn't much crying and all that, because they know how much you hate that crap. You try to make jokes about getting sponge baths and the horse pills. You got two nurses, a fat black woman and old white woman who calls you captain. You had been the captain of the vice squad back in the fifties, your wife had told them. Captain, she calls you.

The black woman carries a big black bag filled with nothing but bottles and vials and needles. One needle is as long as your forearm.

"What's that for?"

"Seizures."

"Calms them?"

"*Mmm-hmm.* Real Good."

About the only action in the whole condo—besides the eating and the talking and the dressing—comes from the maids. Man, how you do love the maids. They are from Eastern Europe someplace, young girls with good bodies and teeth, tanned and curvy and shy in that sexy kind of way. They don't look like maids.

You have never seen maids like that.

When they look at you, you wink and tip the brim of your Irish cap. One of them, a dark girl with a nice tan, winks back. Man, that makes your day.

"Just why are they here?"

"Everyone needs a job," your wife says.

"With bodies like that, they don't need to be scrubbing toilets."

"They're nice girls."

"You see the fella who runs this place?" you ask.

"No."

"He's suspicious."

"Everybody is suspicious to you."

"He's mobbed up. You take my word for it. He's mobbed up."

"Why do you say that?"

"The Albanians and all that shit are running the show now," you say. "Don't you read the papers? All the old grease balls are dead. They don't have the stomach for it."

"Please don't embarrass me."

"Can I just make an observation?"

YOU START TAKING some pleasure in watching him. You learn his name is Fatmir. Which is pretty funny since he's bloated in the face and porky in the body and wears satin track suits and gold jewelry. You tell your wife that maybe he learned to dress like a mobster from watching American TV.

"Maybe he likes track suits."

"Yeah, he looks like the physical fitness type."

"You want something to eat?"

"Let's go down to the diner. What's that place called?"

"Pete's."

"Yeah, yeah."

"What are you thinking?" she asks.

"Ham and eggs."

"What are you thinking?"

"I used to run bastards like this."

"What has he done?"

"You bet your ass he's done something."

YOU HAVE THAT old white nurse wheel you out around the swimming pool and out to the pier and she's chattering on about the *blattedy-blah-blah* about the winter in Florida and how all her friends were jealous back in Buffalo or Cleveland or some place. And the thing about being old and dying is that you don't have to act like you give a rat's ass about any of it.

"Would you like something?"

"A cold beer," you say.

She laughs like it wasn't a real request and you wait till she's gone to turn down the oxygen tank and take off that fucking mask and light up a Backwoods cigar. You smoke it down a good halfway when you see Fatmir roll up in a metallic green Humvee with chrome wheels. Two girls are with him, one is the maid who winked at you and some other young good-lookin' gal.

They're not dressed as maids. They wear tight halter tops showing off belly rings and tight blue jeans with high heels and you roll forward a bit in the wheelchair staring through the open space of the parking garage facing the pool.

The girls, looking damn near identical, peel off a roll of bills from tight jean pockets and hand over a cut.

They don't notice you.

When you're a decrepit old man, no one does. You kind of wished you'd had this disguise when you were busting up the old Bolita racket in Ybor City. Back then they saw you and Buddy and from a mile away, hearing *Tres Canejos! Tres Canejos!* The Cubans figuring if you were a rabbit, then your buddies were, too.

You wonder if you could still tap a phone line, thinking about it, till you spot Fatmir's fat ass pull out a cell phone from his track suit and make a call. So it's just surveillance. It was always just surveillance back then, too.

"YOU WANT ME to turn on the TV, Dad?" your daughter asks.

"Fetch me a beer."

She doesn't give you shit. She's a good daughter and grabs a cold Budweiser. She props you up on a deck chair on the little balcony overlooking the vacant lot. She says her goodbye, a little teary eyed, and you promise not to die overnight if you can help it. And she grabs her keys to head back to the motel.

You don't feel so great. But you don't feel like you're dying. Maybe that's the bitch of the pills.

You doze off and wake up sometime in the middle of the night, maybe three in the morning. Two men are arguing in some foreign tongue down in that vacant lot among all the stunted trees and palmettos growing in that sandy soil. You spot their thick shapes in the moonlight and a flash of bright red from a jacket. They're carrying something heavy, bitching at each other in that foreign speak about who's holding the most weight, tossing what they got over a long wall made of cinder blocks.

One of the men disappears and then comes back with two shovels. It's windy up on the balcony and smells of salt water and dead fish.

The men light up some cigarettes and rest, leaning against the wall. You run your hands over the wheels of your chair and roll forward, trying to be quiet and slow but damn if you don't knock what's left of your warm beer through the balcony railing.

The men look up after the glass shatters.

Fatmir cranes his fat neck and has a good look at your face. He doesn't look happy.

"MAYBE THEY WERE fishing," your eldest son says.

"With shovels?

"Couldn't have been poles?

"I got cancer, not brain damage. Jesus."

"It's dark. Tough to see."

"When's Buddy coming?" you ask, yelling back to your wife. She's frying bacon and eggs, making coffee.

"Tomorrow."

"Get his ass on the phone."

ACE ATKINS

BUDDY WEARS AN orangish Hawaiian shirt with seagulls and palm
trees and water and bullshit. You remember the time he got into a scrap
with a greaseball heavy named Cowboy Ippolito and Buddy tossed him
through a plate glass window. When was that? Fifty-eight?

He's grown fat and bald in the last fifty years.

"You look fat," you say.

"You gonna eat that?"

"No," you say. "Take it."

Buddy reaches for your bacon at Pete's diner, having wheeled you into
the end of the booth. The anchor tattoo on his hairy forearm has faded
a great deal.

"This place reminds me of that place? You know?"

"Ayres Diner," you say.

"Ayres Diner."

"Buddy, you bring a gun?"

"You said you wanted a .38."

"Where is it?"

"I don't have a .38."

"Couldn't you have brought any goddamn gun?"

"I don't want to be a part of what you got planned."

"Son of a bitch. You, too."

"Not like that."

"You think I'm gonna shoot myself?" you say. "Sheesh."

"What should I think?"

"This guy Fatmir wants me dead. I was watching the sunset last night
and he comes over to me like we're old friends and puts his hands on the
grips of my chair. He smelled like a dung heap. His breath like dead
shrimp and cigarettes."

"I can't believe it."

"Since when am I wrong about crooks?"

"I can't believe you watch sunsets."

"Bleh."

"SWEET MOTHER OF God," Buddy says.

You two are watching the sunset and drinking cold beer, a fishing pole
in each of your hands. Buddy has turned away to watch two maids, different
girls, ditch their working clothes for string bikinis and baby oil. One is
blonde and the other brunette. They are tanned, narrow at the waist and
curvy in the hip and ass.

"I'd like them to clean my toilet," you say.

"They speak English?"

"Does it matter?"

"You could bounce a ball off that woman's stomach."

15

"You could bounce a couple of 'em."

"You say they're whores?"

"Wait a second and they'll get a call. They always write something down, like an address, and take off real fast."

"Where's the big man?"

"He'll be around."

"Where's that hole he dug?"

"*Shhh*. Be quiet."

You reel in your hook and bait and see that the shrimp has been eaten away, leaving only an empty transparent head. "Son of a bitch."

"ARE YOU SCARED?" Buddy asks that night, wheeling you along a sidewalk snaking along the main road from town, out of the condo complex and down to the empty lot, separated with the wall of concrete blocks. Lots of cars speed past you, blowing up grit and trash into your face but you keep on rolling ahead. There is a single light up on a telephone pole and out into the lot, you see a cat hopping around, trying to catch a lizard.

"He's gone. Don't worry."

"I mean about dying."

"Push me to the edge there."

"Can you walk at all?"

"Yeah, I just like you to push me around for fun."

"Are you scared?"

"I don't know, Buddy. God damnit. Over there, you see that?"

You point out a spot about three by six where the soil had been turned over. Buddy mops the sweat from his face and cleans his glasses with a clean handkerchief.

"I'm not afraid," Buddy says. "You want to know why?"

"Don't tell me you've gotten religion on me."

"It's the most important thing I've ever done," he says. "I haven't missed a Sunday in ten years."

"*Bleh.*"

"Right there?" Buddy asks.

You hand him the shovel and point. "Come on. Come on."

THE COP IS green as goose shit. He's young with a hairless face and a two-dollar haircut. You asked for a detective and you get a kid on traffic duty, taking notes on a fucking computer instead of writing stuff down for a man. It's nearly midnight before he shows up.

"Something funny?" he asks.

"Just never seen anyone take a report that way."

"I can file it by pushing a button."

"So this is just a report? I asked for a detective."

"Yes, sir."

"They buried someone back there."

"Where you found the bottle."

"The bottle had a note inside."

"And what did it say?"

"What did it say, Buddy?"

"It says *mascara*," Buddy says.

"And you know what that means, kid?" you ask the boy on patrol. His fingers stop typing. He drops his eyes, looking down from where he set up on the trunk of his cruiser. "It means asshole in Albanian," you say. "Look it up. Hey, they moved the goddamn body."

"Is there a bathroom around here?"

You toss your thumb over your shoulder at the toilets by the pool. Buddy watches you open up the patrol car and look around giving a low whistle, reaching into the front seat. Buddy taps your shoulder as he spots the boy coming back, zipping up his fly.

You close the front door. The boy studies you.

"Hell of a machine. Me and Buddy were cops way back when."

"I think I got what I needed," he says, reaching for the door handle. "Thanks."

He drives slow down the condo parking lot and turns on the signal to make a turn.

YOUR WIFE PICKS up two T-bone steak dinners the next day from a place in Clearwater. They look and taste like elephant ears and the medication is making you nauseous. Early evening is slow; the kids have flown home. Buddy is gone, gripping your hand for a long time, crying a bit telling you he'd try and stop by before you left. Hospice has bathed and dressed you earlier, piling you into two thick shirts as you requested because it makes your bony frame fill out and because it feels so damn cold all the time. You add the Irish cap.

"You want dessert?" your wife asks.

"He wouldn't even get me a piece."

"A what?"

"A gun."

"We have ice cream."

You shrug. "It was nice to see the kids," you say.

You two eat ice cream in silence so damn still that you hear each scrape of the spoon.

SHE'S LEFT YOU to smoke a Backwoods cigar at the pier, promising to return after a quick trip to the grocery store. It's late, maybe seven o'clock at night, and the sun is long since gone and the only show comes from some ratty pelicans trying to sleep on the pilings. There's a speed boat some asshole had tied up where you like to fish and your eyes grow heavy as the hull slaps up and down in small waves. You dream you are alone, detached and drifting, nothing but water and fog around you until you're back in that '54 Ford unmarked unit running wires off telephone lines listening in on Charlie Wall dropping the dime on greaseballs before he got his throat cut, or parked outside Santo Trafficante's ranch house in Palma Ceia before he escaped to Cuba to run Havana with Meyer Lansky. You smoke cigarettes, drink Old Forester in the old sheriff's office in the jail by the city graveyard. Your short-sleeved dress shirts and pants are pressed and your wingtips shine. You wear a .38 Chief's Special on your hip when you make those midnight meetings with Pelusa Joe at that old kiddie park, Fairyland, talking about the old Italians pushing out all the Spaniards and Cubans, blood wars heating up over gambling and bootlegging.

You feel as light as a goddamn balloon.

A girl cries.

You open your eyes and the whole damn scene doesn't seem real to you. All that fog and floating made sense and then you get mad a little, knowing it was the meds making you go nuts.

You wheel yourself over to the woman sitting on the edge of the diving board. Her long tan legs are knocked together at the knee below a miniskirt. Her head is in her hands with hair spilling down in her face.

"You okay?"

She looks up and you expect her to be prettier.

Her face is a goddamn mess. Split lip, eyes busted. Her arms and neck are bruised. Her face is wet from the crying and blood and she pats a paper towel to the marks. You figure the guy was wearing a ring.

"You speak English?" you ask.

She nods.

"Fatmir?"

She nods.

"I saw you with another girl," you say. "She looked like you."

She says it was her sister.

"What happened to her?"

"Who are you?"

"I used to be a cop."

She nods.

"What happened to her?" you ask.

And she tells you.

Six girls brought in from the old country. They scrub toilets and screw men until they pay off Fatmir. The girl who'd winked at you had gone off the plan and Fatmir choked her out while polishing the bastard's nob. There are five girls left and all of 'em scared shitless.

They can't go to the cops.

The girl says home is even worse.

There's more. But it boils down to Fatmir being a first-class shitbag.

YOU FEEL LIKE a million bucks as hospice bathes and dresses early the next morning, buttoning you up in pajamas and placing your meds in a paper cup. They've started to corrode your insides, giving you some bad indigestion at night and you ask what if you skipped them for now.

"The pain will be something else," the black nurse says.

"You won't be able to focus, enjoy the time you have," says the white nurse.

You take the pills with some bad Florida water. They set you into your wheelchair, spiffy and clean and ready for presentation. The black nurse has left her black bag open, that big ole horse needle sticking out of the top.

"HAVE I BEEN a pain in the ass?"

"When?" your wife asks.

"Always."

"Pretty much."

Both of you sit at the condo kitchen table. She's signing thank you letters for all the cards you've been getting.

"But you love me?" you ask.

"Don't be silly."

"Me, too."

"I haven't been a pain in the ass," she says.

"Hah."

"What do you want to do tonight?"

"Get drunk, go dancing. Stay up all night."

"Order in?"

"You wheel me down?"

"The pier again?"

"Nice sunset."

"What did they do with my husband?"

"I like the colors."

"How corny," she says.

FATMIR WHEELS IN that big green Hummer about an hour later, strutting out in a black muscle shirt and big puffy pants and sneakers. He's unshaven and fat and wears a lot of gold. At the edge of the parking lot, he lights a cigarette and begins to urinate against a fence.

He checks his watch, punches some numbers with both hands, still pissing, and starts to talk. You move the wheelchair back from the light, shadowed in the edge of the parking garage, under a tennis court. A ball

THE LONG LAST RIDE OF EL CANEJO (OR SUNSET)

thwacks and pops above you. The wind off the Gulf is cold but smells like summer.

Fatmir starts to yell and puts the phone back in his pocket, looking up to the fifth floor and cursing for someone. He curses some more and heads to the elevators just as you wheel out into the wide parking lot and find the passenger door of the Hummer, staring up at the chrome handle as it were the moon itself.

That goddamn door handle is a mile away and it takes about every inch of you, your spine cracking as you stretch, to reach it and push, unlatching the door, finding purchase on the armrest and pulling yourself up and into the car. The girls have to work for him for two years or they get shipped back. There's other stuff, expected stuff, like drugs and pornography. Most of the money getting rolled in real estate, the same as the Italians did over on Treasure Island and Passe-A-Grille fifty years ago.

You make it halfway, your chest against the seat, your old useless legs hanging out into the window, wheelchair knocked down and away, hoping he can't hear shit from five stories up. But you finally right yourself sweating and nearly passing out, trying to catch your breath like a beached fish, hands jittery, and spitting up blood into your fist.

You're fucked now.

You lean your head back into the headrest, steadying your hands into the leather jacket over your pajamas. You've worn your Irish cap down in your eyes and you like the look of yourself staring into the rearview and then up to the fifth floor where Fatmir heads out from a condo and heads back to the elevator. You nod as you wait, wondering if he'll see your wheelchair toppled over into the empty parking space.

But he's a dumbshit and a minute later, Fatmir jerks open the door and jumps inside, breathing heavy and sweating and it's a solid couple beats before he notices the old man in the pajamas sitting beside him. Out of habit, he puts the key into the ignition.

And that's when you lash out at the son of a bitch, stabbing him hard in the neck with the horse needle you stole and dropping that plunger down with your thumb. Fatmir holds his neck and screams at you, touching the blood in his neck and wanting to know what you've done.

You take that moment to snatch up his right wrist and click on the cuffs you stole from the patrolmen. You click the other end of the steering wheel.

He can't believe it. He can't fucking believe it.

You wink at him. *Goddamn, you're having fun.*

Whatever was in the needle has gone to work. You reach for the keys and crank the ignition, the big engine coming to life. He flops his fat head against the seat and lolls sideways, eyes wavering but on you. The windshield is wild and brilliant with gold and purple and blackness edging the horizon. You think it's a shame that the pretty scenes are wasted on the assholes of this world.

You knock the car into drive and use both hands to move your foot to the pedal, pressing down with all you got onto your left knee, the big sonofabitch Hummer heading through the parking garage, out the exit, busting through a wooden fence and across the polished pool deck. The light is so damn bright that you have to squint to steer, Fatmir's big shoulder rolling against you as the wheels bump and shutter over the path, crashing down the concrete steps and heading flat out onto the wooden pier.

That light so gold and bright, blue and black, that all of it the sea and earth and air looks like one goddamn thing.

The crash into the Gulf takes a lot out of you, the inch of wind you got in your lungs gone for a good long while. But you recover, pushing Fatmir against the driver's window that's half covered in seawater, the shiny hood nosing down, currents pulling you along.

You've brought your last Backwoods cigar for such an occasion and light it up with a Bic, making a show of blowing the smoke into the man's unshaven face. Water rushes at your feet and through cracks in the back windows.

Fatmir isn't talking.

"Look at those goddamn colors," you say.

"Why," he asks. "What does it matter?"

"Bleh," you say, water edging your chin and the orange tip of your cheap cigar. "It matters."

STIFFS

BY NEAL BARRETT JR.

STEED AND MAXX stared down at the dead and frozen bodies. The mediks had taken a look, then screwed the glass lids tight. Now they stood aside and waited for the kops to go away. There was nothing left to smell, but the kops wore lip-loppers, nose-buggers and goggle-stuks because that's what kops did. The mediks grinned behind their backs. They thought the kops looked like ducks.

"What I think happened," said Steed, "is Marlow and Chin were poisoned eighteen to twenty-seven hours before they left Earth. At a guess, I would say 9 to 11.5 millizacs of tribiorectum solution or air injection of chlorio-hotchagotus. Or, possibly both."

"Yeah? And why's that?" said Maxx.

"Well," said Steed, "obviously, no one gets aboard without a full nanocheck, so it happened before that. And I mention the two poisons because it had to be something godawful strong. Marlow and Chin are both 179. They're already full of plastic, mastic, putty and tin, iron, copper, polymer and peat, arsenic, nickel, bromo-tactiumitus and two-percent meat."

"You mean *you* don't know which? I can't fucking believe that."

Maxx's look was enough to slay a roomful of rookie kops, but nothing offended Steed.

"Actually, I don't have the answer to that, Inspector. It could be either one. But I *do* know who killed them."

"You what?"

"That's pretty obvious, isn't it? Marlow and Chin are 179. That ties them at number nine. Crane is second with 215 and Brinsley's fifth at l90. At the top, of course, is Arlo Hoop at 222.

"So it's Sheriden C.B. Brinsley, of course. He's doing them in one by one, working his way up to old Hoop. At the end of the convention he'll be number one, the world's oldest living assassin."

Maxx laughed. "That's ridiculous, Steed. No one is going to bring down Hoop. Not Brinsley or anyone else."

"No one but us," grinned Steed. "You, sir, and your humble aide, lackey, minion, your faithful squire—"

"Steed—"

"—We'll *do* it, Inspector. We'll track that clever bastard down and toss him in the slammer. And you know what, sir? I'll bet you half a crown Sheriden C.B. Brinsley already knows we're on his trail …"

HE STOOD ALONE at the Dan'l Boom Bar off the hotel's lobby. He was alone, because that's how Brinsley liked to be. It wouldn't be hard to take him out in the half-dark room, but he was C. B. Brinsley, and he knew no one would dare to try.

The pert, near-naked cutie set a crystal glass of Pakistani Scotch before him and trotted off. Brinsley took a quick swallow and set the glass back on the fancy napkin. The napkin was black, made of linen stock, lettered in silver, and read:

Welcome to the
BLINK AND DIE ASSASSINATION SOCIETY SEMINAR

The girl had left a black and silver lapel button on the napkin. It read: BADASS.

Brinsley studied the pin a moment, then stuck it to his lapel. It never hurt to look like one of the guys. They respected you for that, and nothing weakens a man more than that foolish look of courtesy and esteem. Brinsley had often used it himself.

Searching in his pocket, he drew out some bills and left them on the bar. It was twice the girl's income for a year. Brinsley didn't notice and didn't care.

He paused, listening, and searching the darkened room with all his senses. He had arrived on the Moon a day before he'd had Marlow poisoned at a hotel in Chicago and Chin in Sapulpa, Oklahoma. The two young men who'd handed them their pens were never seen again.

MAXX THOUGHT HE might throw up at his first breath of the Great Pacifica Resort. The place was a dump. Cots, crates, and corrugated walls. Steed made a fuss but Maxx didn't complain. No one was going to put up kops in a decent hotel. The magnificent Crater Inn was for zillionaires, almost as fancy as the Tennessee Towers, the convention hotel where the really big boys stayed. That's where Brinsley and his cohorts would be. All Maxx had to do was figure a way to get to him through impossible hotel security.

Maxx hated the Moon. Couldn't stand it. God had put it there to look at. Like the stars and planets and stuff. You weren't supposed to really *go* there.

Besides, he didn't think he could take another day of Steed. Maxx was seventy-two and Steed was fifty. A pompous little bastard. A kid maybe what—forty-, fifty-percent meat. Worse than that, Steed was smart. A fucking genius who could outthink Maxx seven ways from Sunday.

Sheriden C.B. Brinsley would know how to knock off Steed. So would Steed, but what good would that do? Maxx's head hurt thinking about it.

THE LOBBY WAS nearly empty. The tacky Moon clock on the wall said 1:00 AM. Brinsley spotted half a dozen media goofs, eight kops, four convention members, and three of something else.

He guessed the assassins at somewhere in their sixties. No winners, but a chance to hang out with the big boys. They wouldn't be here if they hadn't paid their dues. He thought he recognized one of the bunch: squat, long arms, one leg of Class-3 steelx in a transparent sheath. Brinsley could see the arterial tubes buried in biajel, the blood and other shit pumping as the guy walked. His head was hard and shiny, sort of urinal-white, with a "Ril-Face" right off the shelf. The poor bastard was scarcely 170 and he'd been through the mill. You could tell a newbie right off. He hadn't made enough kills to cover up the bad stuff you picked up in the trade.

No one glanced at Brinsley, or they pretended they didn't. It was partly a sign of respect, partly to let him know they weren't dumb enough to look him in the eye.

Brinsley turned away toward the elevators, caught the scent of the restaurant nearby, thought he smelled clams, lamb, ham, boa, and badger pie, liver-ripple ice cream—stopped, froze, came to a halt, went rigid as only Brinsley could, caught the reflections in the darkened glass by the lobby doors, turned, and, in less than an instant, brought the irritation and urge to kill under control.

Taking a deep breath, he stalked by the hotel guards and into the supra-cooled, polargated, double-defriga-mated lunar air that flowed through the vast, inner workings of the Moon. It was pure and free of all viral and bacterial intrusions of every kind. To Brinsley, it smelled faintly like a men's room he recalled east of Bismarck, North Dakota.

The two men were standing by the curb. One was plain fat, the other looked like a stick.

"What do you want," asked Brinsley, adding a dozen new smells to his growing inventory.

"We are officers of the Lunar American Police, Special Extension. We would—"

"LAPSEX," said Brinsley, "I know who you are. You're Inspector Maxx, he's Detective Steed. I know when you arrived. I know you're living in a sewer. When do you intend to leave?"

Steed looked offended. Maxx, an old pro, showed no reaction at all.

"As I'm sure you know," Steed said, "we are here to arrest you for the murder of Thomas Marlow and Sidney Chin. Will you come with us quietly, or should I call for officers to assist?"

"No."

"No, what, sir?"

"We mean no offense," Maxx broke in. "This is a professional matter, not personal."

"Goodnight," said Brinsley, and turned back toward the hotel.

"Just a moment," said Steed. "We're not finished here!"

Brinsley kept walking.

"If you cooperate," Steed said, "it's possible that could have some bearing on your case."

"To some extent," Maxx added. "You should keep that in mind."

Brinsley disappeared past the lobby doors.

"It's hard to reason with the criminal mind," said Steed.

"You'd do well to remember that, Detective. It will serve you well in your career."

IN HIS ROOM, Brinsley scanned the list of convention participants. Names and pictures flashed across the screen. The one he was looking for didn't appear. No big deal. All you had to do was be on the list, one way or another. About half the members used a different alias and a face to match, because the kops on two planets had their names.

He stopped at GARFENO RIGG. He didn't know Rigg but he recognized him from the members in the lobby. Jug-head, cheap face, bad leg. He punched in statistics for Rigg:

Height
Weight
Heartbeat (normal walk)
Sub-atomic structure
Biological sounds and rumbles
B.A.D.A.S.S.RATING: Number 17
Age: 168

Hey, why not? Something to do. Better than hanging around in the room. Brinsley inserted three dozen microboomers at different points on the sole of his left shoe. He carried the shoe with him to the entry corridor where guests passed on the way to their rooms. There, he replaced the shoe on his foot, and made a careful but erratic walk around the hallway. Each time he stopped, one near-invisible particle stuck to the floor. Each was the size of the fecal leavings of a flea.

Brinsley stepped back, studying his work. A thousand guests would pass by that evening. Many would step on one of Brinsley's devices. Only one, with the exact sub-atomic characteristics of Garfeno Rigg, would react to the tiny specks Brinsley left there. The act would send hordes of officers from hotel security, MOONPRIX, LUNA-TECS, and other agencies into a frenzy. Brinsley hoped it would give Maxx and Steed a chance to earn their salaries from LAPSEX, and buy a decent meal.

THE GIRL WAS sitting cross-legged on the floor in front of his door. Long legs, hands in her lap, fingers bright with silver rings. When she saw him she rose, rising like a dancer, uncurling from a fine and practiced move. Her hair was long, black, and in careful disarray. She smiled in a lazy, gentle manner, without looking up, as if she had expected him to be there, just as she was at that time. When their eyes met, he was slightly taken aback, for there was the hint of an invitation, unexpected in a woman he had never seen before.

"Good evening," he said, "I don't believe we've met."

"I guess we have, now," she said. And as she spoke, he sensed every inch of her body, clothing, jewelry, perfumes, and natural body fluids. He found no dangers of any sort, only rather intense and cautious emotions. He was scarcely surprised that she was a normal woman, and not a member of his profession.

"You look right through a person," she said.

"So do you," said Brinsley."

"But not quite the same way." She patted his arm, something he would never have allowed if he didn't know she was clean.

"I didn't mean to be rude," she said. "It's just that I know who you are. You're rather famous, Mr. Brinsley. Near the top of the list."

He looked at her without expression. "And you're a fan of our group? You're interested in assassins?"

"Some. Not all."

"And what do you want with me?"

"That depends. I'm sorry. My name is Jeannie. Jeannie Real-Parts."

Brinsley tried not to smile. "And which parts are we talking about?"

"Which ones do you like?"

"Which ones have you got?"

Jeannie shook her head. "May I come in, Mr. Brinsley?"

"Surely." He stepped aside. "Forgive me."

She brushed him lightly as she passed, and flowed onto the couch in that dancerly manner he so admired.

"If I'm right," he said, pausing to fix drinks at the bar, "you'll find a rarity in parts among this group."

"Does that mean I'm wasting your time?"

"None of your business. For your information I've been luckier than most. What I haven't got, you don't need to see."

Brinsley laid her drink on the table before her. A chair was handy but he stood instead. Something about her, something more than her perfect features, her breathtaking beauty, left him with an odd sense of irritation. She was too content, too easy. In some way, life belonged to her and she knew it.

"I shouldn't say this," he told her, "and I'm not a guy that's rude to pretty girls. But I look at you …"

Brinsley paused. "I'm suddenly thinking what you know and I know but no one thinks about much. Everyone lives forever, thanks to the science jerks who gave us this—this gift.

"We've got it, but what do we do with it? See, I'm intruding on you here and I don't have any business doing that. You, lady, are so goddamn adorable, so—Is this what you're going to do forever? You going to be a hundred-year-old hooker? Think you can handle that?"

"You going to be a five-hundred-year-old killer? That working out for you, pal?"

Brinsley stood by the edge of the couch.

"I don't know. It's something to do."

"Man, there's a bright answer for you."

Brinsley frowned at that. When he faced her, those goddamn crazy eyes knocked him for a loop again.

"Is that all? Is that all, really?"

She stood, close. So close he could smell her breath, her hair, taste the magic of her skin. He wondered how this could happen, just *happen* like that. He could control his body, his senses, probably better than any man anywhere. At the moment, he had no desire to do that. Instead, he set down his drink and watched her, knew where she was going, and followed her there, his heart beating out of control, something that scarcely ever happened to C.B. Brinsley in the most dangerous, violent profession in the world.

The explosion shook the room at 4:23 AM. The girl gasped, held him. He shook her off, was halfway dressed before she caught sight of him again.

"Don't worry," he said, "be right back."

"Oh, good," she said.

GARFENO RIGG WAS scattered in a number of disgusting pieces. At least, Brinsley guessed part of the mess was Rigg, for there were half a dozen more chunks and puddles scattered about. Brinsley was puzzled by the mess. He'd never had trouble with the microboomers before. He hoped the other casualties had been tourists, and not members of BADASS.

A crowd was gathering, as crowds will. A number of the gawkers were kops, including two he knew well.

"There's no chance of a deal now, Brinsley," said Detective Steed. "We've got you cold. We've got the proof, the facts, the evidence, the whole kit and caboodle, as they say. We're taking you in now. I wouldn't resist. That would be futile."

"It would," added Maxx. "I can get a hundred officers here with a snap of my fingers."

"Why?" said Brinsley.

"Why?" Steed's face began to cloud with anger. He gave it his best and startled Inspector Maxx, who had never seen Steed rise beyond the edge of irritation.

"Don't play the fool," said Steed. "We're arresting you for the brutal murder of one Garfeno Rigg and persons unknown. Give me your shoes, Brinsley. Now!"

"No, thanks. I wouldn't walk in this mess without shoes."

"Don't argue. Give them to me now." Steed took a menacing step forward.

"Do something with him, Inspector. Help him leave here in one piece."

Maxx stepped between them. "I have a better idea. We'll go through everything in his room."

"All right," said Steed, "but I like the idea of just stripping down the bastard now."

"I think we'll go for the room," said Maxx.

"OH, MY GOD!" Steed cried out, and turned the other way. Maxx took a good look, a professional to the core.

Jeannie Real-Parts had not bothered to pull up the sheet. She was propped on a pillow, reading a magazine she'd found on the floor. Maxx made a note of the title: MOON BABES!

"Ma'am, I assume you have been here since approximately four AM on. Am I correct?" said Maxx.

"Didn't check the time," said Jeannie.

"Surely you simply choose not to remember," said Steed.

"Get out of here," said Brinsley.

"Not without your clothing and shoes," grinned Steed.

"You find any?" said Maxx.

"Uh, no. And that means he did the crime with the clothes *and* shoes he's got on!"

"He's got you there, Brinsley."

"No."

"No? You saying no to an officer?"

"No. Just saying I want you to do the strip job, Steed."

The color drained from Steed's face. "Don't you move. We'll have guards at the end of the corridor until a special squad arrives."

"Good idea," said Maxx, who urged Steed to the door.

"What did you do with them?" Brinsley asked her.

"Threw them out the window," said Jeannie.

"Shit. Everything I own? Great." He peered out the door. No one at either end. "I'll be gone for a while."

"Okay."

"Will you be here?"

"Should I be?"

"Yes indeed."

She smiled and picked up her copy of MOON BABES! "Good. Then I will."

BRINSLEY HADN'T BEEN in the place before, but he'd heard about it for years. Every pro in BADASS knew the Tennessee's Bar & Grill was the most exclusive retreat on the Earth and the Moon. It was said God couldn't get in because he couldn't afford the drinks.

The décor was something else. The room was a replica of a 1920s small-town garage. Antique cars in various stages of disarray were scattered about. The floor was concrete artfully painted with grease. Dust imported from Highway 65 south of Pine Bluff, Arkansas, was sprayed on the walls. Tools lined workbenches apparently worn and stained from the years. Behind these benches were barmaids clothed in old-fashioned overalls that scarcely covered any area concerned with heat, lust, buggery, frenzy, nookie, or passion of the flesh.

Comfortable, specially tattered easy chairs surrounded pot-bellied stoves that burned authentic-appearing wood.

There were couches for members who could no longer sit due to replacement of muscle, bone, nerve tissue, organs, or bodily fluids. There were also special devices designed to support the body in a comfortable vertical position. These fine artifacts were made by Burmese nuns who were taught this art from birth.

When Brinsley entered, all eyes took him in, then quickly glanced away. They could list his hits from memory. They knew about Chin and Marlow. They weren't at all certain about this Rigg character. What was the deal on that?

Brinsley saw Crane, number two, nodded at Bobby James, who was third. James was with an old, torn-up guy Brinsley had never seen before. Whoever he was, he gave Brinsley a black as thunder look.

Before Brinsley could look back, two hefty guards grabbed him with respect and tossed him down at Arlo Hoop's table.

Arlo hollered and shooed away two cuties in coveralls.

"God A-Mighty, it's good to see you, C.B. How long has it been?"

Brinsley had no idea and it was clear Hoop didn't care. Whatever the time, it hadn't been kind to Hoop. He'd made his big kills in the early days and easily looked his 215 years and his position as Numero Uno. His head was a gator jaw stuck on his neck with dia-mole and plutz. Most of his body was pluto-pork, muckalot, and hydro-tinitus. Brinsley wasn't sure about the legs, but had an idea '98 Fords had come into play.

"I've got to talk to you, C.B., no offense, so don't drop me on the spot. I understand Chin and Marlow. Distraction, right? Used it myself. This Garfeno what's-his-name. What is that shit? The guy wasn't your target. You just give the club a bad name."

"Okay, I was wrong, Arlo. Got bored, sitting around. So?" Brinsley gave him a hard look.

"Hey, pal. I'm number one, I can ask any fucking thing I want. You lookin' to climb? You want my job? You working your way up from five?"

"Hell no, Arlo. I'm just doing my job. Got these LAPSEX jokers on my back. Don't want to be two or three, either."

"You don't want to be four, either." Hoop made a face. "That fucking Rastov. One up on you and I wish he was in Cleveland. Pain in the ass is what he is. You know him?"

"No, he here?"

"Over there, with Crane. Another asshole."

Brinsley turned and saw the Rastov guy staring right at him, giving him another dark look.

"I don't know him. But he doesn't care for me."

"Don't feel left out. Doesn't care for anyone knockin' 'round on the same planet he's on."

"You've got a great bunch of guys here, Hoop. I was you, I'd find me a cabin somewhere and haul ass out of this business."

Hoop gave him a look. "You sure you're not working your way up, C.B.? Padding your scores, maybe, to get to old Hoop?"

Brinsley laughed. "I don't want to be a big shot. Told you that, right? So—"

Brinsley stopped, jerked around as a waitress screamed and dropped her tray. Drinks went scattering as a man blasted through her, tossing her aside. Brinsley saw at once it was this Rastov, heading right for him, limbs jerking this way and that, eyes wild with terror. He gagged, twisted, shuddered and jerked, then dropped like a rock.

Guards surrounded Hoop. Hoop let out a yell and dove for cover.

The guy on the ground was scarcely two feet from Brinsley. His face was ripped, mangled, torn, as if someone had run him through a thrasher … and, as Brinsley watched in alarm, half his features oozed away and slid across the floor.

Brinsley felt something turn over in his stomach. He had never seen Rastov before he sat down with Hoop, but he knew the real face that was visible now. He had memorized all its features before he left Earth. He was James McCarty Simms III, from Allentown, Pennsylvania.

He was the man Brinsley had come to the Moon to kill.

NO ONE SAW him leave. Chaos was the name of the game in the Tennessee's Bar & Grill. The members of BADASS had nothing against death. It was how they made their living. The idea that someone might do the same to them—it was frightening, irritating, and totally uncalled for. It didn't seem fair at all.

Brinsley paused for scarcely a moment—taking in the street outside the hotel, the windows, the few people walking about. He was moving before anyone could remember he was there; down an alley beside the hotel, up a street that led to a row of elegant shops. The avenue was too bright, and he circled back through a spacious park that featured fake plants and trees from Earth. It was darker there, and the shadows gave him time to think.

Clearly, something had gone terribly wrong. His target had discovered *him*. Which meant someone else had known who he was. Who, though? And, more bewildering still, someone had saved Brinsley's life before the man could reach him. This whole business was getting more bizarre by the minute.

Brinsley wondered if he could somehow get back into the hotel and learn what was going on. He wondered if the girl was still in his room. It didn't much matter. Going back inside was out of the question.

The place would be swarming with kops, including the irritating Maxx and Steed. Right now, his very presence on the Moon might be hazardous at best. He could get on a ship, but he'd have to be careful, maybe even change his appearance the way Rastov had done. The very idea brought a bad taste to his mouth. He'd be damned if he—

"You're fast, but you're not that fast," said Inspector Maxx. "Don't move an inch, Brinsley, just stay right where you are."

"I've got to be slipping," said Brinsley. "This is very embarrassing to me."

"Don't be. I've been in the business a long time myself. Just hug that tree, don't turn around, and listen. There's a lot you need to know if you want to get off this world alive."

"And what? You're going to help me do that?"

"I already have, Brinsley. I shot that son of a bitch in the bar. I think that's worth a little gratitude."

"Why would I think you'd do that? Who was it, you or your toady Steed?"

"Steed's got nothing to do with this. This is my business, not his. I told you to listen," Maxx said harshly. "I don't want to kill you, you're worth a lot of dough to me."

Listening sounded like a good idea.

"I've been a good kop a lot of years. Not always, and not tonight. I'm earning a fat payday for watching your ass. Mrs. James McCarty Simms III wanted her old man dead, and my job was to see you stayed alive long enough to do it. You screwed up, and I intend to ask for a bigger piece of the action."

Brinsley was tempted to turn around and stare at Maxx. Tempted, but not much.

"And now what? We hold hands and dance away the night?"

"Now I decide whether to earn Mrs. Simms' money or dump you out topside and see how long you can hold your breath. It's a close call, Brinsley, a fucking close call!"

"Yeah, well, if there's anything I can do to help—"

BRINSLEY KNEW THE taste in his mouth the moment he opened his eyes. Krepto-mi-napalot, a pretty heavy dose if was right. He knew, too, that his face was sticky and his nose was full of wax. Fake! All of it fake, just like the late James McCarty Simms III. Somewhere, Inspector Maxx was laughing in his beer, thinking about the fifth most famous assassin on two worlds plastered up like a clown.

Wiping the gunk from his eyes, he could see the rows ahead and knew the ship was only half full. The screen up front showed a pearl-bright vision of Earth, which was still halfway from the Moon.

Great. The sooner the better. Get back and straighten all this shit out and get back to work. Whatever came next, it sure as hell would be on good old Earth somewhere.

First off, he needed to explain to the widow Simms what had happened up there. There was time to work out a good story, but it had to be a good one. He had the best reputation in the business and couldn't let this thing screw it up …

"Having a good trip? My, you look nice, love. Who does your makeup?"

For an instant, Brinsley was startled. He knew her voice, her touch, the exotic scent of her flesh. He also knew she ought to be back on the Moon, not halfway to Earth.

"What's up, Jeannie? Business laying off on the Moon?"

"That's not very nice, C.B." She moved in closer to his seat, and rested her hand on his knee. "You never complained when we had our little affair."

Brinsley moved her hand off his knee. "I'm not complaining now. Just think it's a hell of a coincidence finding you here, at a kind of crucial moment in my life."

"Oh, that." Jeannie laughed. "I can't *stand* those freezy things. Gives me the creeps. I'll take the long way any time. Like you."

"I didn't ask if you liked third class or first. What are you *doing* here just when I'm getting the fuck off the Moon?"

"Oh, well …" Jeannie stretched up closer, until the warmth of her body touched his, and pressed her lips firmly against his. She held him close until she ran out of breath, sat back and sighed.

"I just wanted you to know I felt something special for you, hon. I haven't known a lot of men like you."

"And somehow you knew one who came to the Moon to kill a man, knew who he was, knew a kop named Maxx, and knew I'd get doped and dumped on a plane back to Earth. That's a lot of something to know, even for a lady in your profession."

Jeannie was silent for a long moment. "There's something else you ought to know, Brinsley. I'm really, *really* sorry to bring this up, but we've all got a job to do, and mine's about done. I'm working for Mrs. Simms too. It was Maxx's job to see that nothing happened to you up there. My job's to make sure no one finds out about poor Mr. Simms. I took care of Maxx before we left. I think he was kind of surprised, you know? He said he thought I was a real nice girl.

"Well, I'm not, actually. Listen, I had a very special substance on my lips when we kissed, C.B. And it was a nice kiss, too. But the chemical on it is working its way to your heart, and when it gets there …"

"You *are* a bad girl, you know?" Brinsley said. "And not a very bright one, either. You need to be careful when you kiss someone in the assassin trade. My skin, bones, musculature, and nervous system are guarded with auro-stiffanil, and every vital liquid like blood, mucous, phlegm, snot and other bodily secretions are infused with tri-demi-yuck-alite, a somewhat deadly combination outside the body it was designed to protect. So you can see …

"Are you unwell, Jeannie?"

"I'm—"

"Yes, you are, and if you don't mind …" He stood, made his way past her, and tried not to look in those lovely eyes.

"Stewardess, I'd like to change seats if it's no problem," he said. "Something farther up the aisle, if you will."

THE END OF JIM AND EZRA

BY C.J. BOX

The Wind River Range, Wyoming Territory, 1835

IT TOOK GREAT determination—almost more than he had left inside him—for Jim not to throw back the heavy buffalo robes and slice Ezra's throat open. His sheathed Bowie knife was in his bed within easy reach where it had been each night for the past twenty-eight years. Jim clamped his eyes shut and stroked the leather-wrapped handle with his fingertips. The blade was as sharp and as long as his thigh and he had used it to cut apart hundreds of buffalo, elk, deer, and bears. It had skinned a thousand beaver and he had shaved with it back when he shaved, and it had pierced the insides of three Indian bucks: two Arikara and a Pawnee. But he'd never used it to kill a friend.

Jim felt ashamed and he opened his hand beneath the robes and released the knife handle.

It was freezing inside the cabin, as it had been every morning for six weeks. The cold had made the chinking between the logs contract, crack, and fall out in chunks. The series of gaps let wind blow through the walls and a half-dozen inch-high snowdrifts had formed across the top of his robes, striping them, making them look, as Ezra pointed out each and every morning, as if he were sleeping under a zebra hide. Ice crystals tipped the ends of individual hairs on the outside of the robe as well, making it look as gray as Jim's beard.

He fought against the urge to grasp the knife again as Ezra's socked feet thumped the rough wood plank floor. Jim listened in tortured silence as Ezra rose unsteadily to full height and stretched. Ezra's bones cracked like the sounds of ice shifting on a lake, a combination of low-grounded pops and high snapping sounds. Ezra growled from deep in his chest and worked a gob of phlegm up into the back of his throat while he sniffed in the fluid of his nose so it could all mix together into a substantial globule he called his "morning mass" because he was

Catholic. Ezra just held it there—sometimes it seemed for a half an hour to Jim—while the man poked and prodded the fire and added lengths of split wood until it took off and started to roar. Waiting for the flames, Ezra breathed raggedly through his nose because his mouth was full. When the fire was intense enough that the metal grate was hot, Ezra spit his morning mass onto the bars of the grate and said, *"Lookit that thang burn."*

Sometimes, Jim could hear it pop.

Jim knew Ezra would then say, *"Jim, come lookit this thang,"* because Ezra said it each and every morning, and had for ninety-two straight days. He said it again.

Ninety-three.

Ezra turned stiffly toward Jim while he pulled a clawed hand down through his matted beard to groom it. He'd once stood six foot four before he got that hump in his back and his legs bowed out as wide as his shoulders. He'd worn the union suit so long his leg hairs were growing out through the fabric. White salty blooms framed the crotch. A tobacco stain looked like a permanent teardrop under his left breast. Both elbows of the suit had long since worn away and Ezra's blue-white joints stuck out the holes.

He cackled and said to Jim, *"Lookit you sleeping under that zebra hide! It looks like a damn zebra hide the way it's all striped like that."*

THE CABIN, CORRAL, fur shack, and loafing shed had been thrown together on the western side of the Wind River Mountains too high up and too far from anyone or anything else. They'd been caught in early September by snow, and Jim could tell by just looking at the sky that more was coming fast, that it was just the beginning of a mean and heartless winter.

They'd been trapped by their own success, a phrase Ezra had latched onto and repeated two or three times a day.

It had been Jim's idea, borne of frustration and lack of beaver in the lowland creeks and streams, to go higher and farther into the mountains than they'd ever gone before. Farther than *any* white trappers had gone before. There'd been a sense of urgency because they were being pushed by newcomers. More of them all the time, flowing west and north across the continent like a plague. The newcomers had no idea how rough and raggedy it had once been, and had little appreciation for men like Jim and Ezra, who had scouted the rivers and valleys and found the beaver and fought the Indians. Jim and Ezra were like the elk. Once plains animals, they'd been pressured to seek higher ground.

It wasn't fair, but Jim had never thought fairness was his due. So many things were working against them. The scarcity of beaver. The discovery back East that silk worked better for top hats than beaver felt. The plummeting price of beaver plews. And their aged and aching bodies.

Three things bound them together, two being their history and their treasure.

The third thing was the fact they were snowbound nine thousand feet in the mountains.

And all Jim could think of these days was how much he wanted to kill Ezra.

THE FUR SHED outside bulged with skinned beaver plews six feet high by eight feet deep. The plews had been skinned, stretched, and bound together. Now they were frozen into bales so heavy it took two men to load them. They were worth a fortune.

The cabin was one room, roughly twenty by twenty feet. There were two frame beds cross-hatched with rope to provide some give, a table that listed to the right, two chairs, a slab-rock fireplace that wasn't tight, and no windows except for the four-inch square in the door covered with bear-greased cotton cloth. Every corner of the structure was filled with snarls of traps and chains. They had one pot, one frying pan, and a tin for coffee and hot water.

It had been over three months.

THEY'D NEARLY MADE up for all of the things working against them the previous fall. They trapped more beaver—thousands of them— than they ever had before as they worked their way up the river to its source.

They called the place Green River Lake and it was magnificent: a huge body of water overlooked by a square-topped granite tower that seemed carved to resemble the massive turret of a German or French castle. Not that either of them had seen a castle, but Ezra had a book with a picture in it. The inlets to the lake teemed with beaver and the lake itself was brimming with plump cutthroat trout.

And once they found the beaver, Jim wouldn't stop. He urged Ezra to stay until the two of them could barely walk due to their arthritic knees made worse by standing thigh-high in freezing water day after day checking their traps. Jim didn't say, "That's enough," until they had to break through skins of ice to get to the drowned beavers.

By then it was too late. Winter was setting in. The logistics of transporting their bales of skinned beaver plews to Ft. Bridger—it would have taken two trips—were impossible. Plus, they couldn't leave their treasure or cache it. Indians would find it and steal it and sell off their year's work. The Indians wouldn't even consider it stealing. They'd consider it "finding." Jim understood that and didn't hate the Indians for the way they thought. They were well aware of the waves of newcomers. And they needed money and guns, too.

So Jim and Ezra built a temporary shelter, until the weather broke. But it never did.

BREAKFAST WAS FATTY beaver tail and the last half of a ptarmigan Jim had shot the day before. The ptarmigan was delicious. Jim watched Ezra eat. Ezra chewed loudly and smacked his lips and his pointy tongue shot out of his mouth to catch droplets of grease on the tips of his mustache. When the bird was stripped of flesh Ezra snapped off every bone and sucked the marrow dry until the bones were no more than translucent tubes on his plate.

Ezra said, "I'd give my left nut for coffee."

Jim said, "Might as well. You got no other use for it anymore."

A gust of wind hit the north wall of the cabin and shot a spray of snow inside.

"Wished I'd done a better job of chinking," Ezra said.

"Me too."

"Got any ideas how we can fix it? Mine wasn't so good."

Jim said nothing. It had been Ezra's suggestion to fill the gaps with bear fat, thinking that the fat would freeze and seal hard as plaster. It worked for a week, until the grizzlies found it and licked it clean. One night, Jim and Ezra sat on Ezra's bed with their .50 Hawken rifles across their knees, hoping the bears didn't push the cabin down around them. They watched as huge wet pink tongues flicked between the logs. They could hear the bears smacking their lips and clicking their three-inch teeth. Jim went nearly mad from fear and impatience and finally went outside and shot a sow to warn them off, but the bears came back that night and licked the rest of the fat clean and tried to smash down the door. Jim and Ezra ate the sow.

"It's gotta stop one of these days," Ezra said, and paused. "The storms."

"It's winter."

"We're trapped by our own success."

Jim closed his eyes. He *knew* he'd hear that one again.

JIM BLEW INTO the cabin from outside with gouts of swirling snow. Ezra looked up from where he sat at the table shaving curls of meat from a frozen deer haunch into the pot for stew. "You look like a damned snow bear," he said. Ezra was always *observing* him, Jim thought. And he never kept his observations to himself.

Jim had to use his shoulder to close the door against the wind and he slid the timber across the braces to seal it shut. He shook snow from his buffalo coat and hung it on a peg. His leggings were wet and packed with snow, and his winter knee-high moccasins needed to be greased because his feet were wet. The snow was six feet deep outside, more than halfway up the cabin. Paths outside the front door—rimmed by vertical walls of snow—led to the corral, the fur shack, and to where the outhouse had been before it got buried. Yellow and brown stains spotted the top of the snow but they lasted only until the next storm. Ezra had stopped going outside several weeks before and had been using a leaky chamber pot he'd fashioned himself from pine staves. It was nearly full. He set it just outside the door each night so it would freeze solid. Unfortunately, he brought it back inside during the day.

Jim said, "Emily's dead."

Ezra shook his head. "How?"

"Froze to death. Hard as a rock. Must have happened last night."

"Wolves get to her?"

"Not that I could see."

"Is she too froze to quarter?"

"Ezra," Jim said, "I ain't eating Emily. She was a good horse. I ain't eating her."

Ezra shrugged. "What's dead is just meat, Jim. You know that. You ate horses before."

"We *had* to," Jim said. "We had nothing else."

"Just thought you'd like something new for a change."

"Not horse. Horse reminds me of Birdwing and all that happened."

The first winter, after they'd gone all the way to the other ocean with Colonel Ashley's merchant party and turned around and struck out on their own to become trappers, Jim had taken a wife. A pretty Crow named Birdwing. While Jim and Ezra were out scouting creeks, the Pawnee had broken into Jim's cabin on the Bighorn River and had taken her. Jim and Ezra pursued the Pawnee for a month and found them and killed them all, only to find out Birdwing had died of disease the week before. On their way back, with Jim mourning and not speaking for days, the Pawnee found *them*. The bucks killed their pack horses and chased them into the badlands, where they'd literally ridden their good horses to death in order to escape. And eaten them.

"Birdwing," Ezra said, after about five minutes of shaving meat into their pot. "You still think about her."

Jim grunted.

"I think about that little whore at Ft. Laramie," Ezra said, smiling manically. "The redhead. I think about her every night before I go to sleep."

Jim took a deep breath, and said, "I know. I'm only ten feet away from you."

Ezra guffawed. He'd never been contrite about that. Even when he worked himself so furiously he sometimes fell out of his bed.

"All I know," Ezra said, "is this is the last of our fresh meat. Unless you can kill us something real soon, Emily might start looking pretty good out there."

"I ain't eating Emily," Jim growled. "She was a good horse."

"And now," Ezra said, "We're plumb out of horses."

"We can get some come spring," Jim said. "We can trade some plews for 'em if we have to."

"Never should have come up this far," Ezra said, shaking his head.

Jim turned away, his rage building.

"Sorry," Ezra said, "I shouldn't have said that."

"You could have left any damned time," Jim said though clenched teeth. "I wouldn't have stopped you."

Five months and Ezra hadn't said it, Jim thought. Five months Ezra had held it in.

"After all we been through together?" Ezra said.

THAT NIGHT THEY ate deer meat boiled in melted snow and didn't say one word to each other. The wind sliced through the cabin and the tallow candle shimmered and blew out. They finished eating in the dark. Jim kept waiting for Ezra to light the candle again because he had the matches. Ezra just ate, and sucked on his mustache and beard for dessert.

Jim didn't have to watch to know what he was doing. He knew the sound. He smoldered.

AFTER EZRA WAS done with the whore from Ft. Laramie Jim said, "Don't forget, our fortune is right outside. I'm sure you want your half when this is all said and done."

Since they'd been holed up there had been an unspoken rule that they didn't talk after they went to bed. Too intimate. Jim had broken protocol but he was still seething.

"I said I was sorry for sayin' that, Jim. Just forget it."

"You could have left anytime. We could have squared up and you could have left."

Ezra said, "It's a cold one tonight."

"You can leave tomorrow if you want," Jim said. "I'll get those plews down myself and I'll sell 'em and send you your share wherever the hell you wind up. Just leave word at the fort where you want the money sent."

Ezra sighed. "You're like a dog with a rag in its mouth, Jim. You won't let go."

Jim closed his hand around his knife, and went to sleep that way.

Lines of snow, like jail bars, formed across the top of his blankets.

THE NEXT MORNING, Jim kept his eyes closed and gripped the handle of his knife while Ezra coughed himself awake, hacked phlegm into a ball in his mouth, and got the fire going.

Ezra spit the gob onto the grate, and said, *"Lookit that thang burn. Jim, come lookit this thang."*

Jim threw his covers aside, sat up, said through gritted teeth, "I'm leaving. I'll be back come spring."

Ezra stroked his beard and squinted at Jim. "How you going to cover two hundred miles in the snow to get to Ft. Bridger?"

Jim gathered and tied up his ropes as a backpack and filled a leather sack with half the pemmican. He grabbed his possibles sack from a peg and stuffed it with half their powder and lead.

"Take more if you want," Ezra said.

"This is fine. I'll manage." Jim couldn't even look at Ezra. He couldn't look at his rheumy eyes or filthy union suit or scraggly beard because he knew if he did he'd kill the man right there. Gut him, and toss the carcass outside for the grizzlies.

"The only way down is through the Pawnee winter camp," Ezra said. "They might not like that."

"Ezra," Jim said, hands shaking, "Get out of my way."

"You want breakfast first?"

"Ezra, get out of my way."

"Just because I spit in the fire?"

"That and every other damned thing."

Ezra stepped back as if slapped.

As Jim pulled on his buffalo coat and clamped his red fox hat over his head, he heard Ezra say to his back, "God be with you in your travels, Jim. I'm going to miss you, my friend. We had some mighty great years together."

Jim plunged outside with his eyes stinging. He convinced himself it was due to the blowing needles of snow in his face.

Through the howling wind he thought he heard Ezra's voice, and he turned.

The wind whipped Ezra's words away, but Jim could read his lips. Ezra said, "We're victims of our ..."

Jim ignored the rest.

THE PAWNEE WINTER CAMP was massive, stretching the length and width of the river valley. There were lodges as far as Jim could see on both banks of the frozen river. Smoke hung low over the lodges, beaten down by the cold. Hundreds of ponies milled in corrals and Jim could hear packs of dogs yelp and bark. Because of the snow and cold he rarely saw a Pawnee venture outside their tipis and when they did it was a quick trip, either to get more wood, water from a chopped square in the ice, or to defecate in the skeletal buck brush.

From where he hunkered down in the deep powder snow on the top of a hillock, Jim tried to plot a way he could avoid the encampment and continue his trek. It had been four days and he'd eaten nothing but pemmican—meat, fat, and berries mushed together into frozen patties— and he was practically out of food. He'd found no game since he left the cabin, not even a snowshoe hare. He'd tried to eat the skin-like under bark of cottonwood and mountain ash trees like elk did, but the taste was acrid and it gave him no energy. A cold breeze from the valley floor brought whiffs of broiled meat, puppy probably, and his mouth salivated and his stomach growled.

He knew from his years in the mountains he was a few days away from death. He had no horse, no food, and he hadn't been able to feel his toes for twenty-four hours.

And he cursed Ezra once again and thought of going back. But he knew if he did Ezra would have to die because he couldn't spend another minute in the man's presence. Ezra had always been just a hair over the line into civilization and it hadn't taken him long to slip back and become an animal again. A filthy pig. Jim wondered why he hadn't seen it before, how close Ezra was to comfortable savagery. He imagined Ezra back in the cabin eating his own leg.

It would be nightfall soon. The winter camp would go to sleep. If he could find their cache of meat, and steal a horse …

IT TOOK A long time to get back to the cabin. Jim didn't know for sure how many days and nights but he guessed it was over a week. Most of the time his head had been elsewhere, for hours at a time, and he sang and chanted and cursed the world and God and those Pawnees who had filled him full of arrows and murdered him for sure.

He lurched from tree to tree on columns of frozen rock that had once been his legs and he peered out at the pure white of the sky and the ground through his left eye because his right was blind. Somewhere along the way he'd lost his rifle and his possibles sack. He thought his knives were still in their sheaths under his buffalo coat but he couldn't be sure and he didn't look.

Jim scooped up snow and ate it as if it were food and it kept his tongue from swelling and cracking. He'd fallen on a show shoe hare that was still warm from being killed by a bobcat and he pulled what was left of it apart and ate it raw.

He thanked God it hadn't snowed hard since he'd left because he could follow his own trail back most of the way.

And he thanked Ezra when at last he smelled wood smoke and meat cooking and there was the cabin, and the fur shack, and the corrals.

Jim wept as he approached the front door and pounded on it.

"Who is it?" Ezra asked from inside.

Jim couldn't speak. He sank to his knees and thumped the door with the crown of his head.

The door opened and Jim fell inside. For the first time since he'd left, he felt warmth on his face.

And Ezra said, "You don't look so good, Jim."

THROUGH THE VIOLENT, roaring, excruciating pain that came with his frost-bitten skin thawing out, Jim had crazy dreams. He dreamed Ezra had shaved, bathed, and put on clean clothes. He dreamed Ezra had re-chinked the logs and fireplace until they were tight with mud and straw and had emptied his chamber pot, swept the floor, and put the cabin in order. He dreamed Ezra awakened without hacking or spitting or even talking.

He thought, *I'm in Heaven.*

But he wasn't.

Jim painfully rolled his head to the side. Ezra was sitting at the table, finishing his lunch of roast Emily. Ezra's face was shaved smooth and freshly scrubbed. His movements were spry and purposeful. His eyes were clear and blue.

Ezra said, "I didn't think you'd come back. I thought you'd make it to Ft. Bridger because you're just so goddamned stubborn."

Jim couldn't speak. The pain came in crippling waves.

"I got the arrows out but your flesh is rotten, Jim," Ezra said. "You know what that means."

Jim knew. He closed his eyes. The pain reached a crescendo and suddenly stopped. Just stopped.

Ezra's voice rose and was filled with emotion. "You ain't exactly the easiest man to live with, neither," he said.

And with that, Jim died, a victim of his success.

OUT STEALING BUDDHA

BY DECLAN BURKE

"JUST THINKING ABOUT it brings on her angina." Dearbhla glanced across, guilty at mimicking her mother's fluttering hysteria. "Just *thinking* about it, she said."

Terry grinned, catching her self-censuring grimace without taking his eyes off the road. "How many's that?" he said. "Three now?"

"Four," she said, and her tone was suddenly sober. "Four in the last six months. And it was only about two miles away, not far from the village." She looked away out the passenger window. Outside was a bleak, blustery December evening, the sun an angry raw sore above the horizon. She shivered despite the drowsy warmth of the car. "She thinks they're working their way up the hill," she said.

"Towards them, like."

"Well, they are at the top of the hill."

"But towards *them*."

She shook her head. "She's not taking it personally or anything." she said. She scratched lightly at her knee. Terry waited. "She says they come down from Dublin," she said quickly, as if admitting complicity. "They drive around in their vans, rob a few houses, and then drive back before anyone twigs."

"Fucking gyps."

"Well, that's what Daddy says. They don't know for sure."

"Someone's doing it," he said. "Someone's driving around in vans knocking off …" He swerved to avoid a plastic bag flapping erratically across the motorway. "Gyps have vans," he said. "And they're thieving bastards."

"You can't just make that kind of …"

"I just did." He flicked his cigarette butt out the window, checked the rearview to watch it spark off the blacktop. "Don't tell *me* about gyps," he said. "I know gyps. Fuckers should be burnt out everywhere they stop, keep 'em moving. The only good gyp is a gone gyp. A next county gyp."

Dearbhla turned her head to check the back seat but the girls had had an exhausting afternoon in the fresh air and were now fast asleep, strapped into their safety-seats, heads lolling with the rhythm of the car. Terry listened while she checked, alert for the sound of Nadia's breathing, the hard-fought half-wheezing, but the country air had cleared her lungs again, at least for another couple of days.

"Sssshhh," Dearbhla said, staring fiercely at the side of Terry's head. "I've told you I don't want to hear that kind of thing around the kids. Okay?"

Terry rolled his eyes. "They'll learn soon enough," he said. "What d'you want, some gyp steals their dollies at school? They'll know then, all right. When it's too fucking late they'll know."

She reached out and tweaked the volume button on the stereo just enough to let him know she wanted to drown him out. But as the motorway narrowed to one lane and he slowed into the roundabout, she turned the volume down again.

"She's worried sick, Terry," she said. "And I'm starting to worry about her. She isn't inventing the angina."

Terry rolled out onto the roundabout, turned off towards town. From the gear-stick he let his hand drift until it found her knee. He squeezed gently. "I know," he said. "We'll work something out."

THE TRUTH WAS, Terry had been thinking about the situation all afternoon. Slobbed out on the couch, almost horizontal, hands joined on his midriff watching the game on TV. The room had been oppressively warm, and not for the first time Terry had wondered if the thick heat was fuelled by the simmering resentment of the man sprawled in the armchair across the room. They rarely spoke, and that afternoon had been no different. Terry didn't mind. He had long ago shuffled away down the beaten track of least resistance; Terry believed that things came naturally or they didn't come at all.

They spoke, of course. They had things in common, like football and bigotry, Nadia and Leticia. But the importance of these things was so ingrained that their communication could be reduced to grunts, nods, and cocked shoulders, so that they only really ever spoke about Dearbhla. This, Terry had lately come to realise, was because Dearbhla was not a common interest. What Dearbhla represented for the fat bald man sprawled in the armchair lay at the opposite pole to what she meant to Terry. To her father, Dearbhla embodied hope and new beginnings; for Terry, Dearbhla had come to represent resignation, looped cycles, and muscles gone slack where they mattered most.

Half time arrived, nil-nil and precious little entertainment on offer. Terry sat up, and more to escape the torpor of the room than from any real need to wet his whistle, he offered to make coffee.

"Aye," Ambrose said, scratching at his chest. He didn't take his eyes from the screen. "A tae'd be nice, Terry, if you're making it."

At the funeral, when he tried to pinpoint the fateful moment when the idea first popped into his head, Terry realised that the fridge had been the catalyst.

IT WAS A big fridge, taller even than Terry, divided equally by freezer and cooler. Terry liked its finish, the way it seemed to be an art-deco throwback to the '50s, when fridges were huge, rounded at the corners, and designed to facilitate excessive consumption. Even fat Ambrose could have squeezed in there. Maybe, Terry thought, an hour of *that* might cool his simmering. He swung the heavy door open, relishing its weight.

He poured the milk and waited for the kettle to boil, and while he waited he tried to remember the last time Ambrose had made the mid-afternoon coffee or tea. He shook his head and gave up. Ambrose was too lazy to walk out to the kitchen, let alone put himself to the trouble of making coffee for anyone else. He thought of Dearbhla and her mother, marching along with their arms swinging, chivvying the girls before them like wayward geese, and realised that the house was wasted on Ambrose. Now that he had retired, Ambrose was as much a fixture in the living room as the fridge was in the kitchen, as squat and as solid, and in the way his fixity suggested that the house had been built around him. Beyond his front door an entire countryside rolled away down the hill to all points of the compass, but Ambrose lolled in his armchair in front of the TV, heedless.

Terry thought of the girls, their complexions illuminated by the garish reds, greens, and yellows dancing on the TV screen as Spyro and Sonic jumped through their hoops, and he heard the sound of Nadia's breathing, the chilling half-wheeze. The ruddy cheeks and dancing eyes when they returned from the fortnightly walk with their mother and Nanna. And he thought again, this time with grim certainty: the house was wasted on Ambrose.

The water rumbled, grumbled, and finally boiled. The kettle snapped off.

"IT'S HIS BLOOD pressure," Dearbhla said. "Ever since he retired he's done nothing but sit around watching TV. But his blood pressure has gone through the roof."

Terry nodded, tapped the remote control, racked the volume up a couple of notches. The picture wavered and danced, then settled again.

"That fucking PlayStation," he said, "has the TV destroyed."

Dearbhla applied three quick deft strokes of the iron to the collar of Nadia's school blouse, stripped it off the ironing board, and slipped a wire hanger into its shoulders. She hung it on the back of the living room door and reached for Leticia's blouse. Terry shifted on the couch, hunching a shoulder, but in the small room the ironing board was an elbow in the ribs.

"We'll have to get them another TV," he said. "A portable. For the PlayStation."

Dearbhla reached for the iron again. "Well, okay," she said. "But where will we put it? There's no room in their bedroom."

"*I* don't know," he grumbled. "But that was a good fucking TV before they started messing with it."

Dearbhla ironed with long, measured strokes. "She's worried," she said, "that if it keeps up, he'll have a stroke."

"What?"

"Daddy. Jesus, Terry—do you ever listen?" Terry didn't answer. Dearbhla turned the blouse over, twitched it flat again. "If something isn't done about his blood pressure," she said, "he's going to have a stroke. The doctor says he's stressed."

Terry struggled into a sitting position, turned to face her. "Dearbh—he sits around all day in that armchair. She feeds him, waits hand and foot. He says fuck all, to man or beast. What difference is a stroke going to make?"

She glared, hefting the iron. "How dare you? You take that back, *right* this fucking second."

"Okay, Jesus." He slumped back against the cushions. "I'm sorry, all right? It's just …"

"It's just *what*?"

"Nothing," he said. "It's nothing." And it was, it really was.

She stood the iron on its end. "If something happened," she said, "out there …" She closed her eyes and shook her head. "It's twenty minutes into town," she said. "That's twenty minutes once you hit the main road. Anything can happen in twenty minutes." She drew the back of her hand across her dry forehead, then let it fall limply to the ironing board again. She opened her eyes. "She's frightened, Terry. She doesn't want to be left alone."

"So why don't they move into town? They'll be closer to us, closer to the …" He was suddenly aware, from the intent way she scrutinized him, that she was every bit as frightened as her mother. He reconsidered. "It'd be more convenient for them," he said. "All the shops are there, all the, eh, facilities. The amenities, like." She nodded him on. "He might even get out more," he said, "go for walks and the like. It can't be good for him, for his blood pressure, lying around all day doing nothing."

"That's what Mum says."

"Has she said it to him yet?"

She nodded, then shook her head. "He won't listen. He says no one is running him out of his house."

Terry nodded. Then he grinned, experiencing a rare moment of empathy with Ambrose. "Can't say as I blame him," he said. "I'd be fucked if I let a load of gyps knock me around."

"Terry." She edged around the ironing board and came to sit on the couch. She perched on the end, looking down at her hands, turning them over. "She's at her wits' end, Terry. She can't take much more. You don't see it. *He* doesn't see it. It's me she tells. *I* have to listen to it every single day. I dread the phone ringing."

Terry said, "It's the waiting that's the worst."

"What?"

"The waiting. The not knowing. Sitting around expecting the worst."

She dropped her hands, looked around and up at him.

"I don't follow," she said, although it was clear to Terry, from the way her eyes narrowed again, that she understood perfectly.

"Maybe," Terry said, speaking to her more cautiously than at any time since he had proposed, "he just needs a nudge in the right direction."

"A nudge?"

"A nudge," he said.

"JUST BE CAREFUL," Dearbhla said. She stubbed her cigarette butt. "You know what his temper is like."

Terry nodded. "We covered his temper on Tuesday," he said. "Wednesday we worked through his blood pressure. Thursday we heard how his grandfather was in the old IRA."

Her face hardened but she took a deep breath and let it slide.

"You have everything?" she said. He patted the pockets of his windbreaker, felt the chisel, the rolled-up ball of stockings, the cylindrical can. He nodded again. She nodded too, lit another cigarette, and turned her face away to exhale out of the open window. She looked back at him.

"Okay," she said.

"Okay," he said. They stared then, mutely, and Terry wondered if it was appropriate to kiss a woman goodbye when you were on your way out to trash her parents' home.

"It's the right thing to do," he said, partly to reassure her but mostly to distract himself from the way his stomach was turning over, the adrenaline curdling.

"Ring me from the road," she said. "After. To let me know that everything's okay."

He nodded. She made no attempt to move away from window. He decided to just go.

TERRY TURNED OFF the roundabout onto the motorway, trying to remember the last time he had seen Dearbhla smoke. As far as Terry knew, she hadn't smoked since she discovered she was pregnant with Nadia, which was almost six years ago now. She'd never been much of a smoker, Silk Cut lights had been her brand of choice. "Sure I'm only smoking fresh air," she'd joked, but even so Terry had never approved. The clincher came when the doctors told them Nadia had bronchial asthma. That was all the reason Dearbhla had needed to pack the smokes in for good. Until, Terry thought, tonight.

He checked the clock. Just after two. The motorway was quiet and shrouded in an unearthly orange light. He shivered, and reached to fiddle with the A/C, but he knew that the shivering had nothing to do with the temperature. The chill of voluntary exile. He slipped the hip flask from his windbreaker pocket and took two quick nips, shuddering as the whiskey burned its way down.

Twenty minutes later he reached the small village that straddled the main road. This was the crucial moment; if anyone saw his car turn off towards the hill ... But the village was silent beneath its orange glow, and so Terry turned off, leaving the car in second gear until he had left the lights of the village far behind. The narrow lane twisted and turned, always upwards, and for once Terry was glad of the challenge of keeping the car between the untended ditches and out of the potholes. He had passed the place where he intended leaving the car before he realised what he was doing.

He reversed, then drove up into the tiny, branch-roofed lane. He parked, switched off the engine, took another couple of nips of whiskey, and tried to smooth the jags of his quick, jerky breathing. Then he pulled the stocking down over his head. When he had no more excuses to remain in the car, he got out and began sidling up the hill.

He was sweating hard by the time he gained the courtyard to the front of the house. He waited a moment or two, trying to identify the unfamiliar shadows and shapes, then tiptoed around to the rear of the house. The dog growled, restless, until he chucked his tongue and whispered its name. Satisfied, the dog whined and settled again.

He unlocked the door with Dearbhla's key and slipped through the gap into the dark hallway, edged towards the kitchen. The only sound the soft scrape of his soles on rough tiles.

A Sacred Heart glowed in the kitchen, its dim smear the only light. Terry slipped past the kitchen table, allowing his hand to slide along the fridge as he headed for the far door. As he padded down the flag-stoned hallway towards the living room, he wondered again exactly what it was he was supposed to steal. He had no intention of trying to get away with anything bulky, a TV or a stereo, but it had to be something that would be noticed in its absence. Something precious, that would cut to the heart of their isolation. And something, he reminded himself grimly, that would not require any kind of light in order to be found.

He thought of it even as he opened the living room door. It sat on the TV, a souvenir of the only time Ambrose had deigned to leave the country: a fat, smiling Buddha. The statue had always irritated Terry, partly because it had been bought in a Tenerife flea market, but mostly because Dearbhla's mother had always said she'd bought it on the strength of its similarities to Ambrose. Terry could see the resemblance all right, in the squat, balding, inanimate lump that served no useful purpose. As for the beatific smile—well, even Terry had to concede that Dearbhla's mother had to have seen Ambrose smile some time, once at least. Terry certainly couldn't remember any such happiness or joy, not even on the day his only daughter got married. And what pleased Terry most about the idea of stealing the Buddha was that Ambrose didn't give a fiddler's fuck for the souvenir, but that he would nonetheless be forced into fretting about its absence as a result of his wife's loss.

He edged into the room, along the near wall, feeling his way with one hand against the dresser that held the fancy dinner service. His toe bumped against the TV stand, and he reached in and picked up the Buddha. It was heavier than it looked, although not so heavy he couldn't carry it one-handed. He closed the living room door, snick-snicked down the stone-flagged hallway again and back into the kitchen. There he stopped, and with the Buddha tucked under his arm he reached into the windbreaker pocket and found the cylindrical can. He shook it, hearing the tinny rattle of the tiny ball inside, then uncapped it and sprayed a sprawling "FUCK YOU" across the door of the fridge. He capped the can again, liking the way each red letter seemed to bleed in the faint, silvery light, and made for the kitchen door. He pulled it to behind him, made some scratches with the chisel in the wood around the lock, and tiptoed out into the backyard again. The dog stirred, restless, until he chucked his tongue, slipping along the back wall towards the side of the house. He turned the gable and the pain hit him even before he heard the shotgun's blast. He slammed sideways into the pebble-dashed wall and slumped to the ground, cut in half.

HE MIGHT HAVE been down for seconds or hours. Time seemed to go on without him. He realised that the right side of his face lay in a shallow puddle; that his left thigh, buttock, and side were burning with an intensity he hadn't imagined was possible to bear and still be able to think, and that the Buddha was still tucked under his arm.

He remembered the shotgun blast. He wondered where Ambrose might be. He thought about how much it was going to cost him to get to his feet, and heard himself whimper. Then he did it.

He stumbled, pitched forward, caught himself and steadied. There was a hoarse, vengeful rasp to the dog's barking, and it surged forward again and again, choking itself on the chain. Across the yard, in the dark doorway of one of the sheds, he could see a pair of feet, soles showing and kicking frantically.

For a split second he thought of crossing the yard but even as he thought that he shuddered, not from pain but the chilly shiver of exile. Dragging his leg, sweating and cursing, he shuffled around the side of the house and eventually gained the lane. From there, at least, it was downhill all the way.

As he sped back to town Terry prayed—and meant it—for the first time in over twenty years. The Buddha on the passenger seat rocked with the rhythm of the car and smiled its beatific smile.

DEARBHLA STARED AT his prize.

"You took the Buddha?" she said. "You took the fucking *Buddha*?"

He nodded, easing himself onto the couch.

"They'll know," she said quietly. "They'll know it was someone who knew them. Who knew about the Buddha."

He grasped at the plural.

"They?"

"Mum and Daddy, Terry. Jesus, who else?"

"Ambrose? He's okay?"

Her eyebrows flickered. "Yeah, of course. Why wouldn't he be?"

Terry shook his head, and the wave of relief even dampened the pain for a moment. Then it flared again, savage in its intensity. He groaned, shifted his weight and pointed at his side.

"He shot me, Dearbh. The bastard shot me."

"Jesus, Terry!" She rushed to the couch, knelt beside it. "Are you okay? Where? Christ!"

He pointed to his side again, closed his eyes, and laid his head back on a cushion. He felt her cautiously lift his sweater, the T-shirt beneath, and if the girls hadn't been asleep, four feet away in the other room, he would have screamed at the sticky peeling. Tears burned. Dearbhla laughed.

"Oh, he shot you all right," she said, choking back the laughter. "He shot you *good*."

She seemed to enjoy his agony a little too much for Terry's liking, but in the end she went for the whiskey and tweezers.

SHE RECOUNTED THE conversation with her mother as she plucked the rock-salt shrapnel from his side and hip.

"She didn't know he'd be out there," she said. "As far as she knew, he was in his room."

"As far as she knew," Terry said. By now the whiskey was kicking in, deadening the pain.

"And he hasn't used the shotgun in years," she said. "Watch—here we go."

Terry winced as the tweezers gouged his flesh.

"Anyway," she said, holding the fragment of rock salt up to the light, "the recoil knocked him off his feet. And Terry," she said, lowering her voice, "he couldn't get back up again." She flattened her lips against the threat of laughter and betrayal. "He's got so fat recently, he just couldn't right himself."

She waited for him to smile along but all Terry could see was a pair of feet kicking in the dark doorway. Mentally he turned away again, and when the tweezers dug into his flesh he welcomed the blunt digging.

"How's his blood pressure?" he said.

"She doesn't know. She can't get *near* him. He's hopping mad." She made a deft twisting motion, plucked another fragment free. "She says she hasn't seen him so alive in years."

Terry nodded, raised the bottle of whiskey to his lips, and gulped down two mouthfuls of the burning liquid. She dug again with the tweezers and he choked, spluttering.

THEY HID THE Buddha on the top shelf of the airing cupboard, under the winter duvets, and life continued on much as it had before. Ambrose dug in, circled the wagons, installed a hi-tech alarm system. Terry shuffled around for a couple of weeks until he lost the limp, and Dearbhla reported back that her mother had started to glow recently.

"I wouldn't be at all surprised," she said, "if they were, y'know …"

Terry shrugged, sipped his whiskey, tapped the volume button on the remote control. He thought his entire respiratory system—lungs, windpipe, throat—had been bent somewhere along the line, so that his entire life seemed to be spent fighting a losing battle against choking.

Three months later, and for no obvious reason, Dearbhla's mother had a severe angina attack. Ambrose being so unsteady on his feet, and the alarm system being so complicated, she had slipped into unconsciousness before he got her to the hospital. She recovered, but she lost forty pounds she really couldn't afford and her skin turned a yellowy shade of grey. The Sunday afternoon walks with her daughter and granddaughters were never mentioned again; instead she slumped listlessly in the living room, absorbing the oppressive heat. It was Ambrose who suggested that they should think about moving into town.

They agreed to Terry's suggestion and moved into the apartment, although it took long, heated arguments before Ambrose finally agreed that Dearbhla and Terry would pay their rent for as long as they lived there. Terry and Dearbhla moved out to the house on the hill, and Nadia and Leticia were delighted by the novelty of having their own rooms. The wide sky and the clear air seemed to ease Terry's choking, and he began to relax; even the pulsing in his gut seemed to throttle down. Once in a while, when the girls were in bed, he would open the freezer part of the pink-tinged fridge and reach way in back to rub the head of the Buddha, for luck.

The following June, when the pollen count was high, Nadia had an asthma attack for the first time since they'd left town. Terry got them all in the car, Nadia in Dearbhla's arms, and put the boot to the floor. He made the roundabout in twelve minutes flat, but as they turned off towards town he heard the child choke hard, convulsing, then stop. Just stop. Dearbhla screamed, the shriek tailing off into a keening wail.

When Terry looked across, the child's face had contorted, her eyes rolled back and dead. The rhythm of the car causing her head to nod gently. As if she agreed with him.

LOVE STORY

BY SCOTT A. CUPP

I STARED DOWN at the body lying in the street and wondered how I would explain it. I could see the headlines. EX-COP SHOOTS DRUG DEALER IN DEAL GONE BAD. Probably actually be a little shorter than that, but the gist would be the same. There'd be a photo of me, probably they'd use the one of me with the walker. It made better "journalism." And there would be one of Eileen, of course. She wouldn't have a walker.

It was all her fault anyway. I was minding my retirement quite well until I fell and broke that hip. Betrayed by my own bones. One small slip and CRACK! Hurt like hell. I found I couldn't walk easily; I had a hard time getting up. Of course, there was no one to watch and care for me. Claire had been gone five painfully long years, sleeping the big sleep. I'd be there soon enough but no fall was going to be the cause. We had no kids, so the doc recommended a rehab facility. I was there, learning to walk around with this erector contraption, trying to keep up some muscle tone, and generally not be a nuisance. I was nearly ready to go back home. Hell, I was ready to go home. Then she showed up. Pretty as a picture, only seventy-five, but abandoned to these vultures.

Her name was Eileen Booker. She had been a teacher—choir and music and you could tell. When she spoke, angels rejoiced. I met her the day she arrived. I was in the lounge area, watching *Jeopardy!* and beating the contestants handily. She was brought in by an ambulance and she was smiling. That smile—it made me want to fight through hordes of Tharks as if I was John Carter of Mars and she was Dejah Thoris. I would cross the whole world to hear her voice and see her smile, fighting every inch of the way.

I spoke to her at dinner that night. She was widowed and alone, same as me. She was in for some rehab, though I could not see that she needed much. She was slender, never lost that girlish figure that probably drove her first husband, Steve, wild. He had gone three years earlier in a car wreck. She was supposed to be along and had deferred, so she blamed herself for not dying with him.

"That's crazy!" I said. "You cannot blame yourself. When you decided not to go, did you know the drunk was going to kill him?"

"No," she replied. "Of course not."

"Then, based on the knowledge you had at the time, the knowledge that you were sick and did not feel like going to his brother's house, did you make the right choice?"

"Yes, I did. I didn't like Fred and Jeanette, his wife, was a terrible cook. And I really did feel poorly."

"So, since you made the best decision you could at the time, how can you fault yourself?"

"It just seems so unfair." She began to quietly cry. "He always took care of me and then he was gone. I should have been there!"

"No, you shouldn't have been there. Steve shouldn't have been there either. But he was," I said. "If you had been, it would have been doubly tragic and I would never have met you."

She wiped her eyes, reached out, and kissed my hand. It was electric! "Thank you for trying to make me feel better," she said. She got up and went on down to her room. I stood up but did not follow. I believe she wanted to be alone.

Over the next week, I learned more of her story. She and Steve had met in college and fallen in love. Steve was an engineer and they lived all over the world before returning to San Antonio (his hometown and the place of their marriage). They had both retired and bought a small home near Castle Hills. They kept a clean house and a small garden. They had no children and had kept various cats, though when the last one died, they did not replace it. I had asked why she was here and she finally told me the third day. It was cancer. They wanted her to keep up her strength through an exercise program and to keep up a social framework with the patients here. She had few friends in their neighborhood. I couldn't understand that. She was amazing. How could she not have friends? But, she said, she and Steve had all they needed in each other. They had many friends abroad and kept in touch with them through email and regular snail mail. At home, they just never tried to socialize. Then when Steve had died, she turned even more inward. She talked to him every day and laughed at his imagined response. When she walked, he walked with her.

I knew I was beat there. Hard to compete with a ghost. I mean, I had seen *The Ghost and Mrs. Muir* several times. The ghost always wins. I soon said goodnight and went back down the hall to my room.

I decided to read a bit before bed. Nothing light and fluffy for the night for me so I decided on some Dickens. I was reading *The Mystery of Edwin Drood*, that last unfinished novel of the Master. I had read it before and even several of the "completions" that various writers did to complete the tale. Dickens had left no outline or notes. The story just stops. Many people think they know his direction but no one can be sure and Dickens frequently turned plots 180 degrees from the anticipated course.

I nodded off about ten PM and slumbered with my glasses on and the light burning. I awoke about one AM and got up to make a pit stop and to turn out the light. As I got to the light switch, I thought I heard a sound outside. I looked down the hallway and saw only one light on under a closed door. I flipped the switch and heard a sound again. I grabbed my robe and walked out into the hallway. The sound repeated. It was a kind of a half sob, half sucking sound. I walked down the hallway and saw that it was Eileen's room. I could hear her crying and that was punctuated by a sucking nose. I nearly knocked but turned away.

Then I smelled it. As Tom Paxton once said, "My nose went up like an infield fly!" The sucking sound was Eileen smoking pot. My cop nose had smelled it many times during the past. I had driven the streets for too many years, busted too many parties, and unraveled too many wrecks to not know that odor. I turned away, disappointed in her.

The next day, I asked her about it. Well, perhaps "asked" is too polite a term. I told her I was a cop and I knew she was smoking illegal drugs and I wanted her to give it to me so I could get rid of it.

"No."

"It's illegal," I said, "and, even though I am retired, I still uphold the law."

She stroked my face. "This is the only thing that helps me make it through the day. The pain is tremendous. And it helps me relax and cope. Yes, it is illegal. Texas does not have a medical marijuana statute. And *that* is a crime in itself! I suppose I could drink myself to sleep, but that really does not help the pain."

I was shocked! She was going to openly oppose the law. I had a brief thought of turning her in, but the sight of her being led away in handcuffs or waiting in a jail cell repulsed me. I did not know what to do. She touched my hand. I stared into her face. She smiled. "You make me feel good, like I don't need the weed anymore. Perhaps, if you were to stay close and talk with me, I might not need it."

Fireworks exploded in my brain. I stayed with her nearly every waking hour. We sat in the lounge area and watched *Jeopardy!* She was better than I was and I was no slouch. We walked though the center's garden, holding hands. I knew that several of the old biddies were talking about us. We didn't care. I knew we could stay together and that it was Love. I don't know if she felt the same yet. I thought she might but there had not been the full *On* indicator yet. We were happy and that was good enough.

She did not give up the weed, though. I could keep her happy and content during the day, but at night, the pain would still come back. She cut back but eventually her stash began to run low.

LOVE STORY

"I need to go out tonight," she had finally said. "I need to go see the man. Would you come with me?" Her eyes pleaded, she squeezed my hand.

To my everlasting shame I said, "Yes."

She drove us to the south side of San Antonio, over off Southeast Military Drive. We stopped at an ATM machine and she got cash, more than she should have needed. We went to a parking lot and stopped. A car drove up and she got out. I got out too and checked the small of my back for my old pistol. You just don't go to a drug buy and not be carrying.

The car door opened and out stepped Ricky Raton. Ricky the Rat, a small-time hood that I had arrested a couple of times in his early days. This was not good. I tried to hide deeper into the shadows.

"Chiquita, you got the money?" he asked.

"A hundred and fifty dollars," she replied. He nodded and pulled out the small package as she handed over the money.

"A hundred and fifty dollars?" I said. "That's highway robbery! It should only be about eighty to ninety dollars for an ounce!"

Heads turned and eyes flashed in my direction. Recognition moved over the Rat's face. "You! You set me up!" he screamed. Slow-motion figures lingered in my brain as I saw his hand and gun move, heard the explosion from his fist and saw Eileen begin to crumble. I felt my own hand buck as it grabbed cold steel and pulled the trigger. Bright flame leapt from the barrel of the gun. I could not even hear myself scream her name. I saw a flash from Ricky's hand and felt the bullet pass through my side.

I fell. Ricky turned and screamed from the impact as his chest flew open. I ran to Eileen but there was no life left. The weed laid on the ground where the bag broke when it fell.

IN THE DISTANCE I can hear the sirens. I'm the only one still left here. They're coming for me.

I decide the headlines are wrong. They should read EX-COP KILLED IN DRUG SALE GONE BAD. Or something like that. I put the gun into my mouth. The smell of cordite is still strong from the previous shot. I hesitate.

Then, I see her again and realize there is nothing to live for. My life was screwed from the first moment I met her and I would do it again. I see the lights just down the road. My finger tightens and I hope I have enough strength left to pull the trigger.

Nothing.

BLAM!

ALL ABOUT EDEN

BY CHRISTA FAUST

I HAVE A much better relationship with Eden now that she doesn't remember who I am.

She called me a little over a year ago, asking me to come down to Palm Springs. She said she needed me again. That was the last time I was really sure she knew me. There've been moments since then. A certain look, or something left unsaid. But those moments are fleeting and far between. Nothing like that call.

"Melanie," she said when I picked up the phone that night. "Baby, I got a little problem."

When I heard that familiar breathy faux-Monroe whisper, my skin went hot, then cold, then hot again. I couldn't help but think of the last time I got a call from her about a little problem.

Of course I came running. I left my rent-controlled San Francisco apartment, my sweet, long-suffering girlfriend, and my plans for a quiet retirement and I never looked back. I guess I always knew it would come to this.

Maybe a little back-story is in order.

Once upon a time, way back in the 1950s and deep in the suburban Midwest, there lived a lonely, awkward fat kid named Steve Dabrowski. Dad, a cement mogul. Mom, a pretty idiot. Older brother, a star quarterback who could do no wrong. And pathetic, clueless little Stevie. Stevie the mistake, the accidental, unwanted pregnancy whose complicated breech birth nearly killed his mother. He had a wide, plain Polish farmer's face like Dad, but framed by thick, strawberry blond curls like Mom. Lanky and broad shouldered like dad, but loved rustling taffeta circle skirts like Mom. Always ashamed. Always, every single day, that shame. That feeling of profound wrongness and hopelessness that never went away.

Well, I guess that's not completely true. That feeling did go away sometimes. It went away when little Stevie snuck into Mom's closet.

Now you have to understand, this wasn't a sexual thing. He wasn't all turned on and furiously jacking off in her frilly panties. Wearing her clothes made him feel right. Terrified of being caught, but right. Like the shame, the never-ending humiliation at the hands of bullies and all those little day-to-day horrors miraculously ceased to exist and he could finally be the person he was meant to be.

As a teenager, Steve started wearing stolen female undergarments under his school clothes. It made him feel safe. A protective layer of secret truth underneath the lie he was being forced to live. He didn't find out how unsafe he really was until a bully tore his shirt during a routine playground beating and discovered a bra underneath. Later that afternoon, the bully and three of his friends found Steve walking home alone and dragged him behind an abandoned supermarket.

They took turns raping Steve in the scratchy autumn grass, laughing and calling him *faggot*. Steve was confused about a lot of things, but one thing he knew for sure was that he didn't like being fucked by boys.

He staggered home, torn and limping. His mom saw the blood on the seat of his pants and refused to take him to the hospital. Instead, she locked him in the bathroom and told him he'd better get cleaned up before his father got home.

Steve ran away that night and never looked back.

He spent the next few years crashing with his mother's sister Irene, a single nurse who worked the night shift and chain-smoked and didn't ask questions. He took a series of shitty jobs and saved every penny and in 1968, he moved to San Francisco. That's where I was born. That's where I met Eden March.

Those two events remain inextricably tangled in my mind, like light and dark halves of a single epiphany. Of course, LSD was involved. Such an embarrassing hippie cliché, isn't it? But hey, that's the way it happened.

At the time I was still trying to be Steve, still pretending, rattling around like a trapped bird inside a cage of perceived masculinity. I wore my hair long and I hid my incorrect anatomy under the colorful silk and velvet fashions of the time, but I was still faking it, still hiding from the truth.

I'd gotten it into my head that I couldn't possibly be a real woman, because I didn't like sex with men. I'd known from my earliest moments of consciousness that I wasn't male, but I didn't think I would ever be allowed to be a woman either. I was sure I was irreparably broken inside, that the rape little Stevie had endured had done something to me that could never be undone. Most of the time I just felt like a freak.

That night I was coming off an epic trip, exhausted but still buzzing, the steep streets still strange and untrustworthy around the edges. At some point the previous day, I'd been struck by this astounding vision in which I saw Steve sloughing off me like a peeling sunburn. It was terrifying because I didn't know who I was underneath that fiction, and I'd tried desperately to hold on to the tattered pieces, but they just disintegrated between my fingers. My girlfriend at the time had talked me through it, telling me it was nothing but a bad trip and I tried to believe her. I really did. Just before dawn, I had decided I needed to be alone for a little while, to ponder the meaning of this revelation without all the white noise of the frivolous, never-ending party around me.

I walked for hours down long, deserted streets that seemed to bear only coincidental resemblance to the familiar streets of my adopted city. I'd been born lonely, felt lonely my entire life, even in the arms of women who said they loved me, but all that loneliness was just a warm-up act for the profound, soul-crushing isolation and alienation I felt that night. Then I turned a random corner, and there was Eden.

Eden was everything the newborn feminist in me had been trained to reject. She was this old-school femme construct of hairspray and perfume. Sleek brunette beehive. Red lipstick. False eyelashes and high, plucked eyebrows. Long, nylon-clad legs. High golden heels with glittering rhinestones. If I had been with my hip, enlightened friends, we would have laughed at her for being so hopelessly out of date, still shackled to the oppressive, patriarchal standard of feminine beauty. Alone, I was utterly, irrevocably smitten.

She was a little tipsy, unsteady on her pretty heels, and she looked up at me with these strange, almost navy blue eyes. They weren't bright or beautiful, those eyes. They were this murky, dead shade like the Bay in winter, like the last color you see before you drown. I've never met another person with eyes that color.

"Hello, baby," she said. "What's your name?"

I tried to say Steve, but when I opened my mouth, something else came out.

"I'm Melanie," I told her. It was the first time I'd ever said that name out loud.

She reached up and touched my cheek. I needed a shave.

"Melanie," she said. "You know this city's full of wolves. Us girls need to stick together."

Looking at it spelled out on the page like that, it seems so trivial and silly. The truth is, I could write about it for the rest of my life and never find the words to make you understand the significance of that moment. For the next forty years, casual lovers, partners, and concerned friends would ask me again and again why I put up with Eden's shit. Why I let her walk all over me and suck me into her endless drama. Why I couldn't just cut her off once and for all. That moment is the answer.

Fast forward to 1981. I'd been living full time as female by that point and had only two months left to go before what I jokingly refer to as

ALL ABOUT EDEN

V-Day. The day I went to sleep with a penis and woke up with a vagina. Eden and I had just gone through our ninth cataclysmic breakup in just over a decade and I was an emotional wreck. She had been teasing me relentlessly about my fear of the upcoming surgery. She'd had her own gender reassignment back in the Christine Jorgensen days and when she got drunk she would lecture me about it like your grandma telling you she had to walk to school through the snow, uphill both ways. Called me a spineless chickenshit who didn't deserve a pussy. I threw all her sparkly shoes out the window and told her to get out of my life. I'd cried so much that week, death from dehydration seemed inevitable. Then, eight days after she left, just after midnight, the phone rang.

"Melanie," Eden said when I picked up the phone. Her words were slurred and juicy. "Baby, I got a little problem."

This little problem was named Fernando. Eden's infidelity with men was the main reason we kept on splitting up, and you'd think I would have told her and her little problem to get fucked. I didn't. I came running, just like I always do.

Fernando had been dead for hours. It wasn't pretty.

This may sound weird, but I was actually okay with the blood. Didn't bother me at all, really. It was the shit that got to me. In the gangster movies, nobody ever has to clean up shit.

Eden was bombed as usual, staggering through the mess and vacillating wildly between hysterical raving and shell-shocked silence. I suppose I should have called the police but I didn't. I couldn't. I knew what kind of tabloid horrors a public investigation would bring for people like us.

The first thing I did was get her cleaned up. Then I wrapped her in a blanket and put her to bed on the crummy sofa. She snored and muttered in her sleep while I dragged Fernando into the bathroom and went to work.

He had been stabbed several times in the neck. There was no sign of a weapon anywhere in the cramped studio apartment. Just two dusty butter knives in a drawer filled with kitchen utensils that looked like they'd never been used.

I didn't dwell on the unanswered questions; I just focused on taking care of the tasks at hand. I poured soda water on various stains. I rinsed the tub with bleach and used a toothbrush to scrub the grout between the bathroom tiles. I went out and bought a hacksaw, then reduced Fernando to six neat black plastic parcels ready to be discarded in various trash bins around the city. It wasn't really that different than cleaning up after Eden when she got blotto and puked all over the house. Sure, it was nasty work, but I did it anyway. Because I loved her.

I still don't know exactly what happened before I got there that night. I probably never will. The next day Eden woke up all hung over and sheepish.

"I really tied one on last night, didn't I?" she said. "I must have had a blast, but I can't remember a thing. Why don't we go out for some nice mimosas, baby? Just to take the edge off."

I'm pretty sure she knew exactly what had happened, but I never called her on it. I never mentioned it again. She moved back in with me the next day.

We broke up and got back together more than a dozen times before we finally split for good in 1998. I hadn't seen Eden in ten years when I got that call, ever since she decided she couldn't stand the cold any more and moved down to Palm Springs. Instead of telling me about it or sending me a letter to let me know she was leaving town (Eden doesn't believe in "the e-mail") she just stuffed all her vintage furs into trash bags and left them on my doorstep. Sarah, my vegan girlfriend, was horrified and made me throw them away. It was tough. They still smelled like Eden.

I did get occasional letters from Eden up until the last year or so. At first she seemed like her same old self, melodramatic and catty as always. But the last half dozen letters were rambling and disjointed, talking about events from thirty years ago like they had just happened last week and complaining about neighbors who were no good and out to get her. The final letter I received from her was almost illegible, the handwriting shaky and oversized. It was a list of items that she claimed had been stolen by her no-good neighbors, including "empty shampoo bottle, Clairol Herbal Essences, 23.7 oz.," "Vogue magazine, March 2001, Penelope Cruz" and "Sheer Energy nylons, tan, size Q."

Of course I was worried. I made some calls and arranged for a nurse to look after her. She hated the first two I hired and refused to let them in because they were "Latins." Eventually I found someone she would accept, a gay man named Bernard, who she claimed looked like a young Franchot Tone and had "real class, not like those Latin sluts."

I'd talk to Bernard every week, just to check in. It seemed like Eden was doing much better under his care. They would watch old movies together and she would tell him outrageous lies about her wild affairs with all the big Hollywood stars. She had stopped obsessing constantly about the neighbors, but also seemed to be growing increasingly untethered from the present day. Still, I felt like she was in good hands.

Fast forward to now. To that phone call. To me driving down the I-5 in the middle of the night, alone with all my doubts and questions.

I'd tried over and over to reach Bernard, but his phone went straight to voicemail. Eden's phone was busy, probably off the hook. No way of knowing what I was walking into.

I hit Palm Springs at dawn. It took me a few wrong turns to find Eden's tiny, Spanish-style bungalow sitting on a quiet block of similar homes that had all seen better days. Several properties had realtor's signs stuck in their patchy lawns, offering quick sale at reduced prices. Eden's neighbors had a foreclosure notice stuck to their door. I figured these must be the same no-good neighbors who'd supposedly been stealing her pantyhose. Their house looked as if it had been abandoned for some time.

There was a red mountain bike resting on its kickstand in Eden's driveway. Obviously not hers. Even when she was younger, Eden didn't believe in exercise. She refused to do anything that couldn't be done in high heels.

I knocked. No answer. Her door wasn't locked.

The nausea and anxiety that had been building in my belly on the drive down evaporated the second I walked into her house. Her powerful, personal scent wrapped around me like one of her vintage furs. Shalimar, champagne, and cigarettes, but underscored with another uglier, yet equally familiar smell. I knew what I needed to do. I'd spent my whole adult life cleaning up after Eden. It was the one thing I was really good at.

Only Bernard wasn't dead yet.

I won't lie. I still feel bad about that sometimes. He was a nice kid. I didn't know Fernando from Adam and even hated him a little because I knew he'd been fucking my Eden. Poor Bernard just wanted to help.

But it's not like I had a choice. He was as good as dead anyway. I just put him out of his misery, like a run-over dog.

After all that had been taken care of, after I'd disposed of Bernard and his bike and scrubbed down every surface of the house till I could see my own determined reflection, Eden did something that kind of surprised me. She pulled me into her arms and kissed me, the way she used to.

We made love that day for the last time.

Naked, she looked like a mummified Barbie doll. Tiny, surgically sculpted wasp-waist and huge, concrete implants shrink-wrapped under sun-baked parchment skin. Without her wig she was almost completely bald. I didn't care. Eden will always be beautiful to me.

As I held her fragile body close to mine, I searched her murky, navy blue eyes for some hint of recognition, some sign that we were connecting in a meaningful way. It was like staring into deep, stagnant water. But her hands, her hands still knew me.

When the cops started sniffing around, I was terrified that Eden might blurt out something that would give us away. But she insisted she had never heard of this Bernard person they kept asking about. She wasn't lying. She didn't know who he was anymore than she knew who I was or who anyone was, for that matter. As for me, I stuck to my story. I told them he wasn't there when I arrived for a visit and that I hadn't heard from him since. I could see they didn't like having to look up to interrogate me and they didn't even bother to hide their sniggers and their freakshow gawking at the ugly old trannies, but in the end they had nothing. The investigation went cold.

I've been living in Palm Springs with Eden for nearly a year. We'll be celebrating her seventy-ninth birthday on Friday, although she still thinks it's 1962. Even though she doesn't remember who I am, she's completely dependent on me now. No more men. No more little problems. Just Eden and me, like it was meant to be. I can live with that.

FLYING SOLO

BY ED GORMAN

"YOU SMOKING AGAIN?"

"Yeah." Ralph's sly smile. "You afraid these'll give me cancer?"

"You mind rolling down the window then?"

"I bought a pack today. It felt good. I've been wanting a cigarette for twenty-six years. That's how long ago I gave them up. I was still walking a beat back then. I figure what the hell, you know. I mean the way things are. I been debating this a long time. I don't know why I picked today to start again. I just did." He rolled the window down. The soft summer night came in like a sweet angel of mercy. "I've smoked four of them but this is the only one I've really enjoyed."

"Why this one?"

"Because I got to see your face."

"The Catholic thing?"

"That's right, kid. The Catholic thing. They've got you so tight inside you need an enema. No cheating on the wife, no cheating on the taxes, no cheating on the church. And somebody bends the rules a little, your panties get all bunched up."

"You're pretty eloquent for an ex-cop. That enema remark. And also, by the way, whenever you call me 'kid' people look at you funny. I mean, I'm sixty-six and you're sixty-eight."

Ralph always portrayed himself as a swashbuckler; the day he left the force he did so with seventeen citizen complaints on his record.

He took a long, deep drag on his Winston. "We're upping the ante tonight, Tom. That's why I'm a little prickish. I know you hate being called 'kid.' It's just nerves."

I was surprised he admitted something like that. He enjoyed playing fearless.

"That waitress didn't have it coming, Ralph."

"How many times you gonna bring that up? And for the record, I did ask for a cheeseburger if you'll remember and I did leave her a

67

frigging ten-dollar tip after I apologized to her twice. See how uptight you are?"

"She probably makes six bucks an hour and has a kid at home."

"You're just a little bit nervous the way I am. That's why you're runnin' your mouth so hard."

He was probably right. "So we're really going to do it, huh?"

"Yeah, Tom, we're really going to do it."

"What time is it?"

I checked my Timex, the one I got when I retired from teaching high school for thirty years. English and creative writing. The other gift I got was not being assaulted by any of my students. A couple of my friends on the staff had been beaten, one of them still limping years after. "Nine minutes later than when you asked me last time."

"By rights I should go back of that tree over there and take a piss. In fact I think I will."

"That's just when he'll pull in."

"The hell with it. I wouldn't be any good with a full bladder."

"You won't be any good if he sees us."

"He'll be so drunk he won't notice." The grin made him thirty. "You worry too much."

The moon told its usual lies. Made this ugly two-story flat-roofed cube of a house if not beautiful at least tolerable to the quick and forgiving eye. The steep sagging stairs running at a forty-five degree angle up the side of the place were all that interested me. That and the isolation here on the edge of town. A farmhouse at one time, a tumbledown barn behind it, the farmland back to seed, no one here except our couple living in the upstairs. Ken and Callie Neely. Ken being the one we were after.

We were parked behind a stretch of oaks. Easy to watch him pull in and start up those stairs. I kept the radio low. Springsteen.

When Ralph got back in I handed him my pocket-sized hand sanitizer.

"You shoulda been a den mother."

"You take a piss, you wash your hands."

"Yes, Mom."

And then we heard him. He drove his sleek red Chevy pickup truck so fast he sounded as if he was going to shoot right on by. I wondered what the night birds silver-limned in the broken moonlight of the trees made of the country-western song bellering from the truck. A breeze swooped in the open windows of my Volvo and brought the scents of long-dead summers. *An image of a seventeen-year-old girl pulling her T-shirt over her head and the immortal perfection of her pink-tipped breasts.*

"You know what this is going to make us, don't you? I mean after we've done it."

"Yeah, I do, Tom. It's gonna make us happy. That's what it's gonna make us. Now let's go get him."

I MET RALPH Francis McKenna in the chemo room of Oncology Partners. His was prostate, mine was colon. They gave him a year, me eighteen months, no guarantees either of us would make it. We had one other thing in common. We were both widowers. Our kids lived way across the country and could visit only occasionally. Natural enough we'd become friends. Of a kind, anyway.

We always arranged to have our chemo on the same day, same time. After the chemo was over we both had to take monthly IVs of other less powerful drugs.

Ralph said he'd had the same reaction when he'd first walked into the huge room where thirty-eight patients sat in comfortable recliners getting various kinds of IV drips. So many people smiling and laughing. Another thing being how friendly everybody was to everybody else. People in thousand-dollar coats and jackets talking to threadbare folks in cheap discount clothes. Black people yukking it up with white people. And swift efficient nurses Ralph Francis McKenna, a skilled flirt, knew how to draw in.

Once in a while somebody would have a reaction to the chemo. One woman must have set some kind of record for puking. She was so sick the three nurses hovering over her didn't even have time to get her to one of the johns. All they could do was keep shoving clean pans under her chin.

During our third session Ralph said, "So how do you like flying solo?"

"What's 'flying solo'?"

"You know. Being alone. Without a wife."

"I hate it. My wife knew how to enjoy life. She really loved it. I get depressed a lot. I should've gone first. She appreciated being alive."

"I still talk to my wife, you know that? I walk around the house and talk to her like we're just having a conversation."

"I do pretty much the same thing. One night I dreamed I was talking to her on the phone and when I woke up I was sitting on the side of the bed with the receiver in my hand."

Flying solo. I liked that phrase.

YOU COULD READ, use one of their DVD players or listen to music on headsets. Or visit with friends and relatives who came to pass the time. Or in Ralph's case, flirt.

The nurses liked him. His good looks and cop self-confidence put them at ease. I'm sure a couple of the single ones in their forties would probably have considered going to bed with him if he'd been capable of it. He joked to me once, shame shining in his eyes: "They took my pecker,

Tom, and they won't give it back." Not that a few of the older nurses didn't like me. There was Nora who reminded me of my wife in her younger years. A few times I started to ask her out but then got too scared. The last woman I'd asked out on a first date had been my wife forty-three years ago.

The DVD players were small and you could set them up on a wheeled table right in front of your recliner while you were getting the juice. One day I brought season two of *The Rockford Files* with James Garner. When I got about two minutes into the episode I heard Ralph sort of snicker.

"What's so funny?"

"You. I should've figured you for a Garner type of guy."

"What's wrong with Garner?"

"He's a wuss. Sort of femmy."

"James Garner is sort of femmy?"

"Yeah. He's always whining and bitching. You know, like a woman. I'm more of a Clint Eastwood fan myself."

"I should've figured on that."

"You don't like Eastwood?"

"Maybe I would if he knew how to act."

"He's all man."

"He's all something all right."

"You never hear him whine."

"That's because he doesn't know how. It's too complicated for him."

"'Make my day.'"

"Kiss my ass."

Ralph laughed so hard several of the nurses down the line looked at us and smiled. Then they tried to explain us to their patients.

A NURSE NAMED Heather Moore was the first one. She always called us her "Trouble Boys" because we kidded her so much about her somewhat earnest, naïve worldview. Over a couple of months, we learned that her ex-husband had wiped out their tiny bank account and run off with the secretary at the muffler shop where he'd been manager. She always said, "All my girlfriends say I should be a whole lot madder at him but you know when I'm honest with myself I probably wasn't that good of a wife. You know? His mom always fixed these big suppers for the family. And she's a very pretty woman. But by the time I put in eight hours here and pick up Bobby at daycare, I just don't have much energy. We ate a lot of frozen stuff. And I put on about ten pounds extra. I guess you can't blame him for looking around."

Couple times after she started sharing her stories with us, Ralph made some phone calls. He talked to three people who'd known her husband. A chaser who'd started running around on Heather soon after their wedding day. A slacker at work and a husband who betrayed his wife in maybe the worst way of all—making constant jokes about her to his coworkers. And she blamed herself for not being good enough for him.

Then came the day when she told us about the duplex where she lived. The toilets wouldn't flush properly, the garbage disposal didn't work, both front and back concrete steps were dangerously shattered, and the back door wouldn't lock. Some of her neighbors had been robbed recently.

The landlord was a jerk—lawyer, of course—named David Muldoon. Despite the comic book surname he was anything but comic. Ralph checked him out. A neo-yuppie who owned several income properties in the city, he was apparently working his way up the slumlord ladder. Heather complained to the city and the city did what it did best, nothing. She'd called Muldoon's business office several times and been promised that her complaints would soon be taken care of. They weren't. And even baby lawyers fresh from the diploma mills wanted more than she could afford to take Muldoon on.

We always asked her how it was going with Muldoon. The day she told us that the roof was leaking and nobody from his office had returned her call in four days, Ralph told her, "You don't worry about it anymore, Heather."

"How come?"

"I just have a feeling."

Heather wasn't the only one wondering what the hell he was talking about. So was I. He said, "You got the usual big night planned?"

"If you mean frozen dinner, some TV, maybe calling one of my kids who'll be too busy to talk very long and then going to bed, yes."

"Maybe watch a little James Garner."

"Yeah or put on Clint Eastwood and fall asleep early."

"Glad you don't have plans because we're going on a stakeout."

"I go to bed at nine."

"Not tonight. Unless we get lucky. Maybe he'll get laid and get home before then."

"Who?"

"Muldoon, that's who."

"You know for a fact that he's got something going on the side?"

"No. But I always listen to my gut."

I smiled.

"I say something funny?" Sort of pissed the way he said it.

"Do all you guys watch bad cop shows before you graduate? Your 'gut'?"

"Most of these assholes cheat."

I thought about it. "Maybe you're right."

"Kid, I'm always right." Grin this time.

Turned out it was the secretary in the law firm on the floor below Muldoon's. Not even all that attractive. He was just out for strange in the nighttime.

We waited leaning against his new black Cadillac.

"Who the fuck are you two supposed to be?"

"We're supposed to be the two guys you least want to hear from." I was happy to let Ralph do the talking.

"Yeah?" All swagger.

"Yeah. You're taking advantage of a friend of ours."

"Get the fuck out of my way. I'm going home."

"It's a bitch getting rid of that pussy smell on your clothes, isn't it? Wives like to pretend they can't smell it."

Dug out his cell phone. Waggled it for us. "I don't know who you two assholes are but I'll bet the police won't have any trouble finding out."

"And your wife won't have any trouble finding out about the snatch in that apartment house behind us, either."

I didn't realize what had happened until I saw the counselor bend in half and heard him try to swear while his lungs were collapsing. He fell to his knees. Ralph hit him so hard on the side of the head Muldoon toppled over. "Her name's Heather Moore. She's one of your tenants. She doesn't know anything about this so don't bother trying to shake her down for any information. You've got two days to fix everything wrong in her apartment. Two days or I call your wife. And if you come after us or send anybody after us then I not only call your wife I start looking for any other bimbos you've been with in the past. I'm a retired homicide detective so I know how to do this shit. You got me?"

Muldoon still couldn't talk. Just kept rolling back and forth on the sandy concrete. He grunted something.

THAT WAS HOW it started. Heather asked us about it once but we said we didn't know anything about it. Heather obviously didn't believe us because two weeks later a nurse named Sally Coates, one neither of us knew very well, came and sat down on a chair next to the IV stand and told us about her husband and this used-car salesman who'd sold them a lemon and wouldn't make it right. They were out seven grand they hadn't been able to afford in the first place but they had to have a car so her husband could get to the VA hospital where he was learning to walk again after losing his right leg in Afghanistan. The kind of story you watch on TV and want to start killing people.

All innocence, Ralph said, "Gosh, Sally, I wish we could help you but I don't see what we could do. There isn't any reason he'd listen to us."

"I can't believe it," Sally said the next time we saw her. "Bob got a call the day after I told you about this salesman. The guy said to bring the car in and they'd get it fixed up right so we wouldn't be having any trouble with it. And there wouldn't be any charge."

"I'll bet you did a lot of praying about it, didn't you, Sally?"

"Of course. We have two little ones to feed. Keeping that car running was breaking us."

"Well, it was the prayers that did it, Sally."

"And you didn't have anything to do with it?"

"Ask him."

I shook my head. "What could we have done, Sally? We're just two old guys."

After she left, Ralph leaned over from his leather recliner and said, "The only good thing about dying this way is we don't have to give a shit about anything. What're they gonna do to us?" That grin of his. "We're already dead."

I DEVELOPED A uniform. A Cubs cap, dark aviator glasses, and a Louisville Slugger. According to Ralph I was "the backup hood. They're scared enough of me. Then they see this guy with the ball bat and the shades—they'll do anything to cooperate." He didn't mention how old we were.

The nurses kept coming. Four in the next three months. A nurse who was trying to get a collection of family photographs back from an ex-boyfriend she'd broken up with after he'd given her the clap, spurned boyfriend stealing the collection and keeping it for her breaking up with him; the nurse whose daughter's boyfriend was afraid to visit because two bully brothers down the block always picked on him when he pulled up; and the nurse who liked to sit in on poker games with five guys who worked at an electronics discount house and thought it was pretty damned funny to cheat her out of forty to sixty dollars every time she sat down. It took her four months of playing twice a month to figure it out.

No heavy lifting, as they say; no, that came with a tiny, delicate young nurse named Callie. We noticed the bruises on her arms first, then the bruises on her throat despite the scarf she wore with her uniform. Then came the two broken fingers and the way she limped for a couple of weeks and finally the faint but unmistakable black eye. A few of the other nurses whispered about it among themselves. One of them told us that the head nurse had asked Callie about it. Callie had smiled and said that her "whole family is clumsy."

It was during this time that both Ralph and I realized that we probably wouldn't be beating the prognoses we'd been given. With me it was a small but certain track of new cancer suddenly appearing on my right thigh; with Ralph it was the return of heart problems he'd had off and on for two decades.

We didn't talk about it much to each other. There isn't much to say when you get to this point. You just hope for as much decent time as you can get and if you've been helping people here and there you go right on helping them as long as you can.

We followed Callie home one night, found out that she lived in a tumbledown farmhouse as isolated as a lighthouse. The next night we followed her home and when she stopped off at a shopping center we waited for her by her car.

She smiled. "My two favorite patients. I guess you don't get to see me enough in chemo, huh?" The cat-green eyes were suspicious despite her greeting. She'd developed another one of those mysterious limps.

"That's right. Tom here wants to ask you to marry him."

"Well," the smile never wavering, "maybe I should talk that over with my husband first. You think?"

"That's what we want to talk to you about, Callie," I said. "Your husband."

The smile went and so did she. Or at least she tried. I stood in front of the car door. Ralph took her arm and walked her about four feet away.

He said something to her I couldn't hear but her I heard clearly: "My personal life is none of your damn business! And I'm going to tell my husband about this."

"He going to beat us up the way he beats you up?"

"Who said he beats me up?"

"I was a cop, remember? I've seen dozens of cases like yours. They run to a pattern."

"Well, then you weren't a very *good* cop because my husband has never laid a hand on me."

"Three restraining orders in five years; six 911 calls; the same ER doctor who said he's dealt with you twice for concussions; and a woman's shelter that told me you came there twice for three-night stays."

The city roared with life—traffic, stray rap music, shouts, laughter, squealing tires—but right here a little death was being died as she was forced to confront not just us but herself. The small package she'd been carrying slipped from her hands to the concrete and she slumped against her car. She seemed to rip the sobs from herself in tiny increments, like somebody in the early stages of a seizure.

"I've tried to get away. Five or six times. One night I took the kids and got all the way to St. Joe. Missouri, I mean. We stayed in a motel there for two weeks. Took every dime I had. The kids didn't mind. They're as scared of him as I am. But he found us. He never told me how. And you know what he did? He was waiting for us when we got back from going to a movie the kids wanted to see. He was in our room. I opened the door and there he was. He looked down at Luke—he's eight now; he was only four then—and he said, 'You take care of your little sister, Luke. You two go sit in my truck now.' 'You better not hurt her, Dad.' Can you imagine that, a four-year-old talking like that? A four-year-old? Anyway then he looked at me and said, 'Get in here, whore.' He waited until I closed the door behind me and then he hit me so hard in the face he broke my nose. And my glasses. He forced the kids to ride back with him. That way he knew I'd come back, too."

This was in the food court of the mall where we'd convinced her to come and have some coffee with us. You could reach up and grab a handful of grease from the air. I'm told in Texas they deep-fry quarter sticks of butter. If it ever comes up here this mall will sell it for sure.

"But you always come back."

"I love him, Ralph. I can't explain it. It's like a sickness."

"It's not 'like' a sickness, Callie. It *is* a sickness."

"Maybe if I knew I could get away and he'd never find me. To him those restraining orders are a joke." Then: "I have to admit there're sometimes—more and more these days I guess—when I think maybe it'd be best if he'd just get killed driving that damned truck of his. You know, an accident where he's the only one killed. I wouldn't want to do that to anybody else." Then: "Isn't that awful?"

"It is if you love him."

"I say that, Tom. I *always* say that. But the woman at the shelter had me see a counselor and the counselor explained to me what she called the 'dynamics' of how I really feel about him. We had to take two semesters of psych to get our nursing degrees so I'd always considered myself pretty smart on the subject. But she led me into thinking a lot of things that had never occurred to me before. And so even though I say that, I'm not sure I mean it." Then, shy: "Sorry for all the carrying on in the parking lot. I attracted quite a crowd."

"I collected admission from every one of them."

She sat back in her curved red plastic chair and smiled. "You guys, you're really my friends. I was so depressed all day. Even with the kids there I just didn't want to drag myself home tonight. I know I was being selfish to even think such a thing. But I just couldn't take being hit or kicked anymore. I knew he'd be mad that I stopped at the mall. Straight home or I'd better have a damned good excuse. Or I'll be sorry. It's no way to live."

"No," I said, "it sure isn't."

"NOW LET'S GO get him."

Callie had mentioned she was taking the kids for a long weekend stay at a theme park, which was why we'd decided on tonight.

Neely didn't hear us coming. We walked through patches of shadow then moonlight, shadow then moonlight while he tried to get out of his truck. I say tried because he was so drunk he almost came out headfirst and would have if he hadn't grabbed the edge of the truck door in time. Then he sat turned around on the edge of the seat and puked straight down. He went three times and he made me almost as sick as he was. Then of course being as drunk as he was he stepped down with his cowboy boots into the puddle of puke he'd made. He kept wiping the back of his right hand across his mouth. He started sloshing through the puke then stopped and went back to the truck. He opened the door and grabbed something. In the moonlight I could see it was a pint of whiskey. He gunned a long drink then took six steps and puked it all right back up. He stepped into this puke as well and headed more or less in the direction of the stairs that would take him to his apartment. All of this was setting things up perfectly. Nobody was going to question the fact that Neely had been so drunk it was no surprise that he'd fallen off those stairs and died.

We moved fast. I took the position behind him with my ball cap, shades, and ball bat and Ralph got in front of him with his Glock.

Neely must've been toting a 2.8 level of alcohol because he didn't seem to be aware of Ralph until he ran straight into him. And straight into the Glock. Even then all he could say was, "Huh? I jush wan' sleep."

"Good evening, Mr. Neely. You shouldn't drink so much. You need to be alert when you're beating the shit out of women half your size. You never know when they're going to hit back, do you?"

"Hey, dude, ish tha' a gun?"

"Sure looks like it, doesn't it?"

He reeled back on the heels of his cowboy boots. I poked the bat into his back. I was careful. When he went down the stairs it had to look accidental. We couldn't bruise him or use any more force than it took to give him a slight shove. If he didn't die the first time down he would the second time we shoved him.

"Hey."

"You need some sleep, Neely."

"—need no fuckin' sleep. 'n don't try'n make me. Hey, an' you got a fuckin' gun."

"What if I told you that I've got a pizza in the car?"

"Pizza?"

"Yeah. Pizza."

"How come pizza?"

"So we can sit down in your apartment and talk things over."

"Huh?"

"How—does—pizza—sound?"

Ralph was enunciating because Neely was about two minutes away from unconsciousness. We had to get him up those stairs without leaving any marks on him.

"Pizza, Neely. Sausage and beef and pepperoni."

I allowed myself the pleasure of taking in the summer night. The first time I'd ever made love to Karen had been on a night like this near a boat dock. Summer of our senior year in college. We went back to that spot many times over the years. Not long before she died we went there, too. I almost believed in ghosts; I thought I saw our younger selves out on the night river in one of those old rented aluminum canoes, our lives all ahead of us, so young and exuberant and naïve. I wanted to get in one of those old canoes and take my wife down river so she could die in my arms and maybe I'd be lucky and die in hers as well. But it hadn't worked out that way. All too soon I'd been flying solo.

Neely started puking again. This time it was a lot more dramatic because after he finished he fell facedown in it.

"This fucking asshole. When he's done you take one arm and I'll take the other one."

"I thought we weren't going to touch him."

"That's why you shoved those latex gloves in your back pocket same as I did. You gotta plan for contingencies. That's why cops carry guns they can plant on perps. Otherwise we'll be here all night. Clint Eastwood would know about that."

"Yes, planting guns on people. Another admirable Eastwood quality."

"Right. I forgot. Tender ears. You don't want to hear about real life. You just want to bitch and moan like Garner. Now let's pick up this vile piece of shit and get it over with."

He'd worked up a pretty good sweat with all his puking. It was a hot and humid night. His body was soggy like something that would soon mildew. Once I pulled him out of his puke I held my breath.

"We don't want to drag him. They'll look at his boots. Stand him upright and we'll sort of escort him to the steps."

"I just hope he doesn't start puking again."

"I saw a black perp puke like this once. I wish I had it on tape."

"Yeah, be fun for the grandkids to watch at Christmastime."

"I like that, Tom. Smart-ass remarks in the course of committing murder one. Shows you're getting a lot tougher."

We took our time. He didn't puke again but from the tangy odor I think he did piss his pants.

When we were close to the bottom step, he broke. I guess both of us had assumed he was unconscious and therefore wouldn't be any problem. But he broke and he got a three or four second lead while we just stood there and watched him scramble up those stairs like a wild animal that had just escaped its cage. He was five steps ahead of us before Ralph started after him. I pounded up the steps right behind him. Ralph was shouting. I'm sure he had to restrain himself from just shooting Neely and getting it over with.

Neely was conscious enough to run but not conscious enough to think clearly because when he got to the top of the stairs he stopped and dug a set of keys from his pocket. As he leaned in to try and find the lock his head jerked up suddenly and he stared at us as if he was seeing us for the very first time. Confusion turned to terror in his eyes and he started backing away from us. "Hey, who the hell're you?"

"Who do you think we are, Neely?"

"I don' like thish."

"Yeah, well we don't like it, either."

"He got a ball bat." He nodded in my direction. He weaved wide as he did so, so wide I thought he was going to tip over sideways. Then his hand searched the right pocket of his Levi's. It looked like he'd trapped an angry ferret in there.

Ralph materialized Neely's nine-inch switchblade. "This what you're looking for?"

"Hey," Neely said. And when he went to grab for it he started falling to the floor. Ralph grabbed him in time. Stood him straight up.

But Neely wasn't done yet. And he was able to move faster than I would have given him credit for. Ralph glanced back at me, nodded for me to come forward. And in that second Neely made his sloppy, drunken move. He grabbed the switchblade from Ralph's hand and immediately went into a crouch.

He would have been more impressive if he hadn't swayed side to side so often. And if he hadn't tried to sound tough. "Who'sh gotta knife now, huh?"

"You gonna cut us up are you, Neely?"

All the time advancing on Neely, backing him up. "C'mon, Neely. Cut me. Right here." Ralph held his arm out. "Right there, Neely. You can't miss it."

Neely swaying, half-stumbling backward as Ralph moved closer, closer. "You're pretty pathetic, you know that Neely? You beat up your wife all the time and even when you've got the knife you're still scared of me. You're not much of a man but then you know that, don't you? You look in the mirror every morning and you see yourself for what you really are, don't you?"

I doubt Neely understood what Ralph was saying to him. This was complex stuff to comprehend when you were as wasted as Neely was. All he seemed to understand was that Ralph meant to do him harm. And if Ralph didn't do it there was always the guy in the ball cap and the shades. You know, with the bat.

Neely stumbled backward, his arms circling in a desperate attempt to keep himself upright. He hit the two-by-four that was the upper part of the porch enclosure just at the lower part of his back and he went right over, the two-by-four splintering as he did so. He didn't scream. My guess is he was still confused about what was happening. By the time he hit the ground I was standing next to Ralph, looking down into the shadows beneath us.

There was silence. Ralph got his flashlight going and we got our first look at him. If he wasn't dead he was pretty good at faking it. He didn't land in any of those positions we associate with people who died crashing from great heights. He was flat on his back with his arms flung wide. His right leg was twisted inward a few inches but nothing dramatic. The eyes were open and looked straight up. No expression of horror, something else we've picked up from books and movies. And as we watched the blood started pooling from the back of his head.

"Let's go make sure," Ralph said.

It was like somebody had turned on the soundtrack. In the moments it had taken Neely to fall all other sound had disappeared. But now the night was back and turned up high. Night birds, dogs, horses, and cows bedded down for the evening, distant trucks and trains all turned so high I wanted to clap my hands to my ears.

"You all right, Tom?"

"Why wouldn't I be all right?"

"See. I knew you weren't all right."

"But you're all right I suppose. I mean we just killed a guy."

"You want me to get all touchy-feely and say I regretted it?"

"Fuck yourself."

"He was a piece of shit and one of these nights he was gonna kill a friend of ours. Maybe he wouldn't even have done it on purpose. He'd just be beating on her some night and he'd do it by accident. But one way or another he'd kill her. And we'd have to admit to ourselves that we could've stopped it."

I walked away from the edge of the porch and started down the stairs.

"You doin' better now?" Ralph called.

"Yeah; yeah, I guess I am."

"Clint Eastwood, I tell ya. Clint Eastwood every time."

Turned out Neely wasn't dead after all. We had to stand there for quite awhile watching him bleed to death.

I WAS VISITING my oldest son in Phoenix (way too hot for me) when I learned Ralph had died. I'd logged on to the hometown paper website and there was his name at the top of the obituaries. The photo must have been taken when he was in his early twenties. I barely recognized him. Heart attack. He'd been dead for a day before a neighbor of his got suspicious and asked the apartment house manager to open Ralph's door. I thought of what he'd said about flying solo that time.

FLYING SOLO

Ralph had experienced the ultimate in flying solo, death. I hoped that whatever he thought was on the other side came true for him. I still hadn't figured out what I hoped would be there. If anything would be there at all.

The doc told me they'd be putting me back on chemo again. The lab reports were getting bad fast. The nurses in chemo commiserated with me as if Ralph had been a family member. There'd been a number of things I hadn't liked about him and he hadn't liked about me. Those things never got resolved and maybe they didn't need to. Maybe flying solo was all we needed for a bond. One thing for sure. The chemo room hours seemed a lot longer with him gone. I even got sentimental once and put a Clint Eastwood DVD in the machine, film called *Tightrope*. Surprised myself by liking it more than not liking it.

I WAS SITTING in my recliner one day when one of the newer nurses sat down and started talking in a very low voice. "There's this guy we each gave five hundred dollars to. You know, a down payment. He said he was setting up this group trip to the Grand Canyon. You know, through this group therapy thing I go to. Then we found out that he scams a lot of people this way. Groups, I mean. We called the Better Business Bureau and the police. But I guess he covers his tracks pretty well. Actually takes some of the groups on the trips. Five hundred is a lot of money if you're a single mother."

The chemo was taking its toll. But I figured I owed it to Ralph to help her out. And besides, I wanted to see how I did on my own.

SO HERE I am tonight. I've followed him from his small house to his round of singles bars and finally to the apartment complex where the woman lives. The one he picked up in the last bar. He's got to come out sometime.

I've got the Louisville Slugger laid across my lap and the Cubs cap cinched in place. I won't put the shades on till I see him. No sense straining my eyes. Not at my age.

I miss Ralph. About now he'd be working himself up doing his best Clint Eastwood and trying to dazzle me with all his bad cop stories.

I'm pretty sure I can handle this but even if it works out all right, it's still flying solo. And let me tell you, flying solo can get to be pretty damned lonely.

NEIGHBORHOOD WATCH

BY CAROLYN HAINES

PENMANSHIP HAD NEVER been her strong suit, but in these days of computer communications, Yvonne knew not to underestimate the power of a hand-written letter.

The black ink flowed across the ecru notepaper in daring loops and swirls.

Dear President Obama,

My sense of irony has been keenly exercised since the brutal murder of my daughter, Rainbow Saffron King. Are you aware that any moron with an IQ in the single digits can buy a gun, yet I have to take a test to keep my driver's license? My neighbors, who are inbred Okies with six toes and rabbit red eyes, all have automatic weapons. Even as I write they are playing shuffleboard in their front yard with weapons trained on my front door.

My poor little Rainbow was planting a vegetable garden to feed the poor when a stray bullet zipped through her heart. Though the police ruled it an accidental shooting and told me there are no laws in Alabama prohibiting folks from shooting weapons in their front yards, I believe Rainbow's death to be a murder. Can you please get those worthless buffoons sitting in Congress to do some work and change the gun laws of this country? A big gun does not make a man's penis a single bit bigger.

Yours truly,

Grace Moncrieff King

Without a moment's hesitation Yvonne copied down the address of her archenemy, Grace Moncrieff King, and sealed the envelope. If the CIA came looking for the author of the note, they'd find plenty to keep them busy at Grace's address.

Yvonne put the note beside two others, already stamped and waiting only on the arrival of Jeffrey, the postman, before winging their way to the White House. She'd written notes to the prior resident of America's first house—with no response. She had higher hopes for the new occupant of 1600 Pennsylvania Avenue. He appeared to have some gumption.

She checked the clock in the kitchen, noting she had forty minutes until Jeffrey was due. She swallowed a handful of vitamins with a glass of filtered water. There was time for one more note. From the kitchen drawer she brought out high-powered military field glasses and focused on the yellow Victorian half a block away. Grace was out in her yard, tending the roses that were her pride and joy.

Yvonne took in every detail. Grace had been to the hairdresser. Her coppery curls feathered around her face, and the color was fresh and perky. At the end of the month, Grace's hair would be faded, sliding toward the natural gray. Grace was at least sixty-two, though she lied and claimed to be only fifty-eight.

Grace lied about many things.

Most especially about her husbands.

After three glasses of wine at a dinner party, Grace had confessed to Yvonne that she'd gone to the altar five times and hoped to make it six. No dummy, Yvonne had searched out Grace's marriage licenses and come up with only two, Anthony Montcrieff, whose name Grace clung to like a favorite pair of panties, and Barney King, her current spouse, who was in assisted living. But Grace was honey to fly-brained men, there was no denying that. Men buzzed around her, intoxicated by her come hither flirtations.

To that end, Grace performed yoga stretches in the window of her second story turret, where any passerby could watch the contortions, which were right amazing for a woman her age.

Old Marshall Binghamton, who owned the property at the end of the road with the fine view of Mobile Bay, walked past Grace's house at least twice a day, eyes out on stems, hoping to catch a glimpse of her antics. Deviant old bastard. When his timing was good and he saw Grace bending and twisting, he'd stop dead on the sidewalk, breathing noisily through his mouth, and sometimes trembling. Oh, he had fantasies of what he wanted to do to Grace.

Which reminded Yvonne to get busy with her letter.

Dear President Obama,

Please consider the injustice of health care in our country today. Insurance companies are villainous in their callous decisions to provide health coverage to policies valuing the penis. Viagra is paid for by insurance policies but birth control pills are not. So men are allowed to have their pleasure (even if too senile to remember it) while young women must risk pregnancy? Foul! I say FOUL!

This is just one example of gender-biased health care in this country. Please level the playing field of sexual misconduct for male and female alike. What's good for the goose is good for the gander. Force insurance companies to cover birth control pills so my teenage daughter can safely continue with her relationship with a sixty-nine-year-old man we are hoping will soon die in a moment of sexual bliss. (He's loaded and she's his beneficiary, the old fool.) But until he croaks, she needs someone to pay for her Yaz because she spends all her money on butt floss undies.

God bless you,

Mable Graham

She signed the note—written on a different type of note card and in a small cramped hand—with a flourish. Mable lived two blocks over and was normally her partner in the weekly bridge games held in the neighborhood. Mable was a good egg, except for her support of the Reverend Bewley Birchwood, a televangelist who promised gold and glory for those who contributed to his TV ministry. To Yvonne's way of thinking, a little CIA intervention might save Mable a shitload of money.

Yvonne placed the stamp, one featuring the black Michael Jackson, on the envelope just as she heard Jeffrey's footsteps on her stoop. She gathered her outgoing mail and went to open the door.

Jeffrey had already dumped his mail sack in anticipation of her invitation for a glass of iced tea. It was their routine. He'd make his report of the neighborhood while he cooled off a little. She admired a man who walked a mail route even in the August heat. The Daphne, Alabama, post office had offered him one of the riding carts, but he said he was holding out for an electric scooter. The truth was, Jeffrey was a conservation nut and walking also gave him an optimal opportunity to keep up with the neighbors.

"Binghamton had a young woman down at his boat dock today." Jeffrey followed Yvonne into the kitchen and took his chair. "She looked to be mid-forties or so. Good figure. She was friendly enough. Blond, about five-five. Beauty mark on her left cheek. It's not even ten o'clock and she had what looked like a Bloody Mary in her hand. Made me think of a good-time girl. Could give Grace a run for her money."

"Grace may have a few more wrinkles, but I'd put my bet on her. She knows every angle in that game." Yvonne could never get over the naivety of men like Jeffrey. They thought it all came down to a bouncy ass and silicon tits. Grace knew moves that would curl Jeffrey's toes, and most of them had nothing to do with the bedroom.

"Old Binghamton seemed mighty smitten. Had that mouth-open, quivery action goin' on." Jeffrey did a fine imitation as he accepted the glass of tea.

"What about Lady Kelley?" Yvonne changed the subject. She didn't like Grace well enough to defend her.

"She's still sittin' in her chair in front of the TV. She won't come to the door, so I can't say if she's cryin' or not."

Lady had lost her husband to a heart attack. Her children had come to visit. Once. Six weeks ago. The ungrateful little miscreants had shown up at the funeral, all weepy and full of woe. Once the will was read and they got their cut, they were gone. Lady, so called because of her genteel personality, had been stripped of financial control. The oldest boy, a sweaty, overweight high school football coach, was in charge of everything. Rumor was the children intended to force the sale of Lady's house and move her to assisted living.

"I'll take her some muffins," Yvonne said as she refilled Jeffrey's glass. "If I hear those kids of hers are coming back, I'll put roofing tacks in the driveway."

Jeffrey wiped the sweat from his glass. "Everything else is quiet. I still say old Binghamton is gonna take up with the younger model. Who'd pass up a T-bird for an Edsel?"

Yvonne had a good laugh. That Jeffrey, he sure knew how to get her tickled. At least once a day he came out with some jewel. She gave him the stamped notes, and he tucked them in his sack before he hefted it and continued on his way. If he saw anything noteworthy, he'd give her a call. Between the two of them, they looked out for the neighborhood.

She put on her athletic shoes, laced them tight, and went to the backyard to call Jethro, her Walker hound/Doberman cross. He'd shown up, starved and abused, in her yard four years before. She'd had him neutered, wormed, vaccinated, and socialized in a matter of weeks, and now he was the best companion imaginable. They walked each day, just before her story came on. Jethro helped her keep the neighborhood safe.

Yvonne didn't bother locking the front door. The neighbors knew each other and who should be allowed to come and go. Any funny stuff, someone would call the police.

Grace was still working in her roses when they marched by. Yvonne spoke—she was always courteous, that was how she was raised.

Jethro was past Grace's yard when Grace called out, "Have you heard Reg Gamble got into some trouble last night?"

It was just like Grace to hold out information until Yvonne had to turn around and walk back. It was a control thing with Grace. Yvonne considered pretending she hadn't heard, but Jethro did a one-eighty. Yvonne had no choice but to follow. Well, she had a little something to tell, too.

"No, I hadn't heard. I hope he isn't sick," Yvonne said, friendly as could be.

"Oh, no. Not unless you count sucking on a vodka bottle as sickness. Got drunk at the sports bar and got a DUI. Cops kept him in jail overnight. I heard he was pitching a hell fit, calling the officers names. His sister bailed him out this morning and took him to the Bradford Center to dry out." Grace's lavender eyes sparkled.

"That's too bad," Yvonne said. "Drinking is an illness, Grace. It's not some kind of moral weakness. Brain chemistry out of whack."

"Oh, posh!" Grace waved airily. "Reg is an old drunk. Mean as a snake when he's on the bottle. Don't try to make excuses for him."

Yvonne let it go. "I hear old Binghamton's got him some frisky blond company. I wondered how long he'd last as a single man. Once his wife died, every widow woman in Daphne took him a casserole. Looks to me like he wanted something more than hot tuna and noodles." Men had once called Yvonne's robust laughter naughty.

"Who is she?" Grace didn't hide her consternation.

"No clue." Yvonne caught a flash of calculation in Grace's expression. "Want to come along with me and Jethro for a walk?"

Grace dropped her leather gardening gloves in the dirt. She dusted her hands and came out the gate. "I need a good stretch."

They strolled down the sidewalk beneath the shade of the live oaks that made Bayside Manor, a gated retirement community, worth living in. The sidewalk was smooth and level, newly built to accommodate those fancy little scooters.

"How come you never married, Yvonne?" Grace rotated each shoulder as if her joints were unhinged.

"Who said I never married?" Yvonne was surprised at the question.

"Well, I just assumed … You don't wear a ring. You never talk about a husband or children."

"Some folks don't need a man to validate who they are. Not one in the present *or* one in the past. What's gone is gone, Grace. So how many times were you married?"

Grace looked confused. "Why do you ask?"

"'Cause you brought it up? How many?"

"Three."

Yvonne nodded. Grace King was a liar. If she was breathing, she was lying. "I never hear you talk about children either."

"Oh, I couldn't have any. I had a delicate uterus. I miscarried three times. My pelvis is so narrow. The doctor said it might break me in two to carry a child, and I was married to Gerard then. A gynecologist. He said I should have it all taken out. He loved me so much he didn't want to risk me."

"Did he work for the health department?" Yvonne was deviling Grace, but she couldn't stop herself.

"Of course not! He had a private practice and was the most sought-after doctor in Louisville."

"What happened to him?"

"It was just tragic," Grace said. "He had a heart attack delivering a baby. Slipped right off his stool onto the floor and he was dead. Like to have broke my heart."

"Was he first, second, or third?"

"Second." Grace looked peeved. She pointed down to the end of the street where the land dropped steeply to the water of Mobile Bay. A wooden pier jutted out. The boat slip was empty. "Marshall's boat is gone."

"He's smarter than I thought," Yvonne said.

"What do you mean?"

"There's a storm brewing out on the open water." She pointed at the dull, flat clouds far on the horizon. "If he anchors the boat right, he can use the motion of the waves to add some punch to his amorous moves. Maybe that young blond won't kill him then."

Grace's mouth thinned into a narrow red line. "I need to get back to my garden." She turned abruptly and strode back the way they'd come.

Yvonne unleashed Jethro. He loved the water. Maybe he had some lab in him somewhere. They had DNA tests for dogs now. An owner could find out the lineage of a mutt. Then again, what difference did it make? Yvonne wasn't certain what her ancestry might include. She liked the water, too.

She sat on a bench and watched Jethro race down the steep steps to the pier. He didn't even hesitate as he launched himself straight off the end in a flying leap to splash in the water. It was good to be young, she thought, remembering her own days of jumping from creek banks into icy streams. Those had been good times.

Now, though, it was time for her program. She whistled up Jethro and headed home. *All My Children* was her lunchtime vice. She'd followed the boudoir antics of Erica Kane since she'd first appeared on the scene. Erica was close to sixty, though she looked no more than forty-five. On *AMC* a character could be a villain one week and a saint the next. Redemption was easy as pie on television.

THE NEXT DAY dawned hot and sticky. Clouds hung over the bay, thick and clotted with rain. A tropical depression was boring up the center of the Gulf of Mexico, and though it was unorganized, there was the chance it could blossom into a monster storm. The August waters, superheated by development all along the coastline, favored such.

Yvonne went out on her front porch and used the field glasses to check up and down the street. To her surprise, Grace was working in her rose garden. It was barely six o'clock in the morning, and Grace was not by nature an early riser.

Yvonne watched surreptitiously as she sipped her morning coffee. Grace was acting strange. She dug in the dirt with quiet fury, and when the sun was full up and Grace had pushed her hair back from her perspiration-dampened face, she dropped her gloves and headed down the street toward the bay.

She was checking up on Binghamton! Yvonne wondered herself if the old boy had made it home. With the storm brewing over the water, he should be docking in safe harbors—but perhaps Grace waiting on the pier was more dangerous than the Bermuda Triangle.

Yvonne took her coffee cup and binoculars inside and wrote a letter.

Dear President Obama,

Are you aware that in the Alabama halls of higher education, female assistant professors make an average of eight thousand dollars less than their male counterparts? Gender bias should not be allowed in institutions supported by state and federal dollars. When the worth—or lack of worth—of an employee is determined by male genitalia—or lack thereof—it's a sad comment on the education and values our young people are receiving.

Does a penis bestow a superior ability to teach? I have not found this to be true.

Please look into the wage disparities between genders in universities and colleges that accept federal dollars. While it is a fact in Alabama, it is likely true in other places.

Thank you,
Marshall Binghamton

She'd typewritten the letter and signed it with a scrawl that could have said anything. Marshall Binghamton would never support equal pay for equal work. He was a chauvinist through and through. Which is why it gave Yvonne an extra boost of pleasure to fold the letter and stuff it in an envelope.

Once it was stamped and ready for Jeffrey's arrival, she grabbed a bagel and Jethro's leash and called the dog. No point missing the fireworks if Binghamton happened to be docked. She wondered if Grace would be so bold as to knock on his front door. Maybe!

With Jethro for a beard and chewing the last of the bagel, she pushed her way through the thick air to the water. The Moon Dancer, Binghamton's boat, was snugged in the little boathouse. And Grace was nowhere to be seen.

Yvonne circled the cul de sac and tried to see past the shrubs to Binghamton's house, but the camellia bushes with their dense green leaves were too thick. Jethro tugged at his leash, but she didn't let him loose to rush to the water. The clouds looked threatening. And she had some errands to run before a big storm came through and knocked the power out for several days.

AT THE LOCAL library she got on the internet and searched for ob-gyn Dr. Gerard in Louisville, Kentucky. She figured Grace was lying, but it was better to check. To her surprise, she found the obituary for Dr. Gerard DeLong, noted obstetrician, who died unexpectedly of a heart attack while delivering a child at Mercy Medical Hospital. He was survived by his wife, Eugracia DeWitt DeLong, and two children from a previous marriage.

Yvonne had not discovered the DeWitt name when she'd first looked into Grace's marriages, and she certainly wasn't familiar with Eugracia, an unusual derivative of Grace. She did a search for Eugracia DeWitt. What came up was the society page of the *Kansas City Register*. Eugracia and her husband, Roger DeWitt, were featured at a party for a local architect. There was no doubt that the woman in the photograph was her neighbor.

She searched for Roger DeWitt. The next mention was an obituary. Roger slipped from the roof of their Kansas City Home and plunged to his death. Eugracia McKenzie DeWitt was his sole survivor. Gregor McKenzie, her third husband, was also deceased. Anaphylactic shock.

So Grace hadn't lied, exactly. Dr. Gerard DeLong, Roger DeWitt, Gregor McKenzie, Anthony Montcrieff, plus the latest, Barney King, a bank manager suffering from premature Alzheimer's disease and living in a facility across the bay in Mobile. Barney had been institutionalized a few weeks before Yvonne moved into the neighborhood. Grace went to see him twice a week, though she said he didn't recognize her.

The doctors said he'd lost the will to live and could go at any minute, which would leave Grace free to pursue Marshall Binghamton full throttle. Yvonne almost felt a dollop of pity for Marshall, but she squished it.

On the way home, she braved the blustery weather and sudden sheets of rain and stopped at the store for coffee, apples, peanut butter, chicken, and frozen dumplings to cook for Jethro, and a bottle of Jack Daniels. She allowed herself one tall Jack and water each evening, and with the storm approaching, she didn't want to be caught with a short supply.

She made it home just as Jeffrey was headed down her front walk. They went inside together, and he played fetch with Jethro while she put the chicken on to boil and made fresh tea. Jeffrey was about to pop with some information, but they had a ritual. When he was at the table, tea in hand, he grinned.

"Old Binghamton was out in his yard this morning when I delivered the mail."

She arched her eyebrows, interested but not too eager.

"Had a pair of red undies hanging from his robe pocket and strutting around like a rooster in a henhouse."

Yvonne poured herself some tea. She really wanted a Jack, but it wasn't even noon. "Did you see the blonde?"

Jeffrey shook his head. "No strange car in the drive, either. Could be she left before I got there."

"Grace is going to take this hard." Even knowing all she did about Grace, Yvonne still felt sympathy. It was humiliating to get beat out by a younger model, as if life experience had no value at all.

"She's dug up most of her front yard. Is she puttin' in a sprinkler system?" Jeffrey asked.

"Burying her high hopes, I think."

He drained his glass, put it on the counter and started back to the front door where his satchel waited. She handed him the letter.

"Only one?"

"Been a busy morning," she replied.

"That storm's comin' in fast. I'd better hotfoot it. I want to get home and make sure everything's secure. You need any help here?"

Yvonne thought about it. "I'm fine, Jeffrey. Thanks for asking."

SOME OF HER neighbors sat in recliners and watched the Weather Channel day and night. Yvonne was determined not to fall into that trap. It was always heat or rain or wind or lightning. The weather bogeyman prowled the Gulf Coast, and it did no good to sit and watch for him. Either he'd come or not. She refused to let her last good years be mired in futile worry about Mother Nature's business.

She and Jethro made a round of the exterior of her house, checking to be sure there was nothing loose to fly through a window. Only one storm in recent history had come directly up Mobile Bay. Most skirted west to Biloxi or east to Pensacola. But if one did come, the bluffs of the Eastern Shore were high enough to prevent flooding. No one could do anything about the wind and rain.

When she stopped in her front yard to double latch the white wooden gate, she saw Grace still out in her yard throwing a shovelful of dirt on a mound already chest high.

"Come on, Jethro." Yvonne opened the gate and let the brisk wind blow her across the street. "Grace! Have you lost your mind? There's a storm coming. Stop digging up the front yard and get your house in order."

Grace looked up, eyes wild. "I have to finish this garden."

When Yvonne got close, she saw that Grace had chopped the root system of several of her prize roses. The woman had gone totally round the bend, and over an old mouth-breather who trembled in anticipation.

"Get a grip." Yvonne was brutal. "Give me that shovel." She took it from Grace's hands. "Now go inside and get ready for the storm. Have you checked on Barney?"

"No. No, I haven't." Grace actually hung her head. "You're right. I'll do that now."

"Are you okay?"

Grace nodded. "Thank you, Yvonne. I don't know what got into me."

She climbed the steps and entered her house. The wind quieted for a moment and Yvonne heard the lock click into place. She and Jethro continued down the street. At the end, she saw Marshall Binghamton out tying lines to hold his thrashing boat in place. Old fool.

She went to the pier and signaled for him to throw her a line. She helped him secure the boat. The water was so rough Jethro had no interest in a swim. He stayed Velcroed to her side.

"Hear you got a new friend," she said when Binghamton came off the boat, his legs shaky from exertion or possibly fear. He'd almost been thrown off the pitching boat several times.

"It's a free country," he said.

"I haven't heard that expression since 1958," she said. "What's her name?"

"Mind your own business." He stormed away through the thick hedges of his lawn and disappeared.

Yvonne almost shot him the bird. Rude old deviant. But she'd been raised better than that. She and Jethro went home. The local news station had gone to full weather coverage, not a good sign, and she decided to watch before the power went out.

Hurricane Francine churned straight toward Mobile on a course due north at sixteen miles an hour. She was a Cat 3 and might strengthen.

Yvonne snapped off the TV and unplugged it. She cooked the dumplings with the chicken and set them aside to cool for Jethro. If the power went out, they wouldn't keep long. He might as well enjoy them while they were fresh.

She made a pot of coffee and considered writing another letter, but her concentration was fragmented. Grace was on her mind. As if she'd conjured her up, Grace's car pulled out of the drive and left the neighborhood. The only places Grace went were the hair salon, the grocery, or to see Barney. Yvonne could only hope she was smart enough not to try to cross the seven-and-a-half-mile-long bay bridge with such a storm bearing down on them. The Jubilee Parkway was high enough to avoid the waves—for the moment—but the wind could flip a car over the rail. And the causeway was likely underwater by now.

Grace finished one cup of coffee and decided to chuck her discipline and have a Jack. Storms somehow called for a bit of drinking. The abandon was alluring—just throwing up her hands and saying, fuck it.

Drink clinking with ice, she went to the telephone table and pulled out the phone book. Only a dozen assisted living facilities in Mobile were listed. She'd never asked which one Barney was in, but she could make a few calls, see if she could get Grace on the phone and talk some sense into her about the storm. The weather was getting worse and worse.

Jethro settled at her feet as she made the first call. She hit pay dirt on the seventh. The receptionist knew Barney King. He'd been her family banker.

"Are you a relative?" she asked.

"I'm a friend of his wife's," Yvonne explained. "I need to speak with her. It's an emergency."

"Mr. King passed away last year," the woman said. "I'm sorry."

Yvonne put the phone down, momentarily stumped. When she picked up the receiver again, she called Louisville, Kentucky, information and asked for Andrew DeLong. She let the operator place the call for her.

Andrew was not at home, but his wife, Judy, had a moment to talk about Andrew's father, Gerard.

"He was a delightful man," she said. "He left a big hole in our family. We get cards from his patients every year saying how much they miss him."

"And his wife, Eugracia?"

"Eu-gracia? The name says it all. Once she had his money, we haven't seen or heard from her." There was a split second of silence. "Why are you asking?"

"She's my neighbor. I know her as Grace King." Yvonne's heart beat too fast and she sipped the bourbon.

"Tell her spouse to be careful. She's a black widow. Andrew thinks she tampered with Gerard's heart medicine."

Yvonne finished her drink in one long, smooth swallow. "Why would you say such a thing?"

"Because he believes it. And so do I."

"Do you have any proof?" Outside a gust of wind blew something heavy onto Grace's roof. The storm notched up, and the telephone line crackled.

"If we had proof, she'd be behind bars."

THE STREETLIGHTS HAD come on though it was only five o'clock. Tree limbs, pitched by the steadily increasing wind, cast strange shadows on the pavement. Yvonne sat at the window, binoculars focused on the yellow Victorian. Grace had returned home, and she was moving about the turret room on the second floor, but she wasn't doing yoga. It looked like she was packing a bag.

She disappeared and the front door opened. She ran out into the rain. Her car backed out of the drive, and she drove toward the cul de sac at a reckless speed.

"Holy shit, Jethro," Yvonne said. She was well into her third Jack, but Jethro never judged her. "Do you think old Binghamton is in danger?"

Jethro didn't have an answer, but Yvonne knew who to ask. Jeffrey. The postman lived only a mile or two away. He was a single man who might enjoy a bit of adventure. She dialed.

"Francine is headed down our throats," Jeffrey said.

"Grace has five dead husbands. She drove down to old Binghamton's like a bat out of hell."

Jeffrey sighed. "Give me fifteen minutes and hope no trees have fallen across the road."

Yvonne found her ex-husband's storm slicker and his .38 that she kept clean, oiled, and in good working order. Marty Jarvis needed neither where he'd gone. She got the leg holster he'd used to carry his second piece.

She was waiting on the porch when Jeffrey pulled into her driveway in his old Pathfinder. Jethro moaned softly behind the closed front door, and Yvonne relented and let him out. He'd stay by her side.

The three of them took off at a brisk walk, the wind pushing them back, making it difficult to gain headway. Jeffrey probably wanted to tell her she was a fool, but she couldn't hear him above the howl of the wind.

When they got to the bluff, she saw the Moon Dancer had broken her aft lines and was slamming against the boathouse. The fiberglass hull wouldn't last long with that punishment. Yvonne was about to turn away when she saw the body floating by the boat.

"Grace!" She shouted into the gale and grabbed Jeffrey's shoulder and pointed.

The body bobbed in the swells, disappearing and then floating back, face down, arms spread. Through the sheets of rain, Yvonne could determine only that it was a female wearing white slacks and a red blouse.

"Po-lice!" Jeffrey pointed to the Binghamton house. "Call po-lice!" He pushed Yvonne in that direction. He started down the steep steps of the pier. Yvonne pulled her cell phone from her pocket. The storm whipped so fiercely reception was nil.

Yvonne grasped Jeffrey's slicker, but it slipped from her hands. He pointed at the house and made frantic dialing motions, then continued his treacherous descent down the wet stairs in the wind.

Yvonne ran. She did it without thought. Jethro right at her heels, she pushed open the cast iron gate, brushed through the camellia bushes and ran across the lawn to the white stucco house. Grace's car was in the driveway. At the door, Yvonne pounded with all her might. It occurred to her she liked neither Grace nor old Binghamton, yet she was risking her life, as was Jeffrey, to save one of them. She couldn't help the way she'd been brought up.

No one answered her banging, but the door wasn't locked. She stepped inside, calling Jethro to follow her. The hound shook, spraying the entrance hall with water. Yvonne crept forward, searching for a phone.

Jethro padded through the foyer toward a closed door. As Yvonne approached, she heard someone speaking. "She threw herself at me," old Binghamton said. "I had no choice."

Yvonne pulled the .38 from the holster on her calf. Jethro nudged the door open and she poked her head in. Old Binghamton and Grace faced each other across a beautiful oak kitchen table. Yvonne was a fool for good wood, and the table was solid and elegant. She forced her attention to the occupants of the room. Both held guns pointed at each other. Neither noticed her or Jethro.

"You killed her," Grace said.

"She was going to tell you." Old Binghamton's gun shifted left to right along with his trembling head. "She threw herself at me and I couldn't resist. She was going down to your house to tell you. I couldn't let her."

"You killed her." Grace sounded like a needle stuck on vinyl.

"There's a price to be paid for interfering in a man's happiness," Old Binghamton insisted.

Yvonne found herself in a quandary. If Grace was a murderer of husbands and Old Binghamton screwed and then killed women, who was she supposed to save? Neither seemed worth the effort.

She grasped Jethro's collar and backed away. The person she ought to be concerned about was her friend, Jeffrey. She found a telephone in a den and dialed 911. She reported the body in the bay and the pending gunfight. When the operator asked her name, she said, "Martha Stewart." She hung up and went back in the storm to find her friend.

YVONNE STOOD AT her kitchen window. Sunlight filtered through the leaves of the live oaks. Across the street, two men unloaded a van full of furniture and carried it into the yellow Victorian that had once belonged to Grace Montcrieff King, black widow. Grace awaited trial for the murder of three of her five husbands. Old Binghamton had been charged with the murder of Lindy Morton.

Hurricane Francine had turned unexpectedly east, walloping Pensacola yet again but leaving Mobile Bay mostly unscathed. Four weeks had passed and songbirds flitted outside Yvonne's window. The first hint of fall spiked the air.

Grace sat down at the table and picked up her pen.

Dear President Obama,

America faces many hard issues, but none so dangerous as the continued overpopulation of the planet. Our tax codes, written and designed to keep an underclass of working poor available to feed the factories of wealthy industrialists, reward Americans for reproducing. The opposite should be true. Americans who do not reproduce should be given tax breaks, especially with the planet groaning under the weight of too many human beings.

This senseless tax structure goes back to the days when a man's virility was judged by the number of children he sired (regardless of his ability to feed and educate said children). It is just another example of policy based on the penis.

Please step forward into the 21st Century and stop this madness.

Yours truly,

Yvonne Jarvis

Along with the note card she inserted a newspaper clipping with a photo of her and Jeffrey Tatano, the postman, receiving the Baldwin County Crime Stoppers award for assisting in the capture of two murderers.

MEMORY SKETCH

BY DAVID HANDLER

"HEY, DON'T I know you?" the kid asked me as he came in the door of Gene's liquor store, bringing the howling winter cold in with him.

"Don't think so," I replied from behind the counter, where I sat huddled near the electric space heater. A Nor'easter was heading our way. They were predicting eighteen to twenty inches of snow that evening along with forty-mile-per-hour winds. Not that I needed Doppler Radar to tell me this. I'd spent most of the eighties working as a roofer in Bozeman, Montana. Whenever a storm was coming my knees and back provided me with my own personalized accu-weather forecast.

"Really?" The kid peered at me from the doorway, unconvinced. "You sure do look familiar. Wait, wait—didn't you used to *be* somebody?"

I didn't go anywhere near that. "You're letting all of the heat out. Shut the damned door, will you?"

He shut the damned door and made his way over to the potbelly wood stove, which helped take some of the chill off the little store. But it was still plenty brisk in there, what with customers coming in and out and there being no vestibule—or insulation to speak of. Gene's liquor store occupied one half of a not very winterized summer shack down on the Shore Road, walking distance from Little Plummer's boardwalk and marina. The other half of the shack was the Clam Bake, a fried everything take-out place that stayed open from Memorial Day through Thanksgiving. Gene's stayed open year round. Not that there was a huge call for frosty cold beer or twenty-pound bags of ice during the winter in Little Plummer, which was one of those remote little Rhode Island coastal towns that jut out into the Sound near Watch Hill. When the weather was warm Little Plummer was mobbed with tourists and boaters and the rich preppy assholes who owned family summer homes there. During the winter its population shrank to a hardy core group of indigenous Swamp Yankees, loners, cheese heads, and wharf rats. There wasn't much in the way of work to be had. And hardly anything stayed open besides Gene's and a skeegie little bar and grill next to Jilly's boatyard called Marty's Hideaway. The boats were all in storage. The tourist shops were boarded up. The summer houses shuttered, the beaches deserted. A biting wind howled day and night, blowing sand drifts across the empty parking lots. Little Plummer had all of the charming ambiance of an arctic outpost in the winter. It was my kind of place. People left me alone. I'd shown up there just after Labor Day. Knowing me, I'd be gone long before the summer people returned.

I sat at the desk behind the counter and watched the kid warm his hands by the stove. He didn't have on gloves or a hat. Just an old navy blue pea coat. I hadn't seen him in there before. He was in his early twenties and on the scrawny side. Didn't work with his hands. They were soft and white. A boy's hands. He was pale, with dark circles under his eyes. He had a wispy goatee. A weak chin. Long, stringy hair that wasn't very clean. A runny nose that looked as if it had been squashed in a couple of fights.

He swiped at it with the back of his hand, glancing over at me uneasily. "What's that you're up to?"

I like to keep my hands busy. It keeps me from thinking too much. "My homework."

"Homework?" he said, his voice soaring upward by at least an octave.

"Damn, you sound just like Maynard G. Krebs."

He shook his head at me. "Maynard G *who*?"

"He was television's first beatnik. A character on *The Many Loves of Dobie Gillis*. Bob Denver played him. The guy from *Gilligan's Island*."

The kid lit right up. "I love *Gilligan's Island*."

"Somehow, this does not surprise me."

"That Tina Louise? Man, she was hot."

"That she was."

He continued to stand there with his hands over the stove. "So why are you doing homework?"

"I'm taking a class at the community college."

"Aren't you kind of old to be going to school?"

"You're never too old to improve yourself. Ought to try it yourself some time."

"What's *that* supposed to mean?"

"Not a thing, Ace."

He considered this for a moment before he decided not to be offended. Lucky me. "What are you studying at this community college?"

"Listen, can I get you something or did you just come in here to get out of the cold?"

"Pack of Camels," he grumbled.

I grabbed a pack from the rack next to me and set it on the counter.

He made no move toward it. Just stayed there by the stove staring at me. "Are you *sure* I don't know you?"

I didn't answer him. Just sighed inwardly. Because he did know me. Everyone knew me. More than forty years had gone by but I still looked exactly like who I was and always will be—Ronnie Ard, the lead singer and face of Ronnie and the Coronados. Environmentalists condemn our society for being so wasteful. And rightfully so. But we're real energy efficient when it comes to our pop culture. We never throw anything away. Just keep recycling it over and over again. If you hang around long enough pretty much everything will come back. My own little contribution to our pop culture kept coming back from the summer of '64. That was when Ronnie and the Coronados released our smash hit surfer single, "Malibu Dream." You remember it. Everyone remembers it.

Hey, it rocks to be young.
On the beach in the sun.
Nowhere to be.
Just hang out by the sea.
Yeah, we're now and we're wow.
And we live for right now.
That's the Malibu Dream.

We were four high school friends from Hermosa Beach who'd learned how to play in my parents' garage—Stu, Rich, Denny, and me. We called ourselves the Coronados until the record company decided I was star material and shoved me up front. The others weren't happy about that but they got over their resentment when the very first song we recorded soared straight to the top of the charts. We played "Malibu Dream" on *American Bandstand* with Dick Clark. They even had us perform it in one of those Frankie Avalon-Annette Funicello beach blanket movies. We were all decked out in our signature matching red blazers, our electric guitars plugged into the sand. I was the tall, good-looking one with the gleaming toothpaste commercial smile and the lacquered blond pompadour. The movie's producers liked me so much they threw me a few lines of dialogue— which made Stu, Rich, and Denny resentful all over again. Especially when it landed me a regular role on *The Adventures of Ozzie and Harriet* as one of Ricky's frat brothers. The record company got us back into the recording studio right away, but by the time we'd cut another single our kind of Born to Be Mild surfer rock had been washed away by a tidal wave called the British Invasion. We talked about changing our sound to keep up with the times. But we were one-hit wonders. One and done.

Not that this runny-nosed kid standing in Gene's liquor store was around in those days. But he didn't need to be. Just last summer one of the big cosmetics companies built a huge TV ad campaign around its new "Malibu Dream" lip gloss that featured not only our song but some old Technicolor footage of me lip-synching it on the beach in my red blazer— intercut with brand new footage of a leggy blonde supermodel romping on the beach in a white bikini. I didn't earn a penny from those commercials. The record company had held onto all of the rights. But they did make me famous all over again to a generation that hadn't even been born when I recorded "Malibu Dream."

"I'll take a pint of that peppermint schnapps, too," the kid said, pointing to the shelf behind me.

"You got it, Ace." I fetched it for him. "Anything else?"

"Yeah, give me all of the cash in your register."

I blinked at him. Well, not so much at him as at the gun he was pointing at me. It was a Smith & Wesson Chief's Special with a stubby two-inch barrel. The gun was wavering in his hand. He was trembling all over, and starting to sweat despite the chill in the air. There was a baseball bat parked under the counter but I didn't make a move for it. Clearly, this kid was strung out and desperate. You don't mess with people when they're like that. I'd made that mistake twice. The first time it cost me four teeth. The second time six weeks in a Mexican jail. There wasn't going to be a third time. Hell, it wasn't even my store. I just minded it a few hours a week for Karen, who'd owned it ever since her husband, Gene, died a few years back. I'd met Karen walking on the beach one crisp October morning. We became friends. Friends with privileges. We'd been living together in her drafty old cottage for the past couple of months.

Karen was very trusting. Maybe too trusting. There was no security camera in Gene's. It was a small town, she insisted. Everyone knew everyone.

"There's not a whole lot of cash in there," I said to him, trying to keep my voice calm. My heart was racing. My mouth had gone dry. My eyes, meanwhile, were studying the shapes and contours of his face. "I doubt there's north of two hundred bucks. Hardly worth the trouble."

"Just give it to me, man." He shoved that gun across the counter at me, his eyes bright with fear. "And stop staring at me like that."

"Like how?"

"I don't know, but cut it out!"

A sudden gust of wind rattled the front window. He whirled, terrified that someone had just come in the door.

"Easy there, Ace. It's just the storm moving in. You seem a bit jumpy. You an old hand at armed robbery?"

"That's none of your business."

"You know, I have a really radical idea. Why don't you just back on out of here and we'll forget this ever happened. It's the Nor'easter. Everyone's acting a little crazy today. I know I am."

"I'm not kidding around man! So just shut up and empty that damned register, will you?"

It's time to go for a whirl.
With a sunshine girl.
Blonde hair and blue eyes.
And she's just the right size.
One big, long kiss.
It goes like this.
That's the Malibu Dream.

After we broke up Stu became a big-time record producer. Rich married into a Ford dealership in Redondo Beach. Denny OD'ed on smack in the summer of '72. He and a half-dozen other people who I knew and loved. Me, I just kept right on searching for my own private Malibu Dream. Which is to say I pretty much stayed stoned for the next ten years. Dropped way, way too much acid. In fact, I still see purple and lime green fireflies on the ceiling in bed at night when I turn out the light. I never picked up a guitar again. The joy that I'd gotten from playing music had left me. I don't know why. It was just gone. I never acted again either—if you can call what I did acting. Although I did appear in *Easy Rider.* Check out the sequence where Peter Fonda and Dennis Hopper visit that commune in the desert. When the camera does a 360-degree pan of those hippies sitting around in a circle I'm right there, wearing a beard, love beads, and a glazed grin. I drifted south of the border to Todos Santos after that and became a full-time surf bum for quite a few years. Came home when my money ran out. But there were too many ghosts in Laurel Canyon so I headed north to Mill Valley, which was where I started working construction. From there I wandered to Seattle, then Bozeman. After that there was, let's see, Austin, then Memphis. Then a musician friend from the old days asked me to help him out on his organic dairy farm in upstate New York. So I made my way up there for a while. But I woke up one morning late last summer and realized I missed the sound of the surf. So I'd ended up back on a beach again.

And I took up with Karen, an aging flower child with dark, searching eyes and a long flowing mane of silver hair. Karen was a Little Plummer local who'd run away to Greenwich Village in her youth. She studied modern dance, taught yoga, made jewelry. Did a whole lot of rootless drifting of her own before she made her way back home and hooked up with Gene, her high school sweetheart. The little liquor store that he'd left her wasn't real profitable, not even during the summer, but she did own the building free and clear. Collected a good rental from the folks who ran the Clam Bake. And she was a licensed massage therapist. Picked up extra cash working part-time at a fancy-shmancy day spa over in Stonington.

Evenings, we'd snuggle in front of the fire, drink wine, and listen to old Neil Young on vinyl.

"Do we have something real going on here?" she asked me just last week as we lay there together.

I didn't answer her.

"When the good weather comes you'll be gone for good, won't you?"

I didn't answer that either.

"You got to learn how to curb this gabby streak of yours, Ronnie. You just babble on and on."

"I might be back, okay?"

"What are you running away from?"

"Myself."

"Will you ever stop?"

"Don't know how to."

"I could show you. I mean, we got us a pretty good thing going on here. You get to a certain point in your life when it's not good to be alone."

Who wants to be old?
All left out in the cold.
Get out and live for today.
It's the only way.
No time for sorrow.
Forget about tomorrow.
That's the Malibu Dream.

"Speed it the hell up, will you?" the kid gulped at me, his finger tightening around the trigger. "I want everything in that register—right now!"

"Whatever you say, Ace."

I opened the register and gathered up what little there was in there. Put it into a meager pile on the counter. The kid stuffed it into the pocket of his pea coat, narrowing his gaze at me. "You'll forget you ever saw me, right?"

"I'm not looking for any trouble."

"Good answer." He backed slowly out of the store, keeping his gun trained on me.

I didn't move a muscle—until he took off into the howling winter cold. Then I went to the front window, exhaling with relief. But I didn't see what he drove off in. He'd parked around in back and taken off that way. I returned to the counter and called 911 before I sat down at the desk and went back to my homework.

It took the state trooper nearly twenty minutes to get there. Little Plummer was too small to have its own police force. He was big and burly, his cheeks all red from the cold. He looked about seventeen to me. I didn't know him, but he sure knew Karen.

"I keep telling that woman to install a security camera," he said, shaking his meaty head. "Nowhere is safe anymore, especially for a lady Karen's age. I mean, heck, she and my grandma Sally went through school together."

"If you're trying to make me feel ancient you're doing a heck of a job."

He took my statement, jotting his notes down in a small notepad, tongue stuck out of the side of his mouth. "Can you describe the fellow for me, Mr. Ard?"

"I can do better than that." I tore a page from my sketchbook and handed it to him. I'd done a detailed portrait of the kid. That class I was taking at the community college was a life drawing class. I've been taking drawing classes for years. Like I said, I like to keep my hands busy.

The trooper gaped at it, awestruck. "Why, that's Petey Battalino. I busted his sorry ass two months ago for ripping off a convenience store in Westerly. He's out on bail now. And I know right where to find him, too. His no-good junkie girlfriend, Darla, has a place. I bet he'll hole up there before the storm," he said as he started for the door. "Thanks a bunch, Mr. Ard."

"You're welcome a bunch."

A few snowflakes were starting to fall. I sat back down next to the space heater and went back to my sketchbook. Or tried to. Word had gotten out about the robbery. A small stream of denizens from Marty's Hideaway started oozing over to hear the blow-by-blow details.

And then Karen made it back from the fancy-shmancy day spa, smelling of China Gel and lavender oil, and I had to tell her all about it. She totally freaked. Hugged me tight. Cried and cried even though I kept assuring her I was fine.

"You're *not* fine," she sobbed, tears streaming down her face. "You could have been shot."

"He was just a scared kid. I'll bet that gun wasn't even loaded."

She touched my face with her fingertips, her eyes shining at me. "You're going to split town because of this, aren't you? I'll wake up tomorrow and you'll be gone."

"Not a chance."

"Do you mean that?"

"I do. There's a major Nor'easter blowing in, remember? I could get stranded in the snow somewhere. The heater in my truck doesn't work. Only a crazy man would think about leaving at a time like—"

She punched me in the shoulder. Hard. "You're a gnarly old bastard. Why have I gotten so attached to you?"

MEMORY SKETCH

It was a habit of hers. Asking me questions I didn't know the answer to.

That young state trooper pulled up out front soon after that and came barging in, his big hat sprinkled with snowflakes. "We nailed Petey at Darla's place," he exclaimed, bursting with excitement. "Recovered the weapon, too. A Chief's Special, just like you said, Mr. Ard. It was stolen from its registered owner in a home break-in two weeks ago."

"Was it loaded?" Karen demanded, hands on her hips.

"Sure was. Petey had a fistful of small bills on him. Told me it was money he'd earned plowing driveways. But get this—tucked in between a pair of ten-dollar bills I found a coupon for a dollar off on a jumbo lobster roll at the Clam Shack. The coupon expired last October. When I asked Petey how it got into his pocket he couldn't explain it. How did it, Mr. Ard?"

"He asked for everything in the register. He got everything."

He grinned at me. "That's using your head."

"If you don't keep using it then your brain turns to jelly. Believe me, I know."

"We couldn't have caught him without that drawing of yours. How did you do that?"

"With a graphite stick. I like it better than charcoal. Doesn't smudge as much."

"No, I mean, what's the trick?"

"There's no trick. You just close your eyes and capture the person's essence."

The trooper frowned at me. "You just ... what?"

"It's an exercise for sharpening your powers of observation. First you study someone's face. Then you close your eyes, focus, and draw what you saw. They call it a memory sketch. I was working on one for class when he showed up." I opened my sketchbook and showed him. "See?"

"Why, that's Karen," he observed.

Karen didn't care for it. "My *essence*," she sniffed, "looks like a decrepit old lady."

"A very hot old lady," I assured her. "*My* old lady."

Now she brightened considerably. "The storm's almost here. Let's close up the store. We can make a fire and pop open a bottle of the Chianti. Hell, you might even get a free backrub."

"Is that all I'm going to get?"

"I just thought of something," our eager young trooper interjected. "The local TV stations are going to eat this story up."

I glanced over at Karen, clearing my throat, before I said, "I'd rather you people didn't call them, if you don't mind."

He frowned at me. "Forgive me for asking, Mr. Ard, but I'm not looking at a twofer here today, am I?"

"At a what?"

"You're not wanted in connection with a crime yourself, are you?"

"No, it's nothing like that. You can go right ahead and check. I'm clean. I just like to keep a low profile, that's all."

He tilted his head at me. "And, yet, I keep thinking your face is familiar. Your name, too. Do I know you from somewhere?"

"Don't think so. I haven't been in town very long."

"But he'll be sticking around for a good, long while," Karen spoke up. "I'll chain him to my bedpost if I have to."

"No need to share the secrets of our love life with the boy."

She punched me in the arm again. Hard. This was another thing she did.

Yeah, we're now and we're wow.
And we live for right now.
That's the Malibu,
Baby, that's the Malibu Dream.

The trooper was still staring at me. The Look. He was definitely giving me The Look. "Wait, wait—didn't you used to *be* somebody?"

I looked out the front window at the falling snow. "Who the hell knows?" I said in reply. "Maybe I still am."

SOME THINGS YOU NEVER FORGET

BY GAR ANTHONY HAYWOOD

VERNON LIKED THE meatloaf. Everything else they served at Winter Haven tasted like day-old modeler's clay, but the meatloaf wasn't bad.

Even Billie seemed to enjoy it. She didn't say as much, because she hardly ever spoke at all anymore, but he could tell by the lack of expression on her face that she wasn't revolted by it, which was more than could be said for everything else about the nursing home.

The walls were gray and drab. The help all wore starched white uniforms and plastic smiles. Old people in various stages of slow death sat in place or inched along in squeaky wheelchairs and walkers that played the linoleum floor like a bad violin. Every now and then, somebody down one hall or another would scream something unintelligible, pissed off or terrified or so bone-deep lonely they couldn't hold it in anymore.

Vernon himself couldn't stand the place, but when Alzheimer's sank its teeth into somebody, this was how they often ended up. Imprisoned in a dump people laughably called a "home," where nurses and aides who'd been paid to give a damn made sure nobody stepped out the front door and either disappeared for days at a time or, worse, tried to cross the street on a red in front of a big rig with bad brakes. Vernon had told himself a million times it didn't have to come to this, that he and Billie had been fine watching out for each other for forty-three years and Alzheimer's wasn't going to stop them from doing so now, but eventually, he'd had to face facts: Billie was slipping away from him. Every time he looked in his wife's eyes, he saw less and less of her, and he didn't want to be at home alone with her when she finally faded out for good.

So here they were at Winter Haven, eating a pathetic lunch together in a dining room crowded with people waiting for death to get on with it, just as they'd been doing every Thursday now for two years. Only today was going to be different. Today was their anniversary, the big number four-oh, and hell if Vernon wasn't going to do something today while they were out on their weekly drive in the car to wake the old girl up a bit. Wipe that sad, vacant expression off her face and bring a smile to her lips, maybe even get her to laugh out loud. Do something, anything, that could remind him of the incredible, ass-kicking woman she used to be before the goddamn fog set in.

She always liked trouble, Billie, and Vernon was just the man to meet her needs. He wasn't much of a criminal in the beginning but his antics were just dangerous enough to give her a thrill. They'd be walking home from the movies and, on a whim, he'd slip a jimmy into the door of a parked car that caught his eye and they'd drive off in it, both of them laughing like kids on a roller coaster. Or he'd break the nose of some little punk, the leader of a band of street thugs who'd mistaken Vernon and Billie for an easy mark, and Billie would lead the way, chasing them all halfway down the block with their own gun. She was crazy. Wild. And she only became more so when Vernon started pulling jobs with Dylan.

Dylan had a mean streak that Vernon lacked, and a need to do things that involved a greater amount of risk than Vernon was comfortable with. But their partnership was made in heaven. They committed crimes together Vernon could have never pulled off alone, and as luck would have it, they got away with every one. Between the two of them, they had both the smarts and the balls to fight their way out of any jam.

Vernon hadn't thought it was possible, but the edge-of-disaster excitement Dylan brought into their lives had only made Billie love Vernon all the more. Sometimes, back in those days, she made love to him with a relentless, unbridled passion that threatened to sear his skin.

Dylan was long gone now, of course, as was Vernon's will to live outside the law, but Vernon believed he still had enough left in the old tank to pull off one more crime all by himself, one more dance with the devil with Billie by his side that might bring her back to life, even if it were only for one brief moment. Today was their fortieth wedding anniversary.

Vernon was going to be goddamned if he didn't make it special.

THEY NEVER WENT far on their little Thursday afternoon outings together and today was no exception. They were lucky Winter Haven let them go anywhere at all together, and Vernon knew it. They drove down to Alpine Street Park a half mile from the nursing home and that was it. It took all of eight minutes to get there and all along the way, Vernon kept his eyes open, watching for the right opportunity to spring his little surprise on his wife. Billie, meanwhile, just sat there in the Impala like always, breaking her silence only to mouth an occasional word or two he could never quite understand.

At the park, they sat on a bench in the shade of a massive oak tree and held hands, watching squirrels skitter across the grass all around them. The only other people in sight were parents and nannies and the little children they were in charge of, none appearing in any way deserving of the cruel fate Vernon had in mind for somebody. Dylan had never given a rat's ass who they victimized, but Vernon always had his limits; he would never have robbed the father of a four-year-old in a public park in the old days, and he wasn't going to do it now. Besides which, Billie would hardly have been shaken out of her shell by an act as ordinary as that.

He had a big steak knife in his jacket pocket. He would have preferred a gun but he could have more easily gotten his hands on a moon rock. Still, he felt like his options in the way of a suitable victim were unlimited. He might be seventy-one years old with knees that barely broke vertical anymore, but experience had taught him that few things closed the gap between a young punk and a slow old man faster than sunlight flashing off the edge of a serrated blade. And if the punk made the mistake of thinking the blade was just for show, well …

Vernon could only wonder about this himself. What *would* happen then? Without Dylan around to do such dirty work for him, could he use the knife if he were forced to?

He hoped he wouldn't have to find out.

He looked over and saw that Billie was smiling, a slight breeze lifting a tuft of white hair off her head like a billowing sail. For a flashing instant, he caught a glimpse of the dark, green-eyed brunette he first met forty-three years ago, waiting tables at a San Pedro greasy spoon he'd stopped in at strictly by chance. But then she sensed his eyes upon her and turned abruptly, and the moment was lost.

"What is it?" she asked.

Vernon shook his head and told her it was nothing. What could he say that would make any sense to her?

The minutes went by without anything changing, the park emptying out until he and Billie were almost the last two living souls in it. Vernon became desperate. By now, he wanted to do something unlawful as much to prove to himself he could as to put a spark back in his wife's eyes for their anniversary. If he failed today, he didn't know that he'd ever have the courage to try something this insane again.

But it was hopeless. There was nobody around to take down … and Vernon suddenly had to pee.

"I've gotta go to the bathroom," he said, silently cursing the mercurial nature of his ancient bladder. Billie nodded, ever compliant, and they stood up and walked together over to the cinderblock lavatories adjacent to the playground.

Outside the door to the men's room, he glanced back at Billie and said, "Don't go anywhere." Issuing an order that sounded more like a joke. Then he rushed inside and made it to a urinal just in time to avoid soiling his pants. It was dark and musty in the place, the floor besotted with water and the walls nearly blackened with graffiti. It was all he could do to breathe without gagging.

He thought he was alone in the room right up until the moment, just as he was zipping up, a man all but leapt out of the toilet stall on his right and said, "Give it up, old man. Hurry, hurry!"

The guy had a gun in his right hand.

Startled and confused, Vernon just stood there looking at him, mouth hanging open as if mounted on a broken hinge. Eventually, the irony of what was happening to him registered, but by then, his befuddlement was mistaken for deliberate non-compliance.

"Your wallet. Your money. *Come on, you old fuck!* "

Vernon's would-be mugger—a swarthy, twenty-something Eastern-European type with a skull cap of black hair—shoved the nose of his semi-automatic into the middle of Vernon's chest, hard, and damn near knocked him backward into the urinal he'd just finished flushing.

Vernon didn't have a wallet. He didn't have any money. All he had was the knife.

He put his right hand in his jacket pocket and filled his fist with the knife's handle as the guy waited, clearly losing patience.

"What's happening in here?"

The man with the gun spun around to find Billie standing behind him, looking like a child who'd just stumbled upon a porn channel on TV.

Without thinking, his subconscious operating under the certainty his wife was as good as dead if he did anything less, Vernon drew the knife from his pocket and lunged forward, looking to put its blade into the guy's back right up to the hilt.

But he was an old man with lousy reflexes, a mere shadow of the hellraiser he used to be, so all he did was clip the guy's gun arm instead. It was enough to make him drop the weapon and recoil, his triceps shedding blood like a slaughtered calf, but that was all. When he turned to face Vernon again, he seemed more inclined toward homicide than ever.

To prove the point, he let out a guttural scream and hit Vernon in the face with a right hand that had the kick of a crazed mule. Vernon went down in a heap, banging the back of his head first on the ceramic of the urinal and then on the floor. He blinked up at a ceiling that was losing focus rapidly, trying to stay conscious, but the outer edges of his vision were already fading to black. His attacker's face loomed over him, a mask of spittle and rage, and all Vernon could think about now was Billie, poor, defenseless Billie, and what this animal was almost certainly going to do to her once he was all through killing her husband.

A loud crack rang out, threatening to shake the mortar loose from the walls of the little public restroom, and at first Vernon thought it was the sound of another punch to his face he was too far gone to feel. But then he recognized it, a virtual blast from his past, and the face above him spasmed and froze, signaling a sudden mood shift in the man to whom it belonged. The face fell away to one side, out of Vernon's sight, and in its place, through the fog of his pain and confusion, he saw his wife, towering over him with the guy's gun in her hand like an avenging angel.

Or at least, he thought it was Billie, until the woman who'd just saved his life put another bullet in the guy on the floor next to him, for no good reason that Vernon could see, and then laughed in a way that sent Vernon back in time twenty years. He couldn't believe it.

His old partner Dylan had returned from the dead.

IT TOOK HOURS to explain everything to the police. The park filled with lookie-loos and television news crews and the questions never seemed to stop. No one doubted for a minute that the dead guy's shooting was self-defense, and both Vernon and Billie were treated with the utmost kindness and sympathy throughout, but getting out of there turned out to be an ordeal all by itself.

Naturally, somebody called Winter Haven and Mrs. Davenport, the home's director, hurried out to the park to make sure Vernon and Billie were indeed okay. More than anything else, the lady was afraid for her job. The pair left the home every Thursday together on her okay and she was terrified she'd somehow be held responsible for the dead man's shooting. The cops finally convinced her she wouldn't be. When they were all free to go, she had insisted on driving Vernon and Billie back to the home, but Vernon wouldn't stand for it. He didn't know how much longer his wife would remain her old self and he wanted to relish the experience of being alone in her company while it lasted. With Mrs. Davenport following close behind in her own car, they drove back to Winter Haven the same way they left it.

Vernon was deliriously happy. Back when they'd first made their Alzheimer's diagnosis, the doctors had told him and Billie that things like this could happen, that months, even years after all memory of the past appeared to be gone, great snippets of it could resurface without warning, for minutes, sometimes even hours at a time. And there was no predicting how or why. The only thing they could say for sure was that, when and if it happened, it wouldn't last.

Vernon didn't care. Tomorrow it would all be over, most likely forever, but today—on their fortieth wedding anniversary!—he'd been with his beloved Billie again. And not just Billie, but Billie at her most thrilling and outrageous, in the guise of the partner in crime she'd eventually become to him, too much the outlaw herself to keep watching Vernon have all the fun. Dylan was Billie on speed, ready for anything and afraid of nothing, and he'd given her the nickname to mark the difference between the two. Vernon and Billie were trouble together, perhaps, but Vernon and Dylan, as a duo, were nothing short of lethal.

Looking his wife over in the car now, with "Tangled Up in Blue" playing on the stereo at her behest, Vernon couldn't tell how much of Dylan was still left. She was quiet, saying little, as she so often did of late when they were together. For all the excitement of the afternoon, the fog was closing in on her again. Vernon could feel it. Almost before his eyes, with a cruel swiftness that brought him close to tears, she was receding into the stranger Alzheimer's had reduced her to over the last fourteen months. A sad, lovely old woman with dull green eyes who always seemed to be on the brink of crying whenever Vernon was around.

It broke his heart.

They pulled into Winter Haven's carport and stopped, Mrs. Davenport's station wagon right behind them. Vernon wanted desperately to say something before they got out of the car, to lift his friend's spirits in some way because she was the only real friend he had and her weekly visits always gave him something to look forward to—but he didn't know what to say. He never did. Maybe if he knew more about her than her name—Billie—he'd have some idea. But she was just some woman who liked to spend a little time with him every Thursday, talking and holding hands. Vernon had no idea why.

"See you next week, love," she said. She leaned forward, away from the steering wheel, and kissed him on the cheek.

Vernon opened the door and Mrs. Davenport helped him out of the car.

"Is it time for dinner yet?" he asked. Whatever he and his friend had done today while they were out, it had made him incredibly hungry.

"Almost. Not quite," Mrs. Davenport said.

Vernon hurried on inside without her, hoping they were serving meatloaf tonight.

Vernon liked the meatloaf.

THE WAR ZONE

BY CAMERON PIERCE HUGHES

I don't want justice, are you kidding, screw justice, we're way past justice, it's blood now ..."

—William Goldman, *Marathon Man*

CHUCKIE "CHEESE" TOWER, nicknamed for his once very blond hair, has had a lot of titles in his life. Bagman. Enforcer. Slum Lord. War hero. Killer. Most of them aren't appropriate for print. He's in his old childhood neighborhood in San Diego's beach suburb Ocean Beach where the '70s decided to take root and aren't budging, on a Friday night. Traffic is surging south to the Gaslamp Quarter's bars and clubs. Couples, of the gay and straight variety, are huddled together to combat the cold. Denizens of the East Coast and Midwest would celebrate the mild weather, but dipping below fifty degrees is polar bear weather in Southern California. Older couples in the suburbs are deep asleep or watching Leno or Letterman or some shit like that by the fire while sipping something warm; maybe some will even make their drink Irish. Most of the houses are cheery and bright in their sparkling Christmas decorations. Chuckie sees a lot of Santas on front lawns as if they're guarding the people inside. Remembers how this neighborhood's street, Newport Avenue, used to be called The War Zone in the '70s when the Hell's Angels were here in large numbers. Chuckie hears a coyote howl in the distance and remembers that he used to hear them a lot more as a child when the city wasn't even a quarter of the size it is now. The prostitutes and drug dealers are out in force and doing business. No one pays attention to the old man that some would say looks like a tired Robert Forster.

Chuckie has a man to kill tonight.

He takes another drag off his cigarette, savoring the familiar rush. On his right wrist is a Timex watch, battered and scratched. He remembers the day in 1968 when he came home from the war after two tours, he had bought it for himself as a coming home present. He had actually enjoyed the war, figuring out early that it was bullshit, so he had had fun firing powerful guns, riding in choppers, smoking fine marijuana and opium, and spending nights with hookers. He checks the time and sees that it's 12:10 AM. *Almost time*, he thinks. Reaching into the waistband of his pants, Chuckie slips out his Beretta. The pistol has only four bullets, one more than he usually uses, but at his age, he wants the insurance. It's gonna be more than enough for this night's job.

I hope so, he chuckles to himself, *'cause I'll be Wally the Walrus's best butt-buddy if I don't get some shelter soon.*

He smiles at the memory of the cartoon walrus that had made him laugh as a child. His family had been one of the first on the block to have a television set. Soon he'll be laughing all the way to Thailand. He had read much about Bangkok in prison. He had acquired certain tastes in Vietnam, and he thought that part of Asia would be a nice place to live out the rest of his days to feed his various appetites. He saw the wrong side of sixty a long time ago and figures he deserves a nice retirement. Home here is a dingy little boardinghouse near the airport. He's been out of prison for four months now.

At 12:15 AM, Chuckie crushes the last remnants of his smoke, flicks the butt into the street, and crosses toward the small two-story craftsman.

The yellow paint is old and faded and has cracks that look like veins, much like Chuckie's old-man skin. There are boards in the second story windows and bars on the first floor. The grass outside is turning brown and looks like it's on its way to an ugly death by neglect. It very much looks like the crack house it used to be. It's starting to rain, which is the first time this year during winter.

Dressed in a simple pea coat and watchman's cap, Chuckie looks like just any old man back from a brisk walk and a nice hit of nicotine. No one pays any attention to old men heading home. It's the perfect stealth.

He clips on a fake police detective badge that he had used on other jobs and rubs his Purple Heart and Bronze Star medals for luck. He waves to the guard seated at the front door reading a Joseph Wambaugh novel under the porch light, calmly walks up the staircase to the second floor of the house, and heads toward the bedroom. His steps are silent in the thick carpeting. Shag? He hasn't walked on shag carpeting since 1982. From the intel he got, he knows the mark is a deep sleeper type of guy. As he gets closer, he curses under his breath. There's a cop guarding the entrance to the room.

Goddamn Murphy's Law is back again to haunt him; it's what made him a two-time loser. The vision of Thailand and its white sandy beaches and exotic nightlife starts to fade away, replaced by the stone walls and guard towers of Pelican Bay or some other hellhole just like it. He would be locked in a cage again. Just another loser among the thousands of losers doing time, taking that third and final fall. Under the state's criminal code, a third felony conviction is an automatic thirty years to life with no parole.

It's either a sure death sentence behind bars at his age or a shiv in the back or gang-raped in the showers. Convicts really hate men like him.

Whatever way you look at it, it's a raw deal. Chuckie doesn't want to cash in on that kind of lottery. Men like him have goals.

The cop, to Chuckie's practiced old eye, is your typical flatfoot. Uniformed in the traditional blue. He has everything you'd expect a cop to have: handcuffs attached to his belt, service revolver tucked in a shoulder holster, police baton at his side. His badge clipped to his leather coat pocket. He even has a small flashlight. His cap is pulled low over his eyes, chin touching his chest.

Damn, thinks Chuckie. *Asshole's asleep. Gotta do him and the mark. This whole deal is going pear-shaped.*

Shooting the cop isn't an option. The noise the pistol would make would attract attention. While Chuckie is here to murder a man, offing a fucking pig is not part of the job. It is, as the saying goes, beyond the call of duty. It only makes the police more determined to hunt you down and shoot your ass, telling the other understanding cops later, *Hey, the motherfucker pulled a gun, what was we to do?*

He doesn't like that scenario. Yet there could be a way to use the pistol. He looks around the deserted hallway. Beads of sweat start to appear on his forehead. Chuckie feels a tightening of his chest. In the pit of his stomach, there's a burning sensation. It'd be really bad for his reputation if he had a heart attack in the middle of committing a crime. Slowly, he creeps closer to the sleeping cop; the moment, he knows, is now. Checking one last time to see if the cop is going to stir, Chuckie slips the pistol into his hand and reverses his grip. He holds it by the barrel with the pistol butt out. Taking a deep breath, Chuckie counts to three. He raises the pistol. Would the cop wake up?

Chuckie reminds himself not to be gentle and to hit with all his might as multiple strikes would be messier than one solid swing. He brings the butt of the pistol down and smashes it into the left side of the cop's skull. The force of the blow knocks the cop down onto the floor and his cap flies off.

Quick. Clean. Silent. Chuckie is feeling pretty proud of himself. The old hitman checks the magazine to ensure the top bullet isn't crimped. He doesn't want the pistol to jam on him. After all, he still has work to do. All that's left is the actual job, using a pillow (he hopes the bedroom has goose-down rather than polyester; they work better) as a silencer to muffle the shot and then walking out and getting lost on the crowded freeway and finding himself in Mexico. By morning, he'll be on a private drug cartel plane to Thailand. *Maybe*, he thinks, *this won't be so bad after all.* He checks his watch. It's 12:20.

He dreams again of Thailand with its bright lights and the beautiful girls there for the taking. He thinks of the last girl he had had years ago before he went to the big house for assault and battery. A stunning young gook girl with long black hair, flawless skin and large brown eyes, and a curvaceous backside. Oh, what a tumble that one was! A real hellcat of a girl! It had been a busy and exciting time in his social life; she had been his sixth lover that year. It's been a long time for him without some loving. Thailand can't come any too soon for him.

Chuckie gets his head back into the game. The mark is inside, probably sound asleep, feeling secure at the thought of San Diego's finest protecting him. Oh, yeah baby! Chuckie's gonna get paid!

One shot, one kill. He has a wide grin. He feels good, a man is at his best when he accomplishes something. His daddy had taught him that. Failing in that household meant the belt and maybe a punch or two; Chuckie feels it made him into the tough old bird he is today.

Then he sees the spot on the wall and that changes things.

The spot is no larger than a dime. It's perfectly round, red in color, and streaks have formed underneath it. Chuckie's no longer smiling; he's seen marks like that before.

He can see small, hard chips that crunch where he touches the impacted plaster. Bone? He smears the fluid along his fingertips. Blood. Chuckie's palms become slick and he almost drops his pistol he's so freaked now. Suddenly that meatloaf special he had for dinner at the early bird special at Coco's threatens to spew forth from his stomach. There are spots in his vision and vertigo threatens to claim him. Chuckie forces himself to take a closer look at the cop.

The first thing Chuckie notices is the exit wound on the back of the cop's head. It looks like a puckered starfish with bits of bone and blood around it. It's small, and he knows instantly what kind of gun causes an exit wound like that. A .22, a professional's cliché, but a practical choice. He curses his old eyes for missing it.

Is another player involved? He shudders at the thought. Ten thousand bones are at stake. His starter money for the rest of his life in Asia. Chuckie needs that money to get out of town. He doesn't want to be trapped in California no more in that ugly little house with all those other losers. Too many people want him dead.

Is it his fault he has needs and was, before he became a two-time prison loser, a competent and in-demand button man known for his efficiency and willingness to take any contract? Kids, women, old men like himself, he'd do anyone and while he's never been particularly expensive like the new kids today, he's worked steady and his rep has been good, even if most of his clients find him distasteful, and given some of his clients, it takes a lot to disgust them.

He steps past the cop, enters the apartment, and tiptoes into the bedroom, a flawless dread buzzing in his skull. It's a simple bedroom with queen-sized bed, a desk with a small TV on it, a chest of drawers, and a small closet. A grandfather clock in the corner by the window.

There's a man lying on the bed. Chuckie sneaks closer and dares to look. The man has a small bullet-sized wound in his forehead. Chuckie would bet his pony-racing money he'd find a wound like a puckered starfish on the back of his head. Weirdly, he's more angry than afraid now.

He didn't wait in Hippie-Ville freezing his balls off half the day and night just to go home empty-handed. Chuckie is so lost in his thoughts that he doesn't recognize the coughing sound behind him.

PHUT! The first shot smacks his right hand, forcing Chuckie to drop the Beretta to the floor. Tears well up in his eyes and he almost screams out. Glancing at his hand, he sees the ravaged muscle, the blood flowing freely into his palm.

PHUT! The second shot tears out bone and muscle from his left kneecap, collapsing him to the floor. Chuckie feels numb. Waves of pain roll over him like a tsunami. He almost screams out again. Chuckie is used to pain though; it's almost like a friend to him, always willing to challenge him. He's a survivor of the state's penal system, serving a total of twelve years if you count the two years at the Hanoi Hilton all those years ago for Uncle Sam. Shivved once, been shot twice, and beaten to a pulp and tortured countless times. Never told Charlie a damn thing.

Chuckie "Cheese" Tower is a man.

He had even survived the time they had called down an airstrike to get the gooks that surrounded him in the jungle. He won't give *this* asshole the satisfaction. Chuckie "Cheese" Tower is definitely a hard man, but when he looks up at the shooter, he's reminded of the all the monsters that had scared him as a child.

There's nothing really remarkable about the blandly handsome man standing over him. He's a man of average height with a sleek, wiry build in a nice but unassuming white Hugo Boss suit and shined black leather penny loafers. Wire-framed glasses highlight an otherwise average and almost pudgy face with pale blond hair and a neat goatee. The shooter could be mistaken for an accountant or even a hip college professor. No one, though, who dared to look into those silvery gray eyes would mistake him for an accountant or a teacher. The shooter's eyes are stone cold, even colder than the rain and wind outside.

"Gallows," croaks Chuckie.

Over the years, Chuckie had heard stories of a freelance hitter who worked for nearly anyone as long as the price was right. Fifty to seventy-five Gs minimum per contract, and like most hitmen these days, Gallows works following a code: no kids. Pussies.

Chuckie had listened to the rumors in the prison yard and the gossip in the bars and pool halls about the urban legend whose name evoked so much fear in the underground and among short eyes. A Fortune 500 CEO with a seat on the Detroit Board of Trade garroted in the back seat of his Mercedes limo while parked in front of the famous Motor City club Envy Inc. Tommy Lau, a Taiwanese Triad boss who had beaten a child porn and prostitution charge, found with his throat and belly slit in a men's room close to the Wonder Wheel at Coney Island. In suburban Bakersfield, a Men of Mayhem motorcycle clubhouse was firebombed with all its chapter's members inside. Angelina Costa, a Mafia princess nicknamed "The Iron Maiden" boiled alive in her pool in her mansion on the Gold Coast in Chicago.

Gallows is an enigma, not only to the police departments all around the country, but also to every lowlife that's brave enough to say his name. All the wiseguys, boyos, and good ol' boys in organized crime have a reason to fear him. Some claimed he was an ex-cop, stripped of his badge after a suspicious shooting of a pedophile that beat the system and skipped free. Others said that he was an ex-spook, out of work at the end of the Cold War and the collapse of the Soviet Union, who found a more lucrative war to fight. One popular theory in the south is that he was an escaped mental patient who made a deal with a demon at a crossroads to make him an unstoppable killer, much like the legend of Robert Johnson's otherworldly guitar skills. Some even speculated he was an angry angel from Heaven in the form of a man. It doesn't really matter which story you believe. Gallows produces results.

Still holding the gun, Gallows steps closer to the now sobbing Chuckie and looks at him like he's curious about something only the old man can tell him.

"Did you think all was forgiven?" Gallows asks softly. His accent is a lilting southern and sounds like a character out of a Twain novel. It sounds like honey on steel. His breath smells like Old Spice and liver and onions.

Chuckie has no idea what the assassin is talking about. Was it about this job? He had accepted the job from Niko Wolfe, a Russian gangster, who was the leader of the Two Crosses. The Two Crosses, a gang formed from the ranks of members of the Mexican Mafia and Russian criminals. They controlled the drug trade in Barrio Logan in San Diego. Everything from coke to smack, they sold it. They even dabbled in the white slave trade. Their profits grossed fifteen million per week, until the San Diego Police Department's Organized Unit and the FBI shut the gang down, seizing over three million in cash and over twenty million in drugs thanks to a tip from a high-ranking confidential informant in Wolfe's organization. He sang like a freaking opera diva. Wolfe and his lieutenants are now locked up at the jail downtown looking at several nasty charges that would put them all in some federal hellhole for a couple lifetimes.

Then what they might call an act of God happened.

The informant was run down by a van as he was coming out of a deli in North Park. After he miraculously recovered in a heavily guarded hospital, a safe house with police guardians was the next logical place for the informant. Looking at RICO charges and the possibility of the death penalty, Wolfe offered a ten thousand dollar bounty for the head of the snitch. Chuckie Tower was hurting for money and looking to collect that bounty. Rumors were floating that Chuckie had gone soft in prison and was out of step and might be willing to do some opera of his own. This job was just as much for his pride as it was for his finances. He needs people to know Chuckie "The Cheese" Tower ain't no joke.

He hadn't counted on Gallows.

"I didn't know—" rasps Chuckie.

"Ignorance is not an excuse, Mr. Tower. You are already dead and on the river Styx. Accept it. This is not about the hit on our friend here. Ten thousand dollars is a pauper's fee for a trained professional. Niko Wolfe is a thug and monster, not the kind of client I'm willing to work for. By the way, does the name Tony Sun sound familiar to you?"

Chuckie shakes his head, more confused than ever.

"Too bad. Tony Sun is a major player on the financial markets. Founding partner and CEO of Sun Mutual Funds. He's also the Bak Tse Sin, the financial advisor for the Four Seas Triad here in Southern California. Takes their dirty money and makes it clean. He has considerable juice from City Hall on down. He's rich and has everything a man could possibly desire. A home in La Jolla Shores, a successful business, and a loving and beautiful trophy wife. Except for one small detail." Gallows produces a picture of the girl seemingly out of nowhere and shows it to Chuckie.

Chuckie's eyes widen and he tries to scream, but Gallows kicks him in the head.

"Jade Sun. Twelve years old. A girl who loved the violin and had a bright future ahead of her. She loved to roller-skate through the city. That's how you found her, correct?"

Gallows then stomps on Chuckie's injured hand, crushing bone and Chuckie's eyes water and he can feel something burning inside him. Once. Twice. Three times the penny loafer smashes onto the old man's hand. Loud snaps can be heard. The assassin looks into the pale face of his prey.

He stares at Chuckie as if looking at a strange animal he's never even heard of, then spits in the crippled man's face. He resumes his talk as if he were giving a class in human rights to a bored classroom.

"You saw her at Crown Point by the bay as she sped merrily in the sun. And why wouldn't she be happy? The world would have been her oyster. That's when you decided to take her." He leans closer as if imparting a secret, "I've survived worse places than you could ever imagine and I made my bones in a trial of fire."

"There's a police officer right outsi—" Chuckie starts to say.

"Do you really think you're so clever that you could gain entrance in here with just an unassuming manner and an old badge? The guard outside has a lucrative side-business of ripping off drug peddlers. We reached an agreement and he was more than happy to have his colleague in the hall take an early retirement since he was getting close to his secret. When I leave, I'll knock him out and that will be his story. With the gentleman in the bed tragically deceased, Mr. Wolfe and his goons will be free, but they will also die within a month of their freedom."

Chuckie cries out a second time as Gallows kicks him in the ribs. Once. Twice. On the third kick, Gallows's shoe cracks a rib. Chuckie wants to faint.

In Chuckie's clouded vision, he remembers Jade. Her smile haunts him at that moment. How he ran his fingers through that silky, black hair. She had begged him to stop, but Chuckie had ignored her pleas and only had gotten more excited. She smelled like lilacs and sunshine and it had driven him crazy. His grunts of ecstasy were loud. Her cries grew weaker as she lost strength to the wire cutting into her neck. Her body wracked by pain. Her innocence taken away by a man old enough to be a grandfather.

In between gasps, Chuckie whispers, "Please, I can explain."

Gallows likes that. He laughs merrily. "Explain? That your hormones overtook your senses? You made a choice, Mr. Tower. You decided to rape and sodomize a little girl not quite yet through puberty. Her choices were taken away by your savagery. When you make a choice, you must live with its consequences. I took Sun's money, but I've donated it to several charities. It's really a pity though that you are more animal than man. A man of your history, if I weren't so sickened by you I'd delight in hearing your stories of war and fire." Gallows's voice stays soft and calm, like he's explaining to a child that lying is bad. It's amazing how polite he is.

Chuckie watches helplessly as the killer removes piano wire from a pocket inside his coat. It looks like something Chuckie had used in Asia as a last resort one time and had found he liked the feel of using it. It looks sharp enough to cut molecules in half. His executioner's eyes show no emotion.

"You chose to kill Jade after you had your fun with her. Tony Sun chose the manner of your death. He could have had you killed in Pelican Bay, but he wanted you to taste freedom again before it was taken from you. You took away the warmth in his heart. Now Tony Sun will take yours."

Gallows yanks the old man up and has him in a kneeling position by the bed, as if he's saying a bedtime prayer. He feels the wire slip around his neck and a terrible yank as it cuts in and starts its work. As Chuckie fades away, he thinks he can feel hands clawing at him, thinks he sees the faces of all those he had killed in Asia and in America's Finest City. God, they're so cold. He thinks he hears a little girl laughing. The rain outside seems to be deafening. Gallows is saying something about Jade and being accepted in some exclusive music school and that her I.Q. had been off the charts. Feels Gallows rip his medals off him.

Chuckie hasn't really thought about God or salvation ever since he found his true self in the jungle over forty years ago, but he's now having what they call a death-bed conversion. He lets out one last gasping scream as he plunges into the hot darkness. His last image is the grandfather clock in the corner. It reads: 12:28.

Gallows gets up, pleased that he doesn't have any blood on his suit and collects his things and walks out, texting Mr. Sun that the job is complete. As promised, he knocks out the cop outside and walks away from the house toward the Ocean Beach Pier, the longest pier on the West Coast, over a mile long. He walks onto it and enjoys the feeling of the powerful winter waves crashing into it as the rain dies down, but not before bathing Gallows. This bustling city, he loves to think, is at the edge of America, right before entering another country much older with an even bloodier history. He loves this time of night, Magic Hour is what he refers to it, when everything is silent and he feels like the only man in existence, free of sin and trouble like a man who can do anything, and all he has to do is choose.

He thinks about the cop he killed tonight, a wife beater who had put his spouse in the hospital more than once. Thinks about the older killer and that he really wasn't lying when he said he would have loved to have heard his stories if things had been different, but like a mad dog, he needed to be put down. It really was too bad; the elderly deserve to be listened to and learned from. He hopes when he's old that others will seek his wisdom, if he even has any to offer. He wonders what it had been like for Chuckie, a hired killer past his prime with dark appetites. He wonders if it stung to have had his abilities as a killer questioned, to watch and feel his body grow old and weak and slow. Killing is a young man's game and Gallows knows it's nearing the time he should consider putting away his killing tools before someone younger and stronger takes him out, much like how he took out Chuckie. Especially in a tough state like

California, the New West, where the elite class joins hands with lowlifes to dance. Where a life can be taken with a simple exchange of money or a big enough favor in return. Gallows knows all the stories about him and thinks it's pretty funny that not one of them is mundane. His favorite, Gallows being a fan of blues and jazz, is that he made a deal with the same demon that Robert Johnson did. No one considers the idea that he's just a dude, like a million others in this world, trying to get by and make a buck in a career he's shockingly good at. No one considers the idea that he could have a wife and kid that depend on him and that he lives in a neighborhood much like this one. That his kid might need braces or that Gallows coaches his Little League team. No one thinks Gallows does normal things, like watch football on Sundays as the Chargers find new and exciting ways to blow it at the last minute. No one even questions how corny it is that a hitman calls himself Gallows. Maybe he's named Frank or Ted.

Five other little Asian girls had died the same year as Jade, all strangled. He'll find a way to link the old man to them, so their parents can have some kind of closure. Jade's father had been the client, but he likes to think he was working for the little girls. He hopes they'd approve of what he did. He stays out there for hours knowing he should have left immediately after the hits, but he can't help himself, it's like he's drawn to the water. Magic Hour is rare for him and needs to be savored. It gives him hope that there's a benevolent force of nature at work out there. He wants to greet the morning as it paints the sky wild and vivid colors as it all turns into the blue sky that makes this city famous. For a brief moment, gone too soon, the whole world looks golden.

He watches as the first surfers go out in their wetsuits for a morning before-work session and the lifeguards take their seats in their towers, like bowmen guarding royalty. Painters are setting up their easels to paint what they see, as if trying to find the secrets to creation in their watercolors. Feeling something close to satisfied, the man who might be named Frank or Ted throws Chuckie's medals into the ocean and walks back into the War Zone.

GILDING LILY

BY JENNIFER JORDAN

I MISS THE moonlight. That deep blue of night that held everything in her dark grip, illuminating just the shadows and suggestions of what creeps from dusk to dawn. Creeps like my friends and me when our wheels took us out of the city and into the freedom of land that still belonged to nature.

Now the dim, yellow streetlights on the outskirts of this decrepit city give a permanent glare to a parking lot and a strip mall. Those are the things framed by my so-called picture window in this cut-rate prison for old people. Assisted living, my withered old ass.

Granted, I need assistance. This for a girl who could take a bike apart and put it back together again in one of those endless summer days youth provides. They called me "Grunt" back then. That was about all you could get out of me when I was working on a bike or a book. I was a looker then. Not beautiful but pretty. Now I look like Joe Perry on a bad day when it's one of my good days. And now endless days are broken up when I have to call someone to help me get off the damn toilet. They charge me when I forget to flush the thing.

I look at the few photos left from that early period and wonder what happened to that lanky, red-haired wench. The smug expression I still have. It is planted firmly on my face, really etched on it, when I watch kids walk down the battered sidewalks, their pants hanging below their asses, thinking the world is theirs to steal.

The older forms of these thug kids are paid to "assist" me here in senior hell. The best of them vacuum the rooms without moving the furniture, leaving fresh paths amidst the dust, and change my sheets when the mood strikes them. They glare at me as they give me my meds and I check those pills before I pop them down. They don't care what they're giving you. All of it is done with a surly lip and an eye roll when I offer my thanks. The things I used to do for myself are now well beyond me even on good days. I have more dependence then I ever thought possible on a stick made of chrome I've taken to calling Edgar. I lean on him to get me from room to room.

If I didn't have Edgar with me at all times, he would have slipped out the door with other items that have disappeared over the last couple of years. The aides tried to convince me I just misplaced them or, in the case of Kitra, that I never had them here to begin with.

"That bracelet can't be stolen," she'd say. "You probably lost it years ago and just forgot about it until now."

"I distinctly remember wearing it just last week!"

"Well, I don't remember ever seeing it and I'm with you most days."

And I'd believe her. I was just dotty enough to think my mind was slipping that much. Hell, I couldn't remember where I put my cup of coffee or set down a book most of time.

But things went too far. One of those little bastards that took the only thing in this haggard old world that really meant something to me. My leathers. Those and the faded tats on my arms marked me as a member of the Warlocks, a group of some of the finest people I've ever met. My arm still sports the dragon twisted around a shield bearing the gang's name and my own from that time: *Grunt*. Ha. A far cry from the delicate flower of a name my parents gifted me with. Lily Tathum. Bah. Only the scant medical staff at this place refers to me with that handle.

Nurse: "Lily, please don't cuss."

Lily: "You don't think God swears when He sees how fucked up things have become on this planet?"

Or worse: the latest and underpaid doctor who knows you only by a file number.

Where was I? Oh, my leathers. Last time I'd worn them they hung on me. It was Kitra who helped me get them on. She actually put her cell phone down long enough to do it. For once she seemed interested in something besides her boyfriend.

"Where'd you get these?"

"The gang I used to run with. When I was about your age."

Kitra gave me a look that seemed to imply I was never around her age. "They look nice."

"They're worth more to me than anything else in the world."

She raised her painted brows, helped me hang everything back up, then went back to texting the boyfriend.

The next day, while I was in the great room listening to some woman from a local church sing Kumbaya, my leathers went for a jaunt without me. I look at those beauties every day at some point, and that evening they were gone.

Picking up the phone and dialing the front desk got me hooked up with some horrendous hold music. I marched down there and saw the one girl on duty on the phone, giggling. She glowered as I approached but didn't put the phone down. Lifting Edgar up, I pounded him down on her cluttered desk.

"Hold on a sec, David." Another arched painted brow. "Yes?"

"Someone took something from my room!"

"Are you a resident at this facility?"

They must have stringent requirements for this desk job. She'd worked here the whole four years I've lived in this nightmare.

"Ms. Tathum, room 107."

"Shit." A short sigh and she was on the move. "I'll have to call you back, babe."

She made a great show of walking to a filing cabinet where she pulled out a sheet of paper, handing it to me.

Printed on the top in barely legible writing it said: Property Loss Form.

"I didn't lose anything, it was stolen!"

Shrug. "You still have to fill out that form. That's the only one I've got."

"Well, aren't you going to call security? Or call the police."

She stared at me a bit slack-jawed for a second. "Well, of course not. Why would I do that?"

"Because someone has committed a crime!"

"So you say."

I'll admit it. At this point, I lost it a bit. Maybe said a few things I shouldn't have. So I did see security. But only when they escorted me back to my room.

When I calmed down a bit, I knew where to look. At the pair of painted brows I'd seen that day. And I had a plan.

I had to wait three more days before Kitra was assigned to my unit again. I buzzed for help from the bathroom, my pants at my ankles like those damn kids. She made her fretful entrance half an hour later. By then my legs had gone to sleep and I was worried that I might have become fused to the toilet. In fact, it took both of us quite a bit of work to get me up. I wobbled for a second, then grabbed on to her to steady myself. And to look her in the eye. I hoped my bullshit detector was still in working order and hadn't gone the way of my pancreas.

"Kitra," I said. "Could you help me into the other room? I want to put my old leathers on again."

For a second I thought that girl was doing a first class Marty Feldman impression.

"Um, you sure you want to do that, Ms. Lily? You've got to be awful tired today."

"Thank you, dear. I am a bit tired. But seeing those leathers will set me right."

I put my arm in hers and steered her toward the bedroom. As we got closer to the closet, I could feel her pulling back. But I kept on my way. When I reached for the doors, I thought that poor girl was going to pass out.

When she saw what was inside, she nearly did.

A full set of leathers hung in the faint incandescent light.

Her mouth had formed a perfect "O."

"Where did you …" Words failed her. It was hard not to cackle like the old lady witch I was.

"What was that, dear?"

"N-nothing. Do you want to put the jacket on?"

"Oh, no. Just seeing everything makes me feel better. I've got to get ready for today's balloon tennis. Could you help me get down to the recreation room?"

"Uh, sure."

She was texting to the boyfriend before the first balloon was in the air.

In Kitra's mind, I would be tied up for a couple of hours. More than enough time for her to have the texted boyfriend show up to get the magical reappearing jacket, chaps, and gloves that any fool with an internet connection and a bad makeup habit knew were worth a few bucks.

In my mind, I had Kitra tied up trying get in touch with the boyfriend, making their way past the paltry security and into my room for at least thirty minutes.

See, once you're in a gang, you're never really out of it. That can be scary but in my case meant that one phone call to an old friend had procured the services of his son, Ogre. Ogre wasn't bright and he didn't talk much, but he seemed to take direction rather well. He was installed in the meager front closet during Kitra's visit and set to move to the bedroom closet when we left.

And if I managed to avoid attracting any attention and my heart didn't give out, I'd make it back to my suite just as introductions were being made.

I'd just made it past the front desk when I heard my name.

"Ms. Tathum."

Well, fuck a duck.

I turned around to see Ted Frasier (a nurse assigned to me and about twenty other people) rounding the desk with a chart in his hands.

"Aren't you supposed to be in Balloon Tennis today?"

"I was. I got tired."

"Let me get someone here to help you back."

Just my luck, one of the only people in this place who actually gives a damn and he's set to ruin my plans.

"I'm okay, Ted. I don't have that much farther to go."

"You look a little pale, Lily. Let me get a chair and I'll take you back myself."

Before I took a breath to refuse him he was coming at me with a wheelchair.

"There we go! Just take a seat and I'll give you the guided tour." He cheerily nattered on as I muttered.

We were at my suite with its mysteriously open door in no time.

"Did you leave this open, Lily? You should be more careful. We've had a few ..." Could Ted think of a politic way of saying thefts? "We've had a few things go missing lately. I'd hate to see something like that happen to you."

As he pushed me in I could see movement in my bedroom. Ted steered me toward it with nary a pause in his babbleogue.

Once there, the tableau was revealed. A Still Life in Idiocy.

Kitra sat on my bed, open-mouthed with her left hand held before her. In front of the closet, what I assumed to be her boyfriend barely stood, his face turning an odd shade of blue. From inside the closet came a large hand wielded by an equally large arm. Ogre seemed to be choking the life out of the pallid boyfriend.

"Ogre!"

An ugly head emerged from amidst the easy-care clothes and the distinctly non-vintage leathers.

"Mmmmmm?" I took this to be Ogre-speak for "What can I do for you?"

"Put the boy down."

A look of extreme disappointment came over Ogre's face, but he let the red-faced boyfriend go.

"What the hell is going on here?" asked Ted.

"You want to tell him, Kitra?"

At least the girl had the grace to blush. Words seemed well beyond her.

"Look." Joy—the boyfriend was up and dissembling. "Kitra just asked me to help her move some stuff for one of her patients."

"Bullshit!"

"Hey, I don't have to put up with this shit." The boyfriend moved to exit stage left.

I brought Edgar up between me and the wall. "According to my cane, Ogre, and the laws of this state, you do!"

The boyfriend's face got redder and a vein began to throb near his throat. "This is all your fault, you stupid bitch!" With that, he went for Kitra, grabbing her by her hair and lifting his hand to strike.

That's when I brought Edgar up between his legs. Maybe hard enough to keep another generation of dumbasses from littering the Earth. He fell to his knees and Ogre rushed forward to grab him.

"Just hold him, Ogre! Gentle."

Ogre eased his grip and awaited further orders.

"What the hell is going on around here?" Ted was clearly not a man of action.

"Ted, grab the phone, dial nine and call the damn police!"

For once, he did as he was told.

KIDS TODAY

BY TONI L.P. KELNER

JIMBO FRENCH, A big man with more than his share of curly brown hair, was ringing up a check for a couple of truckers when I walked into French's Restaurant on Monday morning, so I just picked up my own menu from the wooden holder nailed onto the wall.

I could have skipped the menu. French's has been there for years, and the food never changes. They serve breakfast all day long, a decent selection of sandwiches at lunch, and at night, dinners like meatloaf and baked ham with two sides. Not that I care about their lunch and dinner. All I ever eat at French's is breakfast. The wife doesn't get moving until nearly noon, which means I get about an hour a day to call my own, five days a week, and I spend it at French's. It's about as cheap as any restaurant is these days, it's reasonably clean, and I don't need a dictionary to figure out what stuff on the menu is. I can't eat ambiance, so I don't see any reason to pay for it.

I headed for my usual table, which is close to the window for plenty of light and far enough from the TV mounted onto the wall that I don't have to listen to the talking heads. It wasn't until I was about to reach for my chair that I realized there was somebody there. A guy in pressed khakis and a dark blue shirt with an alligator on it was giving Sunny his order.

I muttered a few choice words under my breath, the way I do at home to keep the wife from hearing. There were other empty tables, of course—it was mid-morning, so the bulk of the breakfast crowd was long gone—but there was nothing open in Sunny's section. Digby, who considers himself the mogul of eBay, gave me a sympathetic look and Lilah May patted the empty chair beside her, but if I'd wanted somebody yammering at me while I ate, I'd have stayed home with the wife. At least the wife didn't expect me to pay attention the way Lilah May would. I just went to one of Marla's tables.

I looked at the menu to make sure that Jimbo hadn't changed anything, then slapped it shut and glared at the guy sitting at my table.

Sunny finished taking his order and came by to say, "Good morning, Mr. Anthony. How's the missus today?"

"Ill as a hornet," I said, "same as always."

"Is her arthritis bothering her again?"

"Nah, she's just mean."

"Let me get this order in and I'll bring you some coffee. Then Marla will be over in a minute to take care of you."

We both knew that a man could die of thirst while waiting for Marla, but Sunny was too nice to say so. Right about then, Marla came out of the kitchen, where she'd probably been talking to somebody on her cell phone when she was supposed to be working. Instead of coming to take my order, she sashayed over to Jimbo and started messing with him, pushing her titties at him as if they were something special.

Don't get me wrong. I'm not so old that I don't still appreciate a good pair, but that doesn't mean I want them shoved up in my face. Not that Jimbo seemed to mind, which the regulars all noticed. Lilah May was watching as if she couldn't wait to tell the story to some other blue-haired old lady, and even Digby glanced over. And naturally the two women who claimed to be sisters, but weren't, had to look.

What was Jimbo thinking, making a fool of himself over a cheap tramp when a nice girl like Sunny was crazy about him? Sure Marla was a good-looking woman, if you liked blondes with plenty of makeup and short skirts, but the wife had been even better looking back in the day and look at what she'd turned into. Sunny was pretty enough, with brown hair kept neat and a good figure. Plus she kept her skirts down where they belonged. I shook my head and opened up my newspaper while I waited for Marla to notice I was there.

Eventually she wandered over and I gave her my usual order: two eggs scrambled, a biscuit with gravy, and crispy bacon. "*Crispy* bacon," I repeated.

"I heard you the first time," she snapped and grabbed the menu out of my hand. "You're the one wearing hearing aids, not me."

Naturally, when she finally brought my food over, the bacon was so limp I could have tied it into a knot. Not that my so-called waitress actually waited to see if I was happy. I think she'd have slung the plate to me like a Frisbee if she could have.

As slow as Marla had been with my order, I wasn't surprised when my to-go order was slow, too. I'd long since finished reading my newspaper and was stuck watching some TV show about which TV star was sleeping with which movie star. Kids today. They think they invented sex. I was tempted to let Marla keep the damned order, but I knew if I showed up back home without the wife's two country ham biscuits and black coffee, I'd never hear the end of it.

Funny thing was, the new guy stayed around as long as I did, even though Sunny had brought him his food right away, the way she did for everybody. He'd pulled out a laptop computer and was typing away as if he was doing something important.

Eventually Jimbo brought over the to-go order because Marla had made herself scarce again. When I went to the register to pay, I said, "You know, Jimbo, I don't appreciate having to wait so long."

"Sorry about that, Mr. Anthony. The kitchen is a bit backed up today." He smiled as if he thought I believed him. He probably thought he'd got all the lipstick off his cheek, too. What a sap.

The next morning the new guy was at my table again, wearing a different-colored alligator shirt. I gave him the hairy eyeball, but he didn't even notice. That meant that once again I was stuck with Marla, my bacon was limp as a dishrag, and the wife's to-go order was slow in coming.

I gave Jimbo another piece of my mind, but he just apologized and gave me the wife's biscuits for free, which wasn't the point.

I made sure to get to French's earlier on Wednesday, and by the time the alligator-shirt guy showed up, I was already at my table crunching on bacon. Lilah May was running late so he took her table, and she had to put up with Marla. Thursday he got Digby's table. It looked like he was well on his way to becoming a regular, and he didn't seem to care that he was throwing off the rhythm of the place. Digby and Lilah May were as annoyed as I was, and the sisters were looking downright hostile. I guessed they were thinking he might be coming after their spot next.

But on Friday, he beat me in and was back in my seat. The bastard gave me a smug look, too, sitting there in yet another alligator shirt. Dammit, there was a limit to how early I could get myself moving in the morning, let alone getting the wife situated. I was never going to get my table back!

I stomped over to Marla's section and stewed all through breakfast. Lilah May stopped by on her way out and said, "It looks like we may be losing a waitress soon."

"Hallelujah! When is Marla leaving?"

She tittered, which is one of the reasons I don't like eating breakfast with her. "No, silly, I mean Sunny. Don't you see how that new guy looks at her? He's smitten. I can read the signs."

How she knew anything about a man was a mystery to me, because as far as I knew, Lilah May hasn't been laid since Truman was in office. But after she left, I took another gander at the new guy. Even though he pretended he was working on that laptop of his or watching TV, every time Sunny came into the room, he was watching her. Unlike Lilah May, I really did know the signs. He was after Sunny, all right, and I had a hunch she'd be gone from French's sooner or later. There was no telling what kind of loser Jimbo would hire next, and I was in a black mood when Jimbo got around to bringing me the wife's biscuits.

I was walking to my car when I saw why Marla hadn't brought me the to-go order herself. She was outside with her cell phone glued to her ear, yakking a mile a minute.

"No, I've got time to talk. Jimbo doesn't mind," she said. "Wrapped right around my little finger … No, not yet, but any day now … Work here afterwards? Not hardly. In fact, I'm thinking we'll sell this place. Jimbo told me one of the chains is dying for the location. I'm not sure which one, but it's one of the good ones, not like this dump … I don't know how much they offered, but it's got to be enough to party on for a good long time."

She saw me listening and didn't even have the decency to look embarrassed. Just made a face and held her hand over the mouthpiece long enough to say, "Go on home, you old fart! And mind your own beeswax!"

I could feel my blood pressure rising as I went to my station wagon. Marla was going to talk Jimbo into selling French's to some damned chain? I wanted to think he'd have more sense, but I knew better. Not only was I about to lose the best waitress I'd ever had, but now Marla was going to take away the one place I could get a decent breakfast and country ham biscuits good enough for the wife. What was I supposed to do? Get biscuits from the Bojangles drive-through?

I sat and thought until the wife's coffee got cold, but the plan I came up with was good enough to be worth her fussing for the rest of the day. Maybe I am an old fart, but I still have a trick or two up my sleeve.

None of us regulars go to French's on Saturday or Sunday—there are too many people who go there for brunch—but on Monday I got the ball rolling. While the alligator-shirt guy sat in my chair, making cow eyes at Sunny, I sat with Digby and laid it all out for him. Come Tuesday, he sat with the sisters to explain everything to them, while I put up with Lilah May long enough to get her up to speed. It was none too soon. We all saw that Sunny was spending more and more time with the alligator-shirt guy, even making some of the rest of us wait for our coffee refills.

Wednesday morning, I didn't even try to beat the alligator-shirt guy to my table. For once, I wanted to be in Marla's section. As usual she was as slow as cold molasses, which meant alligator-shirt guy was long gone by the time she brought my to-go order. I said, "Huh, must be nice."

"What?"

"To have plenty of money."

"Like I'd know, working here."

"If that new guy keeps tipping like that, you can ask Sunny what it's like. He just slipped her a twenty."

"What?"

Since most of us only left a couple of dollars, a tip that big that sounded awfully good to Marla. I added, "Of course he didn't start out giving her that much, and it's not every day. Still, even twice a week is pretty good."

"I think you need to get your eyes checked, old man. Twenty dollar tips in this place?"

I just shrugged. "Just don't expect me to start throwing my money around like that."

"As if!"

The next day, when I sat at what was becoming my regular spot, Sunny came right over to get my order.

"Where's Marla?" I asked.

"Oh, she's here," Sunny said. "Jimbo rearranged the sections a little." She looked wistfully at the new guy, who was looking put out at having Marla waiting on him. But Marla was doing her best to show him how good a waitress she was—running back and forth every few minutes, bringing him fresh coffee whenever he took a sip out of his cup, and of course, shaking her booty for all she was worth. When he only left a so-so tip, she let her smile slip for a second, but since I'd warned her that he wasn't overly generous every day, she just sucked it up and kept on flirting.

The next couple of days were like musical chairs, with the alligator-shirt guy trying to make his way back to Sunny's section while Marla chased him around the dining room. I'd been hoping that he'd go ahead and fall for Marla, but he only had eyes for Sunny, no matter how many blouse buttons Marla left undone. Plus he hadn't left Marla any monster tips, so she was losing interest. That meant we were going to have to move on to the next phase first thing Monday morning.

This part involved all of the regulars. We were all used to Digby talking about the stuff he bought and sold on eBay, and he was always telling us what our clothes and cars were worth. Now Digby told Marla how expensive alligator-shirt guy's watch and cell phone and computer were. He also made up some tale about the man owning his own business and being independently wealthy. I thought he was laying it on too thick, but Marla swallowed it hook, line, and sinker.

Since Sunny was still interested in alligator-shirt guy, too, she had to be redirected. Lilah May took on that job. Her being such a gossip anyway, it was only natural when she said, "You know, Sunny, maybe I should warn Marla about that man over there. Since he started eating here, I've heard him on his cell phone out in the parking lot making dates with three different women."

"Really?" Sunny said. "He seems so nice."

"Nice is as nice does," Lilah May said. "Now if I were a few years younger, it's Jimbo French I'd be looking at. He's a steady, trustworthy man. Cute, too."

"You're right about that," Sunny admitted.

Then, as if it had just occurred to Lilah May, she said, "You know, you two would make a real cute couple."

"I don't think he's interested in me."

"He could be. If you'd just wear a tiny bit of makeup and maybe spend just a little more time talking to him, I bet he'd be head over heels for you in no time."

"You think so?"

"I know so!"

Sunny had nearly given up on Jimbo because of him panting after Marla, but Lilah May's encouragement was all she needed to make her hopeful again.

As for Jimbo, he might not have been the brightest bulb on the circuit, but even he could tell that Marla was chasing alligator-shirt guy. So when Sunny started making an effort, it had an effect pretty quickly.

That left alligator-shirt guy, who still didn't like Marla, and that was the trickiest part. Since he never bothered to speak to any of us regulars, we couldn't very well suddenly strike up a conversation with him. Nor could we start yelling at one another across the tables, because the wrong people would hear what we were saying. That's where the sisters came in. They were both a touch deaf anyway, so they usually spoke a little loud anyway and their table was the closest to alligator-shirt guy.

The brunette one said, "Have you seen what Sunny is up to this time?"

"Don't tell me she's catting around after another man," the redhead said.

"You know she is! This time it's Jimbo."

"I thought it was the cook."

"Oh, he was last week. You know she doesn't let moss grow under her."

"What about that linen delivery man?"

"He was just a one-time thing, I think. She kept the dairy man busy for nearly a month, but that's probably over now."

"I wouldn't put it past her to be seeing two at the same time."

"Two? Try three or four!"

They laughed.

I'd told them to not even look in alligator-shirt guy's direction, but I kept an eye on him as best I could over my newspaper. I don't think he wanted to believe them, but I caught him watching Sunny when she was talking with Jimbo, and I could tell he was becoming more and more convinced.

Of course, just chasing him away from Sunny wasn't enough. If he just stopped coming to French's, Marla might start up on Jimbo again, and Jimbo might drop Sunny, and we could still end up losing our restaurant. So now we had to get alligator-shirt guy hooked on Marla. Making that happen took all of us regulars.

First off, the sisters started talking about what a sweet girl Marla was. "She told me that she attends church every Wednesday night and Sunday, too," said the redhead. Since we weren't sure what alligator-shirt guy's leanings were, we'd decided to take a chance and made her Protestant, which fit well enough. I figured Marla would be protesting as loud as she could if we ever tried to drag her into a church.

Next Lilah May shared a table with Digby, and of course she brought up the subject of Marla. "She's such a lovely, unspoiled girl," she said, emphasizing *unspoiled* enough that even a dummy would know that she meant Marla was a virgin. I had a hard time keeping a straight face at that—chances were that Marla hadn't been a virgin since her age hit double digits.

Then Lilah May said, "I just wish she'd dress a little differently. She's so innocent that she doesn't realize the effect her unfortunate outfits have on men."

I hadn't been sure that alligator-shirt guy would swallow that, but Lilah May can be pretty convincing when she wants to be.

The next day, Digby invited me to his table, saying he wanted to talk about something, man-to-man.

"You'll have to speak up a bit," I said. "My hearing aid battery is about to run out, and I didn't bring any spares."

"I've been thinking about asking Marla out," Digby said. "You know, like on a date."

"I can't say as I blame you," I said. "I'd ask her out myself if it weren't for the wife. Well, that and being forty-five years older than she is." Forty-five years older than she pretended to be, anyway. We went on to discuss where Digby might take her on this theoretical date of theirs, but I kept glancing over at alligator-shirt guy's expression. He wasn't liking our conversation one bit. There's nothing like a little competition to get a man riled up.

As for me, I sprinkled conversations with random facts about Marla, saying what a shame it was that she didn't have any family in town and didn't even have a pet in the apartment where she lived all by herself. The other regulars weren't sure why that made Marla more attractive until I spelled out that it meant that he wouldn't have to get her parents' approval, didn't have to deal with a dog or cat in case he had allergies or phobias, and that they would have a place they could be alone. Even Digby got what they might want to do in private.

After a week and a half of our play-acting, I came into French's and saw that not only had Marla not come into work that day, but alligator-shirt guy never showed up either. None of us regulars said anything, but we were all grinning to beat the band.

Of course, that meant Sunny had to handle the whole dining room so she wasn't quite as good as she usually was, but that was only for a few days. A week later, when Marla still hadn't shown, Jimbo hired Annabelle. Annabelle wasn't as good as Sunny but she was a big improvement over Marla. After that, things quieted down other than us regulars trying to guess when Jimbo was going to pop the question to Sunny.

Except a week after that, alligator-shirt guy showed up again. At my table. And while I was glaring at him, he was concentrating on Sunny. The other regulars were all kinds of agitated, wondering what was coming next, and Lilah May kept trying to get my attention to come talk to her. I acted as if I didn't see her, just read my newspaper and thought about the situation. By the time Annabelle brought me the wife's biscuits, I had my plan all worked out.

When I went to pay my bill, I said, "Jimbo, did that gal Marla ever pick up her stuff? I lent her a magazine right before she disappeared, and I was wondering if she left it here."

He looked doubtful, probably about the idea of Marla reading anything, but he said, "I don't know what she had. Sunny packed her stuff into a box in case she ever shows up. But she can forget ever getting her last paycheck, leaving me in the lurch that way." I had to listen to him complain about her for a few minutes, but in the end, he brought over a cardboard box that had once held bags of potato chips and said I could look through it myself.

I went slowly, knowing he'd eventually have to go check things out in the kitchen, but once he was gone, it didn't take me but a minute to find what I needed. I covered up what I took with my newspaper, and then headed for my station wagon to wait. When alligator-shirt guy came out and drove away, I followed his van, hoping he was going home. Luckily, that's where he went. Since my memory isn't as sharp as it used to be, I made a note of the address on an old envelope before heading on home myself. Of course, the wife fussed and fumed about her coffee and biscuits being cold, but I just heated it all up in the microwave, put it in front of her, and turned off my hearing aids.

The next day, I didn't go to French's, even though it was a Thursday. That is I went, but I didn't go inside. Instead I drove by to make sure alligator-shirt guy was there at my table. Then I drove back to his house, and left a little something under some leaves on his lawn. It took some doing to make sure it was visible, but not too obvious. I'd have been worried that somebody would see me, but naturally enough, alligator-shirt guy had an isolated house with no other houses near by.

Then I went looking for a public phone, which wasn't easy—the phone company doesn't have many anymore, because everybody uses cell phones. I found one outside a busy grocery store, where nobody took any notice of me as I called the police and said I'd heard screaming coming from alligator-shirt guy's house. They wanted my name, but I hung up and went into the grocery store to get something the wife could eat instead of her country ham biscuits. She wouldn't like it, but she could lump it this once.

By the time I got back out to my wagon, the police were at the phone trying to get fingerprints, and I wished them luck. What kind of moron leaves fingerprints in this day and age? I'd even wiped off the quarter I'd use to pay for the call.

And wasn't French's buzzing when I got there the next day? The regulars were all sitting at the same table, something I'd never seen before, and the sisters waved me over to join them.

"Did you hear the news?" Lilah May asked, her eyes wide.

"I just got here—you know I haven't read the paper yet."

"They found Marla!" she said.

"Don't tell me she's coming back to work here."

"She's dead!" Digby put in, earning him a dirty look from Lilah May for spoiling her story.

"What was it? Drugs?"

"No," Lilah May said. "It was that *man*. The man with the alligator shirts. He kidnapped her and took her back to his house and he did *things* to her."

"You're shitting me."

"No, it's true," the sisters said in unison.

"And you know the worst part?" Lilah said, lowering her voice to a stage whisper. "Marla wasn't the first."

Digby jumped in again. "The police found remains of three other women in his basement. Word is that they'd all been interfered with."

Why he couldn't say *raped* like anybody else, I'll never know. Jimbo and Sunny came out of the kitchen then, and I thought they were going to take my order, but no, they pulled up chairs so we could go over it all again.

With everybody talking over one another, I got most of the details without even opening the newspaper. The cops received an anonymous tip yesterday about screaming from alligator-shirt guy's house. The guy had just gotten home and said he didn't know what the police where talking about, but then a cop found a French's nametag with the name "Marla" on the ground in the front yard. They called Jimbo, who told them what he knew, which was enough to make them suspicious. When they went inside, they found what was left of Marla and the other women, and now alligator-shirt guy was in jail where I hoped he never got a bite of crispy bacon again.

It took another week or two for things to really settle down. Sunny was upset, feeling guilty about Marla, so Lilah May pretended to be, too. And I saw Digby swiping some menus and things from French's, probably to sell on eBay. Some people will buy anything. The sisters told anybody who'd listen that they'd known all along that there was something *terribly wrong* with that man, though they'd quickly change the subject when asked why they hadn't warned anybody. And of course nobody mentioned our efforts to point the guy toward Marla.

As for me, after that one day, I went back to my own table to eat my breakfasts all by my lonesome while the other regulars kept on bleating about the horror of it all. Idiots! I'd known what the new guy was that first week. The signs are easy enough to spot, if you've got half a brain, and half a brain is all Lilah May had, thinking he was hunting for a wife. He'd been hunting all right, but not for a wife.

I couldn't believe what a fuss everybody was making anyway. Four women? Big fat hairy deal! Back in my prime, I went hunting every month, and I still managed one or two hunts a year—I'd have to check my scrapbook to find out what my latest tally was, but I was getting pretty close to triple digits.

Kids today. They think they invented serial killing.

THE OLD MAN IN THE MOTORIZED CHAIR

BY JOE R. LANSDALE

MY GRANDFATHER, STUBBLE Fine, used to work for the cops, but he didn't get along with them so he quit. He opened a detective agency, but he didn't much care for that, even though he was good at it. Well, to be honest, he was great at it. But he didn't care. At heart, he's lazy.

No man in my memory has more looked forward to retirement than my grandpa. And as it turned out, he pretty much had to retire. His legs played out and he spent his days in a motorized chair, in front of the television set. His wife, my grandma, left him early on, well before he retired, and she died of some kind of disease somewhere in Florida. We never met.

On the day I'm telling you about, I was visiting his house, which is a three bedroom that looks a lot like the three bedrooms along his street and across from it. He and I get along well enough, considering he doesn't really like much of anyone, and hates the human race in general.

But, I get my fill of him plenty quick, and I think the feeling is mutual, though it's more about his personality than about anything I might do or say.

I was pretty close to making my escape, as it was a Saturday, and I wanted to have a nice day on the town, maybe go to the mall, see if any good-looking women were hanging around, but fate took a hand.

Grandpa was watching his favorite channel, one about reptiles and insects and animals. He loved the episodes with alligators and lions, and especially snakes. The ones where adventurers went out and showed off poisonous snakes and told you about them and handled them in precarious and irresponsible ways to show you how knowledgeable they were. Grandpa watched primarily in hopes of seeing someone bit.

So he's settled in with a snake program, waiting on another, 'cause it's some kind of all-day snake marathon or such, and just as I'm about to put on my coat and go out into the winter cold, the doorbell rang.

Grandpa said, "Damn it."

I went over to the kitchen window for a look. The sheriff's car was parked at the curb, and behind it was a big black SUV splattered on the sides and all over the tires with red mud. I went to the door and opened it.

Standing there beside Jim was a young woman, who was, to put it mildly, a stunner. She looked like a movie star to me, even though her hair was a little tousled, like she had just gotten out of bed. She was wearing jeans and those tall boots with the white fluff around the tops, and she had on a well-fitting dark jacket with the same white fluff around the collar.

I invited them into the house, said, "Grandpa, it's the sheriff."

"Oh, hell," Grandpa said.

Jim looked at me. "Cranky today?"

"Every day," I said.

"I heard that," Grandpa said. "I got my hearing aid in."

We went over to his chair. Grandpa said, "Today is the all-day snake marathon, and I don't want to miss it."

"This is kind of important," Jim said.

"So's the snake marathon," Grandpa said. "It shows next time six months from now. I may not be here then."

I thought: Now that's silly. If you're not here, you're not gonna miss not seeing it.

Grandpa turned his head slightly, looked at me, and said, "I still want to see it."

"I didn't say anything," I said.

"Yeah, but you were smiling, like what I said was silly."

"It is," I said. "Why don't you just record it and watch it when you want?"

"Don't have a recorder."

"I bought you one for Christmas."

"That's what's in the box?"

"That would be it. I'll hook it up."

"Not today you won't."

"Well, it's still silly," I said.

"Not to me," Grandpa said. He put the TV on mute, looked at Jim, said, "Well, get on with it."

"Mr. Fine. Good to see you," Jim said, reaching out to shake hands. As he did, Grandpa sniffed, and smiled.

"Call me Stubble or Stubbs. It's not that I feel all that close to you, but Mr. Fine makes me feel more senior than I like. Besides, I see you from time to time. So we know one another."

"Very well, Stubbs—"

"Wait a minute," Grandpa said. "Never mind. Call me Mr. Fine. It sounds better coming out of your mouth."

"Okay, Mr. Fine."

"What's the problem," Grandpa said. He said it like a man who might already know the problem. But that's how he was, a know-it-all, who, much of the time, seemed in fact to actually know it all.

"This is Cindy Cornbluth," Jim said. "Her husband is missing. I had her follow me here to see if you could help us out. I know how you can figure things, how you can notice things the rest of us don't … Like … Well, you know, there was that time with the murders in the old theater."

"And all those other times," Grandpa said.

"Yes," Jim said, "and all those other times."

Cindy leaned forward and smiled a smile that would have knocked a bird out of a tree, and shook hands with Grandpa. I thought he held her hand a little too long. Before he let it go, he gave her face a good look, and when she stepped back, he gave her a good once over. If he thought what I thought, that she was as fine a looking woman as had ever walked the earth, he didn't let on. His face looked as sour as ever.

"Give me the facts, and make it short," Grandpa said. "They got a round up of the top ten most poisonous snakes coming on next, in about fifteen minutes"

"Jimmy … Sheriff. He can't possibly help us in fifteen minutes," Cindy said.

"That's how much time you got," Grandpa said. "You already made me miss the part about where one of the snake wranglers gets bit in the face."

"You've seen this before?" Jim asked.

"He has," I said. "But he never tapes it. Won't hook up the machine. He likes to symbolically capture the program in the wild."

"They got this one snake," Grandpa said, "bites this fool messin' with it, and they can't get its teeth out. It won't let go. The guy is going green, even as you watch."

"You enjoy that?" Jim said.

"Oh yeah," Grandpa said. "Rule of thumb. Don't mess with venomous snakes. Okay now, tell me what happened. Chop, chop."

"I woke up this morning," Cindy said, "and Bert was gone. That's my husband. I don't know where. I didn't think much of it. I thought he might be surprising me with doughnuts."

"Doughnuts?"

She nodded.

"He do that often?" Grandpa asked.

"Now and again," she said.

"So, Saturday, that's his day off?"

"Not usually. But he decided not to go into work today. He can do that when he wants. He owns his own business. Construction."

"Heard of it," Grandpa said. "Cornbluth Construction. Got some big deals lately. Saw it on the news."

"That's right," Cindy said.

"Would you say he's wealthy?" Grandpa asked. "That the two of you are wealthy?"

"He's been fortunate," Cindy said.

"So, tell me the rest of it."

"I got up this morning, he wasn't home, and I waited around until noon. Then I called the sheriff. I was worried by then."

"Did you think he might have gone in to work?"

"No. It didn't cross my mind."

Grandpa looked down at Cindy's feet. "Nice boots."

"Thanks," Cindy said, and looked at Jim perplexed. Jim smiled. He knew how Grandpa was, knew he had round-about ways, provided he was in the mood to help at all.

Grandpa called me over, said, "Get your digital camera, go out to her car …" He paused, looked at Cindy. "I did hear right that you followed Jim over?"

"That's right," she said, "but what has that got to do with anything?"

"Maybe nothing," he said. "Get photos of the car, all around."

I found the camera and went out and took photos of the car. When I came back in, I leaned over Grandpa's shoulder and he looked at the digital photos on the camera's display. He took off his glasses and rubbed his eyes and sighed. He put them back on, glanced at the TV and pointed.

"That's a black mamba," Grandpa said.

"What?" Cindy said.

"The snake," Grandpa said pointing at the silent TV. "Very deadly. Hides in the grass, and then, BAM, it's got you. You're dead before you can say, 'Oh, hell, I'm snake bit.' "

Grandpa said to me, "Grandson, turn up the heat."

I thought it was pretty warm, but I did as instructed.

"So, you two," Grandpa said to Cindy and Jim, "did you know each other before today?"

"Yes," Jim said. "In high school."

"Date?"

"Once or twice," Jim said. "Just a kid thing. Nothing came of it."

He looked at Cindy, and she smiled like a woman who knew she was beautiful and was a little ashamed of it, but … not really.

Grandpa nodded. "You know, the dirt around here is white. Except up on Pine Ridge Hill. The oil company did some drilling up there, and it was a bust. I heard about it on the news. They had to close it down.

They say the old ground up there is unstable, that it's shifting, that a lot of it is going down the holes that were meant for oil drilling. It's like a big sinkhole up there, a bunch of them actually. Saw that on the news, too."

"Okay," Jim said, "But, Mr. Fine, so what?"

"Here's the deal. Cindy has a rough place on her hand. Felt it when we shook. But I'll come back to that. She's also got red clay on her boot. The left one. I think she may have stomped some of it off, but there's still a touch on the toe, and a bit she's tracked in on the floor. So, she's been out there to the old oil site. I believe that she's got a bit of pine needle in her hair too, twisted up under the wave there, where it got caught in a tree limb."

Jim leaned over for a look. I gave it a hard look from where I was standing as well. Didn't that old codger wear glasses? How in the world had he noticed that?

"I drove up there the other day," she said. "I was looking for pine cones, to make decorations. I haven't washed my hair since then. I was hanging around the house, didn't have anywhere to go."

"Gonna spray them pine cones gold, silver?" Grandpa asked, not looking away from the TV.

"I don't know," she said. "Something like that."

"On your ear lobe there's a dark spot. Noticed it when we shook hands. I'll come back to that."

Jim gave that a look too, said, "Yeah. I see it." Then, appearing puzzled, he unfastened his coat, took it off, dropped it over the back of a chair.

Grandpa grinned. "Warm, son?"

"A little," Jim said.

"Well, now, Jim," Grandpa said. "I've known you a long time. Since you were a boy."

"Yes, sir."

"I believe you're a good man, but she didn't call you this morning. She lied and you let her."

"Now wait a minute," Jim said.

"When you shook hands with me I smelled her perfume on your coat. A lot of it. I don't think sheriffs are in the habit of comforting women with missing husbands with a hug so intense it gets on their coat, and in their hair. And she called you Jimmy."

"Well, we know each other," Jim said. "And I did comfort her."

"Another thing. There's what we used to call a hickey on your neck."

Jim slapped at his neck as if a mosquito had bitten him.

"Not really. Just kidding. But here's what I think. I think you've been having an affair. If she had called the Sheriff's Office to get in touch with you, and the two of you were not an item, you wouldn't have come to me right away. You were hoping it was simple and I could solve it without involving the Sheriff's Department. That's why you had her follow you in her car, so she wouldn't be in your car.

"And Mrs. Cornbluth, that smile you gave me, the one that was supposed to make me weak in the knees. That seemed out of place for the situation."

"People respond in different ways," she said.

"Yes, they do," he said. "I give you that much. Would you like to take your coat off?"

"I'm fine."

"No, you're not. You're sweating. In fact, it's too hot in here. Grandson, turn down the heater, will you."

"But you just told me—"

"Cut it down," Grandpa said.

I went over and did just that.

"When you and me shook hands," Grandpa said, "there was a fresh rough spot on your palm. That's because your hands are delicate, and they held something heavy earlier today, and when you struck out with it, hitting your husband in the head with whatever you were using … A fire poker perhaps? It twisted in your hand and made that minor wound."

"That's ridiculous," Cindy said.

"It certainly is," Jim said. "Okay, Mr. Fine. Me and Cindy had a thing going, but that doesn't mean she killed her husband."

Grandpa said. "Jim, you came by her house. Just like you were supposed to. I don't mean you did anything having to do with Mr. Cornbluth, but Cindy was expecting you. You had a date with her because Bert was supposed to be at work, but when you showed for your date, she told you he had stayed home, and she hadn't been able to reach you, and now he was missing and she was worried. That it wasn't like him. Right?"

"How could you know that?" Jim said.

"I guessed a little, but all the other facts line it up. After she hit her husband in the head with something or another, she wiped up quick."

"But why would I kill him?" Cindy said.

"That's between you and your husband, but if you were having an affair, it might be you weren't that fond of him, and he found out, and you didn't want to lose all that money, and you thought if the body wasn't found, you'd get insurance money and no jail time. The murder was quick and spontaneous, done in anger, and afterward, because Jim was coming, you had to do on the spot thinking, and it was stupid thinking.

"You drove the body out to the old oil well site this morning, dumped it, drove back and cleaned the car, the house, and maybe you were cleaning yourself when Jim showed up. You had to wipe yourself down quick. But that spot of blood on your ear. You missed that. And one more thing, Mrs. Cornbluth. You're sweating. A lot. That's why I turned up the heat. To see if you'd take your coat off on your own. You didn't. That made me think you had something to hide. Like maybe the blood that splashed on you from the murder wasn't just a drop on your ear, and you didn't have time to change before Jim showed up. So, you threw a coat on over it. Was she wearing it in the house when you showed, Jim?"

Jim nodded, looked at her. He said, "Cindy. Take off your coat."

"Jim, I don't want to."

"Jim isn't asking. The sheriff is. Take it off."

Cindy slowly removed her coat. She was wearing a gray, tight-fitting, wool sweater. There were dark patches.

Grandpa said, "Those wet spots on her sweater. I think if you check them, you'll find they're blood. And if you check up at the old oil site on Pine Ridge Hill, you'll find her husband at the bottom of one of those holes. You know, they were supposed to fill those in next week. If they had, good chance that body would never have been found. That's how you got the pine straw in your hair, wasn't it? When you were draggin' Bert from the car, through the pines, to the top of the hill? And Jim, when it all comes out, that you were dallying with a married woman while on the job ... Well, I hope you keep your job."

"Yeah, me too," Jim said taking out a pair of cuffs. "Put your hands behind your back, Cindy."

"Jim. You don't have to do this. Bert found out about us—"

"Shut up! Just shut up. Put your hands behind your back. Now."

She did. He handcuffed her. She looked at Grandpa. "I hate you, you old bastard."

As they went out the front door, which I held open for them, Grandpa said, "Lots do."

Grandpa turned up the sound on the TV. Just in time. The countdown of the world's most poisonous snakes was just about to begin.

ANGEL OF MERCY

BY RUSSEL D. MCLEAN

For the real Renate—
tougher than just about any hardboiled hero you could name.

IT WAS A glorious day for a funeral.

Might sound selfish, but it was good to be outdoors. Away from the home and the gardens. Somewhere new.

If it wasn't for being shoved around mercilessly in a wheelchair by a criminally bored and underpaid twenty-something who talked to me more like I was a child than a grown man, I might have felt the years just falling away.

In the church, they had me next to Renate Oks (pronounce it like Ox, or God help you), who had been dragged—protesting like hell—into my life (and, sure, those of the other residents) maybe six months earlier.

I didn't know why she was with us. She had more energy than some of the staff: those allegedly young and fit folks who were supposed to care for us oldies. But all the same, I was glad she'd moved in.

In an institution like Craws Creek Retirement Home—we called it simply, The Craws—you start to crave the company of friends. Being in a home can be like prison. But worse, because you're never quite able to figure out what you did to deserve incarceration.

Other than get a little old.

A little dottery.

A little reliant on the help of others.

As the last of the mourners piled in, Renate leaned across and whispered conspiratorially, "Margaret-Anne gave me the new series of *24*." She had a DVD in her room. Even knew how to work the damn thing. Hell, she could work the computers in the rec room better than someone half her age. One of the other residents called her "an unusual lady," and I think they meant it as an insult.

To hell with them.

It was good to have someone in the home who didn't meekly accept the platitudes and the pity of the staff, who was out to prove to the world that she was still as alive and kicking over seventy as she had been under thirty.

I looked across the assembled. Saw Jimmy's family sitting down in front, their heads high and their eyes red-raw. Not crying, but on the verge. I wanted to go over and offer my condolences right then, but I was dependent on my bored, gum-chewing nurse to actually be arsed into wheeling me across.

So I didn't say anything. Figured I'd wait until the service was over.

Renate leaned over again, said, "Butter wouldn't melt."

I looked to where she jerked her head. The new orderly stood calmly at the end of a pew, his features suitably solemn.

Right enough; *picture of innocence*.

Except Renate and I knew the truth.

Moon-faced moron was a killer.

Had murdered Jimmy.

And three others. That we knew of.

It was just a matter of proving it.

WE REALISED THE truth during a 24 marathon a week earlier, two days before Jimmy finally snuffed it of "natural causes."

The middle of the second set, I'd been perturbed by Jack Bauer's daughter's encounter with a cougar and Renate was trying to convince me that I needed to lighten up, get more into the spirit of the show.

Guess I was still thinking about all the people who'd died in the last month. Sure, get to our age and maybe you should expect it. All the same, so many deaths in one go seemed like a punch from above.

Renate picked up on this, said, "You know your problem? You think too much. Too seriously."

I laughed. "On the show, if so many people died in such a short space of time, Jack would be interrogating everyone in his path to get to the truth."

Renate hit the remote. Queuing up the next episode.

Sure, we were hooked.

I'd watched a lot of the TV over the years. This was the first show I'd watched in a long time where I genuinely couldn't tell you what was going to happen next.

Call that a novelty.

A knock at the door timed with the beep of the countdown on the TV. Renate and I both looked up as the pale, round and sickly looking David Connor walked in. As though he owned the place. "You two doing okay?" He didn't look directly at us. More like he was inspecting the room. "Not interrupting anything, am I, Mrs. Ok-us?" He spoke slow and loud as though we were mentally impaired.

Christ, I could have gotten out of my chair and throttled him. It wasn't just the tone. The one that said, "what a terrible shame that you're so old and useless." No, everything about him screamed, "arsehole." He was perfectly ironed. Not just his shirt; his whole damn appearance was without creases.

"I hope we're not going to have a repeat of the other night," he said. "All that commotion."

"Mrs. Simpson is an interfering busybody," said Renate. "The only reason she heard anything was that she lives with a glass against the bloody wall!" These last words were shouted in the general direction of Mrs. Simpson's room.

"Just keep the volume down," Connor said. "I worry about you two watching all this violence. It's not good for you to get over excited."

I imagined I was Jack Bauer, torturing the smug, patronising shite by hooking up an electric charge to his genitals.

From the look on her face, I figured Renate was thinking the same thing, too.

As he left, Renate said, pointedly, "And it's pronounced *Oks*." Waited until he was gone before adding, "Pillock."

As the clock counted down at the end of the first hour—forty-three minutes, really, when you took into account the space the Americans left for their commercials—Renate said, "I'd leave tomorrow."

"Why don't you?"

She shook her head. I knew I was blushing furiously, feeling like an eejit. There were certain rules of etiquette in Craw's Creek. The big one: you never asked anyone why they were here. Don't ask me how that got started. I always guessed it was because there are enough sob stories going around a place like Craw's without adding to them.

"Not all of the staff are arsebuckets," I said. "And probably his heart's in the right place." Sounded weak, all right. But it seemed the right thing to say.

Not that Renate gave a monkey's, of course. Tell it like it is? She knew how to cut through the shite. "He looks at us like we're already dead. Beyond taking care of ourselves."

I looked down at my useless legs. At my chair. Old, unreliable. I could be talking about either.

Renate noticed my gesture and laughed. "Rubbish," she said. "A wheelchair? Young people have them, too, and most of them do all right."

I laughed. "D'you think Jack Bauer would kick as much arse in a chair?"

"More, probably," she said. "It would just make him angry."

Silence.

Not uncomfortable.

Finally, I said, "He was on duty when Jennifer died." Talking about Connor.

Renate didn't say anything. Maybe because she'd heard the gossip about me and Jennifer in the halls. Retirement communities could be every bit as bad as schools. Worse, maybe.

"I hate the idea that his was the last voice she heard."

Renate was looking at the screen, now. Focusing on the split screen action that started the next episode. She said, "He was there with Jimmy, too, so I heard."

I tried to pull myself out of it. Made a joke I knew was in bad taste before I uttered the first syllable. "Probably listening to that dull toerag's voice was what finally did them in."

We both laughed. No humour. Just release.

And then I made the mistake of thinking about what we'd said.

Counting the deaths that had occurred since David Connor started to work for the home.

All of them "natural."

All of them on his watch.

AFTER THE SERVICE, I was rolled out past Jimmy's family. Shook hands, accepted kisses on the cheek and in return muttered my condolences. After a few funerals, your words feel useless and you wonder whether they ever do any real good.

Like sticking plasters on the stump of a severed limb.

My nurse left me outside so she could go and have a smoke round the side of the church. I encouraged her. Wanted to have a chance to talk to Renate, who'd already agreed to wheel me for a while.

She wheeled me among the graves. The grass was wild, but not uncared for and it felt good to be away from everyone else, even for a few moments.

She said, "The more I look at him, the more certain I am that he's up to no good."

I nodded. "Do you think maybe we're getting paranoid?"

"No," she said. "No, I don't think so."

BACK AT THE Craws, she showed me some printouts from various sources: BBC news, daily newspaper websites. All that information sitting around, freely available to anyone who cared to find worried me. But then, the whole idea of the internet made me uneasy. That's the way it is with some people. New ideas seem incomprehensible or terrifying, so we try to ignore them.

Renate spread the papers out on her desk, the one next to the window that looked out across a flat extension roof and onto the rear gardens. I wheeled across, took my reading glasses out and skimmed the more pertinent details.

Feeling like a detective.

Thinking of myself as Bogart or one of the guys I grew up watching in the cinema. A black and white hero, digging for proof to stop the murderer. Sure, Bauer was a class act, but it was the old heroes I truly aspired to.

And, stealing a glance at Renate, I had the broad all sorted, too.

My heart beat a double-quick rhythm. My hands shook, ever so gently. A coldness ran up my arms. I tried to ignore the sensation.

The articles covered common ground: nursing home deaths in suspicious circumstances. Going back about ten years. Up and down the country.

I looked up at Renate. Feeling a moment of doubt about what we were doing. Said, "People die all the time."

She nodded. "I had Margaret Ann do me a favour." She selected out a particular printout. Not a news article.

At the top of the page: Craws Creek's official letterhead.

I saw the name on the RE: line.

David Connor.

And a list of employers and dates.

She said, "You wanted to know why I'm here? At least part of it's to do with my daughter working for their HR department."

Renate talked me through the chain of evidence, how everything linked to our man's previous employment records. Connor had been employed at every one of the homes around the time of the deaths. And he always left right before anyone became suspicious.

I nodded as she talked. She had me more than convinced. Talked with the kind of passion that could have led people on marches.

I could have got out of the chair, run down the hall, beat a confession out of Connor.

That was the strength of her conviction.

THE PROBLEM WITH getting old is that you feel everyone should respect your advanced years. Your experience. Your wisdom. And then you realise that, honestly, no one gives a shite.

The revelation is painful the first time, soon becomes a minor annoyance and then merely slips into the background hum of your life.

Homes like Craw's Creek only reinforce this sensation no matter how noble their intentions. You become isolated from society, start to believe that there must be a reason why people talk to you like you're a moron, why they keep you away from all the young and healthy people out there.

So when Renate decided we'd gathered enough evidence to approach the manager of the home, I felt strangely elated. Here was the chance to prove that we were not useless, past our sell-by date.

That feeling lasted right until we finished outlining our suspicions. When I saw the look in the big man's eyes.

He was the kind of blowhard perfectly suited to a management role. He came to work wrapped up in a pinstripe, a white shirt, and a tie with two colours so he could pretend to have personality. He also sported a ridiculous walrus moustache.

Did he look at himself in the mirror?

Who told him that was a good look?

After listening patiently to us—well, mostly Renate—outline our suspicions about the home's very own Angel of Death (Renate assured me that was the name for a certain type of serial killer) the big man looked at us both, his eyes settling for a few seconds on each of us in turn.

And then he smiled.

The kind of smile that yelled, *patience.*

Made me feel like a doddering old fool.

Think how he saw us: two bored old folks (one of them who dreamed of the days when he had mobility and could stay up past midnight) who spent too much time watching TV shows about coverups and conspiracies together.

Two seniors behaving like wrinkly teenagers telling the owner of the home where we lived that we suspected he had hired a serial killer on staff.

Oh, aye, he was going to take us seriously.

He said, "David came to us highly recommended."

Renate countered, "By whom? Have you looked at his record?"

"Yes." He nodded three times. Then regarded us with those tiny, dull eyes that stared out from deep inside his fat face. "And that leads me to ask … how have you seen his record?"

Renate sputtered.

And that was when everything came apart.

BACK IN RENATE'S room, she raged.

I sat there (given the chair, what choice did I have?) and listened.

When there was a suitable gap—when she finally took a breath—I said, "Maybe he's right."

That got her.

Just as good as if I'd slapped her once across the face. Not that I ever would, you understand. I've never been for violence. Especially against women.

She sat down on her bed, kicked her heels.

I could imagine her as a teenager.

Rebellious.

You knew that just to look at her.

I said, "We're bored, you and me. Cooped up like this. Looking for release, right? They treat us like we're mentally deficient but we both know that we're as sharp as ever."

Renate grinned and tapped her head. "A few memory problems," she said.

I slapped the arms of my chair. "Some mobility issues."

"But otherwise right as rain."

I nodded. Felt that cold pain in my arm again. Had been getting worse over the last few days. I coughed as though I might dislodge something.

When it was done, I said, "So maybe we're just looking for trouble. To keep ourselves busy."

The cough again.

The pain shot up my arm. Along my chest.

I was sweating.

My breathing was all wrong.

Renate came across and laid the back of her hand against my forehead. "Are you all right?"

"Fine," I said. But it wasn't true. Even though I was in the chair, my balance was shot. I was about to slide out and crumple on the floor. The pulse that banged on the left side of my forehead pumped even faster. "Honestly, just … the excitement must be—"

That was when I heard the gunshot. At least I thought I did. The bullet ripped through my heart. *Dead* in the heart.

"It's okay," I said. "Jack Bauer's had worse."

My hearing went, then. I thought I heard her say, "You don't know Jack," but I couldn't be sure of anything.

I gripped at my chest to massage my heart, keep it going. But I knew it was a feeble gesture. The last-ditch attempt of an old man who perversely wanted to hold onto a life he had come to despise.

At least until he finally found someone he could bear being around.

SOMEONE WAS HOLDING my hand.

That was all I knew at first. Just the sensation. Heat. Pressure.

Then I realised my head was on a pillow. Soft. Light. Supportive. I wanted to stay this way forever, resisted the urge to ask if this was heaven—even if it was, I'd have felt like a berk if those were my first clichéd words in the afterlife—and finally opened my eyes.

Renate smiled at me. Squeezed my hand even tighter. Said, "I know I'm a knockout, but …"

I tried to laugh, but even the idea hurt.

ANGEL OF MERCY

A nurse—not one of the carers from the residential wing, but a real honest-to-God nurse—stopped by the bed. Made some cursory physical checks.

When she asked me how I felt, I said, "Like my heart stopped." Sounding grouchy with it.

She said, "The good news is you're still with us."

"But for how long?"

I meant it as a joke, but when I looked at Renate and saw her features pale and drawn, the years suddenly apparent where I had never seen them before, I felt a tug of guilt.

"No, I'll be fine," I said. "Strong as an ox." Meaning it like a pun, a play on her name. She didn't smile.

Maybe I just wasn't that funny.

WHEN RENATE WAS gone, the nurse gave me a quiet ticking off.

I should have seen this coming.

Had been through it before.

Had been ignoring the signs.

They were the same lies anyone would tell themselves. Who wants to admit to their own mortality? Their own weakness?

My left side was entirely numb. I could move, but with little more prowess than a fish flopping on the sodden floor of a boat.

And maybe half the strength of that.

I kept drifting off, too. Not unusual, but I prided myself that I could usually stay awake through a whole conversation. Not like some of the other brain-deads I shared corridors with in the Craws.

The nurse gave me drugs at regular intervals.

Thank God she allowed me to take them orally.

I drifted on a chemical cloud. Lost track of time.

But I was too tired to care.

WHEN I OPENED my eyes again, it was dark.

Someone was leaning over me.

Their breath was on my cheek. Hot, stale, ragged. Coming in short, heavy bursts. Sounding … excited.

"It's okay, you don't have to be scared."

Connor.

He gripped my arm. His long, bony fingers were unexpectedly powerful. I thought of crab's claws pinching at me.

There was a jab from a needle in the fleshy part of my upper arm.

Cold.

Not unpleasant.

And then not much of anything at all.

I drifted on that cloud again.

But this time was different.

I was moving further away from the world. It was a comforting experience. I found I didn't care much if I just left everything behind. It was enough to simply float.

"It's no life, to be old," Connor said in a strange sing-song voice that I realised was supposed to be reassuring. "The spirit of death always around the corner. Nothing else to live for but the view out of the window and the next call from a relative who feels guilty for shutting you away from prying eyes."

I tried to say something.

Only croaked.

Tried to move, realizing at long last what was happening. The panic started to pull me back to the world. I felt weight again.

But I couldn't find the strength to say anything, to move my body.

Something clattered. Wheels squeaked.

The cold had me surrounded. Was inside me, now.

I wanted to speak. Not cry for help, just let him know how I felt. He continued his gentle monologue, as though to a baby or an invalid.

I closed my eyes.

Imagined my hands around his throat, his eyes bugging, his lips going blue, his cheeks turning purple.

It was a beautiful vision.

I'd have been happy if it was what I finally took with me.

My body was utterly numb, now. No feeling left.

"Don't think of it as something being taken from you." His voice was muted, now. If I kept going, I think I might have been able to get away from his constant drivel. No such luck, of course. He kept going: "Think of this as a gift. Your final freedom. Your reward for a long life, for all the things that you did with it. While you still could."

His voice was softer, now. Close and yet so far away.

I drifted again.

An illusion. My mind's way of coping with what was happening. I had to remember that. I had been a staunch realist all my life. My own murder would not turn me into a believer.

Then something pulled me back down.

A noise.

A crack.

A cry.

The world rushed back.

A hand grabbed at my arm, pressed down as though whoever had reached out was trying to use me as a lever. The sensation was light, as though there were layers between my arm and the hand that curled around it.

Then:

"Stay down, you bastard!"

Renate.

Slowly, I turned my head. She was standing beside the bed, holding a metal bedpan. Her jaw was open, almost cartoonish, like she was doing a double take in some unsubtle sitcom.

I could still feel someone holding onto me. Looked down and saw a hand reaching up from underneath the bed.

Then the fingers slipped and the hand drifted away into the shadows.

I looked back at Renate.

In the half-light, saw dark blood congealed on the edges of the bedpan that she was still holding like a weapon. A club.

She was utterly still, like she'd shocked herself with what she'd done.

I smiled. Or at least tried to.

She dropped the pan. The clang as the metal hit the floor reverberated beautifully through my skull.

Reminded me that I was still alive.

I wasn't going.

Not yet.

I said, "Is he dead?" Croaking like I'd just gargled with gravel.

Renate didn't respond straight away. Then she looked at me as though she'd only just realized I was in the room. She tried for a smile. *Reassurance.* "I'm eighty years old. If they don't believe me, that I was acting in self-defence of a friend, what are they going to do? Put me in jail for life?" She laughed. Wouldn't have won any Oscars.

The room was getting darker. The lights?

Or my vision finally giving out?

I blinked to keep Renate in focus.

Said, "Thank you."

But she ignored me.

And then I realised I wasn't speaking any more.

There was no more cold. No more heat. No more sensation.

And the world was fading out.

I said, "We did it, though, didn't we?" and wanted to scream when she didn't respond.

The lights came on in the room. The halogen hurt my eyes. Fuzzed out the details.

People were shouting, their voices all over the place. I couldn't make out words. Didn't recognise anyone.

All the faces that leaned over me were blurs.

Except Renate's.

Hers was the last to go.

MISS HARTLY AND THE COCKSUCKER

BY DENISE MINA

THE TRICK TO becoming invisible, she had learned over a lifetime, was to stay in character and be dull. Now that she was in her sixties the important thing was to ask questions.

Miss Hartly liked shoes that fitted around her feet, forgiving shoes. Too many people these days, far too many people, made their feet fit the shoes instead of the other way around and they'd be sorry in the future. They would. She knew a lot of people who were crippled because they'd squashed their feet into inappropriate foot wear and gave themselves bunions and wasn't that a shame?

He wasn't listening. A red-faced businessman, slip-on shoes slipped off, hands clasped across his belly, waiting for the next whiskey. It was, Miss Hartly admitted to herself, a bit fucking cheeky. She'd been listening to him bum his load for a full forty minutes. He was a success, seemed to be the essence of what he wanted to tell her. A great success. Everyone said so and he had the money and the ex-wives to prove it.

His eyes were half shut, his head tipped back, looking straight forward to the screen, taking in the image of the giant airplane looming over the entire Atlantic, following a red line from Heathrow to La Guardia.

They were flying into the sunset, chasing the tail end of the day, flying east. A red sun sat just below the horizon, the low clouds smeared with red blood and yellow stain. Night would come to them and everyone would sleep, try to sleep in their bed chairs. There would be an hour when everyone was asleep. Miss Hartly had charted it: someone, certainly one of them, would fight to stay awake but they would finally lose that fight.

They'd had their nuts, their glass of champagne—he asked for extra and she gave him hers—and now they had just a little while to wait for the rigmarole of the meal. It was a ridiculous fuss really, the meal. The stewardesses in first class liked to make eye contact as they handed over knives and forks and spoons, as if they were being photographed for the brochure. Miss Hartly met their eye, held their eyes for too long, thanked them and began again with her questions.

She started each flight with small questions: How long until we land, dear? Is there likely to be turbulence? When is the meal to be served? What are the options? Oh, they're in the menu, I see, thank you. I don't have my glasses, could you read that for me, dear? Oh, fish, lovely. No, I think I'll have the chicken.

Even before the meal they were losing patience with her. She could tell by the way they blinked slowly, rolling their eyes back in their heads. She saw them give rictus grins as they came to turn off the attendant call button and listen to her inane queries: How does the television work? Did they have *Midsomer Murders*? What a shame. *Antiques Road Show*? Oh dear, those were her favourite shows. That's a shame. She liked playing the old lady.

This crew were already losing patience with her before she upped the ante by making requests: could you do me a favour, dear and check for certain that my suitcase is on the plane? My niece, that's who I'm visiting, has just had a baby and my suitcase is full of presents for the baby and I need to be sure that it will arrive with me. She lives very far upstate and—I'll check that for you, Miss Hartly. Would you mind very much making sure that the disabled support is going to be waiting for me at the gate because my knees are not too bad but they do tend to go if I walk too far—they were tired. They didn't want to help her. They wanted to sleep walk, smiling, through the procedure of the meal, the drinks, the giving of pillows. They were ideal.

Finally, she achieved invisibility: they were avoiding looking at her. When she saw one of them coming around the partition to their little preparation kitchen area Miss Hartly leaned out from her seat and looked needily at them. They began to slip her eye.

In that quiet moment, before the ceremony of the meal began, she looked around the cabin. It was a small plane. First class was sparsely populated. Mostly businessmen, their seats paid for by someone else. Fat men. She thought successful people were supposed to be thin nowadays.

A young man, dressed inappropriately in a loud T-shirt and skip cap, looked resolutely out of the window. She smiled to herself. Him. He'd get it. She licked her lips at the side. He'd get it and she felt that he deserved it for dressing without decorum. Miss Hartly had been travelling the world for a long time, flying for a long time. She remembered a time when it was customary to dress up in a new outfit to fly across the Atlantic. It was an event, not something to be tolerated and slept through. The boy had baggy trousers on, a loud blue check. People flew in their pyjamas.

No sense of occasion. Anyone could fly nowadays.

She looked at the businessman next to her, the successful businessman. He was pretending to be asleep. He'd pretend to wake up when the food came, sit up and pretend to be startled, oh food, good. He was avoiding her too. Ideal.

She looked down at her lap and allowed herself a smile.

The meal came, was delivered with the usual nonsense, a million questions, gravy? Gravy? Gravy? Would you like a drink, Sir? Would *you* like a drink, Sir? Sir, would you like a drink? They delivered the meal as though it was a gourmet feast, course after course, small salad, a roll— bread for you, Sir? Some shit with bits of chicken stuck in it. A pudding. Cold chocolate mousse.

The first class meal was perfect for Miss Hartly. Not only were the courses small, which she liked, but the attention of the stewardesses was deeply distracting, the preposterous nonsense of asking question after question: Tea or coffee?—chose. Sugar?—chose. Milk?—chose. By the time they reached the complementary chocolate all the passengers were yearning to be let alone.

They reached the final gathering of the detritus of the meal, napkins, empty cups of coffee, and everyone settled back. Miss Hartly kept her chair upright because, she told the uninterested man next to her, she had a bad back. Gardening, she did love her garden. He pointed to his earphones and nodded. She told him again, my back is bad, she said.

"I can't hear you. I'm watching—" he pointed to his screen.

At this Miss Hartly feigned hurt, and smiled suddenly, as if she was covering it up. "Oh."

The lights were down. They were asleep. Everyone was asleep. A collective hush filled the cabin. She looked back. Not one of the screens was blinking bright light at the passengers.

As a tester Miss Hartly leaned out into the aisle and caught the eye of an air hostess. Just the corner of her eye. The air hostess deliberately turned away and then, very gently, pulled the curtain on the preparation area shut.

Miss Hartly slipped back into her seat and smiled. The drone of the engines filled her, tingling her fingers. It sounded like permission.

Silently, she slipped her buckle open, silently, and set the two sides of the belt on either side of her seat, doing it carefully so that she wouldn't need to fumble for them when she sat back down.

She stood up gracefully, more nimble than her support stockings would suggest, and then, once in the aisle, she reached up to the overhead cabin and felt inside.

LA GUARDIA AT midnight. Five AM to the UK passengers. They were befuddled and defenceless.

It didn't go well for Miss Hartly. On a dream trip, an ideal trip, everyone got off the plane, tramped up to the passport control, waited, and walked through, by which time no one on the airline really cared about them. Their contract was fulfilled. They had delivered them. And Miss Hartly would be wheeled through on her way, her heart in her throat, headed for Manhattan and a short, enjoyable stopover before beginning her driving tour of bed and breakfasts in New England.

But it didn't go well.

She waited back, always the last off, waiting for the disabled support to arrive with her chair. Everyone was standing in the aisle, stretching out their legs and ready for the off when the red-faced businessman's breathing changed. He gasped, slapped his heart, panted, looked around wildly. He crouched in the aisle, recklessly unzipped his wheelie bag and rummaged. The wildness of his movement attracted the attention of the stewardess.

"Can I help you, Sir?"

He stood up, looked through her. "My money is gone."

Happily he was at the back of the cabin, near the pilot's cabin and the stewardess didn't like him, distrusted him. They were going to let the others off but the man protested, "Don't you dare let them get off! Someone has taken my money, one of them has taken my money."

The other passengers turned on him. They had connections to make. They had paid for first class precisely so that they could get off first. This was nonsense. He'd misplaced his wallet.

Furious, the man opened his wallet and pointed it towards them. It was empty.

The stewardess took his arm, "Where was your wallet during the flight, sir?"

"In my bag! In my flight bag."

She looked tired under her makeup. "And where was your bag, sir?"

"In the overhead cabin! I put it up there ..." Woeful, sad, he pointed a small bent finger up at the cabin above Miss Hartly's head. He looked distraught.

Miss Hartly watched them, her hand folded over her lap, tiny handbag sitting on her knee. She had an anecdote about losing her purse on holiday once, a long dreary story that went nowhere and ended with her finding it had been handed in to a police station in Rome but not getting it back because she had left for home by then and the post wasn't as efficient in Italy, well, you know Italy. She used that sometimes, when things went wrong, but it didn't seem right this time.

She looked up at him and pressed her lips together in a consoling smile.

The man scanned the other passengers. "*You*," he said to the young man with the loud T-shirt and skip cap. "I saw you moving around during the flight."

"Excuse me?" He was American, assertive, indignant. He didn't look American, wasn't beefy or shaved. His accent was very East Coast. The man knew he had made a mistake and faltered.

"I saw you on this side when you were sitting on that side. What were you doing over—"

"I beg your pardon, are you accusing me of stealing from *you*?" He pulled a satchel in front of him, a leather satchel with a monogramme on it. Miss Hartly had felt the quality of the leather when she reached into it. She knew it was as soft as butter but hadn't realised that it was his bag. She thought it belonged to the older man next to him. It had a brick of thumbed cash in it as well, smelled of cigarettes and whisky, like gambling money. Miss Hartly knew suddenly that he was slumming it here, in first class. The boy was from money and he was taking a chartered flight and dressed like that because for him it was like going on a bus. He would usually take a private jet. The businessman had made a bad mistake.

"I saw you in the aisle, over this side of the compartment …" He doubted himself for a moment, and in that moment everything changed.

The boy sniggered at him, "You're out of your mind, man." He turned his back to leave and the stewardess hurried forward to fill the businessman's vision. "Let's have another look, it can't be far."

She stood on the side of an aisle seat and felt inside the compartment, a flat hand slapping down on the plastic, coming down empty. People were leaving.

"Ma'am?" Another stewardess, coming up the cabin, her hand gently brushing Miss Hartly's elbow. "Your wheelchair assistance is here, Ma'am."

"Oh, dear me, oh, dear," wittered Miss Hartly as she stood up, "This poor gentleman seems to have misplaced his wallet somewhere and he can't seem to find—"

"If you could just come with me, Ma'am." A firmer hand on her elbow. An order.

Miss Hartly nodded sadly and followed her, clutching her tiny handbag in front of her.

WAITING IN PASSPORT control. A long snaking line. Behind her the wheelchair pusher was a grotesquely fat woman, short, she breathed noisily, shifted from foot to foot as they waited, her hips must be aching, thought Miss Hartly, from carrying all that weight.

She looked up at the long queue leading to the non-resident passport control. They were working quickly this evening. Not too long a queue. Not bad at all. The red-faced businessman was nowhere to be seen. She looked for him. He'd still be in the plane, looking for the nearly seven hundred pounds that had slipped out of his wallet.

Strange: there, beyond the desk for U.S. citizens, stood Skip Cap and he was staring at her. He was holding his navy blue passport, satchel strap slung across his body. She narrowed her eyes to see his face in the shadow of the cap. He was smiling straight at her, his big American teeth white as bleached bones. He saw that she was looking back at him, widened his crocodile smile and raised his hand in a jaunty salute. Then he turned softly and walked away.

A cold dread shivered down her back. She sat up straight. U.S. Marshal, an air marshal? No. They didn't sit in first class. They didn't fall asleep either. But she had been seen.

Defensive, afraid suddenly that her fake passport wouldn't get her through, that he'd reported her, she shifted in her seat. No noise. Startled, she shifted again. No noise, no crumple of notes and American Express, no prods from the corners of cards in her girdle.

It was all gone.

The word was out of her mouth before she caught herself, "COCKSUCKER!"

"*Ma'am?*" The fat woman pushing the chair had heard her, Miss Hartly could hear the delight and disbelief in her voice.

Miss Hartly covered her mouth with her handbag, "A stroke." She said. "I … had one … before."

"Oh." The fat woman was laughing at her. She could feel the aftershocks rippling through her massive fucking body like the aftershock from an earthquake.

Bunch of cocksuckers.

SOMETIMES YOU CAN'T RETIRE

BY MARCIA MULLER

SOME MORNINGS I feel every one of my 102 years. Actually I'm only seventy-two, but my life, it's been rough.

Thing is, you never know what to expect. Comes up, blindsides you. Of course, I should've realized that. But I didn't, oh, no.

I wanted to be of help. Wanted to ease them out of their pain. Ease out the others who were causing their pain. Damn, though, it wasn't pleasant work. It took too much out of me. I decided to stop, and I did. You can't save everybody no matter how much you want to.

There are some things you just can't retire from.

BOSTON, MASSACHUSETTS—A long time ago.

Woman on Charles Street. Furs wrapped around her neck like they were clinging there for their lives—only they were dead, stone dead. She had a fat, smug face, too much makeup for somebody her age. Sixty, seventy—does it matter? Little yappy dog on a leash—shit-zoo, one of those silly breeds. Its little legs were working hard, but not fast enough to keep up with her. She jerked on its lead till it near choked.

The sidewalk was crowded with people stopped at a crosswalk. When the light was about to change, the woman lurched forward in front of a bus. After her body was removed, the ASPCA came for the dog.

HOUSTON, SUFFOCATING HEAT and humidity.

The brown Labrador—dragged by an impatient, Spandex-clad male jogger—was breathing hard, heaving. They paused at an intersection near Rice University, the jogger bouncing from foot to foot and making the dog's head bob. Then the jogger stumbled out into traffic. Brakes screeched and there was the sound of something being smashed like a Halloween pumpkin.

SOMETIMES YOU CAN'T RETIRE

VENICE BEACH, CALIFORNIA.

The standard poodle was being run too hard by the guy on Rollerblades. Drool dripping off its jowls and a dazed, coated look in its eyes. The guy didn't notice, just kept zipping along, dodging pedestrians, other skaters, and tourists. As dusk was setting in, he veered off into a video store, came out with a plastic bag, and tugged the animal toward an alleyway.

Venice Beach is not a very safe place at night. Gang violence claims many.

SO NOW YOU'RE wondering what happened to the canine victims. Well, they're safe now. I made sure of that.

The shit-zoo got adopted before I had time to go to the animal shelter. A good thing, too, I can't stand that yapping. My work as a structural engineer took me from Boston to Houston, where I acquired Sam the Labrador. It was a few years later, after I'd moved to LA, That I rescued the spaniel, Delia, from a pet adoption agency.

Now I'm retired, live in Los Alegres, California, a small town in the Sonoma County wine country. I've had other pets along the way: An abused German Shepherd. Three cats whose owner was caught dropping them off in a Dumpster just hours after their birth on a 102-degree day. A parrot that was clinging to the inside of a screen door of a house in West LA, screaming "Help me, help me!" More dogs, more cats, even a rabbit—all of them needing good homes.

Mr. Bleeding Heart they call me.

Life here in Los Alegres is pleasant. People are friendly, but pretty much mind their own business. The streets are tree-lined, the homes well kept, the gardens tended. There're a couple of good dog parks, and my vet gives me a discount because I've got nearly a dozen animals—mostly cats, a couple of dogs, the parrot, two white rats, and Ambrose the Snake. Ambrose is gentle, but the mailman sure gets shook up when he slithers up the window screen and looks out. I even have a girlfriend, Marilyn, who works at the animal shelter and alerts me when a promising adoptee comes in.

One day in September Marilyn came over as she often does after work. She looked troubled.

"Charley, you hear what Supervisor Lambruschi is up to now?"

"No good, I assume."

Marilyn unwound her scarf and dropped it, then her coat, on my couch. Scout, the yellow cat, immediately went and sat on them. Marilyn is a hefty woman, with long gray-blonde hair, plain but goodhearted. She bent down to pat Godwin, a terrier, and her sweat pants strained at the seams. Doesn't matter; I like them with some meat on their bones.

"Charley," she said, "Lambruschi is trying to enforce the three-pets-per-home ordinance."

Leo Lambruschi. My next-door neighbor. New to the city council this year. He'd also—so far unsuccessfully—tried to get the council to approve a ruling changing the animal shelter's policy from no-kill to euthanizing after thirty days.

This latest action was aimed directly at me.

"If he's successful, you'll have to move out of the city," Marilyn added.

I considered that. A place in the unincorporated country outside of town sounded good to me, but no way could I afford the inflated prices, even with what my paid-for 1930s bungalow would bring. I could buy in one of the less expensive and less populated northern California counties but, dammit, Los Alegres was home. I'd moved around enough in my time. No more.

Leo Lambruschi …

He was a mean, petty little man who wore his city council membership like the mantle of some king. He hadn't tried to poison my pets or trash my yard or beat me up. In fact, he struck me as a physical coward. But I hadn't counted on him burning the midnight oil while poring over obscure city statutes.

Leo had a handsome collie, Jewel, and took her everywhere with him. I mean, everywhere. Work, shopping, jogging, the post office; in cold weather he even sat in the outdoor section of our local pub, where dogs are allowed. But there was a downside to the owner-pet relationship: Leo drank, and he was an angry drinker. Sometimes in the night I would hear Jewel crying as if afraid.

Leo and Jewel would set out for his insurance agency at eight o'clock sharp every morning. By that time I'd let my golden retriever, Bella, into the yard, and when they went past she'd go off: barking, leaping at the fence, snarling. Bella's normally a docile animal, but there was something about that collie. Or Leo.

Jewel would cringe and cower, and Leo would stare, first at Bella and then at my house, his dark eyes burning with little pinpricks of rage. He started leaving notes on my gate.

"Curb your dog." Ridiculous; she was in her own yard.

"Keep that damn dog in the house!" Well, no, I wasn't about to do that. She's a big dog, needs room to stretch her legs.

"If you don't shut that dog up, I'll call the cops about the noise." Yes, our city does have an ordinance about barking dogs, but apart from when Leo and Jewel walked by, Bella hardly uttered a sound.

Did I say people mind their own business here? Well, most of them do, but one day I'd come home from the grocery store and found Leo snooping around my front porch, peering through the living room window. I kind of sneaked up on him, but that wasn't what made him rear back. No, it was Ambrose. He was sunning himself on the window seat along with two of my cats and when Leo peered inside, Ambrose slithered up against the glass to see who this might be.

Leo kept backpedaling and smacked into me. I dropped my grocery bag, it split, and cat- and dog-food cans, fish flakes, and bird seed spilled onto the porch. Leo whirled, stared at me, then looked down at his feet. When he raised his eyes to mine, they were knowing and accusing.

"Charley," he said, "how many damn animals you got in there?"

I didn't answer. Tell the truth, I was trying to calculate.

"That snake. Fish, apparently. Those cats. That dog."

"Two dogs," I corrected.

"Anything else?"

"A parrot and—"

At that moment Miles the Parrot started yelling "Help me, help me!"

"I'll help you," Leo muttered. "I'll help you all right out of here."

LOS ALEGRES IS a former farming community. Still plenty of agriculture on the flatlands to the east, although a lot of acreage has been developed into shopping centers and tract houses. Every year some silly bastard who bought a home overlooking a plowed field writes a letter to the editor complaining about the "awful" fertilizer smell and asking why the city "doesn't tell them not to do that." Like people who buy a house directly under the flight path of the local airport and then want the planes to stop flying over.

I live on the west side, but animals are plentiful here—and welcome. A neighbor up the hill from me keeps two fat sheep. He's partially disabled and can't cut his lawn, but they do a fine job. Another neighbor keeps chickens and hand delivers a basket of fresh eggs every week or so. At the top of the hill, horses graze, and I can hear cows bellow and goats bleat not far away.

So why, in 1980, did the city council enact a dumb-ass law about allowing only three pets per household?

Well, with all the new development, they were trying to go upscale, like the cities down in Marin. Reaching for a new image. But the sheep and chickens and horses and cows and goats were grandfathered in—meaning you can't kick 'em out if they're already there. And if a sheep dies and you replace it with another, who can tell the difference? We've got some of the oldest livestock in the world here in Los Alegres.

Leo's challenge to my owning all these animals was as petty and mean as he himself.

A week after Marilyn told me what Leo was up to, an order came from the city to find new homes for all of my animals except three. But they were my family—the only one I'd ever really had. Sweetheart the Rat was old and arthritic; nobody would want her, and the shelter would euthanize her. Leo'd see to that. The cats—people favor kittens over adult cats. Miles was too loud and sometimes crapped on the floor when outside the confines of his cage. Ambrose was … well, creepy to most people.

There was a hearing. Leo self-assured and condemnatory. Me nervous, trying to plead my case in stammering sentences. The judge took pity on me, gave me ninety days to find new homes—for my animals or all of us together.

The day the ultimatum came down, Marilyn provided a solution. "I've got an idea, Charley—you and I could move to my ranch."

Marilyn had inherited a small dairy ranch in the countryside to the west of town from her father. The cows had been sold, and the property was just sitting there, vacant. It would be an ideal place for pets, but …

"I don't know," I said. "I've always lived alone, except for my animals."

"It's a big house, and I work long hours. You'd be alone as much as you want."

It sounded like a plan, so I told Marilyn to start packing, and I put some things in boxes myself. But before I went anywhere, I had to do something about Jewel, the handsome collie who had her special table at the pub. Jewel, who went to work every day. Jewel, who cried at night while Leo drank and raged.

I WAS WAITING at the light at Main and D Street—center of town—all newly redeveloped and shiny, a reflection of what Los Alegres would become, no stopping progress. Cars, trucks, buses speeding by, going too fast as usual.

In front of me Leo, with Jewel on her lead, bounced on the curb, impatient to get on with his run. I'd staked out this intersection for two weeks, I knew the traffic patterns.

And soon it happened: the red Corvette, its driver seeing the amber light and speeding up to get through before it turned.

A shove, so slight that no one in the knot of pedestrians noticed it.

Leo stumbled forward in front of the Corvette.

I grasped Jewel's leash to prevent her from running off. She shivered and leaned into me as we moved through the excited crowd. But she'd be all right once she joined my other liberated animals.

Like I said before, some things you just can't retire from.

THE INVESTOR

BY GARY PHILLIPS

THE THREE WALKED through the refrigerated rear section of Limoli's Quality Cuts, passing hung sides of beef and pork. Past the carcasses, Jill McCory turned her head at the whine of a band saw. One of the butchers was cutting into a slab to make individual ribs for barbecuing. She grinned weakly at her boyfriend, Reny Paulski, and he squeezed her hand for reassurance. Tal Shanko, the third member of the trio who walked behind the other two, continued to scan the surroundings, his face impassive. They cleared the work area and to their right was a set of swing doors with smeared windows they went through.

"What can I get you guys?" the pleasant and pretty twenty-something woman who greeted them asked. She was dressed in low-rise, hip-hugger jeans and a lightweight sweater top with a modest neckline. She was fit, no muffin effect of fat flopping over her pants' waistline. It was warm in this part of the shop. Seen through her tangle of dark brown hair, one of her ears had several silver studs of differing styles.

"Nothing, we're fine," McCory said.

"I'd like coffee if you have it," Shanko countered. "Black, please."

McCory turned in profile to show him her annoyance. Paulski worked his jaw muscles but remained silent.

"Sure," their greeter said. "Right this way." She turned and walked to a closed unmarked grey-colored door she opened and said, "They're here," to the two men sitting inside the office. She stepped aside and the trio entered.

The inauspicious office was of the home improvement store wood-panel variety complete with framed reproductions of race horses and a LeRoy Neiman print of the Foreman-Frazier fight in Kingston, Jamaica, in 1973. There was also a flat screen TV mounted on a wall.

Joe Gentenilli sat behind the sole desk in the room, and he looked from the man sitting across from him, Rafe Barata, to the three who stood. His eyes momentarily rested on Shanko as he noted the other man regarding the Neiman work.

"You into boxing?" Gentenilli asked.

"I like it fine," Shanko said flatly. The young woman returned with the coffee in a Styrofoam cup and handed it to him. "Thanks." He took a sip and looked at McCory, who they'd agreed would lead the negotiation. Given there were only two chairs in the room, and those seats were occupied, it didn't seem to him the two others in the room expected a meeting of give-and-take. He was right.

"Mr. Gentenilli," McCory began. "We want to work out an understanding on this biodiesel matter. It's not now or in the future our intent to cut into your rendering business." She smiled thinly, making a gesture with her hand. "There's plenty of grease for everybody."

"That some kind of ethnic slur?" Barata cracked, pointing at her. He had a diamond ring on his little finger and another gaudy ring on the finger next to it. There was a heavy gold link bracelet around his thick wrist.

McCory frowned. "Of course not."

"Just funnin' you, girly," Barata chuckled. He was a heavyset man in his fifties and he shifted his bulk in the over-sized chair. It creaked.

Paulski touched McCory's arm, a signal for her not to react to the remark. He said, "Okay, we came here at your invitation to work this out, not get into trading barbs."

"Then how do we keep you off the street?" Gentenilli said in an even tone.

"What?" McCory said.

Gentenilli went on, "You started out a couple of years ago collecting grease, for free, I note, from the shops not in our association. Doughnut and fast food chains around here," he tapped his index finger on the desk.

"We get our used grease from all over," Paulski corrected. "Even over in New Hampshire."

"Whatever," Gentenilli said with a curt chop of his hand through the air. "The fact remains you were, but it was just converting the stuff for your own use in your cars. Fine. But now all of a sudden you got people talking about manufacturing biodiesel."

"You're not," Shanko pointed out.

"Who are you?" Barata said, moving his heft around again, aiming his jowls at the interloper.

Shanko said, "An investor." He had more of his coffee. He liked the brew. It was good coffee.

"That's what I'm talking about," Gentenilli said. "Now you're making some kind of Mother Earth friendly heating furnace, that it?"

"Yes," McCory said. "We're concerned about the environment."

"We're concerned about our environment too," Sabarge quipped. "Our economic one, understand?"

"I'm not following you," McCory said. "Ultimately what we're doing is going to be good for your business and our business. On average something like two point four million gallons of fuel oil are consumed each winter in the New England area. You have contracts to collect the grease and you turn around and sell what you render. We're trying to make and market a new type of furnace that can utilize a heating oil with a greater percentage of biodiesel content. The thing is, traditional furnaces aren't designed to handle that kind of fuel."

"Fact is we're creating a market," Paulski added.

"See, that's the problem," Gentenilli said, glancing at Barata. "We're forward thinkers too."

"Exactly," Barata echoed.

Paulski made a face. "You're going to make furnaces?"

Gentenilli looked aghast at such a prospect. "Hell no."

"They're setting a bad example, that it?" Shanko said.

"You're who again?" Barata challenged. McCory and Paulski were in their early thirties, Barata and Gentenilli in their fifties. It was hard to tell about the compact, loose-limbed Shanko. His grey-white hair was brush cut precise, his boots scuffed and weathered. He could have been forty-five or he could have been sixty and then some.

His expression remained staid, and he didn't respond as he enjoyed more of his coffee.

"My father and Tal were," Paulski began.

"Friends," Shanko finished.

"Listen, we don't have a problem with you three being jolly green or whatever the hell you call it," Gentenilli said, leaning forward. "But for all concerned, it would probably be better if you maybe saved the trees some other way."

Paulski and McCory exchanged glances. "You can't threaten us," she said.

"I didn't hear no threats," Barata said as if testifying on the stand. "Who the fuck is threatening?"

"This is simply a conversation about business," Gentenilli added. "Colleagues, I note."

"Well, we're not doing anything wrong or interfering with you," McCory said.

Gentenilli looked at her blandly. "Appreciate you coming," he said.

McCory started to respond but Shanko cut her off. "Thanks for the coffee." He walked over to the desk. Though there was a wastebasket next to it, he placed his empty cup on the desk. Gentenilli and Barata glared at him. Shanko turned and walked back to the younger couple.

"Let's go," Shanko advised. The three departed the Quality Cuts office.

"So what the hell was that all about?" Paulski asked when they were walking to their van parked on a pay lot. Painted on its side in stylish letters were the words, "Maple Leaf Furnace Factory."' Leaning on the "Y" was an anthropomorphic smiling turtle holding a wrench resting on the shoulder area of its shell. They got in the Toyota van and drove away.

McCory nodded toward Shanko. "What Tal said. The way they see it, if we're successful then others might be inspired or to use the mainstream framework, imitate us."

"So?" Paulski said.

"We're collecting the grease for free, Reny," McCory said.

Paulski came to a red light. The French-fry smell from the converted van's tailpipe tantalized pedestrians in the crosswalk as they passed by the vehicle. "Oh, right," he muttered. Across from them was the partially finished shell of a mixed-use development in what had been redubbed the Newmarket District by the tony crowd, but was still called the Meat Market by old schoolers and the boyos in Boston.

Paulski continued when the light changed and he drove forward. "They get a certain price for the rendered grease and want it to stay that way. More green tech means less demand for their services and their product."

"Yes," McCory agreed. She glanced back at Shanko. "But we're the small dogs when it comes to WVO." She used the shorthand for waste vegetable oil as this was how the used oil was referred to by the enviros. She and Paulski had rehearsed not to use jargon at the meet.

"They reached out," Shanko noted. "They wanted to send a message."

Paulski said, "Going green is getting co-opted like everything else in this country, Tal. These old-time castoffs from bad mafia movies can't hold that back. Gangster capitalism is always absorbed into white collar capitalism."

"Usually not without casualties," Shanko observed quietly.

McCory grimaced.

THE FOLLOWING WEEK Lilly Densmore, who attended MIT studying mechanical engineering and worked part-time at the Maple Leaf Furnace Factory, was driving in Somerville after making a repair call. She'd driven out in the company van to recalibrate a dual set of their furnaces installed in a lamp and lamp parts supply warehouse. She was listening to a Massive Attack CD when she turned off Middlesex Avenue heading back to the shop and slammed on her brakes. A red child's wagon suddenly rolled into the roadway in front of her. The car behind her also had to brake hard and slammed into the van's rear bumper. A toolbox flopped over and noisily spilled its contents.

"Aw, shit," Densmore swore. She looked back and then got out of the van. The other driver was out too.

"What the hell, huh?" the other driver, a tallish man in shirt and tie, said. He still felt the warmth of his Benz's heated interior even though the temperature was in the mid twenties.

"It wasn't me," Densmore said, pointing toward the front of the van. She looked around for kids playing but didn't see any. She walked over to the wagon and her eyes got wide. She said "Shit" again.

In the bed of the wagon was a large turtle on its back with a hunting knife plunged through its underside.

TWO WEEKS AFTER this incident the Maple Leaf Furnace Factory, a former bicycle sales and repair converted storefront near Cambridge Square, was firebombed. Two potential customers, a lesbian couple who owned and operated a sandwich shop, were being shown the company's new industrial furnace. A man in a winter coat and gloves entered. He was a bland looking individual with thinning brown-blond hair and glasses.

"Be right with you," McCory said to him, talking to the sandwich shop owners. She was the only staffer there.

The man shouted, "Take the hint, cunt." He took his gloved hand out of his pocket and threw a grenade-shaped device onto the floor. This exploded in sparks and flame as he ran out. McCory, fearful the heat would ignite the biodiesel fuel in its metal drums in the rear equipment and processing area of the shop, dashed for the fire extinguisher.

One of the other women, who'd been taking Muay Thai, mixed martial arts lessons, ran after the arsonist. She didn't get a chance to test her skill but did get a partial plate number as he left in a new dark-red Cadillac CTS coupe driven by another man.

Inside the shop, McCory got the fire out before the fuel went up. Later, after the fire department had come and gone and there was a conversation with the insurance carrier, she and Reny Paulski talked matters over at their apartment. They sat at their kitchenette table.

"Aren't we being hypocrites, Jill?" Paulski rubbed his jaw with a calloused palm.

"'Cause we're tree huggers we're just supposed to pucker up and take it?"

"I'm just sayin'." He smiled weakly.

She put a hand on his. "I know."

Though hesitant to do so, the couple decided to called Tal Shanko, the major investor in the Maple Leaf Furnace Factory.

"THE FUCK IS this?" Robert "Squid" Sparda mumbled when he came out of the Pink Slipper strip club on Bower Road in Quincy. He'd gotten a blow job in the VIP Room so was in good humor. Now propped on the windshield of his dark-red Cadillac CTS coupe was a teddy bear. Had one of the girls in the club left it? He picked it up and could see a note card attached to the stuffed animal. Curious, he read it.

"I got this for you to snuggle with, faggot. Leave the kids alone."

Shaking the teddy bear in his hand, wondering what hump would have the nerve to have left this, he then noticed his four tires were slit. Roiling inside, cold air hissing from his flaring nostrils, Squid Sparda twisted the bear's head off. The thing exploded with a flash and a bang, temporarily blinding him. The stuffed toy also released a dye pack like what was used by banks to booby-trap their canvas money bags. Purple ink was sprayed on his face and expensive camel hair coat, ruining it.

"Motherfucker," Sparda screamed, stomping and groping about on the icy slush coating the parking lot. He lost his footing and went down hard on his backside. He continued to swear and promise reprisals.

"THE GIRL," BARATA was saying, "we don't know much about. Hell, there's a half a dozen McCory's up and down this block. But one of the old soldiers over at the hall told our guy this Paulski is the kid of Mike Paulski from the boilermaker's local.

Gentenilli asked, "Paulski, the father, I mean, he around?"

"Naw, he made enough on the Big Dig to retire, him and the second younger wife, not the kid's mother. Someplace out in California is the way I heard it."

Considering this, Gentenilli sipped his coffee and brandy. Since the exploding teddy bear the day before with Squid Sparda, the Maple Leaf Furnace Factory was closed and secured. The two young proprietors had not been seen around there or at the apartment they shared in Dorchester.

"The tough guy, the one that inked Squid," Barata began, aware of the irony, "we got squat. He ain't from around here but the Paulski kid says he was friends with his dad."

"Yeah." Momentarily Gentenilli worried his bottom lip. "Must be some California connection."

"Must be," Barata agreed. "You want Squid and Dink to make a house call?"

Gentenilli had more of his spiked coffee. "Do that. Mike Paulski needs to be reminded how things work. He can set his kid straight."

Barata nodded quickly and got busy on his cell phone. The chair creaked under him as he moved his bulk.

"PLACE DON'T LOOK like I figured," Squid Sparda remarked, looking out the passenger side of the rented Lexus. The dang Jap car had more leg room than he'd imagined.

"Look at that one," Francis "Dink" Hullson said behind the wheel, nodding in the direction of another McMansion. "Swank," he monotoned, admiring a large home on a small lot that looked to be a mélange of French Chateau and Cape Cod in design. Two Priuses, white and black, sat side by side in the driveway. A bumper sticker on one of the cars read: "Stop the War," though wasn't specific about which one or whose.

"This town wasn't even on the goddamn map we got from the airport," Sparda said. They'd flown into San Francisco International and knew from the internet to drive to Redding. From there they got directions at a café to Northpitch, some seventy miles to the west of Redding. "But it looks like they got money around here. "Is this where actors or those computer fucks are moving to or something like that?"

Dink Hullson, more contemplative than his fellow soldier Sparda, said, "I don't think that's it."

"Well, it's something." He looked at the paper again, the one with the address they'd obtained from their guy at the union with Mike Paulski's address on it. This was where he received his pension checks. He pointed, "Here's the street." Hullson made a right and the two found themselves on a cul-de-sac. At its end was a modest abode, at least compared to the other houses they'd seen. There was a worn pickup truck parked in front.

Hullson parked the rental in the empty driveway and the two got out and walked to the front door. Sparda knocked. He'd used various face creams and astringents and had managed to fade the dye splotch on his face and neck. But there was still enough color on his skin that it looked like a runaway birthmark.

At first there was no answer and he knocked again. A male voice from inside said, "Come on in."

Sparda grinned wolfishly at Hullson and entered the house. The aluminum bat swung by Tal Shanko went right across Sparda's chest, knocking the wide-eyed hoodlum back. Before he could recover, Shanko stepped forward from where he'd positioned himself beside the doorway. He whacked the end of the bat on the side of Sparda's jaw, cracking the bone in two places.

"Christ," Sparda exclaimed as he went sideways, stumbling into and upsetting a stand with a vase of freshly cut fire witch and sunflowers in it.

Dink Hullson had stepped back out of the way and now had his gun in hand. He shot twice at Shanko who, upon seeing he hadn't knocked Sparda into him as he'd intended, had run and dived through an interior open doorway.

"Get up," Hullson blared, reaching his free hand out and helping Sparda to his feet.

"Cocksucker," Sparda said, putting a shaking hand to his damaged jaw.

"Worry about that later," Hullson advised, already heading the way Shanko had gone. "We gotta get this civilian."

Sparda followed and the two went through a study outfitted in the latest in home entertainment gadgets, including a video game paused on the flat screen TV. A lone controller rested on the coffee table before the screen. The game was something about knights and fire-breathing dragons, they noted absently.

The two soldiers went through a large kitchen with an island to spot an open back door. This let them out onto a deck containing a built-in barbecue grill and uncovered hot tub. There was also a small guesthouse in the far end of the green thick yard, bordered by a cinder block wall.

"Where is that bastard?" Sparda had his gun out as well. The anticipation of inflicting painful revenge on his attacker ameliorated his own agony.

Hullson made his way toward the guesthouse. Sparda fell in beside him. Behind them was a splash and they both turned toward the hot tub but saw no one in the water. In contrast to back east, the temperature was in the high seventies. They eased closer, the idea having come to them that maybe Mr. Baseball was hiding under the water. Closer, they saw several avocados floating in the hot tub. They looked up to the leafy braches of an avocado tree overhanging from another yard.

"Fucking Californians and their goddamn vegetables," Sparda said, talking causing him to wince.

Hullson didn't correct him that avocados were considered a fruit. As one they turned and rushed to the guesthouse, using their shoulders and body weight to crash through the lightweight door. They could see where Shanko had gone through a rear sliding glass window over the bed. He'd moved the bed aside and had climbed on a chair to reach the opening.

"Fucking guy," Sparda muttered between tight lips. One side of his face was swelling.

On the chair looking out, Hullson saw that the guesthouse butted against a portion of the back wall. Beyond was an open field where several abandoned and rusted hulks of farm machinery resided. Oddly the grassy field was tended and not overgrown though it seemed the useless equipment had been purposely left in place. To his left heading for a stand of trees, he spotted Shanko's retreating form. He ran at a steady clip. Hullson described what he'd seen to Sparda as they exited the guesthouse.

"He's like sixty or something isn't he?" Sparda remarked as they saw a way to the field between the houses once they were out in front. "Probably eats that damn tofu and shit," he said derisively. "Motherfuckin' rabbit."

Hullson wondered what else they didn't know about this Shanko but kept it to himself. They took off for the field on foot. There was no way to take the car in there as it was hemmed in mostly by low mountains.

"At least it isn't snowing like back home," Sparda whispered as the two entered the leafy area. He could barely open his mouth over clenched teeth. Where they were wasn't so much a forest as it was trees sparsely separated and a lot of brush. There was a distinct aroma in the air.

"Hey, that's weed," Sparda declared quietly.

"That's what it is about this town," Hullson said in a low voice. "All those damn new big houses around here."

Sparda snickered then grimaced due to his jaw. "Everybody's in pocket around here."

Hullson glanced sideways at his partner. "That's what I'm worried about."

The two continued their search heading in a direction toward the mountains. The smell of flowering pot plants intensified. Walking several paces apart, Hullson paused at a sound to his flank. He held up a hand and pointed for Sparda's benefit. They went through the undergrowth and came to a series of razor wire fencing enclosing a cultivated field of crops neither foot soldier could identify. Though they knew the squat plantings weren't marijuana.

Suddenly a German shepherd appeared on that side of the fence, barking at them.

Sparda stuck his gun out at the dog. "Shut the hell up," he lisped.

His footfalls on the dry fallen leaves and brush masked by the barking dog, Shanko came within the orbit of the two men quickly. He brought the bat down full force on Sparda's gun arm. Shanko broke his wrist and Sparda yelped as he let go of his piece. Hullson was about to shoot him but Shanko had pulled free the mouth of a soaked paper bag tucked under his belt.

He threw it underhanded smack into the gunman's face. Hullson shot his gun but his vision was blocked and he missed the fleeing Shanko as he gagged. There was cow droppings in the burst bag, and some of the waste had gone into his mouth. The logo of a fast food outlet was on the paper bag.

Sparda held his damaged wrist as Hullson spat and wiped at his mouth using tufts of grass he plucked from the ground. "I'm going to kill that comedian," he grumbled.

Squid Sparda picked up his gun with his left hand. If he didn't hurt so much, he would have laughed at Hullson. Instead he asked, "Now where?"

The dog sat on its haunches looking quizzically at them, then got up and trotted away.

"Anywhere," Hullson angrily replied, still wiping at himself. He went in a direction and Sparda joined him. They weren't in control, clearly on someone else's playground and the unease of the situation bothered both men. A moroseness descended on them. Sparda was used to Hullson being dour, but he found it a gigantic drag.

"Maybe we should hole up, get ourselves cleaned up and what have you and call in reinforcements. We got friends in the Bay Area."

Hullson put glittering eyes on him. "No goddamn old hippie is gonna get the best of me." He stomped forward. Back in deep brush again, the two heard the whine of an engine but then it cut off.

"Was that a motorcycle?" Sparda muttered.

Hullson kept quiet and alert. They came out of the brush and into a clearing. Around them were the stumps of cut trees and the smell of fresh wood permeated the air stronger than the essence of pot plants. The two gaped at the structure before them. It was as if they'd stepped onto a new Las Vegas themed destination.

"That's the Raj Hall," Sparda said.

"Taj Mahal," Hullson corrected.

"Yeah, like the one in Atlantic City."

Hullson, splattered feces drying on his face and sport coat, glared at Sparda. "That's a casino with a few minarets in front. This looks like the one from the pictures."

Before them was a modified replica, down to the reflecting pool leading to it, of the famed seventeenth-century architecturally arresting mausoleum in Agra, India. The building before them was four stories high. There was scaffolding framing the central structure, and several ATVs and pickups were parked about the area. Nearby the two could see several cottages mirroring the main building's style with other sections marked off in the dirt with wooden stakes and twine.

"Some kind of resort," Hullson guessed.

No workers could be seen or heard. The nearly finished faux Taj Mahal and the stonework bordering the reflecting pool gleamed bright white in the sunlight. This copy with its dome minarets and wall engravings was concrete and stucco rather than the marble of the original.

"I don't like this," Sparda said. Everything on him ached and he wanted a drink.

"Too late now," Hullson said, heading toward the front.

Standing at the entrance before a set of carved double doors, Sparda wondered, "Maybe we're supposed to say open sesame."

Hullson snorted then looked wide-eyed when the doors swung inward. He and Sparda raised their guns on Tal Shanko standing in the darkened interior, his hands on the door handles.

His composed features gave them pause. Shanko smiled crookedly. The two representatives from Boston looked around at the sound of splashing, like at the hot tub. Only this time it was not an innocuous occurrence. Emerging from hiding in the reflecting pool were three individuals, two men and one woman. They wore snorkeling masks and breathing tubes, and aimed assault rifles at the two North Shore mob emissaries.

"Fuck me," Sparda managed, his jaw so swollen, one of his eyes was shut.

"I WANT IT categorically understood I'm not happy with this."

"I know, Joe," Vincent "Swan" Argostino said. He broke off a piece of one of the chocolate chip cookies on the saucer and chewed it slowly, contemplatively. "But this decision is bigger than you or me." He sipped some of his espresso. The two sat at a small table in the Golden Strike Bowling Supply and Trophy concern in Charlestown.

"What kind of message are we sending here?" Gentenilli said.

"That we're not about to commit time and resources over bullshit." He had another bite of his cookie.

"I'm just sayin', is all."

"Look, weed is a money maker." He pointed out beyond the walls. We don't grow it, but every damn mook under forty around here smokes it, plus you got the aging whatchucall baby boomers toking too. All through the New England area.

"I don't need to remind you," he added, breaking off more cookie, "it's not an enterprise we get any action off of. Yet."

"That mean getting in bed with Shanko? He's reached out, hasn't he?" Gentenilli said.

"It means since the FBI patted themselves on the back for running that scumbag snitch Whitey Bulger out of town, we've been sitting sweet. We don't need the DEA or any other government alphabet running around sniffing up our asses."

Gentenilli wasn't quite sure how to interpret that, but he was clear he was to lay off the little shits of the Maple Leaf Furnace Factory. He'd also been informed that Tal Shanko was a player among the pot growers of the so-called Emerald Triangle, the area encompassing parts of Humboldt and Mendocino Counties of Northern California. Marijuana was a business earning millions. And the man sitting across from him, Swan Argostino, was an underboss who liked earners—and the potential therein to earn.

"I suppose then I gotta accept this … peace," Gentenilli relented. "Dink is, well, Dink. But Squid, you know."

"He's not to be a problem," Argostino declared.

Gentenilli spread his hands. "He won't be."

Argostino finished his espresso. Gentenilli left. A sudden shift in the wind made him look around quickly as he stepped to his car. A hint of burning marijuana had come and gone and made him leery. The other thing he'd learned about Shanko was he'd been in Vietnam, one of these crazy bastards they called tunnel rats. Soldiers sent down into smelly and scary Viet Cong tunnels after Army engineers blasted them out—their thankless tasks to clear them out. Never knowing when a spike was going to spear you in the eye or get gut shot in that crawl space, bleeding out while Charlie hacked your balls off for fun.

Fuck, Gentenilli reflected. Shit like that did something to your outlook. Mike Paulski had been in 'Nam too, though just a grunt. But that's where he'd met Tal Shanko. They'd been in the same platoon it turned out.

Frowning about Shanko, about how he could have killed his soldiers but didn't so as not to escalate the situation but made it plain he could have, got Gentenilli muttering.

"I note this fucking guy is going to be a real pain one day." He drove away, a light flurry starting up, dusting his car pristine white.

BILL IN IDAHO

BY SCOTT PHILLIPS

I HAD ORIGINALLY considered my young assistant to be a species of imbecile, and hired him out of pity because in that day and age, since the arrival of the dry plate, the duties of a photographer's assistant didn't demand much in the way of brainpower. In the course of time he revealed himself to be a relatively bright lad, however, and a decent photographer in his own right. It was his look that gave the impression of intellectual debility: a tendency to breathe through his nose combined with frequent lapses into daydreaming, which taken together gave him the look of someone trying hard to remember how much a whole bunch of nines was.

His name was Jimmie, and I never knew why he stayed in Bainer, as there were so few women a poor boy like he had no hope of finding a wife, which was what he wanted, by his own admission, more than anything else in the world. My own wife had recently left me to go live in Kansas with our son; she had been crankier and crankier about the rustic quality of Idaho living over the past three years, and when the first cold snap hit at the end of August she packed her trunk and left. "I suppose you've heard that great swaths of this country have been settled and civilized by now," she said before leaving, but she didn't try to convince me to leave with her. There was no mention made of divorce, this being by my count the sixth time she'd left me over the years, and in any case we hadn't ever bothered to get married, my marital status and hers having both been complicated since our meeting thirty-five years ago.

A COUPLE OF months hence, on a cold bright day in November, poor Nettie Oliver, née Cass, crossed the studio's threshold looking ragged and drunk. "Howdy do, Bill" she said, the boy staring at her as if at a ghost.

"Hello, Nettie. It's been a little while." It had been six or eight months, though by appearances it might have been ten or fifteen years. She'd lost a couple of teeth on top, an incisor and a premolar, and one of her eyelids had taken on a droop I didn't remember from before. Her smile was lopsided in a way that suggested injury rather than coquetry or wit, and there was no sign of the child who was shortly due at our last meeting.

"I was just wondering if you might help a lady out of a fix."

I fished four silver dollars out of my trouser pocket and placed them in her outstretched palm. "What happened to Mr. Oliver?" I asked. This would be Lester Oliver, a chief compressor operator at the Lucky Seven silver mine; having taken a special interest in Nettie some time before, he'd married her in the fall of '07 and shortly thereafter decided he couldn't continue to live in a town where his wife had been known as a working girl, and so he arranged for a job in Butte for less money and a lesser title. Nettie was delighted to be leaving Bainer, Idaho, behind, and though she promised to write and send pictures of the child once it arrived we all suspected we'd heard the last of her.

"Mr. Oliver don't claim me no more."

I didn't ask about the child. "Have you arranged a place to stay?"

"Looks like it'll be the bawdy house again."

Young Jimmie's eyes looked fit to burst from their orbits. He had come here from a town of Mormons near the Montana border and was still easily shocked, or as in this instance, titillated; I suppose at heart there's not much difference between one and the other.

I nodded and tried to muster an encouraging smile. There'd be few takers for her in this state, and Mrs. Corbin at the Paris wouldn't likely take her back on. That left the Royal Crown two doors down, a lesser establishment that catered to a rougher and less exacting clientele, and where the turnover rate was determined more often by mortality than by opportunities for betterment.

When she was gone I sent the boy into the darkroom and went down the street to the barber shop for a bath. I had lately become the subject of a certain amount of good-natured fun in the shop for my eccentric habit of bathing every other day or so. Before my wife's departure we had a house with running water and it was no one's business how clean I was, or how filthy, but with her gone I no longer required as much space, and I broke the lease and began sleeping in a small room above my shop, taking my meals in the Excelsior restaurant around the corner.

Marty Conlon greeted me on my arrival, his face white with lather, and Bert Naymon, the barber, grunted and jerked his head toward the washroom in back.

"Nettie's back," I said, knowing her to have been a favorite of Conlon's.

"Is she now?" he said.

"You keep talking while I'm trying to shave you," Bert said, "you're going to end up with your jugular spraying the room red and me springing for your funeral."

"She's not with Oliver any more."

"That no-account, he didn't deserve her. Not a lick of it."

I couldn't disagree. Oliver was a blusterer and a heavy drinker who had taken a lively dislike to me when he saw that I was friendly with Nettie, dating back to an earlier departure by my wife that had lasted all of six months. Mistaking my cordiality for a lingering erotic interest he forbade her to speak to me, and when they wed there was no photographer to record the ceremony.

While I bathed I thought not of Nettie but of my reason for bathing: a pending rendezvous with a lovely, forty-seven-year-old widow named Mrs. Hinds, whose erotic interests were varied and enthusiastic to a degree that might have been considered pathological by one of the European alienists currently coming into intellectual vogue. For my part I found her perfectly sound of mind, the only spot on her rationality being her choice of a grizzled old goat of sixty-three as her backdoor swain. This was a Thursday, the night she dismissed her servants early to permit my undetected entry into the premises, and since I had only one opportunity per week to slake my thirst I tended to stay up all night long, waiting for her to think of something she hadn't tried yet and might enjoy.

WHEN I WAS clean and dry I walked down to the Excelsior and ordered a plate of roast chicken accompanied by a cup of coffee. I finished the coffee before the meal arrived and ordered a second, an amount sufficient to keep my senses sharp for the evening but low enough that its diuretic effect need not spark the sort of rivalry between bladder and prostate that I knew from experience could complicate an amorous encounter.

The chicken was scrawny but well-seasoned, and before I was finished Wally Finn stepped through the front door and took a table without waiting for the overburdened waitress to seat him. Finn was the managing engineer of the Apex silver mine and had in that capacity supervised Lester Oliver, so when I finished my meal I approached him and mentioned that Nettie was back, and wondered aloud whether Oliver might not follow her back from Butte.

Finn was by then well into a plate of bleeding roast beef, and as he spoke he chewed, holding his fork and knife pointed upwards as if to ward off an attack, the white linen napkin stuffed into his shirt collar stained pink. "What I heard was, he left Butte a while back. Thought the men at the mine were looking sideways at the wife, got it into his head they all knew she'd whored here in Bainer. Took her away after a month or so, this is the first news I've had of either one of them."

"Did you hear whether the baby was born in Butte or not?"

"Don't know one way or the other. Don't much care either. Man was a good enough on the compressor but he kept getting persnickettier all the time. She's more'n likely better off away from him."

THAT NIGHT AS I lay sated beneath Mrs. Hinds's bedclothes I mused on the fate of Nettie's child. My hostess was sound asleep beside me, exhausted, the clock on the mantel set to chime at four-thirty so as to allow my discreet egress via the kitchen door before the return of the servants at breakfast time, and her occasional contented sighing put me in mind of the sounds babies make in their sleep. What depravities had Oliver committed that would lead Nettie to abandon her child?

Before my departure Mrs. Hinds commented on my pensive demeanor and I explained the situation to her.

"But that's awful. A man who beats a woman will certainly not hesitate to strike a child."

"That's the way of the world as I've observed it."

"Well, you must do something about it. Find out where the man lives."

"I suppose I could try and get Nettie to tell me, but even if she does I can't just go and take the child by force."

"You could do it by stealth. You say the man's a drunkard, why not wait until he's unconscious with drink?"

"It's child stealing, my dear Mrs. Hinds. And what would I do with a child?"

"The child would live with me as my ward and heir. And here's what you'll do: you'll offer the brute money. Two hundred dollars."

"I believe the buying and selling of babies is illegal as well, and in any case I have no reason to think he's become destitute. I doubt very much that your two hundred dollars would induce him to part with the flesh of his flesh."

She was becoming indignant, and annoyed at my intransigence. "All right, Mr. Ogden, offer him one thousand dollars."

I knew when I was beaten, and in any case I needed to be on my way to avoid detection. And next Thursday would roll around in due time, and I did want to be on her good side then.

"All right, Mrs. Hinds, I'll have a talk with Mrs. Oliver about the whereabouts of her husband."

OPTIMIST THAT I am I tried the Paris first. There was a piano player having a hard time learning a rag tune when I sat down with Mrs. Corbin in the parlor for tea. Part of the pianist's problem was that the instrument was sadly out of tune—no piano tuner had passed through in a year or more—but everything else about the Paris was first rate by the standards of the Coeur d'Alenes. Mrs. Corbin shook her head and made a clicking sound with her tongue and palate. "Poor thing looks like she's been in a fight with a bear, doesn't she?"

"She's a mite the worse for wear," I allowed.

"I'd love to help her out but this isn't the rescue mission. I gave her six bits and sent her down to the Royal Crown."

The manager of the Royal Crown was the sort of fellow who gives pimps a bad name. Though emaciated it was easy to see that he had once been a handsome devil, born to lead innocent women astray, his nose aquiline and his jawline strong beneath rheumy yellow eyes. "If you want a piece of ass it's five bucks."

I happened to know that the going rate at the Royal Crown was three, but I didn't press the matter. "I just want to talk to her. Is she here or isn't she?"

"Talking or banging, it's a sawbuck either way."

He was chewing on a toothpick, and I thought for a second about taking it from him and embedding it in his eye. Though thirty years younger than me he was built like a child, scrawny and tubercular, and I took no pride in the thought that I could best him physically. But battering the fool wouldn't help Nettie's situation, nor that of her babe, and so I handed him a half eagle and brushed past him into the musty disgrace of a parlor. It too had a piano, with the keyboard lid propped open to reveal a number of its yellowed faux-ivory inlays broken off to reveal the common, dirty wood beneath.

He led me up the stairs to a dismal hallway and opened the first door on the right to reveal a shapeless woman of indeterminate age, sitting on a bed whose rusted springs creaked to the time of her absent-minded rocking. A creature better suited to a lunatic asylum than a bordello, she took her time in looking up at us, seeming to register only dimly our presence, and she grinned at me and then at her pimp.

"Here you go, champ," the pimp said.

"This isn't her," I said.

"For five dollars you take what I give you," he said.

If I'd been feeling ungallant I would have pointed out that there wasn't a woman in his stable that a sane man would pay five dollars to lay with, but as one of said women was sitting next to us, admittedly either demented or narcotized to the point of imbecility, and I held my counsel. Instead I took him by the throat with my right hand and shoved him against the peeling, browned wallpaper and squeezed until his eyes started getting wet.

"Listen here, you miserable little lunger, I gave you what you asked and I mean to see Mrs. Oliver." I never would have pulled such a stunt over at the Paris, where the bouncer was a good-natured six-foot, three-inch tall Swede and a zealous defender of his mistress's girls. The Royal Crown was a different story, though; this enfeebled scarecrow was what passed for a protector, and the establishment had lost at least five girls since I'd been in Bainer to violent johns. The police handled these cases with indifference, and in one case where the miscreant escaped and made his way to Tacoma, Washington, where it was reported that he was shot by the police there in a scrape following a similar offense.

I let the pimp go and he collapsed to the plain wooden floor coughing and crying, the whore looking on in delight as though at a Punch and Judy show. Clutching at his throat he pointed down the hall.

"Nettie?" I hollered, and a door came open twenty feet down and to my left. Nettie peeked through the crack and at the sight of me opened up.

"Bill, you old dog, come for a taste?" She beamed at me, her sunny demeanor undoubtedly opiate-derived, but it was still good to see her smile. She wasn't much healthier looking than she'd been the day before, but her burdens seemed partially lifted.

"Just came in for a talk," I said.

"That's all right, some do that." She closed the door behind us and sat on the bed. The room was scarcely nicer than the one I'd just left, though perhaps a bit cleaner. Nettie sat down on the bed and patted the spot on the mattress next to her. I sat down and leaned forward, noting the half-empty laudanum bottle on the nightstand.

"Nettie, I'm wondering about your baby."

"Oh, she's with her papa."

"Where about?"

"About the cabin." Her eyes were dilated to near blackness and her expression that of a dreamer. I was loath to disturb her euphoria, since a darkening mood might make her suspicious and stubborn.

"I want to help the baby. There's a wealthy woman here in town, Mrs. Hinds, who'd like to take her on as a ward. She'd live a life of comfort and ease and I'd see to it that you saw her any time you wanted."

Nettie closed her eyes as though imagining it. "Mmm. That sounds just fine, Bill."

"Can you tell me how many days off is the cabin?"

"Mmm-hmm."

THE NEXT DAY I hung out a shingle telling potential customers that I was off for the rest of the work week. I consulted with a local physician about what goods I would need to care for an infant of perhaps five or six months of age, and then set out to procure the necessary items at Mrs. Hinds's expense. She had also provided me with a thousand dollars in gold certificates as a bribe. I packed a rifle and two revolvers, one for Jimmie and one for myself, and more ammunition than I imagined we'd need. Then Jimmie and I set off for Oliver's cabin, two and a half days distant.

There was snow on the ground before the trail had taken us up much more than five hundred feet higher than the town's altitude, crunching hard snow that looked to have been down for a week or more. I spent a great deal of time that day trying to make myself believe that I might convince Lester Oliver that he should give up his daughter for the child's own sake, but I knew that more than likely I'd have to kill him, and to my shame I found myself seriously contemplating the notion of an ambush. I had no wish to die, though, nor any to see my young assistant cut down, and by the end of the second day's frigid ride I had not yet abandoned the idea.

On the morning of the third day we awoke before dawn and left the horses and supplies, heading up the trail on foot in hopes of spotting the cabin's smoke before Oliver could see us. With luck we might find a better way to approach it than by the trail.

But there was no smoke coming from the cabin when the snowy clearing in which it sat came into view. All I could do was hope that when Oliver departed he left some indication as to his destination, otherwise the only alternative that presented itself would be a return to Bainer and then off to Wallace to catch a train for Butte.

We were nonetheless cautious upon our approach to the cabin, a shoddily constructed thing of mismatched woods and a three-by-four piece of sheet metal hammered onto one wall where the rotted wood had collapsed. The window on the eastern face of the shack had been similarly covered by a large square piece of grey plywood.

Both our guns were drawn when I pounded on the cabin door. Getting no response I kicked it where it joined the wall, and it splintered and fell inward, one of the leather thongs holding it to the frame tearing right out of the wood.

Day had broken but the sun hadn't yet crested the mountainside and the interior of the cabin remained dim. The smell of a large dead thing became overwhelming, even in that cold, and in something of a panic I circled around the house and pulled that plywood off of the east window, and looking in through the glassless frame saw what was left of Lester Oliver, lying face up on a bed not much nicer than Nettie's at the Royal Crown. He had been shot through the temple, and judging by the undisturbed bedclothes and the clothing folded by the side of the bed, it had happened while he was asleep. At that temperature, who was to say how long he'd lain there?

Jimmie was still waiting outside before the front door, timorous as a rabbit now that we were in the presence of the dead. I went inside, and in the sad blue light from the paneless window I noted the presence of a cradle in the furthest corner of the room.

Inside it was a girl child about twenty inches in length, dressed in a fine bonnet and a baby's dress of good quality, the only items in the cabin that bore no signs of decay or overuse. The child's eyes were sunken and her mouth frozen slightly open as though in sleep, which gave me some slender hope that her death had been painless. In fact I had no way to prove whether the child had died of natural causes, upon which Nettie became deranged and killed her husband, or whether Nettie had poisoned her, smothered her or simply abandoned her to starve and freeze to death in the room with her defunct father.

IT TOOK A good while for the fire to really get going, but once it caught the cabin was a smoldering pile of ash within an hour, and though I didn't quite have it in me to poke through the cinders to make sure, I felt confident that no evidence remained of Nettie's crime.

THE NEXT DAY, after a long silence on the trail back to Bainer, Jimmie finally asked me what the sheriff would do to Nettie when he found out what had happened.

"He won't find out."

The boy nodded, and I imagine he was relieved. "What about that Nettie, then?" he asked. "Oughtn't she to pay for what she done?" I had no answer, except the idea that turning three-dollar tricks in the Royal Crown probably amounted to a kind of damnation.

After a while I got to thinking about what lie I was going to tell Mrs. Hinds, and then about the grinning madwoman down the hall from Nettie, wondering what kind of story had led her to that barren room, and whether it was any worse than the one we'd just laid waste to.

WHEN WE GOT to town I stopped at the studio first thing. Once I'd unpacked and eaten a decent meal at the Excelsior I went over to the barber shop for a bath, and once the road grime was washed off of me I thought it time for a shave and a haircut as well.

"Where you been these last few days?" Bert asked me, adjusting the sheet over my shirtfront. "Missed all the excitement."

"How's that?"

"That whore you're so fond of, she tried to cut a john with a razor, and when he run off she drank a whole bottle of laudanum in one draught, or so the paper said."

I WENT OVER to the Royal Crown and knocked, hoping one of the girls might give me a more or less straightforward account of the matter. The little pimp answered the door, though, and shut it immediately back up when he saw me. I was about to knock again more insistently when it reopened and the little bastard handed me a folded up sheet of paper.

"Here," he said. "Stay away from here on out. You're bad luck."

Dear Bill, you know I been jueced ever sincet I got back to town. After you come see me I sober up + rememberd where you was goin + am fixin to take a jon or two to hell with me. Not yr falt yr tryin do the rigt thing by my litle girl but two late. Yr Nettie

THEY BURIED HER in Rosemont Cemetery alongside the town's founders and most respectable cadavers, beneath a granite headstone paid for by a kindly widow who had come to believe that the girl child had gone away with the abandoned Mr. Oliver to be raised by relatives in Nebraska.

"Oh, Bill, think of it," Mrs. Hinds said when I relayed that bit of fiction to her. "She died without even knowing that her precious child was going to be all right."

"I'm sure she knows it know," I answered. It was Thursday night again, and after that I took the widow to bed and forgot about the whole business for a few hours.

ZYPHO THE TENTACLED BRAINSUCKER FROM OUTER SPACE VS. THE MOB

BY TOM PICCIRILLI

THE MOB SHOWED up on the set of *Zypho: Critter from Another Universe* while I was in the rubber Zypho outfit trying to stick my tentacles up a naked sorority chick's nose. Barry screamed, "Higher, higher, really jam them up there! Don't forget that you're sucking out her brain juice!"

I hadn't forgotten. I'd written the script. It had started as a coming-of-age story about a father-and-son camping trip and had somehow turned into a soft-core science-fiction horror flick with me wearing the monster outfit. I had stopped reworking my Oscar acceptance speech. And now the mob was here.

No one else on set seemed to care much, not that there were many of us. My agent Monty Stobbs had managed to pull together a group of fallen B-actors in various states of alcoholism, drug addiction, and suicidal depression, and then put them to work carrying the lights, holding the booms, and doing other grunt work in between their on-screen cameos.

Barry asked me, "Are her tits too big? Is that what's distracting you?"

They were too big and they were distracting. I couldn't remember the name of the co-ed in the bathtub that I was currently hovering over despite the fact that I was intimately familiar with her nostrils. She'd only been on set for twenty minutes and she'd only had one line in the movie, which was, "Eeeeeee!" Monty was banging her. Or maybe Barry was.

Either way, I wished I didn't have to wrestle with her in the soapy water. I wished I hadn't retired from teaching high school English after a mere thirty years. I wished that I hadn't moved from New York to East Hollywood to kick start my screenwriting career, which had done nothing for me so far except kick back.

ZYPHO THE TENTACLED BRAINSUCKER

In this instance, the mob was comprised of Big Big Phil Compansano and Jack "the Jackal" Hinks. I wondered if there were any syndicate boys called Joe "No Nickname" Smith. Big Big Phil and the Jackal had been shouldering their way into Barry Copeland's operation for a couple of weeks now. They called themselves union representatives but never said from what union. They wanted a flat off the top percentage of the flick's budget and weekly protection payments to make sure nobody set the place on fire. I was glad that Barry had been paying so far. The place was my apartment.

The budget was beyond low. This was no-budget filmmaking at its most mediocre. It was also pretty smart filmmaking. Barry would get a cable distribution deal and a DVD package just for showing 38Cs and some Karo syrup blood and gore. He was guaranteed a minor hit and a major return on his very small investment, which so far had turned out to be about what most people had in their change jugs.

Barry Lesterfield was maybe twenty-five and had been born and raised in Malibu, coddled in the soft arms of wealth thanks to his father, the world-famous director Lyndon Lesterfield. When Monty had told me that Lesterfield was interested in my coming-of-age screenplay I naturally thought he meant Barry's dad. Even after the truth became apparent I still naively believed this might be an in to at least meeting the auteur. It wasn't until weeks later that I learned Barry had been caught sleeping with his stepmom and had ripped his father off fifty Gs for a Colombian coke deal that had gone sour at the border. The auteur would not be stopping by the set to encourage me anytime soon.

But the mob boys didn't want to hear about Barry's troubles. They showed up every few days and strong-armed him and whistled at the scream queens. Monty had paid them off a few C notes here and there, but I knew they weren't happy with it. They were idiots who expected anybody with a SAG card or 35mm camera to be connected to Paramount.

Big Big Phil wasn't even big, much less big big. He stood about five-seven and came up to my shoulder. He topped out at maybe an hundred and fifty pounds sopping and dressed the way I did, like a transplanted East Coaster who just couldn't get into the swing of things where California weather was concerned. I either underdressed or overdressed and Big Big was doing the same. He stood there in a cheap suit and a bad Hawaiian shirt. I could see the bulge of a .357 under his left arm. He thought it made him look intimidating. It just made him look uncomfortable. He had to keep shifting his stance to balance out the weight of the piece. He was the backshooter, the talker who'd pretend to be your buddy, asking you about your wife, your kids, then get up behind you and put one in your head.

The Jackal looked more like a bulldog. He was the enforcer, the legbreaker. He went six-five and three hundred pounds of muscle going to fat. He was a little starry-eyed on the set and kept smiling at the girls in a shy sort of way. I put his IQ at roughly the same as your average mollusk. He carried a pipsqueak .32 at the small of his back. I knew he carried it because I'd seen him showing it off to one of the girls the last time he and Big Big Phil had shown up to shake Barry down.

Barry said, "All right, cut! Cut! Let's break for lunch, then we'll reset the cameras and come back for the pickups."

I climbed off the co-ed and pulled my tentacles out of her nose. It caused her to go into a sneezing fit, which really juggled her merchandise. I reached for my handkerchief before remembering I didn't have any pants on. I stepped out of my tub carefully and offered her a towel. She dried her hair and wrapped the towel around it and walked out of my bathroom naked. Big Big Phil said, "Hello there, Peaches," and the Jackal just guffawed and toed the floor acting all gee-willikers.

I reached for the zipper that ran up the back of the suit but couldn't get to it. My sciatica was killing me and it was about a hundred degrees inside the full-body Zypho rig. I lowered the toilet lid and sat down. I was fifty-nine years old and having one of those illuminating moments of astonishing clarity when I wondered what the fuck had gone wrong with my life.

I called Monty over. "Get me out of this thing."

Monty was a slick little hustler in a power tie who had promised me the moon and handed me a burning bag of dog shit. It was my own fault. I knew what he was when I met him but my mid-life crisis had matured into outright terror as I thought about the approach of my sixtieth birthday. My old man had died at fifty-six, my mother at fifty-eight. Ever since I'd hit California I'd been having vivid dreams of all my lost loves and deceased family members pulling up to my front door in a tour bus and beckoning me on board. I'd awaken in a pool of sweat and listen to screams of the cats next door stuck up in the pomegranate trees.

He grabbed the zipper, strained and grunted. "It's really stuck!"

"Keep trying."

"It's not moving."

"Get somebody to help you fix it."

"Who?"

"I don't know who. Call Barry."

"He's busy with the boys."

"Who else is here?"

"Most of them went out to lunch already. I think Suzy's getting dressed in your bedroom. I'll go check."

I knew if Monty wound up in my bedroom with an overstacked voluptuous co-ed would not be returning forthwith to aid me. "Jesus Christ. Monty, when you promised to sell my script and told me that I'd be invited on set to meet all the stars, this really wasn't what I was expecting."

"It never is," he said. "You all right in there?"

"I'm dehydrated. And my back is a wreck."

"Can we fit a straw through the mouth-hole?"

"There is no mouth-hole, it's just tentacles."

"How about the nose-holes?"

"There's netting across them, same with the eye-holes."

He shrugged. "Well, this may not mean much to you at the moment, but the film is very realistic. There's a genuine veracity. It's authentic. I feel that there's an intrinsic—"

They were eight-dollar words he had picked up reading this morning's *LA Times* film review column. I walked away from him.

Out in my living room, Big Big Phil and the Jackal were in the midst of threatening Barry. They hissed in his face and talked about cutting off his nuts and mailing them to his sister. I sat on my couch and tried to get to the zipper again. I hadn't cried in fifty-two years and thought I might finally crack. Monty went to my fridge and grabbed a beer and stood in the middle of the room drinking it and going, "Ahhh, that's good." I sensed our professional relationship was about to end.

When the mob started bouncing Barry off the wall Monty hit the front door at a solid sixty miles an hour, his power tie trailing over his left shoulder. He'd taken my last beer.

Barry dropped to the floor with blood trickling out of the corner of his mouth. The Jackal picked him up and swatted him down again. As far as ass-beatings go, it wasn't much of one. But Barry had no real point of reference and started crying. Big Big Phil let loose with a callow giggle and kicked Barry in the side. Barry howled louder.

I was struggling so hard to get out of the rubber outfit that my tentacles were clapping together.

Big Big Phil pulled a face and looked at me. "What the hell are you supposed to be?"

"That's a good question."

"Got a good answer?"

"I'm supposed to be Zypho the tentacled brainsucking critter from another universe."

"You're a moron."

"You're probably right. How about if you let him up now?"

"You telling me what to do?"

"Yes."

My sciatica was killing me. I stood and stretched my legs and said to the Jackal, "Hey, you think you could help me out here?"

"What?"

"The zipper is stuck."

"Your fly?"

"Not my fly, the zipper in back of this suit."

"Who are you?" he asked.

I sighed. It was difficult sighing without a mouth-hole, but I managed it. "Well ... you know that actor ... the one from your favorite movie?"

"Lance Corwin? From *My Dog Red: An Alaskan Odyssey*?"

It figured. "Yes. That's me. Lance Corwin."

An enormous smile split the Jackal's craggy face and he immediately got to work trying to fix the zipper. "It's really stuck, Lance!"

I looked down at Barry. He wasn't quite sobbing but he was on the verge. I thought, You're lucky, buddy. If that Colombian deal had gone through they would've chopped you into pieces and scattered you all over Newport Beach.

Big Big Phil got in close, like we were buddies. It was the only game he knew how to play. He kicked Barry in the face and Barry's nose started leaking like a low-running faucet. Big Big Phil put an arm around my alien shoulder, leaned in toward where an ear should be and whispered, "It's called blood, Lance. You want to see more of it?"

"Yes," I said.

A wild keening shriek went off like a siren. The cat next door would never learn not to climb up the pomegranate tree.

Big Big Phil said, "Jesus, what was that?"

"It was a scream," I whispered. "Want to hear more of them, you simpleton prick?"

He went for his piece. I wasn't all that worried. He was small and fast but a .357 in a shoulder holster would take a tiny fucker like him about ten minutes to pull and aim. I'd lived in Brooklyn most of my life. I'd been around men like these since I could remember. My family had owned a grocery store that had been squeezed from every angle. My grandfather had paid them off and my father had paid them off and my uncles and brothers and sisters had paid, and in the end everyone had worked themselves to death or were practically at the door after giving too hefty a wedge of cash to assholes like these.

I thought of the thirty years of high school mischief I'd endured. The apathetic students, the boring meaningless tests, the great works of literature that had been ignored each day, my failed novels, my failed scripts, my failed memoirs, the wife I'd lost a decade ago to a sporting goods salesman, the children I'd never been father to, the dreams that had died hard and those that were still twitching. I thought of my mother on the bus, waving to me from the window.

Behind me, the Jackal was still focused on the Zypho rig and kept trying to work the zipper. "Lance, I can't get it!"

"Keep trying."

Big Big Phil came up with his pistol. It was practically as long as his arm. I jammed my tentacle up his nose and he yelped. He dropped his .357 and it hit the floor as heavily as a cinder block. Barry yipped like a Chihuahua and jumped out the open window. It was a two-story drop and when he landed I heard his ankles crack like overheated glass.

I turned and snaked my hand around the Jackal's waist and got hold of his popgun .32. He thought I was giving him a hug and he returned it with fervor. I thought, *Whoever this Lance character is, he certainly instills a lot of loyalty in his fans.* I withdrew the gun and shot the Jackal in his knee, then turned and shot Big Big Phil in the left foot.

They were both lightweights who couldn't take much pain and after a little screaming they passed out quickly. I tried to call 911 but I couldn't work the miniature keypad of my cell with the Zypho hands.

My bedroom door opened and Suzy stood there in black leather short-shorts and a blouse that wasn't much more than a lace bikini top.

She didn't say "Eeeee!" this time. In fact she didn't say anything at all. She walked over and stared at the mobsters out cold with their blood leaking all over the floor and started to squirm a little. She let out a giggle and fidgeted some more. I could see her large hard nipples pointing at me like the accusing fingers of circuit court judges. She was possibly the sexiest woman I had ever been so close to. I hadn't had a painfully turgid hard-on in at least ten years. I was getting one now. It made my sciatica worse.

And I was still trapped in this fucking suit.

TRADE SECRET

BY BILL PRONZINI

I WAS SITTING in one of the canvas chairs on the back deck, adjusting the drag on my Daiwa fishing reel, when I heard the car grinding uphill through the woods.

My cabin is on a backcountry lake, pretty far off the beaten track, and the gate across the private road has a No Trespassing sign. The only visitors I get are occasional tradespeople from the little town a dozen miles away, by invitation only, and I wasn't expecting anybody today. I got up, slow—now that the cool early fall weather had set in, my arthritis was acting up—and shuffled inside for my .30-06. Then I went out front to find out who it was.

The car that rolled out of the pines was a shiny new silver Lincoln I'd never seen before. Illinois plates—that told me something right there. The driver was a man and he was alone; the angle of the sun let me see that much. But I didn't get a good look at his face until the Lincoln swung to a stop alongside my Jeep and he opened the door.

Surprise. Easy Ed Malachi.

He hadn't changed much. A little less of the dyed black hair, a few extra wrinkles in his jowly face and another ten pounds or so bulging his waistline. Dressed same as in the old days, like an Armani ad in a magazine—silk shirt, Bronzini tie, a suit that must've set him back at least three grand. But the outfit was all wrong for a trip into this wilderness country. That told me something, too.

Malachi was smiling when he got out, one of those ear to ear smiles of his that had always made me think of a shark. I leaned the rifle against the wall next to the stacked firewood, moved over to meet him when he came up onto the porch.

"Hey, Griff," he said, and grabbed my hand and pumped it a couple of times. Sunlight glinted off his gold baguette diamond ring, the platinum Patek Philippe watch on his left wrist. "Hope you don't mind me just showing up like this, but you're a hard man to get hold of. Long time, huh? Must be, what, six years?"

"More like seven and a half."

"Some place you got here. Middle of nowhere, not easy to find."

"That's the way I like it."

"Sure, you always were your own man. But I never figured you'd turn into a hermit."

"People change."

"Sure they do. Sure. You're looking good, though, fit as ever. Retirement agrees with you."

"You didn't come all the way up here to make small talk," I said. "What do you want, Ed?"

"How about a drink for starters? I been on the road five hours, I can use one. You still drinking Irish?"

"Now and then."

"Spare a double shot for an old friend?"

We'd never been friends, but there was no point in making an issue of it. I led him inside, poured his drink and a dollop for myself while he looked around at the knotty pine walls, the furniture and bookcases I'd built myself, the big native stone fireplace. "Some place," he said again.

"Suits me."

"I see you got a phone, but I couldn't find a number."

"It's unlisted. I don't use it much."

"Where's your television? Bedroom?"

"I don't have a TV. Or want one. Can't get reception up here anyway."

"Yeah? So what do you do nights, winters?"

"Read, mostly. Work puzzles, listen to CB radio. Fall asleep in front of the fire."

"The quiet life." Malachi's expression said what he meant was boring life. He couldn't imagine himself living the way I did, without luxuries and all the glitz he was used to. "What about women?"

"What about them?"

"You always had one around in the old days."

"That was the old days. Now I like living alone."

"But you don't always sleep alone, right? I mean, you're not even seventy yet."

"One more year."

"Hell, sixty-nine's not old. I'm sixty-five and I still get my share." His laugh sounded forced. "Good old Viagra."

"Let's take our drinks out on the deck," I said.

We went out there. Malachi carried his glass over to the railing, stood looking down at the short wooden dock with my skiff tied up at the end, then out over the mile and a half of glass-smooth lake, the pine woods that hemmed it on three sides, the forested mountains in the near distance.

"Some view," he said. "Anybody else live on this lake?"

"No. Nearest neighbors are two miles from here and they're only around in the summer."

"You do a lot of fishing?"

"Fair amount. Mostly catch and release."

"No fun in that. What about deer? Catch and release them too?"

"I don't hunt as much as I used to."

"How come? Still got your eye, right?"

"My eye's fine. Arthritis is the problem."

"But you can still shoot? Your hand's still steady?"

"Steady enough. Why don't you get to the point, Ed, save us both some time?"

He took a swallow of his Irish, coughed, drank again. He was still smiling, but it looked as forced now as his laugh had been. "I got a problem," he said. "A big problem."

"You wouldn't be here if you didn't. And you wouldn't've come alone."

"I don't know who to trust anymore, that's the thing. I'm not even sure of my bodyguards, for Christ's sake. Things've gotten dicey in the business, Griff. Real dicey."

"Is that right?"

"Might as well tell you straight out. Me and Frank Carbone, we're on the outs. Big time."

"What happened?"

"Power struggle," Malachi said, "and it's none of my doing. Frank's gotten greedy in his old age, wants to expand operations, wants full control."

"Why come to me about it?"

"Why do you think? Do I have to spell it out?"

"Contract offer? After all these years?"

"Sure, a contract. Best one you ever had."

"I'm an old man. Why not bring in some young shooter from out of town? Detroit, Miami, LA."

"I got to have somebody I know, somebody I can trust. I could always trust you, Griff. You never took sides, never rocked the boat. Just took the contracts we gave you and carried them out."

"That was a long time ago," I said. "I've been out of the business almost eight years."

"Not such a long time. I'm betting you're as good as you ever were. The best. Not one screw-up, not one miss. And you always had an angle nobody else thought of. Like the time the cops stashed that fink Jimmy Conlin in the safe house with half a dozen guards, and still you found a way to make the hit. How'd you manage it, anyway? I always wondered."

"Trade secret," I said.

Another forced laugh. He gulped the rest of his drink before he said, "Fifty K was the most you ever got in the old days, right? For Jimmy Conlin? I'll pay you seventy-five to hit Frank Carbone."

"I'm not interested."

"What? Why the hell not? Seventy-five's a lot of money."

"Sure it is. But I don't need it."

"Everybody needs money. Sooner or later."

Well, he was right about that. I was down to only a few thousand stashed in the strongbox under the bedroom floor, and the cabin could use a new roof, a new hot water heater. I could use a bigger skiff, too, with a more reliable outboard. But money and the things it could buy weren't important to me any more. I could make do with what I had, make it last as many years as I had left.

"No sale, Ed."

"Come on, don't play hard to get. Seventy-five's all I can afford. Think what that much green'll buy you. Round the world cruise. Trips to Europe, South America, anywhere you want to go."

"There's no place I want to go," I said. "Everything I want is right here. I haven't been away from this wilderness in five years, not even for one day, and I don't intend to leave again for any reason or any amount of money. I'm staying put for the rest of my life."

"Bullshit, Griff. Can't you see how desperate I am?"

"I see it, but the answer is still no."

Malachi's fat face was a splotchy red now—anger, fear, the whiskey. "Goddamn you, I done plenty for you in the old days. Plenty. You owe me."

"No, I don't. I don't owe you or anybody else. I paid all my debts before I retired."

"You better take this contract," he said. He pointed an index finger at me, cocked his thumb over it. "You hear me? You know what's good for you, you take it and you do it right."

"You threatening me, Ed? I don't like to be threatened."

"I don't care what you like. You got to do this for me, you got to hit Frank, that's all there is to it. If you don't and I have to take a chance on somebody else—"

"Then that somebody hits me too. That what you're saying?"

"Don't make me do this the hard way, that's what I'm saying. I like you, Griff, I always have, you know that. But you got to take this contract."

I gave him a long look. His words had been hard, but his eyes were pleading and he was sweating into the collar of his expensive silk shirt. I said, "I guess I don't have much choice."

"Neither of us has. So you'll take it?"

"Yeah. I'll take it."

"Good! Good man! I knew you'd come around." Malachi's big smile was back, crooked with relief. He used a monogrammed handkerchief to wipe off his sweat, then clapped me on the arm. "How about we have another drink," he said, "seal the bargain?"

I said that was fine with me and went inside to refill our glasses. Before I took them out to the deck, I made a quick detour into the bedroom.

"What's that you got there?" Malachi asked when I handed him his drink. He was looking at the wicker creel I'd slung over my shoulder.

"Creel. I'm going fishing after you leave. Let's take our drinks down to the dock."

"The dock? What for?"

"Nice by the water this time of day, good place to talk. There're a few things I'll need to know about Frank and his habits. Besides, there's something I want to show off, something I pulled out of the lake."

"Sure, okay, what the hell."

We went down the back steps, across to the dock, out along it to where the skiff was tied at the end.

Malachi said, "So what's this thing you want to show me?"

"Down there, in the skiff."

When he turned and bent to look, I took the silenced .38 out of the creel and shot him twice point blank. He fell over into the skiff's stern, just as I'd intended him to. Neat and clean like in the old days.

I climbed down and made sure he was dead. Then I stripped off his diamond ring and the Patek Philippe watch, put them in my pocket, and covered him up with the tarp. Later I'd run the body out to the middle of the lake and weight it and drop it overboard. I'd have to get rid of the Lincoln, too, but in mountain country like this it wouldn't be too much of a chore, even for an old guy like me.

Back in the cabin, I put in a long distance call that got picked up right away. "I changed my mind," I said. "I'll take you up on that contract offer after all. But it'll cost you seventy-five."

"For you I don't argue," Frank Carbone said. "Seventy-five it is. But how come you changed your mind? You told me before you're never leaving that retirement place of yours."

I didn't have to, now. Didn't have to worry about having enough money to last me the rest of my life, either. But all I said was, "Send somebody up with the cash in a couple of days. I'll have proof the job's done in exchange."

"A couple of days? How you going to do it that quick?"

"That's my business."

"Sure, sure. Same old Griff. Trade secret, huh?"

"That's right," I said. "Trade secret."

THE SUMMER PLACE

BY CORNELIA READ

THIS IS HOW old I am: I remember when country roads consisted of three tracks worn into the grassy earth, not merely two. The long-missing center path had been, as E. B. White would later write, "the one with the marks of hooves and the splotches of dried manure." My approximate age and the fact my brother and I have always despised one another is all you need to know.

We only summered in the country, of course. Every June travelling north to Canada in our father's Pullman car, every September descending southward for New York once again, the train's basso rumble beneath our swaying berths deepening sleep as surely as telegraph wires swooped from pole to pole beside the tracks.

That private railcar is gone of course, as is our house facing onto Central Park. What my brother and I have left of halcyon childhood is the cottage Grandfather built on Campobello. Perhaps our neighbor Mr. Roosevelt's own attachment to the island allowed us to preserve it, despite everything else his New Deal would strip from our shared tribe.

There is something else I share with Franklin: in the summer of 1921 he lost the use of his legs.

Although we'd immediately been forbidden to swim by our parents and Mamzelle, my brother enticed me to race him through the woods of Campobello one afternoon—pulling ahead at the final moment so that he could push me into the iron-red waters of Glensevern Pond. It was his dark hope that I, too, would contract what we then called infantile paralysis.

In that, as in no endeavor he's attempted since, my brother Malcolm achieved success. Once the threat of my death had receded, I realized that polio had robbed me almost entirely of the use of my arms.

I was sixteen years old, but can certainly claim to have adapted to my changed circumstances most tremendously well.

I learned to drive a series of specially customized cars, the steering wheels of which are located on the floor, with brake and accelerator operable within their circumference. I guide a horse well enough with my legs that I can still ride to hounds. Indeed, I rarely think of myself as a woman impaired.

The project I find I must complete by the end of this summer, however— some fifty years following that during which Malcolm knocked me into the infected pond water—has been hindered by it tremendously.

It is now nearly August, you see, and I have not as yet managed to kill him.

I lack the strength necessary to employ a gun, a knife, or (most assuredly) a bow and arrow to achieve this end. Neither do I possess the dexterity required for the admixture of say, bleach, into, say, the gin fatuously smug Malcolm now sips beside his radio, while Curt Gowdy chronicles the Red Sox' miraculous fifteenth-inning fight against the Indians.

It would not be suitable for me to request the aid of our staff, though I doubt they harbor the least affection for my brother, and would perhaps not entirely disapprove of my designs on curtailing his longevity.

But the help have this evening off, and Malcolm's lovely girls and their even lovelier daughters have gone to town for dinner. I now have a mere two hours left to me before my nieces are due to return. As I treasure them more dearly than he ever has, I consider that an appropriate deadline for the conclusion of my work tonight.

I stand on the unlit front porch, gazing through a moth-bedizened window screen as my brother chuckles to himself and swills more gin, the ice cubes melodic in his tilted glass.

The cool night air smells of pine sap and low tide, and I know that fireflies hover and dip among the rosebushes behind me.

This is not a misadventure I've been plotting for the past half-century. Indeed, I have always considered my brother more pathetic irritation than anything else. He is merely a failure, a blowhard, a buffoon. Not intelligent enough even to personify so much as an iota of true malignance, outside his one episode of evil intent towards me all those years ago.

But he is our father's male descendant, and as such was given the power to fritter away the last meaningful vestige of our family's long history—this house, and the hallowed ground upon which it stands.

He has announced to me the intention to dispose of it come September, and I cannot allow that to happen.

I've been thinking these past months about the poignance of summer places, those locales we bond with in early childhood: cabins or beach houses or rented cottages which ever afterwards imprint us with nostalgia for fireflies and the sandy back seats of station wagons, for sudden squalls and having to wait a whole half hour before we can go back in the water before being told we must come out again far too soon because our lips are blue—these destinations so indelibly treasured their very shining distance made us chant "Are we there yet?" with such brimming expectancy, because it always took so very long to arrive.

My own wonder is chronicled in faded leather albums on the game-room shelves. Malcolm and I in sepia, standing on the long front porch in tiny straw sunhats and white batiste dresses, so young Mamzelle must be holding us each by the hand to keep us upright. The pair of us posed in our scarlet pony cart—my brother by that time handling the reins. Mother and Father on wicker chairs, our Scotties Towser and Ponto drowsing on the dappled grass at their feet.

Two albums later the images become black-and-white, then finally bloom with color. Generations and decades, death and birth.

I have watched my nieces and their daughters learn all the secret places I believed my own as a girl—out in the woods on days that were fine, inside the rambling house on rainy afternoons. I shall not lose this, nor will they.

One imagines that even the poorest of urban children hold dear some beloved talisman of fleeting summer youth. Perhaps the fire hydrant most often prized open during heat waves, or the melody of some approaching Good Humor truck whose icy wares they can only occasionally afford.

Indeed, once I am at the helm of our family trust, I may well establish a charity to honor my brother's memory: The Malcolm Standish Farnsworth Foundation, "Popsicles for the Deserving."

One last healthy sip and Malcolm has again drained his cocktail glass, having this evening consumed the contents of what was a half-empty gin bottle at the front of the bar shelf. Now he must reach behind that drained bottle for a fresh fifth of Gilbey's, and I know he is already far past noticing that its pink-paper seal is no longer intact.

I could not have managed to fill Malcolm's glass with bleach quickly and surreptitiously while ensconced in the same room with him this evening, but the long afternoon afforded me plenty of time to wrestle a wide kitchen funnel into that second bottle's neck, and to untwist the Clorox bottle's cap with my teeth while its base was pressed firmly between my knees.

After all, neither of my nieces drink gin, and Malcolm has certainly never bothered with lime nor tonic.

I bid goodnight to all the girls hours ago, calling to them down the long upstairs hallway from bed before the sun set across the Bay of Fundy outside my windows.

One by one, they ducked their lovely heads inside my doorway to wish me sweet dreams, each seeing the high collar and full sleeves of my white pintucked nightgown, and the bangs that Claire, my ladies' maid, had pinned in their nocturnal curling papers before going home for the night.

I waited until full dark before turning back my covers and moving carefully across my bedroom floor, then down the hallway for the servants' back stairs.

The kitchen was dark, and I left its screen door propped ajar with one of my bedroom slippers, the better to quietly shoulder it open to let myself back inside the house.

Once Malcolm has sampled the drink he's about to pour himself—an eventuality I have no interest in watching—I'll wait in the kitchen until everything is quiet before climbing back upstairs.

Simple enough, really. And of course it's not as though my fingerprints will be found on either the gin or the Clorox bottle.

Suppressing a contented sigh as Malcolm stands up, I savor the sight of him shuffling sloppily back toward the bar, glass in hand.

I turn to slip quietly down the wooden porch stairs, wincing only a little when the front path's gravel nips at the sole of my tender bared foot.

Our rose garden looks rather lovely in the moonlight, and I was right about the fireflies.

WARNING SHOT

BY JAMES REASONER

WALT PARKER HAD to dry his sweaty hand off on his pants before he trusted himself to draw the gun holstered on his hip. He didn't want to drop the Smith & Wesson.

Whoever had broken into the darkened furniture store moved again. Walt heard the scurrying footsteps. He might be old, but there was nothing wrong with his ears.

He stood behind the railing at the edge of the mezzanine and peered down at the main sales floor. A night light burned in the office, way off to the left, but the big room with its long aisles of divans, armchairs, china cabinets, coffee tables, kitchen tables, and lamp tables swallowed up that faint illumination in a hurry, leaving the displayed furniture draped in shadows.

Walt had been getting a cup of coffee in the little mezzanine lounge when he'd heard the tinkle of breaking glass a couple of minutes earlier. His heart had started to thump hard right away. He had known when he took the job at Hammersmith's Furniture Store that sooner or later he might have to deal with burglars, and the thought scared him.

But jobs of any kind weren't easy to come by these days, and President Hoover was wrong when he said that prosperity was just around the corner. In Walt's experience, most of the time the only thing waiting around the corner was more bad news.

Like your boy, your only son, and his wife were both dead, killed instantly when some drunken bastard driving a cattle truck crossed the center line on the Fort Worth highway.

Walt held the pistol in his right hand and gripped the mezzanine railing with his left. Who the heck broke into a furniture store, anyway? It wasn't like you could put a divan in your back pocket and carry it off.

Hammersmith's did a pretty good business, though, even in hard times. Whoever was sneaking around down there might think the day's receipts were still locked up somewhere in here. They weren't, of course;

WARNING SHOT

Mr. Hammersmith took all the money home with him every day. But the burglar might not know that.

There it was again, the sound of shoe leather slipping along the linoleum floor! Walt took a deep breath but had a hard time getting it past the thick lump in his throat. He looked toward where he'd heard the sound and saw a shadow moving.

His eyes followed the shadow, locking in on it until he could make out the man-shape slipping along one of the aisles from right to left. Walt extended the hand holding the gun and tracked the burglar's progress. The man was heading toward the office. Yeah, he was definitely after the day's receipts, thought Walt.

There was no point in waiting. The burglar was right in front of him. Walt would stop him in his tracks. Show him that he meant business.

Walt swallowed hard, forcing down that lump in his throat, and shouted, "Hold it right there!"

And then he fired a warning shot over the burglar's head.

Only, just as Walt pulled the trigger, the man did something that Walt never expected him to do.

He stood up.

The thud of a bullet striking flesh and bone mingled with the echoes of the shot as they bounced around the cavernous showroom. The burglar dropped instantly, falling out of Walt's sight behind some dressers. Walt stood there, trying to wrap his stunned mind around what had just happened.

The burglar had been crouched over, bent almost double as he made his way along the aisle toward the office. Startled by Walt's shout, he had straightened up without thinking ...

Right into the bullet that was supposed to go over his head.

Walt groaned as he realized that he'd shot the man. Without thinking about what he was saying, he muttered, "Oh, shoot, oh, shoot," as he hurried toward the stairs. He took them as fast as his sixty-five-year-old bones would let him. He didn't want to trip and fall and shoot himself with his own gun.

The stairs were in the middle of the showroom. He had to go all the way down to the end of the aisle by the office and then past a couple of rows of furniture to reach the aisle where the burglar had fallen. As he trotted along, trying to keep his breath under control, he fumbled out the flashlight he kept in his pocket.

As he rounded the long rows of furniture, it occurred to him that the man might be just wounded, not dead. He could be waiting around there with a gun of his own.

That thought made Walt slow down and then stop.

The burglar had to be dead. The thud of the bullet hitting him just *sounded* deadly. But Walt was going to be careful anyway. He crouched and leaned forward to peer past a big armchair. He stuck the flashlight around the chair and turned it on.

The beam lanced along the aisle and wavered around for a second before coming to rest on a sprawled figure. The man wore dark clothes and lay on his side with his head toward Walt. Walt couldn't see the burglar's face, but he could see the pool of dark liquid around the man's head.

No, the burglar wasn't a threat anymore. He never would be again.

Walt sighed and straightened up. He turned toward the office, where there was a phone, and went to call the sheriff.

MAUREEN DIDN'T LIKE him working nights. She said she missed him being there beside her in the bed, even though he did snore and hog the covers.

"Just goes to prove a body can get used to anything," she always said.

She had supper waiting for Walt when he got home every morning, and breakfast ready at the same time for Joel, their grandson. It was a crazy way to live, but then, times were crazy, weren't they?

Walt was running a little late this morning because of having to tell his story so many times, first to the deputies who showed up in answer to his call, then to the sheriff himself, then to Mr. Hammersmith, and finally to the sheriff again. Tom Mulhoite wanted to make sure his story hadn't changed significantly from the first time he'd told it, Walt figured. They'd known each other for nearly forty years, ever since Tom had been a little boy growing up in Lockspur and had been friends with Walt's boy Doyle, before Tom's family moved to the county seat. Tom and Doyle had stayed in touch. He'd been at the funeral for Doyle and Catherine. He still called Walt "Mr. Parker" even though he could have gotten away with calling him by his first name. Tom was the sheriff, after all.

Joel came out of the house just as Walt was parking the Packard in the driveway. He had his books in his arms and was on his way to the high school four blocks away. Nothing was very far from anything else in a town the size of Lockspur.

"Hey, Gramps, you're late for supper," Joel greeted him.

"Yeah, and I reckon your grandma's gettin' impatient, too."

"She said you probably stopped to talk to somebody. Said you lose track of time when you're talking."

He'd been talking, all right. Talking to folks about how he'd shot and killed a man.

The breath seized up for a second in Walt's body as he looked at his grandson. Joel looked so much like Doyle had at that age. He had the Parker build, a little under medium height and a little chunky, not fat, mind you, just naturally chunky, that made him a good player in the line for the high school football team. The same thatch of sandy hair that had to be slicked down with Brylcreem to make it presentable, and even Brylcreem couldn't tame that wild cowlick on the back right corner of the squarish head. Walt had had the same cowlick until his hair thinned out so much.

Yeah, Joel looked so much like Doyle that sometimes it made Walt's heart hurt with loss. But at least he and Maureen still had the boy. At least Joel had had somebody to take him in after the car wreck when he was still in grade school. He had been with Walt and Maureen longer than he'd been with his own parents.

"You all right, Gramps?" Joel asked now.

"Yeah," Walt told him. "Your grandmaw was right. I got to talkin' and lost track of time." He swallowed. "You have a good day at school."

"Thanks, Gramps. See you this evening."

Joel headed down the street. Walt went inside, through the side door that opened into the kitchen.

"Well, I was about to put the food up, either that or give it to the dogs," Maureen said from the stove where she was stirring something in a pot. She glanced around, then looked again as she saw that Walt had sunk heavily into one of the chairs at the kitchen table. "Walt? What is it?"

They didn't have any idea, he thought. Jack Lindquist didn't deliver milk here on Thursday morning, so Maureen and Joel wouldn't have seen anybody to talk to since they got up unless one of the neighbors came over. They wouldn't have heard the shot in the middle of the night like that, either, not through the thick walls of the old store and all the way down here at the other end of town.

"I shot and killed Champ Drummond last night," he said.

The spoon clattered on the stove as Maureen dropped it. "Oh, good heavens," she said. "What happened?"

"He broke into the store. He was headed for the office, I guess to see if he could steal the day's receipts. I called out for him to stop and fired a warning shot over his head, and he ... he stood up. I wasn't aiming over his head after all."

Maureen's hands bunched up in her apron a time or two. "Oh, my. Oh, my." She came over to him and put a hand on his shoulder. "Are you all right, Walt?"

"Yeah. There wasn't a shootout or anything. Just the one shot." He lifted his hand and tapped his forefinger against the center of his forehead. "Right there, slick as you please. Tom Mulhoite said he must've died instantly, so there's that to be thankful for. I wouldn't want even a Drummond to suffer."

Maureen pulled out another chair and sat down beside him. "Champ, now, isn't he the youngest of the Drummond boys?"

"Yeah. He was, what, five or six years ahead of Joel in school?"

"That sounds about right. Didn't he *know* there was a night watchman in Hammersmith's?"

"I don't know. Maybe he didn't. Maybe he knew and just didn't care."

"I hate to speak ill of anybody, but those Drummond boys were always no-account. I thought maybe since Champ was on the basketball team he'd amount to something, not like those brothers of his."

"Well, it got him a nickname when they won district," Walt said. "His real name was … Arthur? Alfred?"

"Something like that," Maureen said. "And you say it killed him?"

Walt nodded. "One shot."

Maureen put a hand on his arm. She was a good woman, but not a particularly demonstrative one. "I'm sorry." She waited a moment. "Do you want your supper?"

"No, I'm not hungry. You can go ahead and put it up. Sorry you went to all the trouble of fixin' it."

"Oh, it was no trouble. No trouble at all. You go get some rest, and maybe you'll feel better when you wake up."

"Maybe," Walt said.

THE INQUEST WAS a couple of days later, over in Prescott, the county seat. Walt drove over by himself. Maureen offered to come with him, but he told her that wasn't necessary.

Mr. Hammersmith had told him to take some time off, so Walt hadn't gone in to work the past two nights. Burl Singletary, who normally worked as the night watchman on the weekends, was covering for him. Walt didn't think it was purely out of a spirit of benevolence that Mr. Hammersmith had given him the time off. He thought Mr. Hammersmith was nervous about having somebody who'd killed a man in the store. He wanted to make sure there wasn't going to be any trouble over what happened before he let Walt come back.

Walt didn't figure there would be any trouble from the law. Champ Drummond had broken a window to get into the store and obviously was up to no good. As an employee of Hammersmith's Furniture Store, Walt had been within his rights to protect the place. Anyway, he hadn't *meant* to kill Champ. That part of it had been an accident, pure and simple. It had been too dark in there to tell that Champ was bending over.

As for the rest of the Drummond boys … Walt didn't know how that was going to go.

"You'd best keep your eyes open, Mr. Parker," Tom Mulhoite had told him that night. "Harvey Drummond is one mean son of a bitch, pardon my French, and Bob and Shank aren't much better."

"Shank's the one who spent time in the pen, ain't he?"

"Yeah, for holding up a hardware store over in Coleman. In broad daylight, the damn fool. Way I hear it, he was drunk at the time. They started calling him Shank while he was in Huntsville. He may be the only one of the Drummonds ever got caught at something illegal, but I'll tell you right here and now, every one of those boys has done that much and worse. Harvey's just been too smart to let 'em get caught until now. I'll bet you he didn't know anything about Champ breaking in here. Champ did that on his own."

It didn't matter who had come up with the idea to rob the furniture store. Champ was a Drummond, and his older brothers would be mad that he'd been killed. Question was, would they try to do anything about it? Tom Mulhoite didn't know, but he thought Walt ought to be careful, and Walt agreed.

He parked the car on the courthouse square and looked around for any sign of the Drummonds as he got out. He didn't see Harvey or either of the other two. Drummonds had a natural aversion to courthouses, he thought. Maybe they wouldn't attend the inquest.

Wouldn't make any difference, after all. It wouldn't bring Champ back to life.

Tom Mulhoite was waiting at the door of the courtroom. He shook Walt's hand and said, "Thanks for coming, Mr. Parker. This won't take long."

Not many people were standing around the courthouse lobby, and that surprised Walt a little. He supposed folks had more important things to worry about than a burglar being shot and killed by a night watchman.

But when Tom opened the door and led him into the courtroom, he saw quite a few people sitting in the three rows of benches for spectators. They turned to look at him and the sheriff.

Harvey Drummond was in the front row, big and blue-jawed with stubborn beard stubble. His brothers Bob and Shank were next to him, and at the end of the bench sat the tiny, dried-out bird of a woman who'd given birth to all of them, and Champ, besides. She had been a widow ever since the boys were little and her husband got his leg cut off by a threshing machine and bled to death before anybody could help him.

Walt took a deep breath and looked away. He knew they were hurting. The Drummond boys might be crooks, but that didn't mean they didn't love their little brother. When you lost somebody, it hurt. Didn't matter who you were, didn't matter who they were. It hurt.

He wished he had just yelled and not pulled the trigger. He wished it for the hundredth time, or more.

Tom Mulhoite was right. The proceedings didn't take long. Walt got up on the stand and swore to tell the truth and told his story as simply as he could. Tom testified as well, and so did the doctor who'd examined

Champ Drummond. Then, after a short deliberation where they didn't even leave the jury box, the coroner's jury returned a verdict of accidental death and recommended that no charges be filed against Walt. The coroner asked if anybody else had anything to say.

Harvey and the other Drummonds sat in stony-faced silence.

The coroner's gavel banged and it was over. People stood up to file out of the courtroom.

Tom Mulhoite put a hand on Walt's arm. "Let's let the crowd clear out first," he said.

Walt knew what Tom meant. Let the Drummonds get good and gone.

"I'm sorry all this had to happen," Tom said while they were waiting. "You, uh, you shouldn't blame yourself, Mr. Parker."

"I don't," Walt said. "I'm not sayin' that it doesn't bother me, knowin' that I ended a man's life, but I was just doin' my job. Nobody forced Champ Drummond to bust into the store."

"That's right. When you come right down to it, what happened to him was his own fault."

Walt nodded. He believed Tom, believed what he had just said himself.

That didn't make it much easier, though.

And it didn't take away the worry about what the rest of the Drummond boys might do.

"Let me go first," Tom said when they left the courthouse a short time later.

Walt was glad to do that. They stepped out onto the porch and started down the steps to the sidewalk that cut across the lawn around the county courthouse.

Car doors slammed.

Walt looked toward the sound and saw Harvey and Shank getting out of an old pickup. Bob opened the door of a roadster parked next to the pickup and got out, leaving his mother alone in the front seat. All three men started toward the stairs Walt and Tom were descending.

Tom went down quickly and held up his hand to stop the Drummonds, saying, "Y'all just hold it right there."

A twinge went through Walt at the way the sheriff had just unconsciously echoed the warning he had called out to Champ Drummond a couple of nights earlier.

"I'm not gonna allow any trouble here," Tom went on as Walt came down the stairs behind him.

Harvey shook his head. "No trouble, Sheriff. We just want to talk to Mr. Parker here for a minute."

"I don't reckon you've got anything to say to him."

Shank said, "This is public property, ain't it? We got a right to be here, and we ain't breakin' any laws."

"You'd know about that, wouldn't you, having been around all those jailhouse lawyers down in Huntsville?"

Shank's face hardened, but Harvey held out a hand toward him, motioning for him to take it easy.

"Listen, we just want Mr. Parker to know that there are no hard feelings," Harvey went on. "It's a damn tragedy, what happened to Champ, but it wasn't Mr. Parker's fault."

Harvey sounded sincere. Bob nodded as his big brother spoke, and he *looked* sincere. Shank still looked mad, but that could have been because of what Tom Mulhoite had said to him.

"If you mean what you say, Drummond," Tom said, "you'll move on and leave this man alone."

Harvey nodded. "Sure. We just didn't want Mr. Parker worrying, that's all." He turned. "Come on, fellas."

The brothers walked back to the roadster and the pickup, got in, drove away. Vanished around a corner on one of Prescott's busy streets.

"Do you believe what Harvey said, Tom?" Walt asked.

Tom frowned and rubbed his jaw. "I'd like to …"

"But you don't, huh?"

"Not really."

"Neither do I," Walt said.

BUT AS THE next few weeks passed, it began to look like Harvey Drummond might have been telling the truth. Walt didn't see Harvey or his brothers lurking around anywhere, and he watched closely for them, too.

He knew that other people gave him looks from time to time, probably even stared openly at him behind his back. He heard whispers and didn't have to understand the words to know what they were saying.

That's the fellow who killed a man, you know. Night watchman. Some kid got into the store, and he shot him dead.

He didn't have any dreams about that night, which was almost as surprising as the Drummond boys dropping out of sight. Walt was glad for any break he could get, though. Life got back to normal. Folks stopped staring and whispering. With the depression going on, they had their own worries. Walt went back to work, said hello to Joel every morning as they passed at the kitchen table, slept good, listened to the radio with Maureen for a while every afternoon before heading for Hammersmith's.

The worry faded away.

Then one night about ten o'clock he was making his rounds through the store when the phone rang in the office.

That *never* happened. Everybody in Lockspur knew Hammersmith's closed at six. In all the time he'd worked here, Walt had never had to answer the phone.

So this was probably something pretty bad, he thought as he hurried into the dimly lit office. He scooped up the heavy black receiver and brought it to his ear, started to say "Hello," then changed it to "Hammersmith's Furniture."

"Walt," Maureen said. "Joel didn't come home."

The Drummonds, he thought instantly. They were finally getting back at him for killing Champ by doing something to Joel.

Maybe not, maybe not. Walt tried to calm his suddenly racing heartbeat. He forced himself to ask, "What do you mean he didn't come home? Where was he?"

"At school. He had basketball practice until late."

Football season was over, and basketball was about to get started. Joel was short for the sport, but Lockspur High School was small enough that if you had any athletic ability at all, you played football in the fall, basketball in the winter, baseball in the spring. Joel was probably going to be a second-string varsity guard.

Unless something happened to him, Walt thought. He tried to shove that possibility out of his head.

"He's probably just with his friends. Maybe they went somewhere after practice."

"No. I called the mothers of all the boys who are close friends with Joel. They all came straight home from practice."

"How long ago was it over?"

"At nine o'clock. I called Coach Summers, just to be sure he hadn't kept the boys later than usual. He said Joel left the gym the same time as the other boys."

"None of them have any idea where he might have gone?"

"They said they didn't," Maureen replied. She sounded more than worried. She was downright terrified.

"All right, take it easy—" Walt began.

"Don't you tell me to take it easy, Walt Parker! That boy is our only grandson. If anything happens to him because … because …"

She didn't have to say it for him to know what she meant.

If anything happened to Joel, it would be all Walt's fault for shooting Champ Drummond.

"I'll get in the car and look for him."

"What about the store?"

"The store will be fine," Walt said. "I'll lock it up. Nobody ever—"

He'd been about to say that nobody ever broke into a furniture store anyway, but of course that wasn't true. Somebody had.

"Just try not to worry," he went on. "I was a boy once myself, you know. He's just out gettin' into mischief somewhere with his friends, and the rest of 'em won't admit it because they know what's up. I'll find him."

"You better, Walt. You just better."

He hung up without saying goodbye and turned toward the open office door.

Something thumped out in the showroom.

The sound set Walt's heart to racing again. Somebody had to be out there, somebody who wasn't supposed to be in the store.

Tonight he wouldn't have to peer through the shadows in hopes of spotting an intruder. The switches that controlled the big overhead lights were here in the office. All he had to do was turn them on, and the whole vast showroom would be flooded with illumination.

His hand had almost reached the switches on the wall when the night light in the office went out. Walt's fingers touched the switches, flipped them up.

Nothing happened.

Bastards cut a wire or pulled a fuse. Walt didn't have to think about who was out there. He stood there in the dark, the breath wheezing in his throat, and knew.

"Parker."

The voice wasn't loud, but it carried well in the long, high-ceilinged room. Walt recognized it as belonging to Harvey Drummond.

"Parker, we know you're here."

Walt turned back to the desk, fumbled for the phone. He found it and lifted it to his ear, but it was dead. Another wire cut.

"Come on out, Parker. See if you can kill us as easy as you killed our little brother."

Did they know he was in the office? Had they gotten inside without him knowing it and been watching him?

If he called out to them, would they aim at the sound of his voice and open fire on him?

"Come on. Three's not as easy to kill as one, but you can do it. You're a big man with a gun in your hand."

I didn't mean to kill your brother. Damn it, I didn't want to hurt anybody.

Then why did you pull the trigger?

He'd been scared. He didn't want to admit it, even to himself, but when he realized that somebody had broken into the store, he'd been really scared and he hadn't even thought that much about what he was doing. He'd wanted whoever was in there to be as scared as he was, and so he had fired the pistol, thinking that would do it …

"You never even said you were sorry, you old son of a bitch," Harvey called out. "There on the courthouse steps, you could have. You could have told us to tell our mother you were sorry you shot her baby boy, but you didn't. Maybe that wouldn't have changed anything in the long run … but it might have."

Walt didn't believe that for a second. The Drummonds stuck together, and violence was second nature to them. Sooner or later they would have come for him, no matter what he'd said that day.

The office door had a lock on it. Maybe he could fort up in here, and they'd go away when they realized they couldn't get to him.

But that wouldn't work, because the door was half glass, with a window built into its upper half so Mr. Hammersmith could sit in here during the day and watch what was going on out in the showroom. The Drummonds could just break out that glass and unlock the door.

He'd be better off out there, Walt thought. At least he'd have room to move around in the showroom.

Moving as quietly as he could, he stepped out of the office and eased to his right.

"Listen, Parker, unless you want something bad to happen to that grandson of yours, you'd better come out and take what you've got coming."

So they had Joel. That came as no surprise to Walt. As soon as Maureen had said that he was missing, that thought had jumped up in the back of Walt's head. The Drummonds had grabbed him on his way home from basketball practice.

Where was he now? Had they left him tied up outside, or had they brought him into the store with them?

Harvey might be lying. They might have killed him already.

Walt reached down and closed his hand around the butt of the Smith & Wesson. He lifted it from its holster.

If they'd hurt Joel, they wouldn't leave here alive, he promised himself. He'd kill them, each and every one of them.

But that was just old man's bravado, he realized. He wasn't sure if he could even pull the trigger again, and if he did, he'd probably miss. They were a lot younger than him, and they were criminals, violent, ruthless men. He was no match for them.

But they had Joel …

Footsteps sounded to his left.

"Damn it, we've waited long enough!" Harvey's voice came from the same direction. "Find the old bastard! Kill him!"

The footsteps were coming in a rush now.

Even with the lights out, Walt's eyes had adjusted to the darkness enough that he could see a little. The streetlights still burned outside, and some of the glow from them penetrated through the big windows in the front of the store. He saw the shapes of the furniture that surrounded him like wild animals closing in on him. His heart jerked and pounded and tried to crawl up his throat. He lifted the gun, aimed toward the rushing footsteps, and started to pull the trigger as he suddenly saw the shape of his attacker.

Instead of firing, he threw himself down. Legs crashed into his shoulders and body. The charging figure fell over him and landed on the floor with a grunt.

Walt pointed the pistol at the ceiling and fired twice.

Breathing hard, he clambered over the fallen form, felt the ropes binding the wrists behind the back, the gag that kept the boy from crying out. He ran his free hand over Joel's head and plucked the wad of cotton from one ear.

"Don't move," Walt breathed into that ear.

On his knees, he started reloading the two rounds he had fired, working by feel and praying that he didn't fumble it in the darkness. While he was doing that, he let out the most pitiful wail he could summon up.

"Joel!" he cried. "Oh, my God! I've killed him! I've killed my own grandson!"

"That's right, old man," Harvey said as he and his brothers stepped into the aisle not far from Walt. Somebody giggled. Had to be Shank. "You gunned down that boy, just like you gunned down our little brother. How does it feel, you son of a bitch?"

Walt's only answer was the roar of gunfire as he started pulling the trigger of the Smith & Wesson.

It was like being in the middle of the loudest thunderstorm of all time. The shots were the thunder, the muzzle flashes that lit up the furniture showroom the lightning. The Drummond boys started shooting back, and that added to the chaos.

Walt could only catch glimpses of them in the flickering, hellish glare, but he saw Bob Drummond double over and pitch forward. He saw Shank stumble to one side and clutch at his throat as blood gushed over his fingers. He saw Harvey standing tall, arm extended, as he fired and fired and fired despite the red flowers blossoming on the breast of his shirt.

Something struck Walt and knocked him over backwards, but as he fell he pulled the trigger one last time—and it wasn't hard at all now that he was defending his grandson—and he saw Harvey sway and then topple like a tree.

Walt had fallen across Joel's body. As the echoes died away, he ignored the terrible pain in his side and rolled over, saying urgently, "Joel! Son, are you all right? Son!"

Joel couldn't answer, of course, because he had a gag in his mouth, Walt remembered. He let the empty gun slip from his fingers and reached up to find the handkerchief that held the wad of cloth in place and clawed it away.

"Joel!"

"I'm all right, Gramps, I'm all right."

Relief washed through Walt, and the sensation was so powerful it took all his pain away.

"I'll get you loose, boy. I'll untie you, so you can get help for us." He started fumbling at the ropes.

"Are you hurt, Gramps?"

"Maybe a little." Walt fought off the weakness until he felt the knots start to come loose.

Somebody began pounding on the front door of the store. "Open up! Open up in there! What's all the commotion?"

"That's the constable, Ed Yantis. You go … you go let him in, Joel. Tell him to … call Tom Mulhoite."

"Gramps!"

Joel's voice was the last thing Walt knew for a good long while.

"THAT'S JUST ABOUT the pure-dee meanest thing I ever heard of," Tom Mulhoite said. "Tied and gagged like that, and with his ears plugged up, Joel didn't have any idea where he was. He just knew he was in trouble, and when Harvey turned him loose and gave him a shove, he took off running blind."

Walt looked up from the hospital bed and nodded. He was in the county hospital in Prescott, all bandaged up like the mummy in that movie with Boris Karloff because he'd been hit a couple of times without even knowing it before one of the bullets knocked him over. The doctor said he was going to live, which was more than any of the Drummonds could claim.

"They came near to spookin' me into shootin' him, too," Walt said. "If I hadn't caught a glimpse of him at the last minute and realized he was too short to be a Drummond, I probably would have." He paused. "I was right this time about how tall somebody was, thank God."

Maureen squeezed his hand. She had pulled a chair close to the bed so she could stay right beside him. Joel was there, too, standing next to Tom Mulhoite.

"That was some mighty fine shooting you did," Tom said.

Walt shook his head. "Luck and God's grace, that's what it was. But I'll take it."

"Yeah." The sheriff shook his head. "After this, nobody'll ever try to break into Hammersmith's again."

"Won't matter to me if they do," Walt said. "I won't be there. I'm not gonna be the night watchman anymore."

"You're not?"

"Nope. I'm tired of livin' backwards from everybody else." Walt smiled at his grandson. "I want to see some of Joel's basketball games this season."

Tom scratched at his chin. "In that case … one of my jailers is fixing to retire next month. You want the job, Walt?"

"You reckon I'll be healed up from these bullet holes by then?"

"I'll hold the job for you, if you want it."

Walt looked at Maureen, who said, "It's up to you. I'd like to have you home again at night, though."

Joel nodded. "It sounds good to me, Gramps."

"Well, in that case ..." Walt looked up at the sheriff. "I reckon you got a deal, Tom. I may be darned near dead right now, but I'm still too young to retire!"

CUTLASS

BY KAT RICHARDSON

THE CAR SPORTED a young man's corpse on its long hood, head down toward the bumper and one foot caught in the busted windshield. The paint had probably been mint green originally; now the oxidized finish was soaking up blood and turning the spinach-colored bodywork the sort of brown you scraped off your shoe. Solis and Brickman studied the car and its macabre passenger from across the street.

Cop cars and barricades cut off traffic for two blocks around the Marine Bank of Seattle, leaving the street a messy tableau of broken glass and near-hysterical bank customers who'd been corralled near the shattered bank doors. A smaller knot of people huddled on the other end of the block, farther from the bank. Some woman near the cars was crying. A Medic One truck, three civilian cars, and two cop cars littered the road. One of the civvie cars was turned sideways to the lanes, creased like an envelope down most of the driver's side front quarter. The car with the corpse had a matching crumple on the driver's side rear and a severe front-end buckle where its passenger side bumper had plowed a parked car before it rocked down and kissed the curb.

"Ten to one the deader's our bank robber," Brickman said as they nudged past the barricades, flashing ID at the nearest patrolman who was holding back the gawkers.

They looked an odd pair: Solis a short, slim, Hispanic kicking middle age; and Brickman a big, blond mutt who still had his college football player tone and 'tude. They presented themselves to the first officer on the scene, a foot-patrol uniform named Gerard, who frowned at Brickman's FBI credentials and addressed Solis instead.

"Bank robbery started about thirty minutes ago, Detective. Ended about fifteen minutes ago. The two robbers attempted to leave the scene in that car," he added, pointing at the body-draped vehicle, "after taking a few thousand in cash from the tellers at gunpoint. That's about when I got here. The driver seemed to lose control or maybe she panicked and

219

slammed on the brakes. Anyhow, one guy fell or got pushed out the door and the other went out the windshield. That's the hood ornament."

Brickman smirked at Solis. "Told ya."

Solis shrugged, dismissing him, and looked back at Gerard. "Where's the driver?"

Gerard pointed at the smaller group near the cars, where the Medic One team was lifting a laden gurney onto its legs. "That's her on the cart. Lois Wilkins. Seventy-two years old." The crying had stopped. "You want to talk to her, you better hurry."

"A granny getaway driver?" Brickman scoffed. "What, crime's the family business?"

Solis shot the fed a scowl. "I don't like it. You take the bank manager, I'll talk to the driver." He ran for the medic team without waiting for Brickman's reply.

The elderly woman on the gurney had her eyes closed and her hands clasped over her sunken chest. If they hadn't strapped an oxygen mask on her face, Solis might have thought she was dead. The medics didn't stop for him and he had to trot beside them toward the bright red Medic One truck.

"I need to talk to her."

"You can follow us to the hospital."

"I can't ask one question?"

"Do it quick."

Solis touched the woman's shoulder to get her attention as the medic lifted the mask off her face. She wasn't nearly as frail as he'd expected, or as small, and he changed his question. "Mrs. Wilkins," he asked, "how did you end up here?"

Her breathing was ragged and after only a single look at him, Lois Wilkins squeezed her reddened eyes shut, tears oozing from the corners and into the thin white hair at her temples. "That awful, awful boy. He wanted my car ..."

LOIS HAD DISLIKED the young man on first sight. It hadn't been the piercings or the ratty hooded sweatshirt, not even the stubby black gun he'd waved in her face. It was the sneering disrespect that really got her goat.

"Nice wheels, gran'ma," he'd said, yanking open the passenger door and jumping in as if she'd stopped at the light only to chauffeur him around town. That was some nerve. "How's 'bout you put the pedal to the metal and take me where I want t'go?"

"Why should I?" she'd demanded. "I have an appointment. I can't be running errands for the likes of you."

The boy's face got mean. "Why?" He echoed. Then he'd reached under the back tail of his shirt and pulled out a compact automatic that he jabbed into her ribs. "Because I got this gun, that's why, you old bitch. Otherwise, I pop a cap in your gray-haired ass, take this fine piece of American steel away from you, and leave you fuckin' bleedin' in the fuckin' gutter. You got it?"

Cars behind her honked impatiently. She started to put her foot into it, knowing the Oldsmobile still had it in her, but the boy'd dug the gun harder into her side. "Nice n'easy, gran'ma. Don't want no cops pullin' you over, now do we? I gots me a 'pointment too."

She'd gritted her teeth and let the car roll out from the line as stately as a presidential limo.

The horrid boy settled in on his side of the car, but kept the gun low and pointed at her. He ran his free hand over the white bucket seat and the center console with its Hurst shifter and fake burl wood trim. "Nineteen-seventy Cutlass Suuuu-preem. Nice. How's a old lady like you rate a ride like this? Huh? You can't barely see over the steerin' wheel."

That was patently untrue as well as unfair. Lois was old, but she wasn't any shrimp. "It was my husband's car."

"You musta took him good in the divorce, am I right?"

"He died."

"Shit. Ain't that the way. All the fine, fine things be in the hands of them what can't appreciate 'em."

"You really are insufferable," Lois snapped at him.

He'd glared and waved the gun at her again. "You keep your eyes on the road, old lady, you know what's good for you. And you gonna have to *suffer* me a little longer. Less you wanna stop sufferin' altogether. Dig?"

Lois bit her tongue. She knew what happened in carjackings.

The thug nodded. "That's better. Now, you got to take me to get my crew."

BRICKMAN CAUGHT UP to Solis beside the owners of the other two cars. The medic unit had rolled and been replaced by the Coroner's team, and the surviving bank robber was already booked and cooling off in holding. Solis was just picking up pieces and looking for a fit. A fine prickling of rain had started up again, making him hunch his shoulders as he glanced at his notebook and walked toward the middle of the street where their conversation wouldn't be overheard.

"Carjacking," said Brickman, shaking his head and making rapid notes so sloppy Solis pitied the FBI transcriptionist who'd be stuck deciphering them. "Jesus, what a pair of dopes. The surviving asshole's a local gangbanger named Jamal Rosewood—'Shotgun Rosey.' Already lawyered up, but he's leaking so fast trying to shift blame to the dead guy, I'm guessing they'll plead out."

"You guys going for felony murder as well?" Solis asked.

"Yup. Always take 'em to the mat and make 'em beg for mercy. And since this is strike two for Rosey, we'll probably end up going for twenty-five in Sheridan. Bet ya he'll be out in less than ten, and swinging for strike three within a year. Your guys'll take the carjacking rap to court, I suppose, but it'll just be icing on the cake."

"So, just the two robbers? No inside guy?"

"Bank manager says no. Just two idiots with guns and the driver."
Solis grunted.

"What did you get on her?"

"Lois Wilkins? Nada. I'll have to try again at the hospital."

"You think these guys targeted this old lady at random?"

"I don't think it *was* totally random."

"So ... you're saying she was in on it."

"No. I think they picked her for a reason: she told me they wanted her car."

Brickman shot a look over his shoulder at the battered Oldsmobile. "That piece of junk? What the hell would they want that for?"

"Because it looks like a piece of junk. You know witnesses are unreliable about cars. One out of ten can't tell you what color a crime car really was, what model or year, how many people were in it, or what the license plate was. You ask all ten, you get ten different answers. If you close your eyes right now, can you tell me what color that car is or how many doors it's got?"

Brickman snorted, turned his back on the car and shut his eyes. "Sure. It's, uh ... faded silver gray, two doors."

"What color roof?"

"Black."

"It got a door pillar?"

"Yeah."

"Anything else you remember about it? Make, model, approximate year, license number ... ?"

"No. It's just some kind of old sedan, like ... maybe mid-seventies?"

"Take a look."

Brickman turned around and opened his eyes. Not turning, Solis began to recite: "It's a 1970 Oldsmobile Cutlass Supreme SX without the badges, faded metallic green with same-color roof, two-door coupe, no door pillar, original Washington plates front and rear, which means Mrs. Wilkins is probably the original owner."

Brickman frowned. "How do you know the badges were removed?"

"Because there aren't any now, but there aren't any holes or signs of recent removal. And that car has the dual exhaust and the Hurst shifter. The car's not a street rod project, so they weren't retrofitted, they're original. The owner must have removed the SX badges when the car was new."

"*If* she did, that's pretty weird."

"Not if you wanted the ultimate sleeper. It's got no hood scoops or striping or anything to tell you it's a muscle car. It looks almost exactly like the base model. Which looked almost exactly like five or six other cars. I'd like to know who Lois Wilkins really is."

"She's a little old lady who got carjacked. What does it matter who she is?"

"Why does an elderly woman drive an old sleeper? So she's an attractive mark for a couple of gangbangers who want a powerful but anonymous car for a bank job? No. She's owned that car for forty years. Why did she buy it?"

"Maybe she was a hot number back in '70. Maybe she just liked it. I don't know."

"Well, I would like to."

"Go for it, Solis. You want to run yourself down on a carjacking rap that'll be buried under the other charges, you do that. But I gotta say, I think you're making a lot out of this old lady. What is it? She remind you of your mother or something?"

Solis frowned. "She does, a little …"

THE BOY WITH the piercings gave Lois directions to an apartment complex on the south end. The city's attempts to make the area respectable had failed again and again and though it was officially White Center, a lot of people still called the area "Rat City." That was how Lois thought of it, too, but it wasn't because of the rodent problem.

They pulled into a graveled parking area across the street, between a school and a park that looked like they'd been dropped there by accident.

Another young man in a similar hoodie ambled toward them from the apartment and motioned them to follow him into the muddy park.

The carjacker twitched his gun at Lois. "Get out th' car, gran'ma."

Her stomach heaved and she knew she would have thrown up if she'd had anything to eat that morning. But she managed to say, "No."

"Say what?"

"I said no. I'm not getting out. You're just going to shoot me and steal the car and I'm not going to make it any easier for you." She was shaking and felt hot and cold with fear, but she sat defiantly behind the wheel and gripped it with white fingers.

He swore, reaching for the keys.

Lois snatched them before he could and tried to nip out the door, but her two seat belts—one across her lap and the other, separate, across her chest—got in the way. He booted the other door open and came around the car to yank her out of the driver's seat as she stuffed the keys down her blouse.

Rolling his eyes, the boy hauled her onto her feet and shoved her toward his friend waiting beyond the fence. "You see what playin' by the rules get you? Fucking seat belt just slow you down. Now we gonna talk to my man, see what we gonna do with you, crazy-ass bitch. And don't think I won't go for them keys, old lady. Your flabby old tits don't scare me none."

He stuck the gun into her back and prodded Lois forward. Her knees were wobbly, but she marched ahead, telling herself if he was going to shoot her, he'd have done it already, and he wasn't half as scary as some of her husband's friends had been ... He was just here and he had a gun and that was bad enough.

"Hey, Ringo, what you bringin' me a geezer for?" the other thug called out as they got near. "What we gonna do with that?"

Oh, goody: another stupid boy who thinks he's a gangster, Lois thought.

"Gonna take the car, man. Right after we ice this bitch," Ringo replied. "What you think? Where the rest of the posse?"

As she'd expected, they were going to kill her. She should have been scared, but mostly it just made her angry to think of these two punks shooting her and stealing Duane's car. They were just kids but they thought they were tough guys and they were going to shoot *her*. This sort of thing wouldn't have happened back in the day. Her eyes prickled with furious tears.

The other boy shrugged. "They ain't comin'. You want t'prove you got the balls, man, you got to do it your own self."

"Fuck!" Ringo shrieked. "Fuck those motherfuckers!" Enraged, he shoved Lois and she stumbled to her knees. "You think I gonna rob a bank on my own, Rosey? Fuckin' errand boy?" He jerked the gun up and pointed it on its side at his friend. "Think I'm gonna make my way dealin' for small change and greasin' motherfuckers for Fat Dog? This my *score*! This my *mark*, man! You gonna come wit me. You gonna crack that bank wit me, or I gonna blow you all over this fuckin' park!"

Rosey shook his head and sighed. "Put the heat away. Ringo, I ain't got no dispute wit you. I come along, you want me to." He shrugged. "But who gonna drive that piece of shit you got?"

"Don't you call my husband's car a piece of shit, you potty-mouthed SOB," Lois muttered. Her chest hurt almost as much as her knees did, sunk into the cold mud. This was doing her health no good at all. She was cold and she was hungry and she wanted to pee. But, maybe, if she played them right, she might still see her doctor tomorrow. Practical, that's what Duane always said: "Got to be practical about these things." He'd said it just before he ratted out his bosses. And about an hour before someone blew his brains out for it. Still, an hour was an hour ...

Rosey and Ringo both stared at her. "What you say, gran'ma?" Rosey asked, turning his head on its side to look at her. He was better-looking than the boy with the jewelry in his face, but still no Rock Hudson, and all he had in common with Rosey Grier was his name and color.

"I said," she gasped, "my husband's car isn't a piece of shit." Lois raised her head and glared at them. "Duane would die if he heard you say that if he wasn't already dead, rest his soul. He loved that car! I still take it to the shop twice a year."

Ringo stuffed the gun into the back of his belt and nodded at his buddy. "She right. Look like crap, but it run nice. An' it a *classic*. We get another couple G for that. Once we done."

Rosey shrugged again. "Whatever you say, dog, but ... who gonna drive it? Can't go park it like a citizen, or bust the bank while five-oh tow your ride."

Lois pushed herself to her feet, panting and wincing from the stiff protests of her joints. "I can drive it."

"You? You crazy, gran'ma?" Rosey inquired. "We ain't takin' no blue-hair on no bank job."

Ringo looked doubtful. "I dunno ..."

"Ringo, you lost your fuckin' mind? She gonna drop us off, then tear-ass over to the po-po turn us in. She a citizen," Rosey added, looking over at Lois. "Ain't you, gran'ma?"

"You ... boys have no idea ..." She tried a grandmotherly smile, but she was pretty sure it looked more like the rictus of a corpse.

BRICKMAN WENT WITH Solis to Harborview. He claimed he wanted to interview the witness himself, but Solis suspected he just wanted to see if the SPD—in his person—fell on its face. On the way, Solis made a lot of phone calls for information on Lois Wilkins. There was something he felt he should know, but he couldn't put his finger on it ...

Mrs. Wilkins' doctor met them outside her room in CCU. "She's not doing well," he warned them. "She missed a cardiology appointment this morning and we were already worried about her. Trauma to the chest from the impact with the steering wheel is making a bad situation worse. So don't upset or excite her. You can have ten minutes, but then you'll have to go. You understand?"

Solis nodded. Brickman was too busy checking messages on his iPhone to do more than grunt. They started toward the room, but Solis's phone rang and he paused to answer it. He listened to the caller, thanked him, and shut the phone off. He looked puzzled.

"It was her husband's car," he muttered. "She inherited it."

"Huh. Who was the hubby?"

"Duane Wilkins. Should I know that name?"

Brickman pulled an incredulous face. "You don't know who Duane Wilkins was?"

"No. Should I?"

"If you ever handled a corruption case in Seattle, Wilkins' name would have come up. He was killed in '73. 'Made man' as the lingo has it. Informed on his bosses during the indictments of '71 and '72. Found in a garage, shot in the head, which was taken as a warning since the usual method of offing rats in Seattle is drowning in shallow water. You should remember that the next time you find a vic facedown in three feet or less."

"I was eight years old in 1973. You weren't even an itch. So how do you know this ancient history?"

"Drugs are still the number one field of study at Quantico. We know every notable mob murder in the last fifty years."

Solis grunted. "Drowning. They used to do that in Cali, too."

"Colombia? The cartel wars?"

"*Si*. My father was a cop in Cali."

"Runs in the family, then?"

"Not so much." Solis turned away from Brickman and went into Mrs. Wilkins' room.

SHE'D SHOWN THEM. First she showed them the gun in the glove compartment. That had been Duane's too, but she didn't feel any attachment to it and she didn't mind so much when Rosey took it away from her. She'd given them the car's registration and her driver's license, too.

"That's insurance," Ringo said, as if it were his idea. "So's you don't run off on us."

Lois pressed her lips together and didn't say a thing.

Then she showed them what Duane had taught her about driving the Olds. It was harder than she remembered, even with power steering, but she did all right. She'd always done all right. Her chest ached, but she ignored it. Another hour and she could go to the doctor. She just had to get through with these stupid boys.

Ringo, the punk with the piercings, whooped it up as Lois maneuvered the car around the streets of south Seattle. "Check it, dog: granny kickin' it old skool!" And he'd laughed at his joke. "You pretty fly … for a old lady."

"I'm old, not dead."

"Yet," Ringo reminded her. "You want t'keep it that way, you just drive that good on the backside of this job. We might even let you keep this fine car. What you think, Rosey?"

Rosey scowled and she knew he wasn't any more taken in than she was. "Whatever you say, bro. Whatever."

Lois kept her mouth shut. Her initial dislike of Ringo had already been surpassed, but she knew better than to talk. Not in Rat City. Driving wasn't the only thing she'd learned from her late husband.

She drove them up to the industrial district, to the Marine Bank, at Ringo's direction. It was an old building and mostly alone in the midst of parking lots and warehouses beside the train tracks. There was plenty of open space to turn the car, even with business traffic, and lots of directions to go once the job was done. She had to hand Ringo that: he'd picked a good spot.

She slid into a loading zone in front, hung up her handicapped placard, and watched the boys run into the bank. She kept the engine running, unlatched her shoulder belt, and started beating the inside of the windshield on the passenger side with the heavy steel buckle.

LOIS WILKINS LOOKED tiny in the hospital bed, though she wasn't really a small woman; she was, Solis thought, taller than he was. But her toughness was failing. The strength he'd felt in her arm on the medic gurney wasn't going to be enough for this fight: he could hear it in her breathing, like he'd heard it before. Her voice trembled as she struggled to answer his questions and her pain made him feel ill.

He tried to ask the questions gently, but he didn't think he'd have time to ask twice. "So they carjacked you and made you drive them to the bank. Why did you wait for them? Why didn't you drive off?"

"They knew where I lived." Mrs. Wilkins whispered. "I was afraid … they'd tell someone to come after me."

"Like someone came for your husband?"

Mrs. Wilkins began to cry. "They said they just wanted the car … But, but … I thought … they were going to kill me. I couldn't let them … take Duane's car …"

THE BANK ALARM started clanging as the two young punks rushed back out, bags bulging with small bills, and Lois was waiting. They didn't notice the crack.

Ringo jumped in first, screaming at her and waving his gun without a care for where he was pointing it. Rosey was a second behind him, but it was a second too far.

As Rosey reached for the car door, Lois stomped on the accelerator.

The Olds burst forward, spinning Rosey onto the sidewalk. Lois gunned the car toward the lane of oncoming traffic as she clawed the unbuckled shoulder belt from under her arm.

"What you doing, crazy bitch?" Ringo shouted, trying to bring his gun to bear on her as the Olds lurched and scraped into the car in the other lane, fishtailing away from the impact. Lois turned her head and body toward the young punk as he was tossed around, unbuckled, in the white bucket seat.

Lois ground down on the gas pedal with one foot and yanked on the wheel, overcorrecting as she turned and whipped the heavy metal end of her shoulder belt into Ringo's face. "Granny's kickin' it old skool, you little bastard!" she screamed.

She lashed the belt across his hand, knocking the gun away as the car careened into another parked by the curb. Then she hit the windshield with the belt as she wound up to smash him in the face one more time.

Blood flew around the inside of the Olds as it rocketed forward, ruining the white upholstery and the fake burl wood dash as the car lurched and slid.

Lois twisted back into her seat and stood on the brakes with both feet, bracing her arms on the top of the steering wheel to protect her head. The disc brakes grabbed all four wheels and locked up, the Olds screeching and rocking up onto its front fender.

Lois slammed forward as the car stopped, banging into the steering wheel hard enough to knock her breathless.

Ringo was flung up against the cracked windshield with a grotesque, wet thud and a snap of his neck. The glass ruptured and he crashed outward in a rain of a million tiny glass puzzle pieces. His foot in its oversized sneaker caught in the twisted frame and his body thumped onto the hood, broken and still.

Blood spread across the faded green paint job …

THE PATIENT MONITORS were screaming. Doctors and nurses rushed into the room, pushing the policemen aside. Solis could barely hear Lois Wilkins saying, "I couldn't let them take my husband's car. He loved that car …"

Brickman backed out of the room shaking his head, dazed. "Jesus. She fucking killed him."

Solis shrugged. "Self-defense. He was going to kill her and take the car."

"That's a bit more than self-defense, man. She laid a trap. She still remind you of your mother?"

Solis nodded. "Yes. My mother killed three men in Cali when I was twelve. They tried to rape her because she was married to a cop they didn't like. All she had was one shotgun shell and a kitchen knife. Imagine what she could have done with a Cutlass?"

CHIN YONG-YUN TAKES A CASE

BY S.J. ROZAN

MY DAUGHTER IS a private eye.

You see? It even sounds ridiculous. She follows people. She asks the computer about them as though it were a temple fortune teller. She pulls out their secrets like dirt-covered roots to hand to the people who hire her. What is private about that? And always involved with criminals, with police! My only good luck, she is not a real police officer, like her best friend Kee Miao-Li. Whenever I see Miao-Li's mother, we give each other sympathy, though I give her the greater amount because her daughter's choice of profession is even more unacceptable than mine.

Although her daughter, at least, is engaged to be married, to a boy of good family, in Chinatown for three generations.

Mine is not.

Not that I believe marriage is the answer to all a woman's problems. I am not a fool, no matter what my daughter thinks. Marriage, if handled badly, can be a source of great distress. This has been the case for Tan Li-Li, a mah-jongg player of my own age—a fact she tries to hide behind black hair dye and crimson lipstick. I would not call Tan Li-Li "friend," although she is among the women I regularly meet with under the trees in the park or at the folding tables of the senior center. It is not easy to be the friend of a woman who eats so much bitterness. Difficulties make many people more kind than formerly; but some are like Tan Li-Li, thinking they can rid themselves of troubles by giving them to others. Tan Li-Li's gloom stems from marriage, though not her own. She is a widow, and as she will be the first to tell you, a widow's lot is sad, to be always alone. I am also a widow, and although I miss my husband, gone these many years, I do not find myself alone. Perhaps that is because I have five children and five grandchildren, all nearby. My daughter, in fact, though her profession is a disgrace, is filial in this: she still lives with me in the family apartment. But Tan Li-Li has only one son, and one grandson, and the marriage that is so bitter for her is her son's.

My daughter, who follows American ways, knows Tan Li-Li and how difficult she can be. She asks me, "Why do you play with her, Ma? When she's there, why don't you sit at another table or something?" If she had a true Chinese understanding, of course she would never say such things. Tan Li-Li was brought into our mah-jongg group by Feng Guo-Ha, with whom she shared a village childhood in China. Even a poor village has its social order. The poorest can be the worst: the smaller the treasure at the top of the staircase, the more fierce the battle on the steps. The Tans were a merchant family, while the Fengs labored in the fields. Feng Guo-Ha, a small, shy woman, tells us that Tan Li-Li was sour, even as a child, and Tan Li-Li treats Feng Guo-Ha imperiously to this day. One thing that galls Tan Li-Li is the contrast between their sons. Feng Guo-Ha's son, like his mother, is friendly and eager to please. He treats his mother well, living nearby, taking her shopping and to the doctor. Often she looks after her granddaughter while her son and his wife are at work. Tan Li-Li's son, in contrast, has for four years ("Such an unlucky number!" Tan Li-Li sighs) been living on the other side of the world, in Beijing, and raising her grandson there.

Feng Guo-Ha cannot enjoy being criticized and given orders by Tan Li-Li; nevertheless, loyalty to childhood friends is never wrong, no matter their behavior, and she remains loyal. Loyalty to friends from adulthood is also virtuous. Feng Guo-Ha and I sewed together in the garment factory for many years, when our children were young. She's my friend, and I won't abandon her to Tan Li-Li's sneering voice.

You can understand, however, what a surprise it was for me when that voice, which I rarely hear beyond the mah-jongg table, issued from the red telephone in my own kitchen.

"Chin Yong-Yun," Tan Li-Li said decisively, as though my name were something I didn't know and would be grateful to be told. "I hope you are well. I am looking for your daughter."

I recovered myself and answered calmly, "Quite well, thank you, Tan Li-Li." Politeness suggested I inquire after her health, also, before reaching the substance of our conversation, but she had not allowed me that courtesy. "I'm sorry, but my daughter is not at home."

"She is not in her office, either. How can I speak to her?"

"If you've left a message, as I'm sure you have, she will no doubt call you as soon as she is able." Unless I spoke to her first myself. Perhaps I could discourage her from plunging into the cloud of bitterness that surrounds Tan Li-Li.

"That is not soon enough. Our matter is urgent."

"Our matter?"

"It concerns my son. As you know, he is visiting me here."

I could not help but know. As if it were not enough to see Tan Li-Li daily parading her three-year-old grandson in the park—grasping the child's hand so firmly I feared it would grow misshapen—she also had spoken of nothing but this impending visit for weeks before Tan Xiao-Du and his son arrived from Beijing. I had expected the visit to lighten her humor, especially since her daughter-in-law had remained in China, but her sourness did not abate. Probably I had been foolish. I had expected pleasure and pride to mark her reactions to many events involving her son: his posting to an important position in China with his American firm, his marriage to a kind and beautiful Beijinger, the birth of their son. Each time, however, Tan Li-Li's reaction had been only darkness. Of his return to the homeland: "How can he leave me here to grow old alone?" Of his marriage: "Now he will never come home!" Of his child: "My only grandson, growing up so far from me!" Xiao-Du had offered to bring his mother to Beijing as often as she wanted, even to settle her there for as long as he stayed. But still, around the mah-jongg table we heard only complaint and recrimination.

"I'm sorry, Tan Li-Li," I said. "I cannot—"

"There, you see?" Tan Li-Li interrupted with a voice of vinegared triumph. I started to ask, "See what?" but she wasn't speaking to me. "I told you, Xiao-Du, that calling Chin Yong-Yun was useless."

I did not want my daughter involved with Tan Li-Li's endless problems, but this insult was unacceptable. Before I could properly respond, however, a man's voice came into my ear.

"Chin Yong-Yun, I hope you and your family are well. This is Tan Xiao-Du."

"Tan Xiao-Du, I and my family are quite well, thank you. I hope your family is, also." The son, teaching the mother courtesy. His Cantonese was good, also. I'm sure his skill didn't make his mother grateful for her luck, although it should have. Many American-born children are poor in Cantonese. My children all speak well, of course. They are talented in languages. I'm sure my choice not to learn English, which made it necessary for them to speak Cantonese at home, played only a very small part.

"I'm sorry my daughter is not available," I told Tan Xiao-Du, "but her services are much in demand, you understand."

"Yes, of course. But this is a very important matter. Isn't there any way we can contact her?" I was reluctant to share my daughter's cell phone number with the Tans, but I couldn't help hearing Xiao-Du's strained tones of distress. Especially when he announced, "It's my son. My son has been kidnapped."

I was briefly speechless, hearing this news. The despair in Xiao-Du's voice, and the situation's dire nature, changed my thinking. It did not, however, change the humor of his mother. "Never mind," I heard her sneer behind him. "I told you, there is only one solution. You will give them whatever they want and all will be well. Do as I say!"

"No!" Xiao-Du responded desperately. "Mother, I can't!"

"Foolish boy! You will not—"

"There must—"

"You are—"

"Come speak to me," I said loudly, into his ear.

"What? I'm sorry, Chin Yong-Yun, what did you say?" I could hear the son shushing the mother as he waited for my response.

"I often work with my daughter on her cases." I am not the sort of person to be unscrupulous with the truth, but circumstances were pressing. "I will collect your evidence, and brief it to her when she is available." My daughter thinks I never listen when she talks about her work. If that were so, would I know the words of her profession?

"Chin Yong-Yun—I don't think—"

"Come, you must hurry if your child is in danger." I hung up the phone. I find this often helps people make decisions.

TEN MINUTES HAD not passed before mother and son were at my door. Of course I had put the kettle on the stove and set out tea cups. I might have expected a small gift of almond cookies or bean cakes, as is customary when visiting, but the Tans arrived empty-handed. Making allowances for the son's distraction and the mother's customary lack of civility, without comment I added a plate of macaroons to the table. As the tea steeped I seated myself in my armchair, instructed them to sit also, and requested that they tell their story.

"I blame myself," Tan Li-Li began, but her son interrupted.

"No, Mother. It is not your fault and this is the time for action, not for blame."

"Nevertheless, I—"

"Please," I said to stop this tiresome argument. "We never involve ourselves in the personal lives of our clients."

"We?" Tan Li-Li's plucked eyebrows arched.

"My daughter and myself. In our investigations. Xiao-Du, just tell me what has happened."

I asked to hear the story from the son, but I had little hope. I poured the tea—first for mother, then for son, and last for myself—and discovered that my assessment had been correct.

"It is, as I said, my fault." Tan Li-Li's shake of the head might have expressed self-disgust, or at least disbelief. However, it was more likely a denial of her son's request to not blame herself, as well as of mine to remain uninvolved in her personal life. "I was in the park with little Bin-Bin while Xiao-Du attended to business for his firm. His position requires him to be available to give instructions to his subordinates at all times. Even when he is overseas with his family." She gave Xiao-Du a look full of maternal suffering and accusation.

"In the park," I repeated firmly. "With Bin-Bin. When was this?"

She turned back to me with narrowed eyes. "Forty minutes ago." She paused before resuming her tale. "Bin-Bin was playing with other boys, and I turned away for a moment to buy roasted peanuts for him, for a treat. No more than a moment! When I looked up, he was gone."

She dabbed at her eyes with a handkerchief.

"What makes you think he was kidnapped?" I asked. "Isn't it more likely he wandered away? Maybe some other grandmother found him. He's a small child who's lived his whole life in Beijing. He doesn't speak Cantonese, or English, does he? He could be at the police station right now, unable to tell the officers even his name."

That was clever of me, to think of that, and I might have expected their eyes to light up and one or the other to call the Fifth Precinct immediately. But the mother looked exasperated, and the son merely sad.

"I got a phone call," he said. "A ransom demand."

I blinked. "Oh."

He waited. "Aren't you going to ask me what they said?"

"Yes. Yes, of course," I said with impatience. "I'm waiting for you to tell me." I added, "It's best to allow people to tell their stories in their own way, without prompting." My daughter has said this, though she thinks, just because I don't stop chopping vegetables when she speaks, that I haven't heard her.

"They said not to go to the police. They said if I do what they ask, my son will be returned unharmed."

"What do they ask?"

He breathed deeply. "My firm develops computer software for foreign markets. Since going to China I've been working on a major project, to enhance the ability of scanners to recognize and read character-based languages—" For some reason, looking at my face, he stopped. "I'm sorry," he said respectfully. "That's technical talk and it doesn't matter. The point is, we're not the only firm working in the area. A successful product, because it will greatly increase computer speed, will be worth many, many millions to the company that develops it. We are the closest."

"Because of Xiao-Du's leadership," the mother put in.

The son just looked at her, then said to me, "That was the demand. To get my son back, they want our code."

"And I say, give it to them!" The mother's face went red with indignation, as though her son's intransigence were willful and unreasonable.

"Your code?" I said. "That is, your solution to your project?"

"Yes. But I can't give it away! I'd be betraying my entire team! Everyone who works for me, trusts me—and my employer, the faith they've shown—"

"You've given them everything they could have asked for!" the mother countered. "You left your home to live on the other side of the world! You work long hours and days, you're exhausted, no time for anyone! Now you must give them your son, also?"

"Of course not, never! But there must be another way. That's why I wanted to come to Lydia—to Ling Wan-ju." He looked at me desperately. "Can you help us? Can your daughter help us?"

"Possibly," I said. "But first you must both answer some questions for me."

"Anything!" said the son. The mother only sniffed and sipped her tea.

"Xiao-Du. First: were you given a deadline for your compliance?"

"Yes, five this afternoon."

"Over two hours from now. Good, we have some time." The mother frowned at that, but I paid her no attention. I asked the son, "Who was it who called you?"

"I don't know. Obviously he represents one of our competitors, but there are a number of them."

"But it was a man?"

"Yes, though he disguised his voice."

"Really? How?"

"He made it low and growling."

"I see. Now tell me, if you do as they ask, what will be the result?"

"Little Bin-Bin will be returned!" The mother could not contain herself.

"My question concerned a different result," I said in a neutral and professional manner. "For you, Xiao-Du. In relation to your employer. What I mean is, why do you not just do as the kidnappers ask, and then explain the dire nature of the situation to your employer?"

The son swallowed. I poured him more tea, in case his throat was dry. "I'd be betraying my firm and my team," he said. "Three years of work, lost. Worse, given away. Even if they understand, they'll have to fire me to save face."

"They will not fire you!" the mother exploded. "Never mind their face. You will resign without explaining anything. With your talents you'll easily find another position, and your firm will continue their work in ignorance. When the competitor brings their product to market, your firm will realize they've lost the race, and consider themselves unlucky. That will be all."

"Even if I could do that," the son said, "lie like that to people who've been so good to me, when the rival system comes on the market, they'll analyze it and then they'll know."

"What of it? It will never be more than suspicion. By then you'll have an important position elsewhere, and no one will speak against you."

"Not in China. In China I'll be finished. Even if it's just suspicion, no one will trust me enough to keep me on."

"So, you will leave China! For your son, is that too big a sacrifice to make?"

Xiao-Du slumped miserably in his chair.

"Thank you," I said. "Tan Li-Li, now I have questions for you."

"This is ridiculous."

"Please, mother," the son begged.

The mother rolled her eyes but turned to me with pursed lips, awaiting interrogation.

"You say you took your eyes off little Bin-Bin for a moment, when you were buying peanuts."

"Just for a moment!"

"I find it hard to believe, Tan Li-Li, that you took your eyes from him at all. I have seen you together in the park. You are the most assiduous of guardians." Tan Li-Li gave me a tight, smug smile. "A bag of peanuts could hardly divert you from your duty to your son and grandson," I continued. "Surely there must have been something else."

Her penciled brows knit. "What do you mean?"

"I am talking about a diversion." Let my daughter claim I don't listen to her! "A noise, a commotion, perhaps deliberately meant to distract you. Can you recall anything?"

After a moment her eyes lit up. "Yes! Why, Chin Yong-Yun, you are correct! A loud argument, three thuggish young men. Near the peanut vendor. Pushing each other, shouting, almost coming to blows. They drew everyone's attention. Then they ran off." She beamed. "Is that helpful?"

"Most helpful. Thank you. Would you like more tea? If not, I am ready to work on your case."

They both looked at me blankly. The son comprehended first. "Come, mother." He stood.

"Where are we going?"

"We're leaving Chin Yong-Yun to her work."

"Chin Yong-Yun?" the mother said incredulously. "What are you proposing?"

"You have hired us," I clarified for her. "Have you not?"

"Yes!" the son said. "Whatever your fee is, I'll pay it."

"Of course," I said. "Now, if you'll excuse me?"

"We have …" the mother stammered. "It was Ling Wan-Ju we—he—wanted …"

"As I said, my daughter is not available, and as I also said, we often work together. Now, come."

"But … the deadline …"

"Yes." I turned to the son. "At the appointed time, if I have not recovered little Bin-Bin, you must give the kidnappers what they demand. No matter the consequences for you. Do you understand?"

He nodded glumly.

"But I don't believe you have reason to worry," I added, to be kind, though my daughter says she never promises a client she will solve their case, only that she will do her best. "Now. Perhaps you should go home and wait by the telephone in case the kidnappers call again."

This time the son looked blank and the mother answered with a cold smile. "They called him on his cell phone. He has it in his pocket."

"Oh. Yes. Of course, his cell phone," I said. "Yes. Still."

I was astonished at the mother's rudeness in forcing me to be so impolite as to ask guests to leave. But time was moving swiftly and I needed to begin my investigation. I walked across the living room and opened the door for them. With glances at each other—new hope in the son's eyes, impatient disapproval in the mother's—but without another word, they left.

ONCE THEY HAD gone I exchanged my house slippers for tennis shoes. I hoped the investigation would not demand a great deal of walking, because my bunions had been painful lately. But I didn't think it would. Except that I didn't understand what "code" was—a detail I regarded as unimportant—the situation seemed clear.

At the bottom of the three flights of stairs I opened the street door and peered cautiously around. The sidewalk held no one unexpected, so I emerged. I looked over my shoulder a number of times as I hurried to the park. I could not imagine who might follow me, with the exception of Tan Li-Li herself. That would be unfortunate, if not entirely unanticipated—clearly she had no faith in me—but she was nowhere to be seen.

In the park I questioned various women looking after their children and grandchildren. The number of people there was less than it would have been an hour ago, when Tan Li-Li had lost little Bin-Bin. By now many children had been taken home for their afternoon naps. Some of the women I spoke to had recently arrived, but still, I found a few who had been there for an hour or more. None of them, however, could give me any information about Tan Li-Li, little Bin-Bin, or any loud argument among three thuggish young men.

I was trying to decide what to do next when my own cell phone rang. I rarely use it, but I accepted it after my children repeatedly insisted. They claimed it would ease their minds to know I could contact them if I needed to. What kind of mother knowingly causes her children unease of mind?

I unclasped and unzipped my purse and pulled the phone from it. Pressing the green button, I said, "This is Chin Yong-Yun speaking," not too loudly, because it's very small.

"Yes, Ma, I know." It was my daughter, no time for politeness, a busy detective. "Ma, I have a call here from a man named Tan Xiao-Du, who says he's the son of a friend of yours and it's urgent. Then I have another from his mother, who says never mind. What's going on? Are you all right?"

"I? Of course I am. Why would I not be?"

"I don't know. It sounded like there was something wrong."

"Do not worry. I am taking care of their situation."

"Their situation? Not your situation?"

"Of course not. I'm sorry, Ling Wan-Ju, but I'm very busy right now. I'll explain later. Unless you're not coming home for dinner?"

"Yes, Ma, I'll be home. Are you sure you don't need me? Or the Tans don't need me?"

"They do not. I do."

"You do?"

"Yes. On your way home, please stop for cabbage."

It is important, under pressure, to be able to do two things at once. Therefore as I spoke to my daughter a decision had taken shape in my mind. Now, having said all I needed to say, I pressed the red button and replaced the phone in my purse, which I zipped. This was unfortunate, because as I was clasping the purse shut, the phone rang again. Ready to tell my daughter I really had no time for idle conversation, I unclasped and unzipped, and took the phone from its pocket. I pressed the green button. "This is Chin Yong-Yun speaking."

I was surprised to hear, not my daughter's voice, but a man's voice, low and growling. "Stay away if you know what's good for you!"

"Who is speaking?"

"You don't need to know! If Tan Xiao-Du wants to get his son back, you'd better leave us alone! Otherwise someone might get hurt."

I asked again who was calling, but the connection had been broken. Many times that is caused by the inefficiency of the telephone company, but I did not think that had happened here.

Once again I replaced the phone into my purse. The voice had been quite threatening, but an investigator cannot allow herself to be intimidated. My daughter has said that many times.

Tan Li-Li's friend, Feng Guo-Ha, lives near the park. I had some questions to ask her, so I proceeded to her apartment without delay.

"Yong-Yun!" Though Guo-Ha smiled quickly, she seemed quite startled to see me. This was unsurprising. I am not the sort of person who appears on doorsteps unannounced; that is rude. However, my investigation demanded certain adjustments and I was doing what was necessary.

"Guo-Ha, good afternoon," I said. "I'm sorry to arrive without an invitation but I must ask you some questions."

"I'm delighted to see you, of course, Yong-Yun, but perhaps you could return later? My granddaughter Mei is having her nap right now." Guo-Ha nodded in the direction of the hallway that led to the bedrooms.

"Oh, Mei is here with you today? What a fortunate woman you are, Guo-Ha."

"Yes, thank you, I am. But Mei has trouble sleeping, so once she settles for her nap I take great care not to disturb her. The slightest sound—oh, dear, I think I hear her crying now. I'm sorry, Yong-Yun, but if you'll excuse me—"

"I don't hear anything." I cocked my head to listen, while delicately placing my foot in the doorway, in case the door shut accidentally. "Oh! Yes, I do. Allow me, Guo-Ha. I'm very successful with children."

"No, Yong-Yun, you mustn't trouble yourself—"

But I was already across the threshold and into the apartment. Guo-Ha's natural courtesy caused her to move aside for me before she quite knew what she was doing. Over her protests I made directly for the rear bedroom, the one that had been her son's. I heard a child's voice behind the door. I have always been able to quiet children when they fuss, but I could hear before I even opened the door that Guo-Ha had been wrong. Her granddaughter wasn't crying. She was laughing. "Hello, Mei," I said, stepping into the room. And to her father, sitting on the floor with her, a picture book on his lap, "Hello, Lao. I'm glad to hear your throat is no longer hoarse." And to the other child, on Lao's other side, "Hello, Bin-Bin."

SINCE BIN-BIN had had his nap and was refreshed, I took him with me soon after. Really, my visit was almost short enough to be considered impolite, but I had pressing business. Clearly, neither Lao nor his mother had been the moving force behind this abduction; they were merely agents, hired for the crime. This sort of thing happens often in detective work, and, as my daughter would agree, it is pointless to go after the smaller criminal. My next focus would be their employer, because, though I had recovered the child, an investigator does not like to leave a case unresolved. But first I needed to return Bin-Bin to his worried father.

Both Guo-Ha and her son were abashed at what they'd done, but I told them, "We will speak no more about this." I took little Bin-Bin's hand and led him out the door. In the park I stopped to buy him roasted peanuts, but we didn't linger. I considered calling my client on the cell phone, but Tan Li-Li's apartment, where Xiao-Du waited, was not far, and while I understand the value of such mechanical devices for people whose lives are as busy as my children's, still I consider them a poor choice for expressing matters of the heart. Also, it irritates me to press those tiny numbers.

The reunion of father and child was quite satisfying. Bin-Bin, who didn't know he'd been missing, squealed with everyday delight and ran into his father's arms. I'm sure he didn't understand the tears of joy, or the many kisses and hugs, or the large, dinner-spoiling dish of mango ice cream that followed.

Through all that commotion and all of Xiao-Du's repeated questions and thanks, Tan Li-Li regarded me with mascara'ed eyes wide in wonder. Finally I was able to convey to Xiao-Du that I was not at liberty to discuss who the miscreants were, but that he had nothing more to fear from them, and also that he would receive a bill for services, payment of which would express sufficient gratitude. After all, would he thank the chef for cooking dinner or the barber for a haircut? Investigating is simply our job at LC Investigations.

Xiao-Du and his son settled down at the kitchen table to happily ruin their appetites together. I said to Tan Li-Li, "I'll be on my way, then. Perhaps you'll see me to the door?"

I should not have had to ask that, but I wasn't sure Tan Li-Li would be courteous enough to accompany me otherwise. She nodded and followed. I stepped into the hallway; she had no choice but to do so, too, shutting the door behind her.

"Chin Yong-Yun," she stammered, "how did you—where did you—"

"Tan Li-Li," I said severely, "I think it's time you accepted that your son's decisions about where to live and raise his family have been made."

"I don't understand."

"Of course you do." I'm afraid I spoke more bluntly than our relationship would have normally allowed, but this was not a time for niceties. "It was a clever plan. And you are fortunate to have in the Fengs loyal friends, to get involved in such business at your behest."

She paled. "They told you?"

"They did not. They remain loyal. I discovered the truth by detecting. Why, for example, did the man who called Xiao-Du disguise his voice? It must be a voice Xiao-Du knows. It was bold of you to have him call me also, but I understand your desperation. He was an excellent actor, by the way. If I hadn't been sure of who it was I might have been frightened. Another thing, no one in the park remembered seeing you with Bin-Bin today. The peanut vendor, whom I spoke to just now, could recall no loud argument among thuggish young men near his stand. You invented that in answer to my question, isn't that correct? Also, I asked myself, why did you leave a message with my daughter telling her to ignore Xiao-Du's call? Finally, I was struck by your insistence that your son resign rather than explain the situation to his employer. That was because, in fact, the code was never going to change hands at all. Xiao-Du's resignation was the solution, but to an entirely different problem."

Tan Li-Li stared at me, her red lips opening and closing like a fish's. It was comical, but laughing would have been unkind and I am not the sort of person who enjoys being heartless.

"You won't tell Xiao-Du?" Tan Li-Li looked truly scared for the first time. If she had appeared at all frightened during our earlier interview, instead of merely short-tempered and aggravated, I might not have understood from the first the situation's true nature.

"I promise I won't," I said. "But you must promise not to interfere with your son's family decisions anymore."

I trained a stern look on her. She nodded.

"Perhaps," I suggested, "you might consider returning to Beijing when your son does, and spending some time with his family there." Uppermost in my mind was how such a decision would strengthen the bonds between mother and son. The prospect of the cheeriness that might result around the mah-jongg table only occurred to me afterwards.

Tan Li-Li nodded again, but said nothing.

I could feel her eyes watching me as I turned and walked away, but a detective has a sense about when she is in danger and I had nothing to fear from Tan Li-Li. I didn't look back. It was time to go home and prepare dinner. I had promised not to tell Xiao-Du the truth about what had happened, but I hadn't promised I wouldn't tell the story at all. It was, I thought, a noteworthy case, and I was sure my daughter would be interested.

GRANNY PUSSY

BY ANTHONY NEIL SMITH

BILL HOLST SAID to the boy, "That's not how you treat an old lady."

Gilley hit the boy again with the walking cane. Third time on the shin. Boy was rolling on the floor like, like, shit, like when Bill used to hit his kids. Bill stood watching with his arms crossed. The boy was crying "Stop, stop, stop!" Not really a boy, but to Bill they were all boys. College kids, fresh out of high school and spending way too much time on the internet, the comfort of their own rooms, getting an itch for fetishes Bill and Gilley used to have to stumble across in grimy stores if they wanted any. But Bill wanted the kid to learn his lesson and make sure all his friends knew. They had the other friend who was in on this out in the car, waiting his turn.

Emma, behind Bill but having a hard time watching, said, "I'm not an *old lady*."

Bill shrugged. "To him you are. Fifty-eight is like an eternity to these fucks, remember."

"It wasn't so bad, what they did. I just wasn't, you know, told about it." She was in her bathrobe, barefoot, and she grinned a little. "I could've."

Bill huffed and thought about the old days. Thought about Emma back in the early eighties, young and able to do things with a cock you wouldn't believe. Still could. But these college boys, Jesus. Guy paid for himself but once Emma got to the dorm room, buck naked on his tiny bed, then the kid's friend showed up and they wanted two-for-one. When Emma said "Every dick pays its own way," they played a little rough with her, pinned her down, called her all sorts of names, but Emma was able to text Bill the distress code on her cell before it went too far. He sent Gilley to the rescue. And here they were, back in the garage at Bill's old car lot. It had been out of business for years, but he couldn't bring himself to sell the lot. He told his children he had, but hid the deed. Vultures, those fucking spawn of his.

This kid was a nerdy bastard. His shins would hurt for a few days, and maybe he'd shit blood from the gut shot, but he'd survive. Bill called

Gilley off and walked over, leaned over, but only so far because his back hurt like shit.

"You get the point, right? That was a no-no."

"I'm sorry, sir, I really am. We didn't—"

"Shut up. I'm keeping your money, and we're going to beat up your friend, but just take one more look at what you missed out on."

He snapped his fingers at Emma, now extra pissed, and she held her robe together tighter.

"Come on, show him already. It'll hurt worse than the cane."

Emma rolled her eyes, pulled open her robe and let the kid get another eyeful of naked. He groaned like he was hungry.

So her tits had sagged, and she had the slightest belly roll on her, and her thighs weren't exactly the leanest in town, not to mention the wrinkles on her hands and around her neck, but Bill could still see why these younger guys would want a piece. Why they'd want to fuck their teachers and their best friend's mom and all of that other stuff out there in pornland that got them jonesing for the real thing. Emma and the other women in Bill's stable weren't tight like *Playboy* models, but goddamn they knew how to *be sexy*, you know? The way they looked at you and moved their hips and worked that lower register when they talked dirty to you. The young women these days, they didn't know squat. They watched rap videos and shit, even the white girls. All the hollering and dry-hump dancing, that wasn't sexy. That was just confusing.

Emma cinched her robe tight again and said, "I don't know, Bill. Maybe, if they promise to be good and pay double—"

"Too late. Gilley, drag this one into the trunk and get the other one."

Gilley cleared his throat. Pretty much the only way he communicated anymore. He grabbed the moaning nerd boy by the arm and helped him up, escorted him out of the garage.

Bill stepped over, slipped an arm around Emma, and said, "The night's still young."

"It's only six-thirty."

"So we've got about three more hours till bedtime. We'll get you some before then."

She played with what was left of Bill's hair. "How about you, babe? You up for me tonight? Go ahead and take that pill?"

Yeah, he wanted to. He'd wanted to ever since he had come "out of retirement" and gotten his girls back on the street—except it wasn't a real street. It was all done by e-mail now. Had to get his grandson to teach him e-mail and interwebs and Facebook and bullshit.

Didn't matter if he wanted to like he did back in the Eighties. His cock hadn't moved in eight years except at night when he wished it wouldn't. Couldn't take the pills due to his heart. He wasn't up to doing anyone, not even jacking off to his precious memories of dearly departed Louisa, who'd passed away from lupus four years ago.

Bill had to blink himself out of it. Looked around the garage, took a moment to remember where he was and why they were there. He slapped Emma's ass. "Now how are you gonna make me money if you're fucking me instead of them? Here we go again."

Gilley had come back with the other kid, taller, beefier, and looking like he could take these old guys, no prob. He even blew a kiss and a wink to Emma. Too busy doing that to notice Gilley swinging the cane at his right kidney.

Kid went spastic, grabbing his side on the way down, Gilley connecting a few more times and breaking the kid's fingers too.

Sure, this bruiser could easily mop up two old men in a fair fight. Gilley and Bill were in their early seventies, for shit's sake. They might have gotten weaker, but they sure as hell got a fuckload smarter than these boys.

As the kid seethed and gripped his hand, Bill said to him, "See, that's not how you treat an old lady."

BEST DAMNED USED car salesman in Sioux Falls from 1967 to 1974. Earned a reputation and even started buying shares in the lot. The heir apparent. The owner's frat boy sons would get to outright own the place, sure, but everyone knew Bill was going to run it. Eventually, patiently, he'd get the whole thing because he knew shit about those boys—one a fag but married, the other maxing out credit cards week after week to keep gambling and losing—that had him sitting pretty.

He took to the bars. He asked his salesmen where they let off steam. He got himself some tail, not too young, not too old. One piece of tail with Kate Jackson hair introduced him to cocaine. Well, fuck me standing up, if that didn't cure some blues … for about a month.

Work, on the other hand, was all pigshit. Turned out the gay co-owner knew about the cocaine and wasn't intimidated. Even got a little flouncy.

It came down to a bad meeting on Tuesday morning when Bill stumbled in late, found the fag sitting behind Bill's desk, feet up. "You want this lot? You're going to have to pay out the ass. You're going to have to work for it."

Bill turned and headed for the coffee pot. "We'll see what your brother has to say about it."

"No need. I bought him out already."

Bill spilled coffee on his hand and bit his cheek.

"Turns out a gambler is more than thankful if you toss over a few grand to keep the bruisers from breaking something. That was all it took. Too bad he probably lost most of it at blackjack the same night."

Bill sucked his burnt finger, couldn't think of anything to say. He stepped back into his office and sat down.

The new owner smiled, straight teeth. "Better me than him, risking it all on two pair or a horse who took a shit before the race."

Bill was never the top salesman again. Wasn't even a top manager. He simply plugged along, a third of the shares, not seeing a dime. He was beginning to think he'd retire a has-been with a coke habit. What the fuck would he do then?

Then he met Patti. Patti had a friend named Emma. And neither one was making much trying to freelance it in truck stop bathrooms. Shit, Patti even cried happy tears when Bill gave her twenty more than she'd asked for. Gave the master salesman an idea. And those two led to Wanda. And eventually to Louisa. Things kept getting better.

HE GOT HOME around ten-thirty and his son was waiting up, of course. Bill Jr. was like some kind of computer genius, supposedly, and barely slept. Caroline had insisted he stay with Dad since Junior, unlike her, was single and mobile and not prone to fighting with Dad as much. The girl reminded him too much of Louisa. And, bless her soul, he was getting tired of hearing women tell him what to do.

"Where were you?"

Not even *Hey, Dad! Looking sharp!* It sucked when the roles flipped, Bill now the child of the house.

Bill said, "The casino. With Gilley."

"Jesus, Dad, like every night with the casino now. Do you ever win?"

Shrug. "Just nickels."

Junior turned back to his laptop. "Gilley might not miss the money, but you've still got bills to pay. And those places get robbed all the time."

"No, not those shitty casinos in town. That's for them, what you call it, doing the meth and all. I'm talking the one out in the corn fields. Jesus. Think I'd wear this to a—"

"Hungry?"

Bill shrank. Sleeves too long. He was cold. Junior turned the heat down when Bill left the house. Christ, all those years he fought with Louisa to keep it cooler, always lost, and now he badly wanted some fucking heat.

He waved off food. Stepped over to the couch, sat down. Looked around for the remote, but it had already begun. The fog. Soon as he stopped moving, stopped thinking about the business, about tricking his kids. Soon as he sat down each night, the fog was there, minutes suddenly turning into hours. He thought he found the remote, because the TV was on. Maybe he'd been watching it for a while. One of those cop shows, the boring ones Gilley and his bitches all like. Not that it mattered. It was a lot of noise, except the news. He could focus on the news, weather, sports. He could even focus on that fucking red-headed kid doing Carson's old job, at least for ten minutes.

It was too hard to keep up. Easier to sink into the fog until it cleared and then enjoy the hell out of his evenings, back on the streets, felt like home. Much more like home than home anymore. It was as if he was watching reruns. Junior didn't look or act much like Bill when Bill was that age, but enough to make him think he'd gone back in time. And Caroline, well, looked almost exactly like her mother. She had for a long time now, and maybe that was fine for a while, but now she was at the age when Louisa had been most bitchy, and Caroline was really bitchy, and Bill was confused for half of all her visits.

Junior's voice blinked him out of the fog. His son was right there, in the armchair, the local news getting started on TV.

"Dad, we need to talk about Jenn."

"Who's Jenn?" Going through his mental files. Patti, Emma, and Wanda Belle. Those were his girls. None of them named Jenn. "Which one is she?"

"The new nurse? She's brunette, the college girl who helps you in the morning?"

Right, got it. Right. The whore with the heavy mascara, always texting when she was supposed to be helping. Barely paid attention. Almost as foggy as he was. She came over smelling like syrup and flowers and cigarettes, always in sweatpants and flip flops, always with her hair wet and stringy.

"She's okay," Bill said. She was something to look at. Reminded him of the girls on TV. "She do something wrong?"

Junior made the face, the same one Bill had made at his kids when they did something wrong the first time but he wasn't ready to take the belt to them yet. It didn't feel good coming back at him.

"She's doing a fine job. A good girl. But, you know … I don't know how to say it."

"Just do it already. Hell, son, did I teach you to namby-pamby like that?"

"Dad, it's hard. She says, you know … says you're harassing her. Touching her inappropriately. Are you getting confused? Playing around?"

Like a vacuum sucking up the fog. That was all it took. Bill blinked into his right mind. "It's a damned lie."

Junior shrugged. "Maybe you were kidding and didn't know how uncomfortable she felt. You can't always say and do the things you used to. It was a different time then."

Bill wanted to punch someone. Start with his dumbass son and move on to slapping this hussy in her lying hussy mouth. He wasn't so far gone as to hit on someone who reminded him of Christmas morning and presents and Easter egg hunts and smiles at the county fair. A kid. She was a kid. A chain-smoking, whore-makeup-wearing *kid*, for shit's sake. He grabbed his son's knee, made the boy jump a bit, and looked him in the eye.

"I'm a perfect gentleman. I have no idea what she's talking about."

Of course Junior didn't buy it. Sweet little piece of ass uses her sad voice on him, and he melts. *Obviously* Dad is a monster. A dirty old man. Poor put-upon caretaker. Bill had three vivacious, experienced women in his stable. He knew how to treat them with respect. He knew what a real woman expected and he knew what powerful spirits they had tucked behind those tits and asses. Put up with Louisa freezing him out, and never once did he *harass* the woman.

"Dad, let me handle it, okay? If you can, remember to leave her alone, let her do her job. We don't want to lose this one."

Meaning Junior didn't want to lose her. Meaning if there was any dirty old man in the house, it was him, not Bill. Men these days didn't take whoever they wanted. They convinced whoever it was that she wanted him just as much. Junior had never married. He got older, but the age of the women he dated stayed the same, and maybe he didn't take the hint.

Bill turned to the TV. The weatherman. Bill couldn't make sense of the numbers anymore. "How much you giving her?"

"What?"

"To shut her up, keep her here. She wants a raise? A payout?"

Junior cleared his throat, crossed his legs so that Bill's hand slid off. "Don't worry about the money. It's all taken care off. Just be good, okay?"

Bill almost laughed. The girl was a shakedown artist. Probably pulled this act on lots of old men. Probably always worked. Smart.

"What's a matter? She can't tell me to my face? Don't I deserve that?"

"I gave her tomorrow off. Don't worry about it. But be nice when she gets back, okay?"

Bill said something like, "Good like her grandpa," but it was lost in the fog again, and Junior wasn't there anymore. And then he was in bed. And then it was dark.

THE WOMEN ON the morning news were cooking but talking too fast to be understood. Bill didn't remember getting here, his couch, a cup of coffee in his hand, but he must've. It wasn't a dream. Muscle memory, perhaps.

Wanda Belle was sitting across from him, her legs crossed like a much younger woman, her usual sexy grin, enough to seal the deal. She was dressed in jeans and an airbrushed T-shirt slit at the collar down to damn near her nipples. She was the oldest of Bill's women at sixty-two, but she had worked hard to make sure it was a Susan Sarandon sixty-two and not a Florida retiree. Real tits, real good thighs, but everything cozy, worn in, and weathered. She kept her copper penny hair cut short so you'd notice her eyes. Magic in those eyes. Hard to believe, but Wanda was his best money-maker with the college boys.

"How's tricks, babe?"

She rolled her eyes. "We're going to have to repeat the whole conversation now."

"What conversation?"

A sigh. The grin never faded. "I've been here twenty minutes already. I sent your boy out for breakfast so we could talk about the business. I'm saying, sweetheart, that it's time to start talking about calling an end to this. How much longer can we pull this off?"

He slammed the coffee down on the end table a bit too hard.

Wanda titled her head. "You already did that."

Stumped him a sec. "I'm strong as a bull. Gilley's stronger. No end in sight."

The expression on her face was one he expected from nurses and doctors, not his best girl. "You said that, too. But you've pretty much got your head on straight three hours a day. Gilley's having heart problems. He doesn't want you to know about them. He's having a ball, but it's killing him."

Sure, things were foggy, but it wasn't like he was totally gone. He knew the day of the week, knew the big news stories, knew the fucking *weather*, right? Knew everyone's names and who they were to him, like Junior ... Emma ... Belle? Wanda. It was Wanda right here with him. The others were Emma and ... shit, the youngest one, like fifty-five. Couldn't remember her name even when he was in his prime. Didn't mean a thing. And the one who was always arguing with Junior ... well, that was easy. It was Louisa. She'd been away for a long time, but she was back now to make sure the boy—was that Junior? Much older now. But Louisa was there, looking like her old self again, to set things straight when the boy got weird ideas, like a retirement home. Retire? Bill? With the car lot still making money? Please.

He blinked and Wanda was beside him on the couch, kicking off her shoes and pulling her legs beneath her. She wrapped her arms around Bill, her head on his shoulder. "It's almost like we've already lost you. Let me take over. I can get the girls out to Vegas or the Valley and make more with DVDs than we can here. Tell Junior to send you out West, and we can keep an eye on you. The very best for you. We can afford it."

It was like magic how the fog lifted. Took a lot of concentration, but say things like "the very best" and "retirement" and "keep an eye on you," and Bill blinked like he'd been catnapping and was now ten years younger, stronger, and with it. He gave Wanda a hug but then pushed her off. He rocked himself off the couch, stood and took in a deep breath. Felt damned good to be a pimp.

"I'm not done yet, hon." Bill thumped his chest. "This ticker's still pumping strong."

"It's not the ticker I'm worried about."

He shrugged. "Some parts you can do without."

Maybe she said something else. If so, he fast-forwarded through it. But the next minute she was smiling with tears running down her cheeks. "God bless you, Billy boy."

"Damn right." He reached down his hand. "Now get up and let me take a look at you. Make sure you're prime rib for the menu tonight."

She took his hand, stood, and took off her clothes. She jiggled in places, but they were good places, and Bill tried to remember what it felt like to get turned on by them all.

THAT NIGHT WAS mostly Wanda. Three gigs, spaced farther apart than in the old days so she could clean herself off and lube up again. Some pill she was taking helped with blood flow, too, so that the friction wasn't so bad while she laid there thinking about what to buy her grandkids for their birthdays. If she was going to get back in the game, she'd told Bill when he came calling, by god she was going to enjoy it.

So she did a college kid, then a guy in his forties who hadn't gotten over his librarian fantasy, and then the last was a grad school lesbian who wanted to be bullied around by a strong, older woman. Wanda came back out to the car after that one shaking her head. "Poor kid. Half the time, I thought I was hurting her. She wants to see me again next week. I don't think I can do that again."

The last call of the night was for all three women, so Bill, Gilley, and Wanda met the other two at Perkins for dinner before setting out. Some kind of bachelor party. They'd done a couple of those before. Left with aching jaws more than anything else.

Patti wasn't so sure she could handle it. "My irritable bowel thing. As long as I have time to use the bathroom first."

The men laughed and the women nodded like they knew exactly how she felt. It was a good night. Bill wasn't missing a beat. So he thought. A couple of times, Emma or Gilley would say something louder than they should have, and Bill wondered if they were repeating themselves. Okay, so mostly good. And no one was scolding him or looking at him like he was a child. He felt good. He ate a sirloin and a baked potato and didn't drip any on his pinstriped navy suit, double-breasted. His sleeves got in the way of his fingers more than they had back in the day, but that wasn't the worst. Wanda flipped up his cuffs and that was that.

They finished their meals and Patti rushed off to the restroom. The others sat around reminiscing. Twenty, thirty years ago. Back when they had all the car lots in town wired, all the bankers and councilmen and school principals. Back when they were doing coke and driving over to the Twin Cities to see Prince and Morris Day before *Purple Rain* had even come out. They would get a line on a party or two over there, grab a couple of hotel rooms downtown, and roll in the big bucks while the record producers and business execs and chefs and politicians paid royally for young, hot, South Dakota pussy.

Before Louisa. Before she came along and changed everything. Not sure what she was getting herself into at first, but then Bill fell for her, and she started doing fewer tricks, and it wasn't long before he'd gotten down on one knee, slipped a ring on her finger, and called an end to the whole side business. Gave the girls a lot back—he'd invested money for them—so they could go on about their lives without having to worry about work for a long time.

Tack on another ten years, and it turned out that Louisa was one of those women who found themselves as better moms than wives. Sex became another chore for her. She'd rather sell Tupperware, Avon, and whatever else was advertised in the backs of magazines. Then she volunteered at the library and that was her first love, her social circle, the topic of conversation.

Not that Bill ever stopped loving her. Quite the opposite. He wanted her even more. His best fucking friend in the world, after all. Who else could he talk to about the news or about B&Bs or trashy novels? Not his dumbass kids, glazed over on MTV and bands wearing Kabuki makeup, Jesus.

He didn't remember exactly any more, but there came a day, the kids nearly done with high school, when she softened to him again. Not sexually. God no, she was done with that by forty-five, thank you very much. Those pipes were dry. But they could talk again. Stay up late watching bad TV. Take weekend trips to the Badlands or up to Lake Country. He didn't even mind holding her purse at department stores.

Louisa. The only one who'd ever been able to rope him in. Lassoed that penis right up, to Wanda Belle's chagrin. They kept in touch some, but Louisa made sure it was casual, short, and very infrequent. And then Louisa left.

At least, Bill thought she left. It was as if the fog was too thick whenever he tried to remember exactly why. They went to bed one night. And for some reason he remembered her sitting up in bed, very early in the morning, and there was fear. It was cold. And then … she wasn't there any more.

He didn't know what he'd done to lose her. Tried to remember, tried to contact her. Got weird looks from his kids whenever he asked, like they were in on it. They said "lupus" as if that explained anything at all. She must have told them not to give Bill her new number. It had to be. Maybe she'd run off with one of those producers she used to fuck. They looked at Bill so sad when he started getting angry about it.

But then she came back. Granted, thirty years younger and just as frigid as when she'd left before, but at least she was around more. Not willing to live with him, instead charging her son—he looked the same age as Louisa, which was weird—with keeping an eye on him all day, every day, except for the trips out with friends like Gilley and Wanda Belle.

Like tonight.

Like when he looked down and realized his glass of tea had slipped through his fingers and tipped over, staining his suit.

The girls were all over him, spotting him with napkins, saying, "It's okay, it's okay. You with us, Big Bill?"

The cold got through to his skin and got him back on track. The girls, looking old and tired but still lovely. Gilley, Jesus, what the fuck had happened to Gilley? Where was his hair? Why were his tattoos so blurred?

Patti came back and said, "That's going to be raw, I tell you. What's going on here?"

"Bill had a spill."

He cleared his throat and remembered the where and the when and the point of all this. "I've spilled worse. Now how about you go get us some and make your man some money, babies?"

Gilley tossed some cash on the table and stood. "These senior discounts are pretty sweet. Too bad I can't spend the rest on anything fun anymore."

Emma held out her hand. "Give me ten bucks and we'll at least have fun trying."

On their way out, laughing like teenagers and swaggering like hipsters, Bill overheard the manager tell their server, "Please, God, I hope I'm dead before I turn out like those guys."

THE BACHELOR PARTY was in a hotel room downtown overlooking the river, and the plan was for Gilley and Bill to get the girls inside, get paid, and then go downstairs to wait, maybe watch the Weather Channel in the lobby. Maybe grab a coffee. But these folks in the room—young tough guys with military haircuts and T-shirts with beer slogans and cartoon characters, all looking new like they'd been bought an hour earlier from Target—set off some sort of alarm in Bill's head, but the noise was buried under blankets, so faint that he couldn't tell if it was for this party or for some other party a long time ago. Maybe this was like *déjà vu.* Maybe. He couldn't remember what he was supposed to be remembering.

The girls filed in behind Bill and Gilley, and the whole room tittered. Giggles hidden behind hands, some guys hooting and applauding, saying

"Hot mamas!" and "Auntie Naughty!" and one guy telling his friend, "I think my mom knows the blond one."

The ladies liked what they saw, far as Bill could tell. They worked the room immediately, not having to fake how impressed they were with all that manhood.

Bill looked around. One of the guys was talking to him, supposedly the dealmaker, but Bill couldn't put the words together. "What's ... going to ... for these young ladies ... party ... night with us?" The second time around, it was Gilley who ticked off the menu on his fingers. Bill was still taking it all in. Six of these guys sitting around. Where was the booze? The music? The porn on the TV? Why was this the lamest party ever, except for his girls in the center of the room now, posing and winking?

Because, of course, finally, the old edge coming back, *this isn't a party at all.*

"Sorry," Bill said. He stepped over to the girls, took Wanda by the hand. "We've got to go."

A big wave of *Awww* from the jarheads.

Wanda Belle pulled her wrist away and started to protest when she caught on. Always the smart one, Wanda Belle. She probably was best suited for the behind the scenes stuff after all, but, god, that body. Shame to waste it.

She whispered to Bill, "Just tell them we dance, then. Just ... I dunno. Maybe Patti can start in with her diarrhea."

Patti said, "Hey! It's called IBS."

Bill shook his head. "Gilley already gave them the rundown. They know. They're waiting for us to agree on the price."

Wanda thought hard. Sure did. Bill could see the wheels creaking up there, slower than twenty years ago but not missing any parts like he was. Made him proud.

"Let me talk to the leader there." She chinned towards the door. "I'll fix this. I can deal with a night downtown."

"Wait, no, what do you ... That's crazy."

"We've done it before, all of us, right?"

Emma and Patti nodded, but neither looked too excited. Patti said, "I'm sure my bowels will act up again. I can't do that in front of other women."

Emma, too. "It's not like the old days, Wanda, honey. What if Alex tries to find me? As far as he knows, I'm at a book club."

"Shit, it'll be the most exciting thing that's happened to him in years."

Commotion at the door. Cop barking. Bill and Wanda turned.

Gilley had made a run for it.

Bill instinctively went after him. "No, wait, don't shoot him!"

Bill made it to the door before a cop wrapped him up. "Chill, grandpa."

He poked his head out of the door in time to see a couple of guys catch up to Gilley and take him to the ground. Bill flinched. He heard the bones pop from down the hall. Gilley wailing as the cops untangled themselves and looked at what they'd done.

One of the cops looked back at the head cheese. "Shit, get an ambulance! Now! Do something!"

Cell phones out, calls got made, while Bill sagged against the cop's arms and watched his helpless friend writhe.

Wanda told the head cheese, "Let's cut a deal here. You see what's going on, right?"

After that, it was all noise to Bill. He remembered himself and Gilley thirty years ago, always with the newest demos from the lot, hot pussy in the backseat, cash burning holes in their slacks. Back then Gilley was like an armored truck. It would've taken a lot more than two cops to bring him to the ground. Shit. You could pound a baseball bat on the man's shins and still not break a bone. And he'd laugh while you did it.

Yeah, Gilley was one tough son of a bitch. Bill wondered what had ever happened to the guy. They used to be good friends. Been a while since he'd heard from him …

BILL WAS GETTING tired of the house. It felt like he hadn't been out for years. He told Junior that and the boy gave him a funny look, then said, "Well, get used to it." Like he was grounded. His own son. Bill didn't buy it. The fuck could he have a son that old? He and Gilley, they were at the prime of their lives. Just sick or something. Maybe that's why he was so weak.

Wanda called in the afternoon, talking about posting bail and taking the rap. She said the cops had laughed about it mostly. There was nothing she could do to keep the story from leaking. He might have reporters asking after him.

"Like there's never been pimps in Sioux Falls before?"

She hesitated, then, "Not one this old."

"Jesus, then they must be starting as pups! What's going on with the kids these days?"

"No, Bill, we're old. The news is going to be all over this, the grandfather pimp and his stable of cougars."

"What's a cougar? What are you talking about? This is a set-up! The cops have got you saying all this. Jesus, Wanda. Put Louisa on. She's okay, right? Let me talk to Louisa."

Another long pause. "I've got to go, Bill. I'm sorry. I'll talk to you soon."

Someone was humming. It distracted him. Like a buzz or a bird or something. He put the phone down, looked around. Coming from somewhere outside the living room. He stood and waited for his head to stop spinning. When had he put on the track suit? He hated the tracksuit. The kitchen, maybe. Caroline, maybe. Listening to her Walkman or something.

He rounded the corner and found some floozy at the dinner table, hunched over a little computer, small enough to fit in her hand. Typing away. Oblivious. She had some wires coming out of her ears, plugged into the computer she was holding. Humming along to something. She was wearing ripped jeans, flip-flops, and a shirt that showed most of her lower back, some swirly tattoo down there. Raccoon eyes. Prime Grade-A fucking material.

He remembered. Clarity like someone ringing a bell. About the cops, about Gilley in intensive care, about Wanda taking the heat, and about this little bitch Jenn trying to fleece him by saying he'd been inappropriate with her.

"You." Waved his hand to get her attention. She had a bit of mouth-breather going on. "Hey, you."

She pulled the wires from her ears, some little nubs at the end. When she spoke, it was loud and sing-songy. "You need something, Mr. Bill? Are you hungry? I can make you some fish sticks."

He pointed at her. "Shut up. I'm old, not stupid. You talk to your own grandpa like that?"

"Yeah. I only see him twice a year, down in Florida. I turn on the charm, he hands out the cash."

"Seems you like the cash quite a bit. What's this about me touching you? All a bunch of hogshit, you ask me."

Jenn rolled her eyes. "Your son told me you had Alzheimer's. Guess you remember more than he let on."

Bill pulled a chair out, sat down opposite her. "Tell me about it."

"I don't know what you're talking—"

"Kid, I'm not going to bust you or anything. Curious, that's all."

She looked at him a long moment, then back at the closed office door, where Junior was supposedly in there working. She turned back to Bill. "Guys can't remember shit, so they don't know if they grabbed my ass or talked dirty, so the family pays to shut me up. I mean, I'm in college, broke half the time. Nice to have some extra money."

"But nobody's ever really done anything to you."

She smiled. "Once. And it was kind of cool. I got a thrill out of this old guy mistaking me for his girlfriend. Wanted me to sit on his face. I told his daughter, and I got five hundred bucks. You know, if he could've taken it, maybe I would've done it, too. One last taste, you know?"

Bill laughed. He liked her. Reminded him of the girls he'd met before Louisa. Hell, more like Louisa than the others, this one.

"Let me ask you," he said. "Ever thought of selling that ass of yours? I bet you could do better than five hundred, and you wouldn't have to lie about it."

"Well, I'm pretty sure I can get a few grand from your son. If I accidentally showed him my tits, maybe five."

Yeah, that was Junior all right. Boy needed to be taught better about business. "You know what I do when I go out at nights?"

Jenn shook her head.

"I pimp some middle-aged women out to college boys who are willing to pay top dollar for a romp in the hay with a naughty teacher or librarian or aunt."

Her eyes widened. "Gross."

"Hey, guys like a woman who knows what she's doing. Right? And I bet a smart girl like you could work on your back a couple nights a week, do some freaky stuff for old guys, and make money like you don't know what."

It was make or break. She'd either shut down or want more. Run screaming and quit right now, or …

"Go on," she said.

Bill's turn to smile. "I'm on the way out, you know. Can't remember shit anymore. But before I go, I plan on teaching that son of mine all about my business, and you would be a good partner. Both of you in charge of a handful of girls, plus my old beauties, well, think about it."

She'd slid out of her chair and slinked over to Bill, wrapped her arms around his neck, breathing heavily into his ear. "Interesting."

He pointed to the office door. "You start with him, go give him what he needs, and then send him out to talk to me. We'll be in business by sundown, missy."

"Him? Not you?" She seemed disappointed.

"Hey, I'll just forget it ten minutes later. Junior's the one who needs to remember."

She started back to the door, a little shy now. Kept looking over her shoulder. No, definitely not Caroline. What was her name? Was she a nurse or something? Jenn. Jenn. Jenn. She knocked lightly on the office door and let herself in. Jenn. Who's Jenn?

Fuck.

He grabbed a napkin and found a pen on the bar, scribbled down something. He started to hear some noise from the back office. Who was back there? Like … someone was getting fucked. Oh yeah. Maybe it was Louisa. It didn't sound like her, though. She was supposed to quit that when they got married.

He sat back down at the kitchen table and waited, looking at the napkin every so often to remind himself. Keeping clear, keeping clear.

Gilley, probably never going to walk again. The girls, probably ready to end their adventure and slip back into normal life. Junior and Caroline and Louisa ... well, Louisa passed on, didn't she? Of course she did. And one day, sooner than later, so would Bill.

When Junior finally emerged from the room, hair and face all sweaty and his eyes glazed over like he'd seen Heaven in Technicolor, Bill had to really concentrate to remember who he was. Another look at the napkin: HE'S YOUR SON. MAKE HIM A PIMP.

Junior caught sight of his dad. Crinkled his eyebrows. "Dad?"

Bill motioned at the table. "Come have a seat. We need to talk."

OLD MEN AND OLD BOARDS

BY DON WINSLOW

THERE'S A SADNESS to sunsets.

People on the beach stop what they're doing, stand still, and watch the sun sink over the horizon. It's pretty, sure, but it's also an acknowledgment of the death of that day, the coming of night, and the relentless passing of time.

You can't stop the sun by looking at it, and that's the sorrow.

OLD MEN AND old boards don't go out much.

They tend to stay in the garage, or maybe on the beach. They're cracked and worn, old men and boards, but they have histories together. They've gone for a lot of rides with each other, those old men and old boards, and they get attached.

Bill Bakke, for example, has had three different wives over the years, but the same board, a 1954 Velzy balsa "Malibu Spoon."

His first wife, Linda, married him because he was the strong silent type and divorced him for the same reason. She left him for a man who talked to her and "shared his feelings." Bill didn't share his feelings, hadn't let them loose since Korea, and wasn't going to. When long, sleepless nights brought Chinese whistles blowing and the mortar rounds exploding in his head, he held himself tight until the sun came up and then took the Velzy out into the water and they rode it out together.

His second wife, Ginger, came and went like a winter swell. She blew in on a drunken weekend and swept out the same way just a year or so later. She basically gave him a choice between her and surfing, and wasn't all that surprised—or even hurt—when he chose his board. No hard feelings, just an *hasta la vista* and a Vegas divorce.

Marion died just five years ago, but ten years after the Alzheimer's took her. She understood his silences and need for solitude, and those mornings when she found him shaking, his arms clutched around his knees, she just handed him a cup of coffee, walked away and didn't embarrass him with questions or offers of sympathy.

She painted while he surfed. Her water-color seascapes weren't very good, but they made her happy and he loved her very much. The last two years when she was in the home, he visited every afternoon, then took his board out onto the water and surfed until the sun set.

He hasn't gone out that much since Marion died.

But this sunset he sits his board just south of the pier and watches the light fade.

BILL HAD TAKEN the Velzy out of the garage and hefted it onto the rack on the old Wagoneer. The board was heavier than it used to be and he was short of breath as he strapped it down. He locked his old service .45 back up in the cabinet, so no kid could come in and hurt himself or somebody else.

It was only a five minute drive down to the beach—the Wagoneer had made the trip thousands of times—and he found a parking spot and took the board down. It was cool for summer, cooler now that the sun was going down, and he thought he should put on a wetsuit but his arthritis wouldn't let him clutch the material so he gave up.

After Korea he swore that he'd never be cold again, but men swear a lot of things.

THIS STRETCH OF coast once was wild and free.

Bill and his buddies cruised it up and down, in the days when you could just pull of the road onto an empty beach and surf wherever you wanted. There were no crowds then on the breaks, no lineups, just him and his friends and endless water and endless time. They bought bags of potatoes and buried them in the coals of open fires, they bought fifteen-cent burgers and ten-cent shakes, they drank beer and played ukuleles and chased girls, and sunset then was just the promise of the next day and there would always be more days.

He came back from the war with his innocence and faith shattered, and all that waited for him was a job laying tile and the board. He took both and built a life. Bought a little house he could afford not too far from the beach, worked his forty, spent his evenings and his weekends with the board and knew himself to be as happy as this life allows. Bill kept the same job and the same house for thirty years, three marriages and one board.

It was a nice neighborhood back then. People kept their houses and their lawns up, the kids were okay to ride their bicycles around the cul-de-sac, the neighbors barbecued together, played cards, and otherwise stayed out of each other's business. They'd stand in the street on summer evenings watching their kids when the ice cream truck came.

Now the kids are grown and can't afford to live in California, couldn't come close to affording a house in this neighborhood anymore, so Bill Jr. is in Arkansas now and Janet lives with her husband in Tucson, and her own kids live nearby. Bill used to drive there once a month but for the past couple of years has found the trip too tiring. The kids call and they keep trying to get him to buy a computer so they can "e-mail" but he isn't so interested. They've each asked him to move to where they are but he doesn't want to leave the ocean even though he hardly goes out anymore.

And he doesn't want to leave his house, even though the neighborhood is going down faster than a winter sun, and the gangs have moved in. If he goes out now in the summer evenings he smells the clouds of dope, hears the bass booming, the coarse laughter and the shouting and the curses. More and more he sits inside and turns the television up. Sometimes he thinks about going surfing instead, but the board gets heavier and his bones hurt, it seems like too much work, and he worries about breaking a hip.

So the old board and the old man sit.

Both knowing they have more rides behind than in front. The truth is that there's a wave out there that's going to be your last, and you may or may not know it. Now, sitting on his board, waiting for the next set to come in, Bill hears the sirens.

THE PADDLE OUT to the break was tough.

Tougher than he remembered, certainly tougher than he wanted it to be. His shoulders ached, his arms trembled, and he felt that scary tightness across his chest. The doctor had given him contradictory advice about it—out of one side of his mouth he advised Bill to give up the surfing, while the other side said it was probably the lifetime of hitting the waves that kept him as healthy as he was.

Janet tried to get him to give it up for good.

"A man your age," she said.

"I'm gonna die doing something," Bill answered. "I'd rather drop dead off my board than off the goddamn sofa."

"Think of your family," she said.

"I am."

THE NIGHT BEFORE had been rough. The Chinese came in waves and Bill had a hard time telling the difference between the exploding rounds and the vibration in the walls from the party next door. Couldn't make out the screams of the past from the shouts of the present.

It had gotten worse lately, with all the noise next door, since the one they called "Z-Jay" moved in. Some kind of gangster, Bill reckoned, he drove his Navigator around the cul-de-sac like a maniac, and Bill was worried that he'd kill somebody someday driving like that, even though there weren't many little kids left on the block riding their bicycles. And no kids waiting at dusk for the ice cream truck. Instead it was kids who would line up outside Z-Jay's to buy his dope.

Then Z-Jay and his "boys" would party all night in the back yard, smoke marijuana and sometimes toss the empty beer cans over the fence.

Bill tossed them back.

Like grenades in a foxhole.

"Just pick them up and forget about it," Janet advised him over the phone.

"Come to Arkansas, Dad," Bill Jr. said.

There's no surf in Arkansas, Bill thought. No sunset painting the ocean. No Marion painting the sunset.

Now he felt the swell building behind him and looked over his shoulder to see a nice set of four waves building nicely. The board beneath him creaked with excitement, an old horse recalling what it was like to be a colt.

The morning had been bad. He sat on his raised patio that he'd built himself and sipped the coffee that Marion couldn't bring him anymore and stared across the fence as if it was barbed wire. The Chinese came and men screamed and men died.

He decided he didn't want to do this anymore.

Didn't want to go through another night like it.

Old and alone.

Decided that if the last wave won't take you, you have to paddle out to it.

BILL REMEMBERS THE day he brought Bill Jr. out to this very spot for his first ride. The boy was excited and nervous and Bill put him on the old board, trusting it to give the boy a steady ride and keep him safe.

It did.

He remembers watching the old board carry his son to the shore and then the boy hopping off and looking back with a big grin on his face and that was maybe the best day of Bill's whole life. The kind of day that gets you through the cold mornings when the past and present won't shake apart but you think you might.

Bill Jr. didn't really take to surfing, though. He developed different interests—cars, girls, friends. That was all right—a father shouldn't impose his own passions on his son. It would have been nice but it wasn't to be.

He would always have that day.

Bill sees the police cars pull into the parking lot, around the old Wagoneer. He knows that he could probably plead insanity, but either way they would lock him up for the rest of his life and that's not the way he wants to go.

So he turns and paddles out, into the waves.

DUCK-DIPPING THE FIRST three, he faces the fourth and largest.

But he doesn't turn to paddle. Instead, he slides off the board into the cold water and pushes the board into the wave. "Go on. Go."

But the old board missed the wave—first time ever—and floated over the backside with him.

"That's the way it's going to be?" Bill asks it.

Seems so.

BILL SPENT THE day doing the dishes, tidying up the house, and cleaning out the garage. He got his papers in order to make sure that Bill Jr. and Janet would get as much as they could from the sale. He was clipping the grass away from the flagstones in the back yard and saw the beer cans glistening in the sun like unexploded shell heads.

That's when he went into the cabinet, got out the old .45 and walked back into the yard. Looked over the fence and saw Z-Jay lying on his lawn chair, his eyes gently closed, a marijuana cigarette in one hand, a beer in the other, the trace of a happy smile on his lips.

From selling dope to children.

Maybe it was that, maybe it was just the beer cans, maybe it was a selfish desire to accomplish something of worth before he left the world, but anyway, Bill rested the pistol barrel on the fence, because it was too heavy now for him to lift and aim with just his right hand. He notched the V on the gangster's chest and yelled, "Hey!"

Z-Jay opened one eye.

"I told you to quit throwing your beer cans into my yard," Bill said.

He pulled the trigger.

Then he pulled it again.

NOW THE OLD man and the old board paddle out toward the last, faint rays.

People on the beach stop what they're doing, stand still, and watch the sun sink over the horizon. It's pretty, sure, but it's also an acknowledgment of the death of that day, the coming of night, and the relentless passing of time.

You can't stop the sun by looking at it, and that's the sorrow.

There's a sadness to sunsets.

AFTERWORD

BY BILL CRIDER

THIS BOOK WAS David Thompson's idea, as I explained in the foreword, and it was one of the things that we talked about the last time I saw him on September 4, 2010, when I was at Murder by the Book in Houston for a signing. David told me how pleased he was with the stories we'd gotten and said that he hoped to have the book ready to preview at NoirCon in Philadelphia.

The book will be ready, thanks not just to David's hard work but also to the efforts of Benjamin LeRoy of Tyrus Books and Sara J. Henry, who contributed so much to the final copyediting.

But while the book will be ready, David won't be at NoirCon to see it. He passed away on September 13, 2010, at the age of thirty-eight. He was one of the creators of geezer noir, but he will never be a geezer. And that's a damned shame, because David was always bursting with enthusiasm and full of ideas and plans, not just for this book, but for Busted Flush Press in its new incarnation, for the bookstore, for the promotion of writers, and for his life with his wife, McKenna Jordan. I can't imagine what he might have accomplished had he lived, but there's no doubt that I would have been impressed.

It's impossible to underestimate how much David will be missed, and not just by his wife and family and the people who worked with him. David was known to mystery writers and fans not just in the U.S. but all over the world. Not all of them had met him in person, but they'd all heard of him, corresponded with him, seen his tweets on Twitter, talked with him on the phone, or read his posts in online forums. His memory and influence will linger for a good long time.

Here's something else David told me the last time I saw him. He said that he was happiest when he was at home with McKenna, when they were on the couch with their dogs nearby. McKenna would be at one end of the couch reading with her stack of books beside her, and David would be at the other end of the couch reading with his stack beside him. It's a picture that will stick with me.

AFTERWORD

David was unique: bright, knowledgeable, outgoing, enthusiastic. He loved reading, writers, conventions, his wife, and the bookstore. Not necessarily in that order. People like him don't come around often. I doubt that we'll see his like again.

Ave atque vale, David.

DAMN NEAR DEAD 2

BIOS

PATRICIA ABBOTT is the author of more than seventy-five stories appearing in literary and crime fiction publications. She won the Derringer Award in 2008 for her story "My Hero." Forthcoming print stories will appear in *By Hook or By Crook, Beat to a Pulp: Round One, Crimefactory*, and the as yet untitled Halloween Noir collection edited by Anne Frasier. She is the co-editor (with Steve Weddle) of a new collection of flash fiction, *Walmart Noir*. She lives and works in Detroit, Michigan.

ACE ATKINS has written eight novels, including his latest, *Infamous*, from G.P. Putnam's Sons. A former crime reporter at *The Tampa Tribune*, he published his first novel, *Crossroad Blues*, at twenty-seven and became a full-time novelist at thirty. While at the Tribune, Ace earned a Pulitzer Prize nomination for a feature series based on his investigation into a forgotten murder of the 1950s—which became the core of his critically acclaimed novel, *White Shadow*. He's now developing a new series set in rural Mississippi, with the first scheduled for 2011. Ace lives on a historic farm outside Oxford, Mississippi, with his family.

NEAL BARRETT JR.'s more than fifty novels and numerous short stories span the field from mystery/suspense, fantasy, science fiction, and historical novels to "off-the-wall" mainstream fiction. Reviewers have defined his work as "stories that defy category or convention." The *Washington Post* called his novel *The Hereafter Gang* "one of the great American novels." He was recently named Author Emeritus at the Science Fiction Writers of America's Nebula Awards convention in Cocoa Beach, Florida.

C.J. BOX is the *New York Times* bestselling author of twelve novels, including the award-winning Joe Pickett series. *Blue Heaven* won the Edgar® Award for Best Novel in 2008, and he's won the Prix Calibre 38 (France) and the Anthony, the Macavity, the Gumshoe, and the Barry awards. His first novel, *Open Season*, was a *New York Times* Notable Book and an Edgar® and *LA Times* Book Prize finalist. The novels have been translated into twenty-five languages. Box lives in Wyoming.

DECLAN BURKE is the author of three novels: *Eightball Boogie* (2003), *The Big O* (2007), and *Crime Always Pays* (2009). He lives in Wicklow, Ireland, with his wife, Aileen, and daughter, Lily, and hosts a website dedicated to Irish crime fiction called Crime Always Pays.

SCOTT A. CUPP is a short story writer from San Antonio, Texas. He has written in the areas of mystery, fantasy, western, science fiction, nonfiction, and music. He has been a reviewer in several venues including *Mystery Scene*. He has been nominated for the John W. Campbell Award for Best New Writer in the science fiction field and for the World Fantasy Award for editing *Cross Plains Universe: Texans Celebrate Robert E. Howard* (Fact/Monkeybrain, 2006) which he co-edited with Joe R. Lansdale. He works with the Missions Unknown and SF Signal blogs. One of his most recent stories is "Johnny Cannabis and Tony, the Purple Paisley (Sometimes) Colored White Lab Rat" at RevolutionSF.com.

CHRISTA FAUST is the author of ten novels, including the Edgar®- and Anthony Award-nominated *Money Shot*, and her latest, *Choke Hold*, forthcoming from Hard Case Crime in March 2011. She lives in Los Angeles.

ED GORMAN has produced two to three books a year, written over a hundred short stories, edited many anthologies, and co-founded and edited *Mystery Scene* since becoming a full-time writer in 1984, after twenty years in advertising. Much of his work haunts that ill-defined land between horror and mystery where the emphasis is as much on fear and shock as on crime and detection. Even his western fiction trespasses into this darkly psychological territory. His one-offs, written as E.J. Gorman, include *The Marilyn Tapes*, *The First Lady*, *Daughter of Darkness*, and *Senatorial Privilege*.

CAROLYN HAINES is the 2010 recipient of the Harper Lee Award and the 2009 recipient of the Richard Wright Award for Literary Excellence. The tenth book in her Sarah Booth Delaney Delta mysteries series, *Bone Appetit*, was published this summer by St. Martin's Minotaur. She is the editor of *Delta Blues*, a collection of stories centered around the Mississippi Delta Blues and a crime/noir element. An animal lover, Haines is active in a number of rescues and operates goodfortunefarmrefuge.org with her friend Aleta Beaureaux to try to help find homes for rescued animals. Her website is carolynhaines.com.

DAVID HANDLER published two highly acclaimed novels about growing up in Los Angeles—*Kiddo* and *Boss*—before resorting to a life of crime fiction. He has written eight novels about the witty and dapper celebrity ghostwriter Stewart Hoag and his faithful, neurotic basset hound, Lulu, including the Edgar®- and American Mystery Award-winning *The Man Who Would Be F. Scott Fitzgerald*. He has also written seven novels featuring the mismatched crime-fighting duo of New York film critic Mitch Berger and Connecticut state trooper Desiree Mitry, with *The Shimmering Blond Sister* (October 2010) the most recent. He wrote the thriller *Click to Play*, and co-authored the international bestselling thriller *Gideon* under the pseudonym Russell Andrews. David's short stories have earned a Derringer nomination and other honors. He was a member of the original writing staff that created the Emmy Award-winning sitcom "Kate and Allie," and has continued to write for television and film. He lives in a two-hundred-year-old carriage house in Old Lyme, Connecticut.

GAR ANTHONY HAYWOOD is the author of eleven crime novels, including six in the Aaron Gunner series, two in the Joe and Dottie Loudermilk series, and three stand-alone thrillers. His first Gunner short story, "And Pray Nobody Sees You," won both the PWA's Shamus and World Mystery Convention's Anthony awards for Best Short Story of 1995. That story is included in *Lyrics for the Blues*, a collection of Gunner short stories published by ASAP in 2009. Gar's most recently published short— "The First Rule Is," which was included in the 2009 anthology *Black Noir* —will be featured in the 2010 edition of Best American Mystery Short Stories. His latest novel is the urban crime drama *Cemetery Road*.

CAMERON PIERCE HUGHES reviews books for *January Magazine*, *Crimespree Magazine*, the pop culture website chud.com, The *Philadelphia City Paper*, and any other publications that will have him. His short story "Moving Black Objects" will be in *San Diego Noir* (Akashic Books, 2011). He has been an internet journalist and blogger since 2006. Like Don Winslow's Boone Daniels, he lives in San Diego. He is twenty-seven years old, and "War Zone" is his first published work of fiction.

JENNIFER JORDAN has articles, interviews, and short fiction in various magazines and a short story called "Bitter Kiss" in the anthology *Stirring up A Storm: Tales of the Sensual, the Sexual, and the Erotic* (edited by Marilyn Jaye Lewis). She is short fiction and special features editor for Crimespree Magazine and was the editor of *Expletive Deleted* and *Uncage Me!* She believes in fairies, is an avid meat eater, and is horribly addicted to caffeine.

TONI L.P. KELNER says that French's restaurant in "Kids Today" is a kind of homage to Finch's Restaurant in Raleigh, North Carolina, where her grandfather ate breakfast every day for years, and Skyland in Charlotte, where her parents eat almost every day. Kelner is the author of the "Where are they now?" mysteries featuring Boston-based freelance entertainment reporter Tilda Harper and the Laura Fleming Southern mystery series, which won a *Romantic Times* Career Achievement Award. Her most recent novel is *Who Killed the Pinup Queen?* She also co-edits urban fantasy anthologies with Charlaine Harris, and their most recent is *Death's Excellent Vacation*, about supernatural beings on holiday. In between books, she's a prolific writer of short stories, including the Agatha Award-winner "Sleeping With the Plush." Kelner lives north of Boston with author/husband Stephen Kelner, two daughters, and two guinea pigs.

JOE R. LANSDALE is the author of over thirty novels and numerous short stories. He has won numerous awards for his work, the Edgar® among them. Some of his works have been filmed. The best known is *Bubba Hotep*. He is at work on a new novel.

RUSSEL D. MCLEAN is younger than most people expect, although since he hit thirty, the grey's starting to sneak through in his beard. He is the author of (so far) two well-received hardboiled PI novels set in the Scots city of Dundee, and his short fiction has appeared in magazines on both sides of the Atlantic. You can find out more about this relatively young whippersnapper at russeldmclean.com.

DENISE MINA has written nine novels, including the Garnethill trilogy, the Paddy Meehan series, and *Still Midnight*, plus three graphic novels for DC. She also writes plays, short stories, and cheques. She has won several prizes but feels that it's kind of vulgar to bang on about that.

MARCIA MULLER, a native of the Detroit area, grew up in a house full of books and self-published three copies of her first novel at age twelve, a tale about her dog complete with primitive illustrations. The "reviews" were generally positive. Since the early 1970s Muller has authored more than thirty-five novels—three of them in collaboration with husband Bill Pronzini—seven short-story collections, and numerous nonfiction articles. Together she and Pronzini have edited a dozen anthologies and a nonfiction book on the mystery genre. In 2005 Muller was named a Grand Master by Mystery Writers of America, the organization's highest award. Pronzini was named Grand Master in 2008, making them the only living couple to share the award (the other being Margaret Millar and Ross Macdonald). The Mulzinis, as friends call them, live in Sonoma County, California, in yet another house full of books.

GARY PHILLIPS edited the well-received *Orange County Noir* anthology from Akashic; *The Underbelly*, a novella about a semi-homeless Vietnam vet's search for a disappeared disabled friend is out now from PM Press; and he's writing the adventures of Operator 5, a Depression-era superspy, part of Moonstone's Return of the *Originals: Pulp Heroes* comic book line. Website: gdphillips.com.

SCOTT PHILLIPS is the author of *The Ice Harvest* (New York Times Notable Book of the Year, California Book Award Silver Medal for Best First Fiction), *The Walkaway,* and *Cottonwood.* Three novels are forthcoming: *RUT*, in October 2010 from Concord Free Press, *The Adjustment* from Counterpoint in October 2011, and *Nocturne le Vendredi* from les Éditions la Branche in Paris, sometime in 2011.

TOM PICCIRILLI is the author of twenty novels, including *Shadow Season, The Cold Spot, The Coldest Mile,* and *A Choir of Ill Children.* He's won the International Thriller Award and four Bram Stoker Awards, and has been been nominated for the Edgar®, the World Fantasy Award, the Macavity, and Le Grand Prix de L'imagination. Learn more at thecoldspot.blogspot.com.

BILL PRONZINI, a full-time professional writer for forty years, has published more than seventy novels, including thirty-five in his popular Nameless Detective series (the most recent of which is *Betrayers*), four nonfiction books, and twenty collections of short stories. In 2008 he received the Mystery Writers of America Grand Master Award. He is also the recipient of the Private Eye Writers of America's Life Achievement Award, three PWA Shamus awards, six MWA Edgar® nominations, and two best-novel nominations from the International Crime Writers Association.

CORNELIA READ grew up in New York, California, and Hawaii, which may have had something to do with why her first husband nicknamed her "the lightning rod for entropy in the universe." Read now lives happily in New Hampshire, thank you very much, and that puling butthead and the Glenn Beck he rode in on can kiss her shapely Edgar®-nominated-and-Shamus-award-winning ass. But she's not bitter.

JAMES REASONER, a lifelong Texan, has been a professional writer for more than thirty years and has written several hundred novels and short stories in numerous genres. Best known for his Westerns, historical novels, and war novels, he is also the author of two mystery novels that have achieved cult followings, *Texas Wind* and *Dust Devils*. Writing under his own name and various pseudonyms, his novels have garnered praise from *Publishers Weekly*, *Booklist*, and the *Los Angeles Times*, as well as appearing on the *New York Times* and *USA Today* bestseller lists. He lives in a small town in Texas with his wife, award-winning fellow author Livia J. Washburn.

KAT RICHARDSON is the bestselling author of the Greywalker paranormal detective novels and a former magazine editor who moved from a tiny apartment in the LA metroplex to a tiny ugly house in Seattle in the mid-'90s. After working for a certain Large Software Company for a couple of years, she felt compelled to be her own boss and sell that darned novel! Five novels, a novella, and three short stories (including this one) later, she is now a self-supporting, full-time novelist. As a result, she is forced to live on a haunted sailboat the size of a very large walk-in closet (what, you thought writing paid well?) with her husband and not enough sexy shoes. She rides a motorcycle, shoots a target pistol, and doesn't own a TV.

S.J. ROZAN, a life-long New Yorker, is an Edgar®, Shamus, Anthony, Nero, and Macavity winner, as well as a recipient of the Japanese Maltese Falcon award. She's served on the boards of Mystery Writers of America and Sisters in Crime, and as president of Private Eye Writers of America. She leads writing workshops and lectures widely. Her latest book is *On The Line*. Website: sjrozan.com.

ANTHONY NEIL SMITH is the author of *Yellow Medicine*, *Hogdoggin'*, and two other novels. He is an associate professor of English at Southwest Minnesota State University, where he directs the Creative Writing Program. He edits the crime fiction ezine *Plots With Guns*. He wishes he could tell a story and drive a boat as good as his grandpa used to.

DON WINSLOW was born in New York City and raised in the village of Perryville, Rhode Island. The author of thirteen books and several short stories, he has also written for film and television. On his way to becoming a writer, Don did a number of things to make a living—movie theater manager, private investigator, safari guide, actor, theater director, and consultant. He now lives on an old ranch in southern California. His first novel, *A Cool Breeze On The Underground*, was nominated for an Edgar®, and a later book, *California Fire and Life*, received the Shamus Award.

BILL CRIDER, editor of this collection, is the author of more than fifty published novels and numerous short stories. He won the 1987 Anthony Award for best first mystery novel for *Too Late to Die* and was nominated for the Shamus for best first private-eye novel for *Dead on the Island*. He won the Golden Duck Award for best juvenile science fiction novel for *Mike Gonzo and the UFO Terror*. He and his wife, Judy, won the best short story Anthony in 2002 for "Chocolate Moose." His story "Cranked" from *Damn Near Dead* (Busted Flush Press) was nominated for the Edgar® for best short story. Check out his homepage at billcrider.com, or take a look at his peculiar blog at billcrider.blogspot.com.

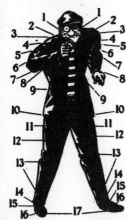